I0662851

Wishing the Moon.
First published in United States.

Text copyright © 2013 by Kendall J. Redburn.

Cover copyright © 2013 by Colton Zimmerman.
All rights reserved.

ISBN: 978-0-9893765-1-8

Published by BitReads LLC
505 Beacon Hill Lane
Plymouth Meeting, PA 19462

For my wife Dorian.

Acknowledgements:

I owe many thanks to my early readers. Dorian Redburn, Mike Coyle, Rebecca Stansel, Stephanie Wykstra, Gene Langenberger, Greg Schauer and John Bieniek. Thank you all for your edits, comments and pushes in the right direction.

If I wish the Moon tonight;

Doubtless, I will get it right.

If I wish to make it so,

To that silver orb to go;

Divine will always grant the boon

For all to visit on the Moon,

Should I desire, without care,

I can join the others there.

– Nursery Rhyme–

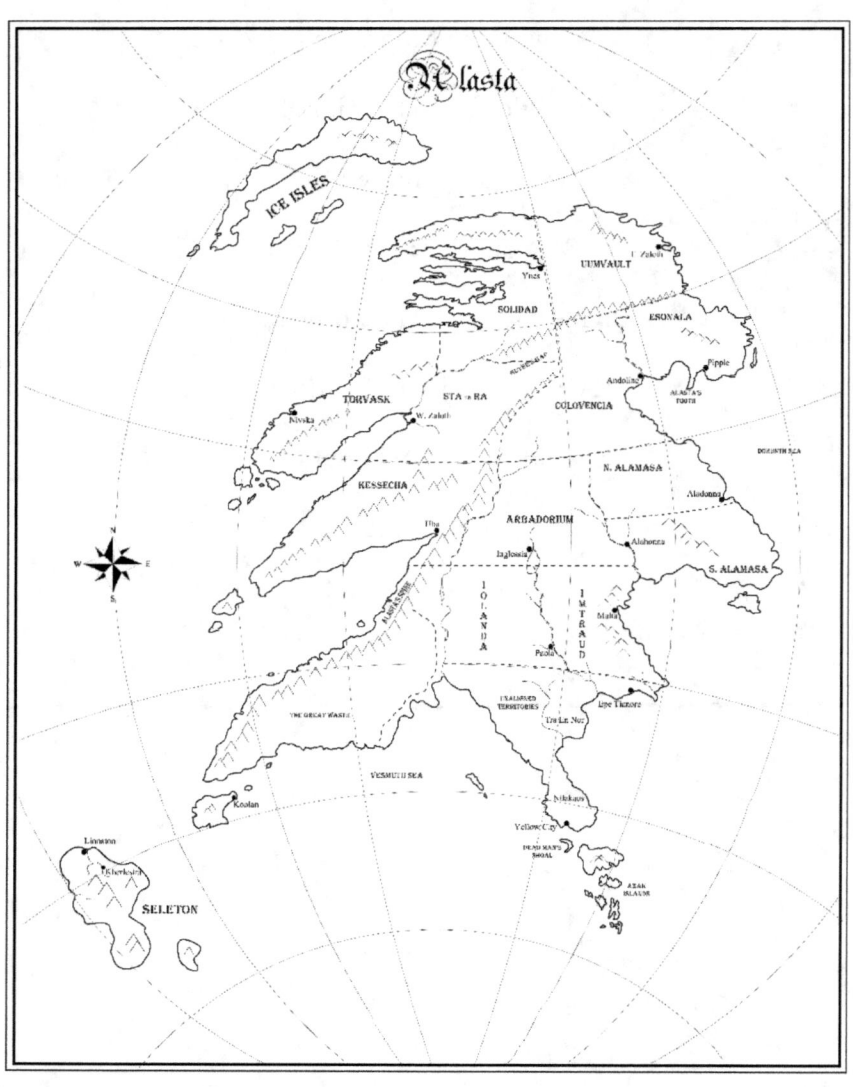

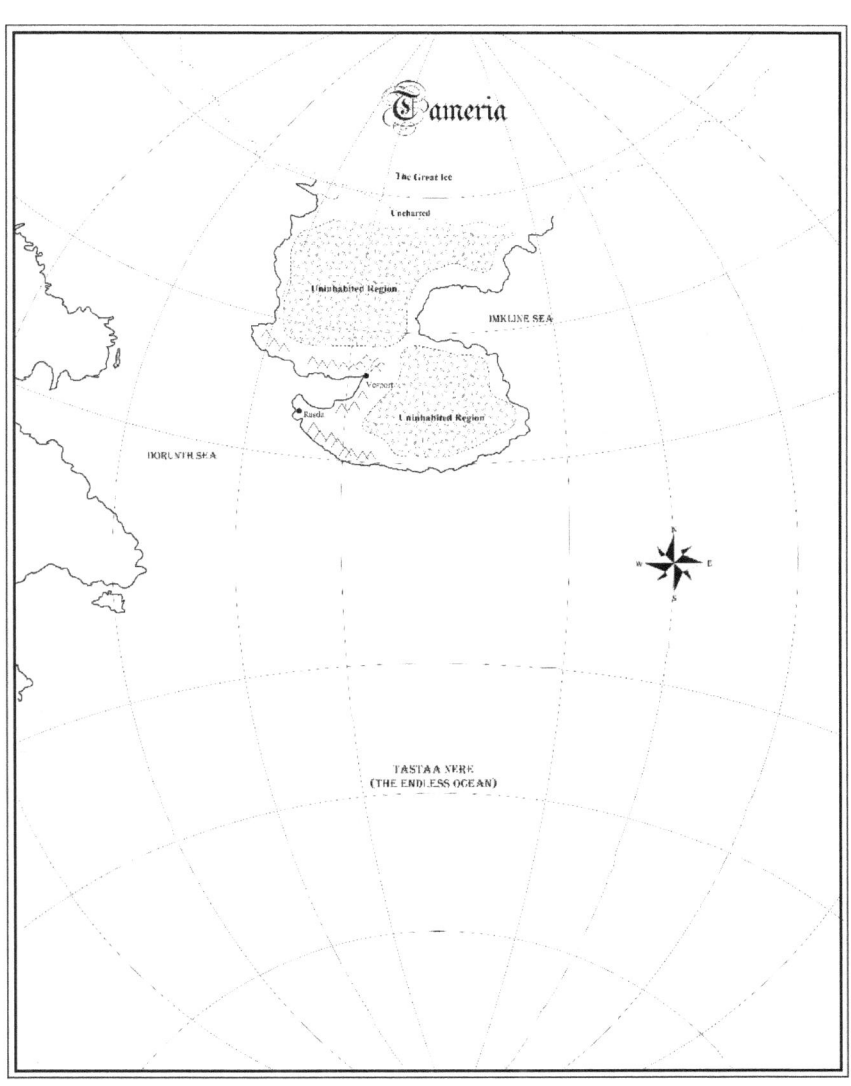

# One.

*He gathered from himself the radiance that separates day from night, and from the light that is life, that is warmth, that is the æther of locomotion, he created the Angels.*

*Book of the Divine.*

**18 Raveen Y.O.D. 742**

## Canter Farm: Southern outskirts of Andoline, Colovencia.

Lanthan Canter lay in his soft feather bed, dressed in his best suit, surrounded by his family and ready to die at the hands of his eldest son. It was his choice, his gift to his family, and Divine rot anyone who would deny him the courtesy of a dignified exit.

He coughed. Short barking coughs that shook the bed. He covered his mouth with a linen, tucked it under the covers—no need to alarm anyone with its contents—and took a drink of warmed brandy and honey that Ella had prepared for him to clear his throat.

He had said his goodbyes during the previous week to his friends and neighbors, and what a time that was. Ella had been a gracious hostess and there had been so much good food and pleasant company that he wished he'd done it sooner. This morning he would make peace with his family and lie next to his mother in the little cemetery at the back of the property by nightfall.

He had a gift, of sorts, for everyone assembled, but maybe not ones they would appreciate right away. In reality, he only had one gift, and that was for his oldest, Derek, and everyone else was just getting leftovers. Regardless, it would have to do.

He had assembled the toys he had played with as a young boy, plus a few more, picked up during those rare occasions when he traveled. These were the gifts for Liam, his grandson, a beautiful mulatto boy with his mother's long wavy hair and his father's deep brown eyes. He raised his hand and called to the boy sitting quietly in a dark suit, over-starched shirt and shiny leather shoes. "Liam."

"The boy jumped down and hurried, clip-clop, clip-clop, to his pop-pop's side, the sound closely followed by the swish of his mother's long skirts, forming a wall of linen behind him.

Derek, Clea and their son Liam had come dressed for a funeral in dark colors and tightly buttoned collars. That was her doing; she would see no cause for celebration in today's proceedings. That was her way, to love so fiercely that it made her seem mean sometimes. At least she had come, but like as not, just to talk him out of this "foolishness."

"You look right smart and fine today young man," Lanthan said.

"Thank you, sir," Liam said.

"Let me get you a healer papa," Clea pleaded.

"Just a moment, Clea dear," he said. "Liam, if you run upstairs, and take your man Jarod to help you, you'll find a trunk at the foot of my regular bed, you know the one?"

"Yes, sir."

"Well, that trunk, and whatever you find inside is yours, so you go on up and look now. Jarod will help you bring it down and put it in the wagon. Mind the cats."

"Yes, sir! Thank you, sir."

"Give pop-pop a kiss," Ella said.

Liam gave his grandfather a kiss on the cheek, and then looked at his mother for permission to leave, fairly bouncing in his eagerness.

"Run along, dear," Clea said. She released her hold upon her son and turned away, retreating from the bed so that she might dab at her eyes without drawing comment.

"Jacob!" Lanthan called. Jacob was his second son and his gift was to inherit the family home. He and his wife Rissanne, both in their thirties, had a single infant child, Mia, named after his mother. Marrying late and having few children seemed to be the way these days, but they both assured him they would have more and name their first son after him.

Jacob and Lanthan shook hands. Rissanne kissed her father-in-law, and laid their daughter into his arms.

Lanthan kissed his granddaughter's cheek, and brushed her dark hair, which had been woven into tight cornrows.

"Jacob, this house is now yours. I have the papers all ready with my solicitor; he will bring them by tomorrow."

"Papa!" Clea cried, and whirled to face him, as if her gaze could dissuade him.

He continued as if she hadn't spoken. "Sell your home and move in here. I will expect you to take good care of your mother and your sister."

"Yes, sir, I will. Thank you, father."

"I know you will, and you're most welcome. Here." He handed Mia back to her mother. "Velda, dear."

His youngest and only daughter stepped to the bedside with her husband Casper, and their two children, Markus and Josia. Lanthan hugged each of the two dark-skinned boys in turn and received their kisses, shook his son-in-law's hand and kissed Velda.

"I have for you two, a gift of seven thousand Suns."

"Oh Papa," Velda exclaimed, "that's too much."

"You're very generous, sir," Casper said. "Thank you very much."

"Nonsense, and additional fifty Suns each for Markus and Josia. It may seem generous now, but it will seem miserly when these boys are grown and this memory distant."

"I assure you good father, your memory will always be blessed in our hearts. Say 'Thank you.' Markus, Josia."

"Thank you sir," the boys chimed.

"Very good," Lanthan said. "Your words are kind and I'll accept them as such. Jacob, would you please escort your mother, and if you would all be so kind, I would like a moment alone with Clea."

Velda and Casper said their goodbyes and ushered their children out of the bedroom.

Ella came to her husband's side and gave a quick smile, but it vanished before it half formed. She dabbed at her eyes with the silk handkerchief he had given her their first night of courting. "May I kiss you, husband?"

"I would be most pleased."

She sat down on the bed beside her husband and leaned against his half-prone body. His strong arms gathered her in, and for the first time in front of their children, kissed her warmly and passionately on the lips. When they parted, both of their cheeks were wet.

Jacob helped his mother back to her feet, the strength she had shown throughout her life suddenly gone. He took her arm, and with her sobbing gently on his shoulder, he guided her from the room while his wife followed with their baby.

"Derek, give me a moment with Clea?"

"Yes, sir." He closed the door behind him.

"You bastard," Clea said, but there was love in her eyes and she sat beside him and took his hands, her white delicate skin folded into his dark leathery fingers.

"You will forgive him."

"No, I won't, or you either."

"You will, but that is for later, I have a gift for you too."

"Oh, it's for me is it? Shall I be pressing the pillow down on your face then?"

Lanthan looked at a paper packet on the nightstand beside the bed. "Those are for you, you will find my mother's rings and jewelry, such as it was, in there."

"That's kind of you, but why won't you get healed?"

"Such a strong will you have, that too is something Derek needs; a woman like you pushing him along. Do you love him?"

She hesitated, and then conceded: "Yes, but I love you too."

"Yes, you love all of us, so stop being such a canker."

She withdrew her hands from his, and folded her arms so that the fabric of her dress—already laced tight—threatened to tear; but she didn't care.

Her anger only made Lanthan smile, but he knew he shouldn't goad her any more. "You must forgive him Clea, for what he's done, and for what he will soon do, but most of all, because he chose you. That other woman, Vellenia—"

"Don't say that name!"

"Oh be still. She's Ra-ken now, and who could blame him for wanting her, but he doesn't, he wants you."

"She never gave him the choice."

"Is that what he told you? Well maybe he did reject her after she hurt him, or maybe she hurt him because he rejected her, and the truth of it is between them and the Divine."

He paused, as if he'd lost his thread.

"I want a promise," Clea said.

"From me?" He gave a little laugh.

"From you and him."

"Oh, so you want to bargain now?"

"I can smother you myself," Clea said, and moved as if to grab the pillow. He caught her wrist and then stroked her arm lovingly.

"I dare say you could. Would this be a promise of prohibition?"

"Yes. He's not to use this ability, in my home, or on any of our family."

"Yes, I can see that would be wise, and if he keeps his promise, will you forgive him?"

"We'll see."

"I can't say I expected better than that as an answer from you, Clea. Now give me a kiss and go, before I die on my own."

Clea leaned forward, and gave her father-in-law a soft, loving kiss on the lips.

"I love you, and I'll miss you." She rose and wiped her eyes.

"So many tears, so many more to come. You may go now."

Clea opened the door and pushed past Derek, her face turned away. She fled up the stairs, perhaps to cry alone or maybe just to find her son.

Lanthan spoke as soon as the door closed. "You are to promise me and Clea, that you will never use this ability within her home, or on any family members. What do you think of that?"

"I think that's reasonable."

"She'll never forgive you if you do."

Derek snorted. "I could just add that to the list."

"Don't! Derek."

"Yes, sir?"

"For Divine's sake, even if you don't, convince her to the best of your ability that you love her, more than you ever loved that other woman."

"Yes, sir, I will."

"Good, now let's get this over with."

"I love you, dad."

"Save your breath son, you know the words?"

"Yes!"

Alright, well I guess I love you too." Lanthan pulled the pillow out from underneath his head and handed it to Derek, then closed his eyes. "Do it."

Derek climbed up onto the bed on his hands and knees, straddling his father; he accepted the pillow, laid it gently over his father's face and then jammed his weight down. At first, Lanthan lay peacefully still, willing, compliant, but when the air burned in his lungs and his resolve waivered and he realized that Clea's offer of a healer wasn't a bad idea. He grabbed at his son's wrists, cried out muffled pleas, and wished he could undo this decision.

Derek held firm as his father struggled, the way they had practiced; using his weight, which was not substantial, his leverage, which was not great, and his years of repressed anger, which were enough.

When it was done, he tossed the pillow aside and looked into his father's eyes, now wide and staring and seeming to say, "now or never boy."

"I wish—" Derek choked. Tears ran down his cheeks.

"I wish." Another false start. He swallowed and then cleared his throat, wasting precious seconds.

"I wish I had the ability to make others speak without reflection."

The rush hit him, the urge, the power, the presence of greater being, a connection with the universe and all other souls within it. He sat back, hands and face raised to the ceiling, his butt resting on his deceased father's shins, and screamed, and laughed, "Yes! Yes, Divine Lord yes!"

The others poured into the room, each with their own wish on their lips—spoken just below the volume of audible—but none of them wanting what they knew they would find.

Jacob gently closed his father's eyes, retrieved the pillow from the floor, and returned it to its proper place under the man's head.

Ella, Velda and Rissanne wept, Clea wept, the children cried; all the while Derek looked at all the sad faces staring at him, and laughed, but not without tears of his own.

Wish-a-day; wish-a-day; wish-a-day;
Gone.

Work-a-day; work-a-day; work-a-day;
Long.

Wish-a-day; wish-a-day; wish-a-day;
Sad.

Love-a-day; love-a-day; love-a-day;
Glad.

Wish-a-day; wish-a-day; wish-a-day;
None.

Wish-a-day; Work-a-day; Die-a-day;
Done.

—Children's hand clapping song —

# Two.

*And unto men, said the Lord Divine, I shall give my gifts, such as they are want, that they might know of me, and worship me, and live in me.*

*Book of the Divine*

## 12 Ahmat, Y.O.D. 743

### East of the Yellow City, Nilakaus

Three men rode along the dusty road; the few clouds drifting lazily eastward managed to avoid casting any shadows that might give Kherlos and his escorts some relief from the sun. The heat was bad enough, but when combined with his clothes—a skirted waist shirt, black-satin trousers, and long black boots—it made him feel like a dandy riding into a funeral pyre. It was, he reflected, a stupid plan after all, but at least the boots were nice.

They were the only part of the costume he felt comfortable dying in. They were a kind of goodbye present from Cordain, his part-time lover and accomplice in this madness. They were made of lambskin, soft and easy to get in and out of. They had been dyed midnight, and had a silver crescent moon motif worked into the leather of the cuffs. Cordain had promised that if the mission failed, he would kill whomever he found wearing them, as well as many other people in general.

Kherlos shook his head at the memory; he could never really tell when Cordain was joking.

Beside him, rode Mekos and Skute, two of Cordain's soldiers, dressed down to play the part of bodyguards. They enjoyed the comfort of utility over style, simple leather jerkins over a cotton shirt, short britches and high-laced sandals. Each man also sported a long hardwood club slung across his back.

Mekos was thin, lanky, with dirty blond hair. He was quick to jape, and could dance a beguiling jig. Skute was thicker, quick to anger but quick to forgive, and easy with money. Both were good friends and good men to have in a fight.

There was little traffic on the road, the smarter travelers having already reached their destinations. In the morning, carts full of grains and goods for sale would crowd the roads into the city. In the evening, those same carts would crawl back out carrying dung.

On both sides of the road were cultivated rows of tall bushes laden with red berries. Children with skinny brown arms darted with sharp knives into the thickets, extracted clusters of ripened fruit and dropped them into woven baskets carried on the backs of their mothers. They all stopped and watched from under broad-brimmed hats as they road by.

"My dad picked cotton," Mekos remarked, "back-breaking labor that is."

"You saying that beats soldiering?" Skute said. "You know you're riding to your death, probably? Right sir?"

"Probably," Kherlos said, "or worse."

"What I'm saying," Mekos said. "Beats picking cotton."

§

The edge of the city was marked with a stone gate, which used to be part of the city wall. The stones of the wall were now visible as part of the buildings crowding together just inside the arch. The arch had the look of a short tunnel after the mountain had been removed.

There were four men lounging inside the shade of the gate, common city men, opportunistic bullies making use of someone else's authority. Three of the men had not bothered to lace up their plated leather armor, and one even left his ponytail unbraided, allowing his long black hair to drift wild.

They appeared to be playing some kind of dice game in the road. All four of them hunched around a circle sketched into the dirt that had been divided into four sections. Suddenly, they let out a roar; one started taking coins from the other three. He had the look of command about him. That is, he had his leathers properly laced and he even wore his cap.

Kherlos halted and waited for them to notice their arrival.

The Sergeant, as Kherlos now considered him, approached. One man took off at a brisk jog, to alert the palace no doubt, and the other two fetched up iron tipped pikes that had been lying inside the arch.

"I am Kherlos Timèatteo. I come bearing tribute—"

"Get down," the sergeant said.

"I'm sorry," Kherlos said.

"Dis—mount." He said it as if it were two words.

16

Kherlos and his men dismounted. The trappings on his horse was supposed to be his safe conduct. Evidently, these men had not been so informed. "I am Kherlos Timèatteo. I come bearing tribute from the Prince Aaron of Tiffaully for your Lord, Ra-ken Bouchard."

The sergeant nodded, as if he knew exactly which prince Kherlos was talking about. He pointed at the satchel slung across Kherlos's chest. "Show it."

Kherlos's men stepped forward and reached for their clubs, but the two city guards were quicker with their pikes.

"Stop," Kherlos said.

The sergeant spat and looked amused. "Normally, I just kill them what raises hand against me." He spat again. "Today I'm feeling generous, been lucky at dice here all morning, and killing might spoil that. So I tell you, and you listen." He jerked his head back. His two men backed off. Kherlos's men lowered their arms and one fetched the reins of the horses before they could wander off.

"It would be my esteemed pleasure to escort you fine gentlemen in to see our Ra-ken Bouchard, or the Butcher, as we like to call him. So toss your billywhackers down on the ground over there, and if you behave, you can have them back when you leave; if he lets you leave that is."

He waited for their decision.

They dropped their clubs into the grass.

"Right, and you?" He poked Kherlos with a thick greasy finger. Kherlos opened the satchel and removed from it, a small box carved from a black wood, inlaid with mother-of-pearl. The sergeant popped the latch on the box and inspected the two rows of gold coins that fit exactly inside.

"Looks a bit light. Lifted a sliver for yourself? No? Bad for you if you did. Bad for your prince too." He closed the lid and handed the box back. Kherlos returned it to the satchel.

"You can see—" The sergeant pulled his knife and placed it against Kherlos's throat. With his other hand, he searched Kherlos until he found and extracted a small purse. He pushed Kherlos back with the tip of the knife and looked inside; it contained a few silver coins.

"What I said, light. Now one thing you learn around here quick as the squirts, is that no one steals from the Butcher, and no one calls him that to his face. That's two, but lesson's over. You bring me this much," he shook the bag, "each time through, and you and your boys here'll be real fine. No problems, no unexpected difficulties along the way here and back." He touched the long blade against his chest. "On my word as a sergeant in the Butcher's army." He even managed to sound sincere.

Kherlos nodded his agreement.

"Right, follow me then. Mustn't keep the Ra-ken waiting."

§

Kherlos had seen slums before. Any normal city had them downwind of the richer quarters. Lathe and plaster buildings crowded together, leaned on each other like a ragged line of refugees; patched up, dirty and thin, like the people who lived in them. They huddled in the doorways of their houses or shops and stared with hollow eyes as they passed.

The wealthy could afford to ride in shaded carts pulled by barefoot boys, but everyone else walked in streets that were equal part boulevard and sewer. He was grateful for his high boots, but pitied his men in their sandals. The city guard didn't seem to notice the muck, and his men knew better than to complain.

As they approached the center of the city the quality, spacing and repair of the buildings improved. They came to a paved thoroughfare and turned north. The road crossed a stone bridge across a wide river. On the other side was the butcher's palace. Kherlos stopped. One of the guards elbowed him.

"Let him look," the sergeant said. "Let him see where his prince's coin is going."

The palace itself looked like it would take ten minutes to walk from one end to the other, and the gardens around it were at least twice as large. He counted three stories to the palace, and figured there were probably more. He could make out scaffolding near the back. The foundations were stone and mortar; the main structure was stained wood. He was surprised that the entire surrounding countryside had not been deforested, and then realized, it probably was, just upstream. Kherlos sighed and moved on. Cordain had warned him this city would not suit him, and he had been right, but he had hoped.

§

They stopped at the steps leading up to the main entrance.

"You and me go up," the sergeant said.

"My men?"

"Unharmed, as long as you follow instructions. Come on."

They stopped at the top step. Eight stout men in yellow silk coats with bright red sashes stood side by side across the entrance. They stood as if statues, with expressionless faces and eyes focused on infinity. When the sergeant reached the top step, the Yellow Guard reacted. Each man, in exquisite unison, stepped slightly apart, grasped their golden scabbards with their left hand, the hilt of their blades with the right, and extracted their blades exactly one hand's breadth.

"Tribute for Ra-ken Bouchard," said the sergeant. No one moved; they seemed not to have heard him. Kherlos looked back. Women in black robes were descending with bucket and brush, attacking the filthy prints they had left on the alabaster stone.

"Good luck," said the sergeant. He then retreated down the steps, taking obvious delight in leaving fresh tracks for the others to clean. The line of men stood immobile, blocking him from making the final step up onto the broad porch.

"Part," a voice called from behind them.

As one, the men took a single quick step back and snapped their swords home. Kherlos was impressed. These men would give even Cordain thistles in his bread.

Another of the ubiquitous servants in black—a man, with a copper badge at his shoulder—put down a stool. "Sit."

Immediately the women went to work on his boots. They lifted each foot, scrubbed and dried it multiple times, each time wiping it with a white cloth. When the cloth came away clean, he was allowed to stand.

"Ra-ken Bouchard does not permit filth inside his home. You are to follow me." The man who spoke was dressed in a black overcoat and black trousers. He wore a silver badge above his breast inscribed with the number twenty-seven.

"I see long hair is in fashion here," Kherlos said. He kept his own hair short, the way a soldier's should be.

As they walked, the man spoke without bothering to turn around. "If you are permitted, you may observe that our Ra-ken is mostly bald. It would be wise not to remark upon this. It has been our custom in this city for quite some time to wear our hair long in this manner."

"Would you cut it if he told you to?"

The man whirled and confronted Kherlos. "Courier, the Butcher provides a simple service to those princes that might desire it. Send tribute heavy by one-eighth Sun and the person who brings it receives a quick execution. Send tribute one-eighth Sun light, and the messenger is left to linger while rats gnaw on his flesh. So why don't we leave the questions until we get to know each other better?"

Without waiting for an answer, Kherlos's guide turned and resumed his progress through what seemed to be an endless series of halls filled with painted blue urns and bronze dogs.

His guide left him to wait in a long chamber with a high vaulted ceiling and matrices of glass panes nestled underneath each arch. Around the room, a single painted mural adorned the walls. It depicted some vast park filled with couples enjoying a day out, as if viewed from a central point inside.

Three times, he circled the room. With each pass, he noticed some new scene, each small vignette depicting some novel way man, woman and beast might congress. It was a single, vast, hand-painted pornographic work of art and one could spend hours inspecting it in close detail and not exhaust its wonders.

Eventually, for he knew no way of measuring time in this otherwise captivating room, the door opened. Another of the Butcher's minions addressed him. "I am to escort you to our Divine Lord, Ra-ken Bouchard. You will enter his chamber bowed low, hands held high, with the tribute in front of you. Do not speak unless he asks you a question, and do not look at his face unless you desire it to be your last sight on Alasta. If allowed, you will address him as Divine Lord. If you turn your back, ever, he will kill you slowly and let you watch as dogs devour your entrails. Understand?"

"Understood," Kherlos said.

"Show me," the man said. Kherlos assumed the position. The clerk pushed Kherlos's back lower, and then tugged his arms higher until he was satisfied. "Come."

Together they entered the inner chamber of the Butcher. Kherlos could only see the ornate carpeting, but he could hear the sounds of many people. His guide stopped and bowed. After a pause, he spoke. "Tribute Lord, from the Prince of Tiffaully."

"Let me see." The voice came from directly in front and slightly above where Kherlos stood. Someone took the box from Kherlos's hands. He lowered them to his sides, but maintained his deep bow.

"Weigh it," the Butcher said.

Kherlos could hear the sounds of many people. Whispers and the shuffle of slippered feet came from around where he assumed the Butcher sat. Black robes moved in and around the periphery of his vision. After a few moments, a voice from the side called out. "Lord, it is correct."

"Exactly?" the Butcher asked.

"No more, no less, Lord."

"Your Prince is a very careful man, clever too, for there are times when we find the tribute has been shaved, and as I am sure you have been informed; no one steals from the Butcher." This remark caused general nervous laughter from the court, the sound of men on edge. One man, he assumed it was a man, tittered.

"Tell me vassal," the Butcher called, "would you care for a demonstration of my power?"

Someone nudged Kherlos. "If it pleases you, Divine Lord," he said.

"It does please me. You may stand." Before he could move, a hand held his head down and a voice whispered in his ear. "Keep your eyes down."

Kherlos stood, and kept his eyes on the floor. He could see a fair number of male feet—one pair had painted toes—and carpeted steps, which he assumed was where the Butcher sat.

"Take down his breeches," the Butcher said.

Kherlos stiffened, but did not resist. Rough hands grabbed him and pulled down his breeches.

"Oh. My," someone with said in a falsetto voice, "I'd tribute that."

"Do you prefer," the Butcher asked, "men or women? You may safely answer either."

"Men," Kherlos replied.

"Can you congress with women?"

"Yes."

"I had meant to return you, a eunuch. I adhere to the principle that men without lust make the most faithful servants. Yet I find myself admiring your…stature. It would be a shame to spoil such beauty, and a cruelty upon your prince, who has shown such punctuality and precision. I would see your full measure." He paused. "Please him."

"Oh yes, my Lord," said the high voice. The man with the painted toenails came and stood in front of Kherlos. He traced his fingers over Kherlos's arms and chest, making soft breathy sounds as he did so. He lowered his hand down onto Kherlos's groin, moved forward and kissed him. It was not unpleasant, but he preferred a more masculine partner.

"Let me see."

The effeminate man moved aside, trailing his fingers as he did so.

"Look at me."

Kherlos looked up at the Butcher. He was a small man, with thinning gray hair. He looked frail, yet his voice was like that of the rough men of the cold north plains: deep and certain. He wore the traditional white robes of the Ra-ken, and the silver double-mooned sigil above his brow. "Vassal, you have amused me, and that is a rare thing. You are to take three of my wives that you might find attractive and fill them with your seed. I will inform your prince that he may tribute twenty less Suns if it is you that delivers it and fifty more if it is not."

Kherlos bowed low at the pronouncement. Cordain would be amused.

"Rise," the Butcher said. The effeminate man giggled at the jest. "I believe I promised you a demonstration." Two bright beams of light leapt from the Butcher's eyes and illuminated the man who had touched him. For an instant, he seemed transparent, then he fell to the ground, a marionette cut free. The others quickly distanced themselves from his body, their nervous smiles conveying the impression that they never really liked him anyway. They had the look of trapped animals. Wolves, Kherlos thought, but then no, wolves can gnaw off their limbs. These men lacked such simple means of escape.

A horde of black robes surrounded the body and dragged it away.

"It is all that I can do," the Butcher said," is to give a faithful servant a quick death at the moment of his greatest pleasure. It is a kindness really, but so few understand that." There were general mummers of agreement, but the butcher waved a dismissive hand. "Pull up this man's pants and get him to my wives before he loses his resolve."

§

In the morning, Kherlos woke to the sight of two yellow-garbed guards at the foot of his bed and the backside of a woman slipping out a door. They stood, arms folded, legs spread, eyes focused somewhere else. He dressed.

The Yellow Guard escorted him to a side entrance, a broad platform that swarmed with black-robed servants. Adjoining, but not touching, was another platform where townsfolk stood and displayed their wares. One man selling onions, picked them out of his cart and passed them one at a time across the gap. A servant inspected each one, and stacked them neatly in red-lacquered crates.

"Hey! Lover boy!"

Kherlos stepped across the gap onto the other platform, pushed his way through the crowd and found Mekos and Skute waiting on horseback, with his own horse held between them. Both men were grinning ear to ear.

"What?" Kherlos demanded.

§

The morning sun rose over the Yellow City with only the smoke from a few fire-gutted houses to mar an otherwise cloudless sky. Twelve men marched in a double line out of west gate. Eight wore worn leather jerkins, short breeches and sandals, and carried long poles with hooked pikes. Four of the men wore loose yellow robes with red sashes and carried sharp curved swords. Leading them was a balding man on a white stallion. He wore a simple white shirt, pants and leather riding boots. On his brow dangled a simple signet of two opposing crescent moons.

North of the wood on the crest of a newly formed ridge, Kherlos and Cordain lay on the ground in shallow depressions perfectly shaped to their bodies. The tall grass and slope of the ridge concealed them from any enemies in the low area before them. They wore flax colored clothes, to blend in with the summer grasses, and hoods with gauzy black veils over their faces. Both men wore gloves. The fingertips on Cordain's right hand were bare, and his fingers pressed into the soil.

"He should have been here," Kherlos said. "I told you this wouldn't work."

"My information is that he's not an early riser, but perhaps he rode south first, and circled behind us and my men are already dead."

Kherlos knew his friend was teasing him. "If we die, we die, but you have no heir."

"There's always an heir."

This was true, but not what he had meant. "You know you will have to touch a woman someday."

"I happen to like women," Cordain said. "What makes you think I don't?"

Well, there's me for one."

Cordain held up his hand. "I feel them coming."

Kherlos felt a shimmer in the ground and saw the grass and the trees around them vibrate. This was Cordain's signal to his men—hidden all around them—that their quarry approached.

Two lines of guards marched into view, their long spears held forward and ready. Behind them rode the Butcher with two of the Yellow Guard marching on each side.

They had set a trap; even a man as powerful as the Butcher could suffer the bite of rats. Cordain had sent men during the night, dressed as drift-folk into the city to break and steal, and then build a campfire by day. Kherlos had thought it too obvious a ploy, but Cordain insisted it would work.

The Butcher scanned the field and surrounding trees. Quick flashes from his eyes lanced all around them and where they touched, woodland animals died. Those on the ground simply lay where they were. Those in the trees fell with a soft thud onto mossy soil. For about half a minute the Butcher stilled the life around them. Kherlos understood; if men had been hiding in the trees, watching, they would now be dead.

"Fan out," the Butcher called. "Advance."

They waded through the knee-high grass. A startled pair of pheasants leapt into the air and the eyes of the Butcher struck them down before they had made three wing-beats.

"Dinner," one of the soldiers cried, then laughed, pleased with his own wit.

The ground shimmered again as Cordain sent another signal. Twelve soldiers—wrapped like ancient desert kings in dirty linen—stepped from concealment at the edge of the wood and kneeled. Each held a circular mess tin, the bottom carefully cleaned and polished to reflect the sun into the Butcher's eyes.

"Kill them!" Bouchard yelled.

Cordain sent a third signal. Now archers, crouched in pits behind low brush, stood up, sighted at the advancing enemy and fired.

The Butcher's men scattered like children. Like any bully, they had not expected a fight.

Bouchard whipped his head around, scanning the surrounding terrain for his true foe.

"Chant," Cordain whispered.

Kherlos chanted. "Divine grant me the ability to smite with death from my eyes."

Men had learned long ago that the Divine was no trickster, no word wrangler that twisted meanings. Some people asked for boons, others put their requests into the form of wishes, but all the mattered was the intent, some form of spoken word, and being first.

Cordain sent his final signal. Eight men, carefully concealed within the ground the night before erupted from their assassin holes. Covered in cloth and dirt to conceal every part of vulnerable flesh from the Butcher's gaze, they rose from the ground, and with the steel of their short swords flashing, they rushed from all sides into the waiting blades of the Yellow Guard.

Even paired, their short stabbing swords were a poor match for the longer, light dancing blades of the Yellow Guard and two of Cordain's men quickly fell. A third ripped the hood from his head, threw it into the face of his opponent, and followed it with a quick thrust.

"Arrows," Shouted Cordain.

The Butcher snapped his head in their direction. The beams from his eyes flashed all around but found no exposed flesh to burn.

Men shouted in pain, anger and surprise. Arrows whisked through the air. Steel rang out against steel. Suddenly, the ground around them heaved and everyone fell down.

The first man to get up was a Yellow Guard with sword in hand and ready to fight. The stallion came up next, angry and snorting it kicked him in the head and then started stamping on his body.

The other two Yellow Guard threw their swords away and laid on the ground, their hands clasped to the back of their heads.

Cordain's men rose.

"Skute!" Cordain called out.

The man who had torn his hood off turned to the sound of his name. "Aye, Lord?"

"He's not dead yet."

"I'll fix that for you then." Skute picked up his sword and stepped over to the Butcher's body. He was lying face down in the dirt, arrows protruding from his back and neck, and a white fragment of bone jutting from his thigh.

Skute dropped to his knees, rolled the Butcher over and stabbed him upward, just below rib cage.

Bouchard opened his eyes.

Skute died.

Bouchard died.

Kherlos chanted. In an instant, the colors of his world inverted. The sun became a black ball hanging in a dark gray sky. Bright colored lights the size of birds circled overhead while the air shimmered with multi-colored motes. Kherlos stood and surveyed the scene. Silver-skinned men kneeled in a field of long gray grasses. Darker shapes, silhouettes of men stood over their enemy. Another shade stood beside him. It reached up, pulled away a mask and revealed the bright golden face of Cordain.

"Spare his men," Cordain said.

"What then?" Kherlos asked.

Cordain reached inside his tunic and extracted a pouch. He pulled open the pouch and extracted a fat pigeon.

"I like birds."

"We all must make sacrifices."

"How do I do this then?"

"You see each living animal as a different color," Cordain said.

"Yes."

"Choose that color, then will it to be dead." Cordain threw the bird into the air.

A great flash of light erupted from Kherlos's eyes and the pigeon fell. His vision returned to normal.

Cordain slapped him on the back. "Welcome my friend; you are Ra-ken, Kherlos Timèatteo. Welcome to the circle of the damned. Shake hands with my men. Some gave their lives here for you. Come honor them." The two men made their way into the field.

The Butcher's stallion was wandering around, grazing, looking for the sweetest grass. The two Yellow Guards stood side by side in a mini formation, their arms crossed, swords sheathed, and their clothes cleaned as best they could. Kherlos men and the city soldiers stood at ease in a loose group chatting while those that were injured were helped to bind their wounds.

Kherlos brushed the grass off his clothes, and put his hands up gain attention. "Hear me. I am now the Divine Ra-ken, Kherlos Timèatteo able to kill with my eyes. You have gained me this ability here today, and you have paid for it with your courage and your lives. I will not forget the sacrifice that you have made for me. Today, we will enter the city and we will make it our own. Tonight you will feast and celebrate my victory.

"Those of you that know me, know that I am a devout man of faith. Tomorrow, I will begin cleaning up the abominations and offenses that the Butcher encouraged under his depraved rule. Tomorrow, I will clean this city of its vermin and filth, but I will not make it my home. I plan to build a new city in a new land far from here. It will be a city where a man may be at peace with his brothers and sisters. Where each may know that the true ways of the Divine are kept according to his law, and not the whims of men. Where the Divine gift I have received here today will not enslave people, but rather keep them free. I thank you for this gift, and I thank the Divine for this day." Kherlos kissed his fingertips, and raised them up to the sky. "Kellen Ra, Oren Mah, Ana moke ku Ah, Ana fetta ku Ah, Ana tonne ku Ah"

"You speak Archaic?" Cordain asked.

"I memorized it for this occasion."

"Well, I'm sure the priests will have you memorizing more."

"Why do you and your Council Ra-ken trust them?" Kherlos asked.

"Every ruler needs a bureaucracy. The priests are literate, and tend not to try to kill you as often. Religious devotion is a powerful motivator and it serves us well."

"I don't trust them."

Cordain snorted. "Of course not, nobody trusts them, we just use them."

One of Cordain's men came over, saluted, and handed something to Cordain.

"Thank you, Captain." He turned to Kherlos. "I believe this now belongs to you." He held a small trinket on a gold chain; two silver crescent moons held together in opposing arcs by tiny silver chains. "Allow me."

Kherlos turned around and allowed Cordain to secure the sigil Ra-ken around his neck.

"Come," Cordain said. "You must make these men swear the oath of allegiance."

Kherlos lifted the silver moons from his breast and marveled at them. He could feel the ability course within him, the divine presence, patiently waiting to be called upon. A mosquito buzzed his ear. He swatted at it, and then realized he had a better way. He called upon his power and looked around, thinking of insects. The lights of the men around him dimmed, while at the same time tiny motes in the air brightened. He focused his attention on them. Die, he thought, the world flashed, and there was Cordain scowling at him.

"Don't…do that," Cordain said, "too much. It will frighten people. Remember, the plan is to convince the Council that you're not a threat."

"Not at all?" Kherlos said, disappointed.

"Well, from time to time you may, otherwise people will start to think stupid things. Look," Cordain clasped his shoulder. "The temptation will be for you to solve every problem with your ability. Resist that temptation. It makes you predictable, and therefore vulnerable." He tapped Kherlos's head. "It's your brains that will keep you alive the longest. Now come, your new men need to swear allegiance to you."

As Kherlos approached, Cordain's men moved away, the city soldiers formed up into a single rank and saluted by pressing the fingers of their hands together in front of a bowed head.

Kherlos saluted with an extended right fist, snapped to his left shoulder.

"I, state your name," Cordain called out, "Do solemnly swear, Divine and brothers all as my witness, allegiance, fealty and obedience to the blessed Ra-ken Kherlos Timèatteo, so long as he does live."

They all swore. Then one produced a sharp knife, and cut his braid off with a quick slice. He handed the knife to the next man, and placed the braid at Kherlos's feet. Each man in turn repeated this action. The two Yellow Guards, which their characteristic synchronization, drew their swords with a flourish, placed the blades behind their necks, and then drew them quickly up an over, neatly shaving a wide swath along the back of their heads.

Kherlos kicked the braids with his boot. "What am I supposed to do with these?"

"Well, err, nothing really, lord," one man offered. "We do this every time, you understand, for each new Ra-ken."

"And then you grow a new one?" Kherlos asked. The men all nodded.

"Is the entire city going to do this? Am I going to be showered with hair everywhere I go?"

"No, lord," the man offered, "Most people will cut theirs as soon as they hear the news. It's tradition to place them before you, not... to ah, throw them at you."

"Why?" Kherlos asked. He looked at Cordain who was trying hard not to laugh.

"It's a way of marking time."

Cordain patted Kherlos's shoulder. "There once was a time my friend, when the Ra-ken walked free, unencumbered by the barnacles of bureaucracy and tradition. Just keep your goals in mind and don't let these things distract you."

"Indeed," Kherlos said, and then shouted, "Men!" His small cadre snapped to attention and saluted, some with his variant, others with the Butcher's version.

"Let's try that again. Men!" This time they all got it right. "Form up. We're going to go claim my city."

# Three.

*So the angels conferred. And it came to pass that there were some among them who asked; Who are these men? And if they are men, then they are not Angels.*

*Book of the Divine.*

**36 Nebut, Y.O.D.743**

## City of Inglessia, Arbadorium

Layton Vernault's home had originally started as a simple two-story lodge nestled between two massive red-barked trees. Now the roof of the lodge was flat and railed and held a number of tables with umbrellas in the center. On either side, a staircase spiraled up around the adjoining trunk in a mirrored symmetry. These ended in railed balconies, from which suspension bridges on either side led back towards the main quarters.

Cordain stopped staring and urged his horse forward. He had heard the house described, but the size and sheer audacity of the structure was stunning.

Two gray-robed priests of the Divine waited patiently by the road. Their heads were almost completely bald, save for a long tassel of neatly braided hair that hung from the side of their heads and ended with a clip-on badge denoting rank.

"Boy!" one of the priests shouted. A youth no older than eight, looking like a miniature version of the one who called him, ran from around the side of the house, over to Cordain's horse, and grabbed its bridle.

Cordain dismounted and handed the boy a small copper coin. "I see you get them young," he said to the older priest.

"Viset see, kellen Ra-ken Cordain Leighland. Ra-ken Vernault is expecting you. I see you are traveling light."

"Thank you, Ahten, but yes, I don't expect to stay long." He turned to the boy. "This is Earthquake, that's his name, but he's really very gentle. Can you brush him?"

"Yes, Ra-ken, I have a stool."

Cordain laughed at the image of the young man balancing on a stool on his toes trying to brush his horse.

"I've never seen a horse this black," the boy said.

"Hold your tongue boy," Ahten snapped.

Bullies, Cordain thought. The world is always full of bullies. The young man would be punished, and any attention Cordain paid to the matter would only increase that punishment. Pretending that the comment was beneath his notice, Cordain stepped away and made as if to inspect himself.

He wore black calf-length boots, black leather riding-britches, a red silk blouse with black embroidered trim, black sheep-skin gloves, which he removed, and his dark brown hair was pulled back into a ponytail and tied with a crimson ribbon. "Am I presentable?" he asked Ahten.

"Does your lord desire to bathe?" Ahten asked back.

"No, if he finds the perfume of my sweat offensive then he can hold a scented hanky to his nose."

"As you wish."

Ahten led the way into the house. The main room was clearly some sort of reception hall with scattered tables and chairs and massive stag-horn chandeliers hanging from the high ceiling. It extended much further back than Cordain had expected.

"This part of the Vernault home extends out over the stables and a small kitchen," Ahten explained. "Additional stables, our quarters and various buildings are all set out of sight, further back in the woods.

"Ah," Cordain said.

Ahten led them to the right. The side of the building encased the trees that anchored it. Thick wooden planks jutted from the sides of the tree and spiraled upward. "Careful, the tree pushes the steps out as it grows. Each year they have to pull them out and refit them. Some might be loose."

"I'll step where you step then."

The stairs ended in a raised platform that circumnavigated the trunk with a suspension bridge leading over to the main living area.

"It must be hard to get supplies up here," Cordain said.

"Oh, not at all," Ahten said, "they have a tackle and pulley, like you'd see on a barn. It's out of sight, behind the house."

The home started some forty feet off the ground, supported by four giant trees that rose hundreds of feet into the air. The main home itself was at least four stories high, with great square panes of glass covering most of the front face. Cordain could see staircases rising up the flank of each tree toward octagonal shaped cottages sprouting from the sides like snails clinging to sea-grass.

"How high are we going?" Cordain asked.

"Oh, just over to the house." Ahten started across the bridge. "Don't look down, or up for that matter, if you're afraid of heights."

"I'm fine, thank you for asking."

§

Ahten lead Cordain into the atrium, and to a small table set with two crystal goblets and a small bell. Dotted around the room were exotic trees with ribbed trunks and leaves only at the top. They grew in giant clay pots and reached almost to the ceiling some forty feet above.

The front and back walls were both set in panes of glass. The wall to his left held row after row of military weapons; pikes, swords, pole-arms, glaives, edge weapons of every variety. On the wall to the right hung a variety of paintings, mostly portraits of men and women in fancy dress, though in the center was a painting of a door. The door opened. A thin man with a gray mustache and long gray curls of hair stood on the edge of the frame and looked down. He wore a dark-brown skirt, brown slippers, and a pale cream blouse with frilled sleeves that ended at the elbows. Cordain forced himself to watch as his host stepped out into the air and gently drifted downward, and was thankful that the skirt material was heavy enough not to lift up.

"Cordain," Layton said as he landed. "How kind of you to come, I trust that your journey was pleasant."

"Yes, thank you. You have a lovely home."

Layton looked around, as if seeing it for the first time. "It is a beautiful house. Baron Ingless himself started it hundreds of years ago. He was a great visionary, a man who truly understood the transient nature of men's lives. I would imagine your own home to be a monument to your ability. Is it not?"

Layton twisted his hips slowly back and forth, as he spoke. "I would expect it to have soaring spires reaching high into the air, supported by massive pillars flowed into the shape of your ancestors, and great columns of marble upholding reliefs depicting all your great military victories. And below, such extensive dungeons, catacombs and layers of winding tunnels that surely they must descend to the very gates of the underworld."

"It is somewhat more modest than that," Cordain said. "Though there has been a trend for the sepulchers of each former tenet to get more and more elaborate. As for myself, I've extended the wine cellar and hardened the earth in areas that were starting to sag."

"Well of course, one mustn't let maintenance accumulate. Will you take wine with me?"

"Of course."

The three men sat at the table. Ahten tucked his tassel back behind his ear as he sat. Cordain noticed the gesture, and realized that each time Ahten moved his head; the braid would pop free again. He resolved to see how often he could make this happen.

Layton rang the little bell. "Please Cordain, do forgive my manners. How is your family? I hope they are well."

"Most well, thank you. Janeth sends her love. Corwin will be finishing his studies this next year, and Embler is looking every bit as beautiful as her mother."

"I'm sure she is; do give them my love as well."

"And I hope all is well with your family as well."

"Yes, I apologize that they are not here to great you, but we'd scheduled a yachting party for Linny's birthday."

"I'm sorry," Cordain said, as if this meeting were his idea, "I didn't mean to inconvenience you."

"Don't be silly, I'm flying down to meet them later anyway."

A young woman, a servant girl, Cordain surmised from her plain brown dress, white apron and cap, approached with a decanter of dark red wine.

"You missed one, Ahten," Cordain remarked. Ahten gave a thin smile, but said nothing.

"I understand you eschew the Servants of the Divine within your household staff," Layton said.

"I do."

"Perhaps Ahten could recommend some to you, I find them most willing and faithful servants."

Cordain looked at the girl.

"Leave the wine," Layton said, and waited until the girl had departed. "You vex me so Cordain, the clergy have valid reasons for excluding women from their ranks."

"Have they discussed them with Vellenia? Tawnya?"

"They have made their feelings clear," Ahten said. "But while we serve the Ra-ken and other blessed, we are not your slaves, and must keep our own council on such matters."

"Perhaps we should make you slaves then," Cordain said with a smile. "Or would your vows be forgotten under the beatings of a cruel master?"

"Cordain, behave," Layton said, "I didn't invite you here to argue philosophy with the clergy."

"No, you invited me here to chastise me."

"Yes, and to warn you." Layton refilled their glasses.

"Warn me?"

"You acted against the Butcher, without the council's permission, and worse, without telling me first."

"Silly me, I thought the Yellow City was outside of the Council's jurisdiction. Have we annexed Vehault recently? And shouldn't you be thanking me?"

"We did thank you," Layton said.

"So why the warning?"

"Ahten," Layton said.

Ahten sat up in his chair, folded his fingers together and leaned in towards Cordain. "Do you remember, of a plan I proposed to the council some years back, to gather the fallen."

"Vaguely."

"We would train innocents, children with no knowledge of the Gifts of the Divine—"

"Yes, I remember that foolishness. What of it?"

"We have both the location and the funds now to proceed, thanks to you."

Cordain sat back, suspicious. "Explain."

"East of Vesport, high in the mountains, the land has been isolated for many generations. The people there know almost nothing of the Gifts. They are the perfect vessels, unsullied by a crass lust for Divinity."

"No, I meant the money."

"Ahh, the funds come from the sale of items liberated from the Butcher."

"That money belongs to Kherlos," Cordain said. "I was not aware the Priests of the Divine stooped to stealing. Perhaps Layton you should not be so trusting."

"We do not steal," Ahten said. "Kherlos is being sent everything that was promised to him, but he has abandoned the Yellow City and left the region defenseless. Besides, my brothers report he is doing quite well in Kherlestra. You should visit sometime."

"I might, and suggest that he look into your bookkeeping."

Ahten shook his head. "Cordain, why do you distrust us so? Kherlos has no cause to complain. We told him our inventory of the palace would take years, even without the interference of those yellow-robed fanatics."

"As opposed to gray-robed ones?"

Ahten harrumphed.

"Enough," Layton interjected. "Cordain, at our next meeting, the Council will formally adopt our plan to build a monastery in the remote mountains east of Vesport, and then to gather there the fallen abilities."

"A monastery, don't you mean a palace?"

Layton shook his head. "No, it will serve as a campus for the students and a base for the priests doing missionary work. You will not believe the levels of superstition and ignorance that exist there."

"I understand most of the people there are dark skinned. Will you be inviting them join your ranks?"

"Of course, we have no issue with the color of a man's skin," Ahten insisted.

Cordain didn't believe him, but could not think of a way to gainsay him, so instead he turned to Layton. "So why tell me now?"

"Well," Layton said. He patted his fingertips together then tucked them under his chin. "I want your support, naturally. Your ability and cooperation will be essential to the project, and you'll be paid well."

Cordain scowled.

"Oh don't be like that," Layton said. "Don't pretend we don't all use our Divine gifts for personal gain. Besides, it's a noble cause, a cause you approve of, or did I misread your intentions in killing Ra Bouchard?"

Cordain stared, took a drink of wine, and said nothing.

"I thought so," Layton said. "You killed the Butcher and sent his ability south with Kherlos. Clearly you share our sentiments."

"I do."

"Yes, and Kherlos is young and healthy and surrounded by loyal guards, but then, so was Bouchard."

"Your point."

"Don't be dense, you know my point. The location of our monastery will be kept secret. It will be difficult to get to even if someone knows where it is, and easy to defend."

Cordain eyed him suspiciously.

"I'm old Cordain, don't mistake that for stupid."

"I don't."

Layton looked doubtful. "I don't intend to bore you with the details, that will be Ahten's responsibility."

"Are you in charge then?" Cordain asked Ahten.

"Yes."

"Of the whole project?"

"Yes, I see this as a divine accomplishment that emanates from humble origins."

"No doubt."

"All we are asking," Ahten said, "is that you help build our facilities, for which you will be handsomely paid."

"With Kherlos's money."

"Well it's the Council's money now," Layton said.

"And these new territories that you intend to liberate. I suppose their incomes will flow into the Council's coffers as well."

"Some of it," Layton said. "But yes."

"And so you're not getting any arguments from Tawnya, are you?"

"Surprisingly, no."

"Will you be adding seats to the Council then?"

"Divine no!" Layton said. "We'll find some Mo-ken to rule each territory, someone we can trust and control, but they won't be given seats."

Cordain nodded, and then realized the true reason for this meeting. "You're going to kill Kherlos, aren't you?"

"We hope that will not be necessary," Ahten said.

"Hope?"

"It will be years before we are ready, and of course we'll try it on the lesser Ra-fel first; to brush the tangles out."

"I can't help you if your plan is to murder my friend."

Ahten started to object, but Layton interrupted him with a hand. "Ahten, isn't Kherlos, if I understand correctly, already attended to by your priests?"

"Yes, I was just going to say that."

"And does he not receive council from them?"

"Yes."

"Including council on the use of his abilities, and the treatment of his citizens?"

"Of course."

"Very well then. Cordain, we share the same goals here, which is peace. I see no reason for the council to seek Kherlos's death."

"Do I have your word on that?" Cordain asked.

"You do."

# Four.

*But Lord, spoke Zaloth, first of the Angels. Thou gives men thy gifts, but not thy wisdom. Surely, the gift of Destruction would be turned against the heavens.*

*Book of the Divine*

**20 Ahmat, Y.O.D. 744**

## City of Kherlestra, North Seleton

Kherlos sat at his desk in his newly finished and furnished apartments, writing a letter to his sister, when a light gray robe of coarse wool appeared in front of him. "Travia, is it time already?" He had hoped to finish the letter to his sister before this appointment, but had difficulty finding the right words. She had written, congratulating him on the anniversary of his ascension to the divine, and offering her regrets that she could not attend the celebration. She seemed eager to know all the details of his daily life, large and small, yet it was always difficult to know what to say and what to omit. As usual, he opted in favor of overkill. He dipped the quill and added three quick lines.

*Sister, before me stands a priest of the Divine who waits on my attention. We are to meet and decide the fate of two felons. I will continue this letter anon.*

"It is, my Lord."

Kherlos stowed his pen and pushed back from the desk "I hear it is a beautiful summer day. Are we meeting outside?"

Travia shook his head as if denying this simple request gave him the greatest sadness. "My Lord, this matter is too delicate for others to overhear."

"Ah, so we have a room that has been finished?"

"Many, in fact."

"I suppose everyone else is already there waiting for me?"

"At your pleasure."

As soon as the two men stepped out of Kherlos's apartments, all activity in the hallway came to a stop. The plasterers on scaffolding lowered their trowels; acolytes in dark robes halted in mid-scurry and bowed their heads. Kherlos and Travia wove their way around them down the hall to the wide marble stairs where two guards stood at attention. From Kherlos's point of view, no one ever did any work.

"I should like to show you a finished section," Travia said.

"Certainly," Kherlos said. He could use the walk. He spent far too much time sitting lately, and worried about developing a paunch. Travia guided him from behind with soft "Left" and "Right" instructions at each intersection. The finished section was a grand hallway with a long patterned carpet, papered walls and lined with slatted suits of armor, enormous blue urns, and woodcuts liberated from the Yellow Palace.

"How many priests were martyred for the cause?" Kherlos asked.

"Lord?"

"I'm surprised the Yellow Guard allowed you to take any of this stuff."

"As long as our feet were clean they didn't care what we took. Do you like it?"

Kherlos shrugged. "It's lovely."

"Excellent, we're just around the next corner."

They entered a large meeting-style room. Five more of his priests waited at the table. Two of the darker-robed acolytes sat at a separate desk with a candle, sealing wax and paddles. All rose and bowed when he entered. Kherlos nodded briefly and moved briskly to the head of the table. He still had trouble telling the priests apart. They all wore the same clothes, the same bald heads, and the same obsequious expressions. Of course he knew who they were, but not always which was which.

"Bring wine."

The large walnut table held trays of grapes and apples, but no cups.

"Water?" Travia asked.

"And water," Kherlos said. He moved to the head of the table, sat, then picked a bunch of grapes and started eating them. A small porcelain bowl appeared at his elbow for the seeds.

"My Lord," Travia began, "As you have heard, we have arrested two persons accused of aggravated theft, though we do not believe their cases are related. We also have a number of minor offenses we would like to bring to your attention."

Kherlos nodded.

"We have been getting complaints about a couple who have refused to place a shrine to your Divine self in their home. This is upsetting their neighbors." Travia paused to see if Kherlos wanted to comment.

"What else?" Kherlos said.

"Three men were observed working during the time of evening prayer. They claim they had gotten behind and needed to finish laying stone before the mortar set."

"What else?"

"There was a woman overheard cursing your Divine self."

Kherlos laughed at this. "I've been cursed before. Invite her to the palace that I might hear her words for myself. I will condemn no one on hearsay. As for the others, I see no need for reprimands. As long as my citizens live in peace and show respect for one another I see no need to dictate the details of their devotions. Do you agree?"

Travia spoke immediately. "We do your Lord. You are a shining example of the Divine's munificence and generosity."

The wine arrived. Kherlos accepted a goblet. The priests, including Travia, took only water.

"Tell me of the theives then," Kherlos said.

Kevlan, the head of security rose. "The first is a woman accused of the theft of a man's purse. We believe that she lifted it off of his person after she had fallen against him."

Kherlos stopped him. "Is she guilty?"

"Yes," Kevlan said.

"Witnesses? Are they reliable and will they testify well?"

"Very well, my Lord."

"And punishment?"

Travia raised his hand and spoke. "We feel she would make a good example, with a public trial, followed by the taking of her hand."

Kherlos mulled this over. "Was she working alone?"

"Probably not," Kevlan said, "but she has not given up the name of her master."

Kherlos scratched his chin and then plucked a few more grapes. If he took her hand, she would be forced to beg or prostitute herself. "Is she local?"

"No," Kevlan said. "We could find no one who had offered her lodging. We expect her to flee back to Linnaton, where we will be able to observe her."

"Yes, I can see the value in that. Give me the warrant."

Travia unrolled a large vellum document and placed it in front of Kherlos, which he then signed with a flourish. The document was then passed to the two acolytes who carefully folded it with the long wooden paddles before adding the seal.

"Next," Travia said, "we have a man who was caught stealing meat. He has been accused of many other thefts as well, but none proven. He is lodged here in the tents, and finds odd jobs of manual labor."

Kherlos smiled; Travia had anticipated his questions. "And?"

"We recommend death." Travia said. The others all indicated their agreement.

"Does he have friends? Family?"

"None that we could discover," Kevlan said.

"No mercy then?"

"That would be your decision, Lord," Travia said.

"Very well, anything else?"

§

Kherlos stood on his balcony and looked over the throng of people assembled below. There were always those who came to perform their morning oblations with him. Today, most of the city attended. Some had been waiting since before sunrise just to secure a spot close to the stage.

He kissed his fingertips, raised them above his head and spoke the ancient words. "Kellen Ra, Oren Mah, Ana moke ku Ah, Ana fetta ku Ah, Ana tonne ku Ah." Below, the crowd did the same. It was a simple request: Blessed Divine, hear me. I act as your servant. I carry your faith. I speak your word.

Kherlos waved and smiled, and returned to his apartments. Takoda was waiting in his office, sitting back with his feet propped up on Kherlos's desk and the beginnings of a new braid laying across the back of the chair.

"Sigil and cloak," Takoda said, as if Kherlos needed instruction on how to dress.

Kherlos smiled. Takoda had served under the Butcher for many years as head of the household staff, using his ability to be elsewhere when Ra

Bouchard was in a killing mood. At first, Takoda had treated him exactly the same way he had treated all the other Ra-ken who had dwelled for a time in that strange palace: servile, obedient and useful. But when he had brought in the clergy, instituted laws, and announced his intentions to leave, Takoda had revealed himself, his ability and his desire to remain in Kherlos's employment. Now they were fast friends, and Takoda japed with him as if they had been boyhood cohorts.

"Are you to dress me now? Where's Desper?"

"Out," Takoda said. He put his feet down and sat up. "Besides, someone has to keep you humble. All this Divine Ra-ken and Ra ku Kellsee starts going to your ego. I've seen it before."

"So you say. Where were you yesterday? I could have used your council." Kherlos walked over to the desk. His sigil was lying near the edge, his fur-lined cloak lay draped over one of the stuffed chairs.

"Wandering around the city, checking for trouble."

"Getting into trouble more likely. Tempting the young women into sneaking away from their aunts no doubt."

"Say not such vile things, my Lord."

"So what you mean is that you had no luck."

"No."

"You need to find a good woman and settle down, be an example for others. I could always arrange one for you."

"My lord, how could I serve both you and a woman?"

"With your ability, you mean?"

"That too."

Kherlos grasped his friend's shoulder and shook him gently. "Do you have any appointments today?"

"No," Takoda lied.

"Good, after we're done with this nasty business I want to go riding. Now you have to help me dress."

"I am always at your service, Lord."

"How is that helping me keep humble?"

"It's my mocking tone."

Kherlos turned and held his arms out. "Be serious, I'm killing my first man today."

Takoda picked up the supple cloak and fastened it around Kherlos's shoulders with a small gold clasp. "Are you killing him in anger, for sport or because you're bored?"

"All of those reasons."

Takoda slapped Kherlos on the back of the head.

"I swear you have a death wish," Kherlos said. "I assume you'll be watching."

"Yes."

"And judging me?"

Takoda combed Kherlos's hair back into place, and finally fastened the sigil Ra-ken around his friend's neck. "Yes. Did you ever hear from Cordain?"

"I did, he says he has to go dig a hole in a mountain somewhere."

"What does that mean? Is that like making love to a fat woman?"

"Have you ever made love to a fat woman?" Kherlos asked.

"No."

"Then yes."

§

Kherlos sat underneath a canopy in the center of the judgment platform with his senior clergy crowding in on either side. Their faith forbade them to cover their heads, which made sunburn a common hazard of their vocation.

The people were quietly waiting for the proceedings. There was very little talking, and then only in whispers. Most of the people wore their work clothes. The city was in holiday during the trials, but most people would return to work as soon as the event was over. Those who could afford to take the day off were more formally dressed; the women in colorful dresses and silver belts, the men in beaded vests and long, striped britches.

Kherlos recognized the different styles of the various sects. There were some ultra-conservative couples; the men wore long greased beards, the women headscarves and long robes. But there were others, men who shaved, as Kherlos did, and women who wore trousers underneath a calf-length skirt. Despite their differences, there was very little tension in the city. They all shared one common desire. Peace. Today they would see two people pay the price for threatening that tranquility.

Travia stepped forward, raised his hands, and waited for silence. "Hear me all of you. The court of our Divine Ra-ken, Kherlos Timèatteo, is now in session. I will lead us now, in supplication." He blessed the Divine and their lord Kherlos, asked forgiveness for the just and punishment for the wicked and wisdom for his children through whom the powers manifest. Then he ended by kissing his fingers and raising them heavenward, intoning the traditional archaic blessing. Peace and love be upon you and our Divine Lord, Ra Timèatteo."

"Peace and love upon you," the crowd echoed.

"Let the judgment begin," Kherlos announced.

The jailer brought up onto the stage the woman accused of theft. He unshackled her wrists and released her.

"You are accused of the theft of a man's purse," Kherlos said. "I would ask you now to answer this charge."

He listened to her tale. She claimed a man had tried to kiss her and had insisted that she return unescorted with him to his home. She had refused, naturally, but forgiven the man for it was clear he was lonely. He had begged her pardon, and given her his purse. He asked her to buy smoked fish. She could buy two fish for herself, and then purchase incense for her shrine. Then without warning, he turned and accused her of taking the purse. He was jealous and angry that she had refused his advances.

Kherlos thanked her for her story, and asked that witnesses come forward.

The man whose purse had been stolen told a different tale. He had not known this woman. It was true that he was unmarried, but desired to own at least two head of cattle before seeking a bride. The woman had fallen into him at the market. He was just about to pay for a rug when the woman, passing by, tripped and fell on him. He caught her, set her up on her feet and offered her peace. But when he reached for his purse, it was missing. He was fortunate that a friend had seen the woman and stopped her. That friend's wife was with him, and found the purse hidden in the woman's clothes.

"Are there any more witnesses?" Kherlos asked.

A portly man came forward, richly dressed in an embroidered shirt, a fur-collared vest and tall, black-leather boots.

"Announce yourself."

"I am the rug merchant," he replied. "I was about to sell the fine man a quality rug at great value."

A few in the crowd chuckled.

"Do you know the man?"

"Only that he is very poor, for he drove a hard bargain and paid very little for my beautiful rug. I made him promise not to tell what a soft head I have."

Kherlos laughed along with the others, but he had heard enough. This play was a tragedy, not a comedy. He looked to the woman; fear and guilt were clear on her face. He looked to his people, the men were laughing, but the women weren't, their eyes were hard, their jaws and minds set.

Twin beams of deadly energy flashed. The woman's hand flared with brilliance and then extinguished, leaving dull gray flesh behind. She lifted her arm, the hand hung limp on the end of her wrist.

"Your hand has offended me with its theft," Kherlos said. "It will serve you no more." He rose from his chair. "You are free to leave us. You would be wise to seek out a surgeon and healer to remove the dead flesh from your body, but seek elsewhere. No man or woman will aid you here."

The jailer appeared on stage again. He touched her gently on the shoulder, and indicated the steps, but she jerked away. She cradled her dead hand against her breast as if it were an infant. Head down, she moved down the front of the platform and then down into the middle of the people. They parted as she passed and would not look at her. After she had gone, they returned their attention to the stage, and waited in silence.

"Bring forth the next accused," Kherlos cried.

As soon as he was free of his chains, the man dropped to the ground and groveled. "Please, forgive me, Divine Ra-ken, I was mad with hunger."

"You stole meat from the market?"

"Yes, I stole it to feed my children."

Kherlos asked, "Was this man fed in jail?"

"Yes, he was fed and bathed," the jailer replied.

"Did he pray to the Divine?"

"No, he cursed me and committed foul acts in his cell."

"Did he receive visitors?"

"No, neither friends nor relatives came to ask of this man."

"Stand this man up and lift up his shirt," Kherlos commanded. The man resisted, but strong arms lifted him and then his shirt. Kherlos called upon his ability, focused his attention on the man's midsection and willed death. "You will hunger no more."

The man might have had something to say, but he seemed barely able to catch his breath. He had lost control of his legs, his bowels and bladder.

"Drag him away, let him lay where the beasts of the forest may feed upon him."

The guards dragged him away; others moved to clean the soil from the stage. Kherlos rose, motioned them back, and spoke to his citizens. "I wish for peace. If you wish to live in my city, then this is to be your wish too. I do not ask that you enshrine me. I do require that you observe a particular orthodoxy. I do require that your offer love, respect, and yes, peace, to your neighbor. The Divine is forgiving, but those who would steal from us and seek to destroy our lives; those who would thwart our purpose and make us suffer; they shall suffer instead. Give to each other your love and we shall prosper, for I am your lord, I am Ra-ken, I am your law, I am your protector, and I am your wrath."

Kherlos returned to his seat. The people cheered, whistled and stamped their feet. His priests congratulated him. Travia mouthed praise and spoke of accomplishment, but he tuned it all out, let it all become so much noise. Words. It was all they had, their only weapon, and so they assaulted him with them. It didn't matter what they said; all words were the same. With his will alone, he could silence them. His will against their words. Silence.

# Five.

*But Lord, spoke Yeywah, second of the Angels. Thou gives men thy gifts, but not thy humility. Surely, thy gift of Creation will upset the balance of the heavens.*

*Book of the Divine*

**8 Hupten, Y.O.D. 744**

## Council Monastery, East of Vesport, Tameria

Fire lit up the mountainside. Dancing shadows among the trees matched the ring of dancing humans. The night air was cool. The moon was rising slowly through the tall thin trees. It was but a thin sliver and its pale rays were no match for the blaze that cavorted below. Around the fire, people moved with the heavy rhythm that shook the trees and echoed down into the valley. Beads of sweat on foreheads and arms reflected tiny diamonds of red and yellow against their dark skin. Gold and silver bangles and earrings flashed great slashes of brightness as their nearly naked bodies gyrated about.

The broad, high plateau they danced upon looked for all the world as if a giant had cleft the mountain with a mighty axe, making two strokes, one vertical, one horizontal, and then had removed the resulting wedge as if it were a cheese. One end of the artificial courtyard ended in steep steps that curved down the mountain and exited through a stone arch into a thick wooded land. On the opposite end sat a large stone temple with immense oaken doors. Between the two ends was an enormous fire, ringed by dancers, who were in turn ringed by priests of the divine in their gray robes, men and women in fancy dress, and finally, almost unnoticed, many dark skinned boys and girls wearing simple shirts, breeches and sandals.

Great tables laden with food and wine had been set up around the plateau. People ate, talked, laughed, and watched the dancers. At their center of all this celebration stood Ahten. This was his night, his party, his vindication. Every finger that pointed, every eye that widened, and each smile on every face was a morsel for his consumption. This was his triumph and every gladdened heart nourished his breast.

A thin man, tall and commanding, approached with a woman on his arm. The man wore a white lace shirt with a black vest, black tights and tall black boots with silver buckles in the shape of rearing stallions. The woman wore a blue satin dress with long sleeves and a revealing neckline.

"Cordain, Vellenia," Ahten cried, "Pench was just telling me about reports from Kherlestra. It seems your boy Kherlos is stirring up trouble."

Cordain took a quick drink of wine from his silver goblet before taking the bait. "Aren't you getting ahead of yourself? Perhaps we should wait until your wishing wheels have proven effective before we start adding more people to the list?"

"Just thought you should know," Ahten said. "In case you wanted to have a word with him. Vellenia, you do look lovely."

"Thank you Ahten," she cooed, "but tell me, don't you priests take vows of celibacy?"

"Divine no! What an odd idea."

"Yet you have no wife. Are all these young ladies in your care, safe?"

Ahten reddened, but from embarrassment or anger, she couldn't tell. "Yes! Of course they are. This project is too important to me to risk it in such a demeaning way. And that goes for all of the staff. The students are allowed liaisons; we're not prudes, nor their parents."

"Relax," Cordain said. "She's just getting you back for what you said to me. We've heard no complaints."

"I should think not," Ahten said.

"Have you seen Xavier?" Cordain asked.

"He's in my office, getting ready."

"Thank you. If you'll excuse me, I need to speak with him before then. Play nice Vellenia."

She pouted. "Not without a kiss."

Cordain kissed her, not long, but just enough to promise more, later. He patted her bottom once and walked away.

"I thought he preferred men," Tawnya Brawley said as she approached the little clique—a short, plump woman in a black ankle length dress, decorated at the end of the sleeves and hem with rainbow colored bands of cloth. Her white hair and pleasant face made her look like everyone's favorite grandmother.

"Tawnya, did you inspect the wishing wheels?" He bowed as he spoke, his face beaming with delight.

"I did, they seem simple enough. I assume the students are ready. Don't go anywhere Vellenia." Tawnya reached out and gently held Vellenia's arm. "I saw him kissing you."

"Everything is quite ready." Ahten said.

"Then I'm going to advise Layton to proceed. I expect our man to be in place within two weeks."

"Excellent, I'm sure everything will go as planned."

"It had better, this place is too chilly to make a good resort. Come Elly, let's go stand by the fire, speaking of which, is Xavier going to start the show or do I have to do it?"

"I'll see what's keeping him." Ahten said.

"Good."

Vellenia waited a moment for Ahten to leave before speaking. "Cordain tells me you've selected our first victim."

"Yes, Jin Yong, he can spit acid."

"Why him?"

"He owes me money."

§

Farther up the mountain, sitting together at the base of a tree, Dharla felt Briana shiver in her embrace. They, like other couples around them had sought a private place from which to watch the coming fire-display.

"I cheat at wishing," Dharla said softly into her lover's ear. "I think the others do too."

"You don't want to be Ra-ken?"

"I do, but I don't want to spit acid."

"I know. How do you do it?"

"I say 'miss' instead of 'wish.' I'm pretty sure that means I can't get it. You know they have to kill whoever has the ability already for one of us to get it."

"Cal told me that. I don't care. What happens if you don't get it?"

"I asked. They put you on another team. Seth says there are going to be many abilities to gather. Oh, look."

Below them, the fire on the plateau flared up and then started to sway back and forth. Around them, other couples were starting to take notice of the changes in the flames. Below them, drums started pounding, and the echoes reverberated among the mountaintops.

They could see the glowing faces of dancers swarming around the fire, jumping and whirling in beat with the drums. The fire joined in with the rhythm, pulsing and swaying in time. A man walked into the light of the blazing pit, naked except a simple loincloth. His body glowed and glistened as if covered with rubies.

"That's Xavier," Briana said. "He likes me."

"He likes all the girls," Dharla replied.

With his arms extended, making a sinuous motion, the man swayed back and forth. The fire matched his rhythm, and together they danced.

"If one of them died," Briana asked, "which one would you want to be?"

"Not fire, or strength, I might want to be able to run like the wind."

The fire gathered itself into a giant red torso rising high above the trees. Whorls of yellow spun from the top of the fiery head, crowning it in gold, while bright blue jets of flame formed its eyes.

"I thought everyone wanted to fly," Briana said.

"I love to run. I would run so fast I could run over water. That would be like flying."

The shimmering giant clasped flame fingers together in front of its face and blew. A stream of sparks leapt onto the ground, touching in three places where bundles of faggots had been tied to a thick post. At each post, a man and a woman— naked above the waist, but painted as if on fire—swayed and spun as the fire danced with them.

"When I get my power, they won't tell me what to do," Briana said.

Below, the drumming ceased. The dancers all bowed to their partners and stepped back into the darkness from which they had come.

Xavier brought his hands down to his waist, and then thrust them high into the air; his doppelganger of flame mimicked the gesture. Showers of sparks flew upward and the hillside became as day.

Another shower of sparks flew up into the air and then exploded high above them. Flowers of flame—of all different colors—erupted into the night while thunder shook the stars and scared away all the game in the valley.

After a time the pyrotechnics ended. The air became still, the mountain silent, and a great cloud of smoke hid the stars. Below the fire demon bowed to an appreciative audience. The master of fire raised his arms, and clapped one sharp tattoo. The fire ceased and the night was pitch.

"We'd best be getting down," Dharla said. Other couples were stirring.

"I'm in no hurry," Briana said. "I'm sleeping on the floor tonight." The girls had been crowded together to make room for the guests. The same was true of the boy's dormitories. Some guests would stay with friends in the village, but most wanted to avoid the hazard of the stairway in the dark.

"Well I'm not; I have a bed waiting for me."

"You could share." They had had this conversation before.

Briana rose, adjusted her thin wool sweater and brushed any loose leaves and dirt off her short skirt. She helped Dharla to her feet. Dharla brushed the back of her clothes, then picked up Briana's blanket and dusted it off.

"I'm sleeping under that tonight," Briana said. She took the short blanket and folded it over her arm.

"I'm sorry," Dharla said, "You know the rules."

"It's okay." Briana moved close and hugged her partner. "Not while the team is active. It's not fair to the others. I could give that lecture from the grave."

"I love you."

"I know, c'mon." Briana said. "Let's go."

# Six.

*But Lord, spoke Xerxes, third of the Angels. Thou gives men thy gifts, but not thy clarity. Surely, thy gift of Divination would raise men up to be your equal.*

*Book of the Divine.*

## 13 Raveen, Y.O.D. 744

## City of Kherlestra, North Seleton

Kherlos appreciated his new office. A few paintings decorated the walls, tall lead-glass windows gathered the morning light, and it had about it a sense of business . It contained a modest oak desk at one end, a few chairs, and plenty of space to hold a small meeting, such as when his head priest Travia and a cadre of acolytes invaded, like this morning.

Kherlos tipped the ornate silver inkwell on its edge, dipped his quill into the shallow remains and tapped it gently against the rim. A large document lay on his desk requiring his signature. He placed the tip against the large parchment contract and drew his name in quick fluid script, each letter flowing down the page into the next. He added the chops and accents to his signature, then dropped the feather into the nearly empty cup, and flexed the fingers of his right hand.

Travia lifted the document carefully and handed it to a clerk seated at a simple folding table. The clerk, with practiced arm, used thin wooden paddles to fold each side inward, creased the seam, and then repeated this action until the document was a manageable flat square. This he wrapped with silk ribbon, and where the ends met, he poured a generous portion of thick red wax. He pressed in the seal of the Ra-ken, and then added the document to an already substantial stack.

Kherlos rubbed his wrist, massaged the tendons in his right hand and waited for the next parchment to appear.

Travia stood placidly in front of the desk, his hands clasped in front of his light-gray robe. "That was the last one, my Lord." Behind him, the troupe of lower functionaries was already packing up.

Kherlos turned his wrists so that Travia could see the ink on his fingers, and the smudges on his white-cotton sleeves.

"My sister made me this shirt."

"I shall admonish the staff to clean it very gently. I shall renew instructions to your valet as to when there will be more documents requiring your signature."

"See that you do."

Travia bowed. As he did so, the single lock of his hair dangled in front of Kherlos like a bell pull, and it was all he could do to resist tugging it.

"Will there be anything else?" Travia asked.

"Yes, find Takoda and tell him I wish to see him."

"Ra ku kellsee, my lord." Travia said.

"Kellsee auch."

The priests and his clerks filed out. For the moment at least, he was alone. There was no end of people who wanted his time, or his advice, or his signature. What they really wanted was his power. But to get that they would have to kill him, and that was never an easy or certain thing.

Takoda appeared in his doorway. "You requested my presence?"

"Come in, sit. Were you lurking outside my apartments and using your ability on me?"

"Nonsense," Takoda insisted, "it's a beautiful day and I know how much you love paperwork. So I thought I would drop by and save your right hand for something more pleasant than signing an endless stream of documents." Takoda flopped down into one of Kherlos's overstuffed chairs.

Kherlos smiled and shook his head. He loved Takoda's bawdy nature and his ability to know what was on his mind. "I did, but I swear you cheat."

"Not at all, I just know you well, that's all. Besides, we've had this conversation."

"So what are my intentions?" Kherlos blanked his mind, he intended to sit there and be stubborn.

"I don't know and I don't care," Takoda replied. "I intend to take you out for a walk, your guards are getting fat and lazy and need the exercise, and if you don't get up and move around more you'll go soft. And then all the young men of the city will lose faith."

"You know," Kherlos stood as he spoke, "it amazes me that you never seem to fear that you might cross the line with me."

"If I feared you, Ra Timèatteo, Ra-ken ka ne caca, or whatever the fel your title is, then I'd just be another one of your sycophants, or hiding under a robe of gray instead of black."

"What did you just call me?" Kherlos feigned anger, a pointless bluff against this man.

"I think it might be better if I let the priests explain it," Takoda said. "Are we walking or not?"

"I'm the one standing."

Takoda pushed himself up out chair. Kherlos motioned him forward, and followed him out. Takoda was taller than Kherlos by almost a head. He was thin, with a neck slightly too long, but it carried an intellect Kherlos both admired and envied.

Takoda stopped at the doorway and glanced down at Kherlos's feet.

"Yes," Kherlos said, "I'm wearing my sandals. You're not the only one who can anticipate the intentions of others."

§

As they wound their way down to the lower levels, they came across two palace sentries.

"You two," Kherlos poked the closest man in the shoulder, "we're going for a walk."

"Sir!"

He turned back to Takoda. "Are they finished with the tile in the front hall?"

"They have planks down. We won't disturb their work."

As they reached the grand entrance, Travia popped out of a side door just in time to intercept them, slightly out of breath, as if he had just been informed that his master was about to attempt to leave the building. "My lord, what a pleasant surprise, have you come to see the mural?"

Kherlos looked around. When he had last come this way, the interior was all rough wood, now the ceiling was covered in gilded plaster, the walls were paneled and workers were finishing the laying of stone tile.

"What mural?"

"Behind you?"

Covering the wall behind him was an eight-foot tall likeness of himself in glowing white armor, surrounded by angels of the Divine—

with yellow suns where their heads should be. He held a golden pike with which he impaled a monstrous, black snake coiled about his feet.

"What is that?"

"My Lord, that is you, slaying the Butcher."

Kherlos smiled; they had certainly taken liberties with the facts.

"Do you like it?" Travia asked, the concern plain on his face.

"If you don't like it," Takoda remarked, "they'll redo it, only bigger."

"Yes, yes I like it."

"And the tile?"

Kherlos looked at the deep red marble tile. It had dark green streaks with flecks of gold throughout. "How am I paying for all of this?"

Travia's face fell.

"Lord," Takoda said, "if I recall, this tile belonged to the Butcher, delivered, but never used. I believe it was found in one of his warehouses, and has but recently arrived."

"Ah," Kherlos said, "Excellent, yes I like it."

Travia cleared his throat. "Lord, I understand you will be traveling, shall I send the carriage?"

"Thank you, no. Takoda and I are going for a walk. I feel the need to stretch my legs."

§

Takoda led the way. He was more familiar with the streets, the people, and anything that was new or interesting. Kherlos had rarely made it outside since the roof had been finished. To him, everything was unfamiliar except the streets, which he had drawn himself on parchment some two years ago.

When they had first arrived, the land had been wild, and they had lived in tents, and then crude cabins. The fields were cleared, surveyed and marked. Ditches were dug and pipes laid, roads leveled and graveled, all in anticipation of a city that was then just markings on paper.

Now those streets were filled with traffic, and lined with houses and shops. Beyond that was a ring of new streets and new houses still under construction, and beyond them, a ring of tents again, where the newest citizens slept.

Takoda guided them from building to building, all in various states of completion, making introductions while Kherlos gave blessings and words of encouragement. They wandered in what appeared to be a random manner amid a sea of strangers.

They came upon what looked to be a rather ambitious building sketchily framed in timber and scaffolding. As they approached, the work ceased and the hammers fell silent. An obese man with a bald head, who had been arguing with a small boy turned and yelled at his men. "Get back to work. What do you think you're doing? I'll tell you when it's time for prayers." The boy tugged at the sleeve of the man's voluminous red and blue shirt.

"Fat Arlond," Kherlos yelled.

Fat Arlond spun around, his face burning. "Kherlos! Lord, Divine Raken ku kellen oh oclo totus. It is such a pleasure to see you."

Kherlos spread his arms. "Give me a hug."

Arlond waddled over gave Kherlos a smothering hug. "Welcome to my home."

Kherlos inspected the building. "You are looking well fed my friend, but your home is looking thin."

"Thank you, lord, but may I tell my men to get back to work?"

"Yes, yes. Everywhere I go people think I'm a walking holiday. If I didn't spend all my days in the palace nothing would ever get done."

"You heard him," Arlond cried. "Get back to work, and put some sweat into it."

"The rains are coming; you'll need a roof before long."

"This is true, lord, but my men say they can only work for me one day out of three, and always there are shortages and high prices."

Kherlos looked at Takoda who nodded in agreement. "Are the suppliers not treating you fairly?" His tone indicated there might be consequences for those who over charged for their goods.

"They charge me no more than any other. They claim the men of Linnaton are to blame."

"Well, I will have the priests look into the matter. Tell me, where is your beautiful wife?"

"Thank you for asking. She is off bargaining for more bricks even as we speak."

Kherlos laughed. "Yes, she will get the lowest price, I'm sure. Tell me, are you still lodging at your brother's?"

"Yes, yes, but he is as anxious for us to be in our own home as we are. His wife is expecting."

"Oh how wonderful." Kherlos said, "Please do extend my invitation to your brother and his wife, the four of you should join me for dinner in the palace."

Fat Arlond bowed. "Yes, Lord."

"This Sunday would be good," Kherlos said, "If it is convenient."

"I am certain it will be, Lord. Blessings of the Divine be upon you."

"Come, show me your inn. This is my good friend Takoda."

Takoda shook hands with Arlond. "Ra ku kellsee, Arlond."

"Ra ku kellsee, Takoda, Ah ku ana fetta moke."

"You speak archaic well Arlond." Kherlos said.

"Thank you, Lord." Arlond led Kherlos and Takoda into the framed structure of the house. The stone foundation and interior load-bearing walls were laid. "Over here," Arlond pointed to a bare patch of dirt, "will be the kitchen, beyond that will be the common dining area. Your shrine will be there, so your divine presence can bless our meals."

"Perhaps you will invite me to bless them in person."

"Of course, of course," Arlond quickly agreed. "Downstairs, will be two common quarters. With bunk beds we can sleep eight in each, one room for the single men and one for the women. Now upstairs, above the kitchen will be our rooms, and a separate room for our daughter and the maids. Then, six private rooms, and finally a single suite at the end, reserved for Ra-ken, such as yourself, or Mo-ken as may be."

"You would keep a room empty?" Takoda asked.

"No, that would be a waste of good money, but it would be let to Ur-non, such as ourselves, only on the condition it is not desired by those blessed by the Divine."

Kherlos looked at the framed space. "Where are the privies?"

"Ah yes, the pipe is installed over there." He pointed to a tarp-covered area. "The ground pipe is laid, one for each floor. They will install the second floor pipes once the frame is completed."

"I don't see a well," Takoda said.

"Dug, but not capped I'm afraid. We are waiting for the pump to arrive from Linnaton, such a fuss those fools make. You would think I was spawning demons with it. It's just a hand pump, not some forbidden mechanical contraption."

"The Divine will not suffer machines to have abilities." Takoda quoted from the Book of the Divine.

"But Kherlos, Lord, you approved it yourself."

Kherlos laughed at that thought. "I am sure I did Arlond, but I am not the one keeping it from you. Takoda, can you look into this matter?"

"Yes, it would be my pleasure as soon as we return."

Kherlos looked around at the skeleton frame and tried to imagine the building as Arlond described it. "This will be a fine addition to our city. I think you will do very well for yourself."

"Thank you, Lord. You are most kind, but still I despair that the roof will not be up before the rains begin."

Kherlos walked them back to the road. "Well, if the roof is not on by the time your brother's child is born, I will find room for you and your family at the palace."

"Lord, you are too kind; I could not accept such an offer."

Kherlos almost believed him. "True, but your wife could." Arlond conceded the point.

"Perhaps there is a favor I could ask of you?" Kherlos asked.

"Yes, anything, name it."

"I am still learning the subtleties of the archaic tongue, would you know the meaning of the phrase 'Ra-ken ka ne caca'"

Arlond's face went white and he dropped to his knees. Work on the house ceased.

"That bad? Come on, get up."

"I would cut out my own tongue rather than say those words to you."

Kherlos glanced at Takoda, who was trying to look innocent.

"Arlond, you knew me before I was Ra-ken, you may speak to me, man to man."

Arlond struggled to his feet again, looked around to see if any women were present, and leaned close to Kherlos.

"It means to know the Divine, in a way that a man would know another man. But not in a kind way. I mean, I know—"

"Thank you."

"You should not let this insult pass." Arlond said.

"I will not, you may be sure of that."

"You will kill the tongue of the man who spoke those filthy words?"

"I am not Ra Bouchard." Kherlos said. Takoda seemed the only one around not interested in this conversation.

"You are most kind, perhaps too kind, my Lord."

"Divine bless you," Kherlos said, "but your men have stopped working again."

Arlond whipped around hurried back towards the house, yelling at the men to get back to work, then, remembering his manners, he turned back and bowed deeply. "Ra ku kellsee" Arlond called.

"Kellst tu, kellst tu auch."

Kherlos turned and clasped Takoda on the shoulder "Let's walk."

He led them out to the edge of the town, and onto the north road towards Linnaton. They walked until the last of the houses were out of sight and the four of them were alone on the road. Kherlos stopped on a stone bridge that spanned the river that brought water to their town. He liked to watch the rushing currents and listen to their soothing rhythms.

"Are you going to build a city wall?" Takoda asked, apropos of nothing.

"No, even stone is in short supply."

Takoda looked around, there seemed to be stone everywhere.

"You know what I mean," Kherlos added. Everything seemed to be in short supply except work and thankfully, food. Fish and game were plentiful, crops grew well in the fertile valley, but most of the easily plowed land was claimed. Those who could work were busy doing so, those who would not were sent away. His thoughts returned to the reason he had come to this spot. Kherlos turned to the guards.

"Soldier."

"Lord?"

"Knock this man down to the ground." Kherlos pointed at Takoda. The soldier nodded, trotted the few steps between and roughly forced Takoda down onto the rough stones of the bridge.

"Thank you, as you were." Kherlos said.

"Sir." The soldier saluted and moved back to resume his position. Kherlos stepped over to Takoda and held out his hand.

"You meant to stop him," Takoda said. "Just before he knocked me down."

"I did, yet somehow I failed to do so."

Takoda lay on the ground, looking at the extended hand.

"Are you going to lie in the road all day?"

Takoda looked around, as if that seemed a fine idea, then he reached up and took Kherlos's hand.

"You owe me an apology," Kherlos said.

"I thought I just did."

Kherlos turned his head slowly back towards the guards.

Takoda made a low bow, "My lord, I most—"

"Apology accepted. Listen, politics are complicated. My people must fear me, just a little—or they will see me as weak. At the same time, the priests must believe they control me. Understand that everything that happens here is reported back to the Council. I can give them no reason to replace me."

"The council is very far away."

"Yes, but not far enough. They're up to something. I don't know what it is, but I want to stay outside of their attention, and to do that I need you and your ability. So stop causing me trouble. Hungry?"

"Yes."

"Good, so am I." Kherlos headed back toward town, walking at a brisk pace. Takoda fell in beside him, and the two guards brought up the rear.

"Now" Kherlos said, "how does that phrase translate exactly." Takoda gave him a wary look but said nothing. Kherlos only laughed.

# Seven.

*But Lord, Spoke Uuvault, fourth of the Angels. Thou gives men thy gifts, but not thy Empathy. Surely, thy gift of Death would be wrought against thy Angels.*

*Book of the Divine.*

**25 Ravee, Y.O.D. 744**

### Tse Lee's Palace, Epe Tianore, Alasta

In his mind, Kim imagined how the events would unfold. He would walk brazenly to the gates of the palace, holding in his right hand, a long sword—with a mongoose etched on each side of the blade—and a curved dagger—subtly poisoned with a narcotic—in his left. The guards at the gate would instantly recognize the danger they were in. One would run for the gong to sound danger, the other would bravely try to hinder his entrance. He would let them both succeed. He would toy with the one soldier, slowly gain the upper hand, and then just as help arrived, dispatch him a quick double back cut through the neck. The others would surround him, armed with spear, blade, and, no wait. Yes, they surround him. He lunges, feints, breaks their ranks and quickly they all fall. Behind them is their champion, a large well-muscled man wearing only an apron, sandals, and the tasseled armbands of his profession. The man is already sweaty, his skin ripples and glistens with a fine sheen. He holds his favorite weapon, a sickle and chain. He is Mo-ken, a healer, and a fighter. He cuts a long line across his chest with the sickle and then heals it closed, so that only an arc of blood shows. Kim bows, honored by such a worthy opponent.

Kim demonstrates his own ability, and fades invisible in the man's mind. This braggartly display is forbidden by his family, but he ignores that prohibition because he is a warrior, and not some ferret that slinks in the dark.

His opponent shakes his head and blinks. All he is able to see are two weapons floating in mid-air. Kim weaves them in an intricate pattern meant to confuse and frighten, but the man is not fooled. Each thrust is blocked, countered and answered. His opponent can see him through the movement of the weapons. The small wounds he is able to inflict, which would distract any other adversary, are healed instantly.

If he were anyone else but Kim, he would lose this fight. He flips his sword up and catches it by the heel of the blade, just in front of the hilt. Now his weapons move wrong. He seems to be taller or facing backwards, or too far away. The chain wraps around the sword, trapping it, and the sickle sweeps through the space where Kim's head should have been, a killing stroke that should end the fight. It does. Kim pushes his dagger into the man's heart and leaves it there, a gift to the worthy opponent's family.

The other soldiers, now understanding whom they face, all kneel in a line along the path, heads extended, awaiting his mercy.

Kim sighed; it would have been an epic battle. He made himself unseen and stepped out from an alley into the street running past the main gate.

As previously arranged, a man with a donkey cart full of melons pulled up to the entrance and argued with the guards about where the produce was to be delivered and who was to pay him. Kim used the diversion to cover his sounds and moved easily past them through the entrance and into the walled grounds of the palace.

A wide red-brick path met and circled a large pool filled with golden carp. In the center, all manner of granite statuary jetted water from green copper pipes into the pool. Two women in bright silk dresses sat on a cushioned bench and fed cracked corn to the fish.

Kim passed by the women, and continued until he found flagstones leading toward a large pond dotted with white and pink lilies. He exited the path and headed for a nearby grove of yellow-leafed trees, where he found a mossy grotto underneath the branches.

The day moved on. As dusk approached, a young couple joined him in his hideout for a moment of intimacy. They made love while he watched. They were clumsy and rushed for time, yet still endearing in their own way. The boy looked to be a stable hand, with straw and smut on his trousers. The girl was some servant from the house. When they had gone, he sat back down in the space where they had lain.

§

A full moon rose above the wall and shimmered gently in the still water. Kim preferred to work when the night was the least threatening and vigilance was relaxed, when the hour was late and the moon high. Kim rose, brushed his clothes and set out for the palace.

The building was three stories tall. Each story was smaller than the one below, and protected by sentry skirts that jutted out over the walls.

Broad steps ran up to a wide porch at the front. Statuary set into small alcoves flanked the large double doors. Two men with pikes and slatted armor leaned casually against the frame and chatted, coming to attention only as the night sergeant made his rounds. Kim would not enter through that door; instead, he would climb a bronze statue of a rearing tiger, near the corner. From there he could step onto the roof and move across its terracotta tiles to a set of shuttered windows. But first he needed a distraction.

"I hate nights like this," the man on the left said out of nowhere. Kim froze.

"Shut up, Rhan," the other said.

"I'm just saying…"

"I don't care. It was your mouth what pulled us a month of nights. You're just lucky we both still have all of our body parts."

Kim watched the two men squabble. He needed to cross the gravel to reach the statues. He would need three steps to do it. He carefully placed one foot out onto the path and eased his weight onto it. On the second step, the night sergeant rounded the corner and headed straight for him. Kim shifted his weight back quickly and balanced up on one leg just as the sergeant moved past.

"Sons of whores," the sergeant growled as he stomped up the steps. "If I thought for one second that the Ice Bitch might be awake I would have both of your asses caned until your short legs fall off." Rhan snapped to attention, remembered his pike, grabbed it and snapped to attention again.

The two men stood rigid. Kim eased his foot down and wondered, did he mean Le Le? Was she here?

The sergeant laughed. "Hut down, boys, I hear she's got herself a new girl, likes to wear them out on their first night." The men relaxed, gave a little smile. The sergeant hung his lamp on a hook, stepped down off the porch and gathered some grass and dirt. He threw the mixture into the air and fixed his will upon it. The debris swirled around and sorted itself quickly into a woman's face. Two black pebbles formed the eyes and the blades of grass formed long strands of green hair. The rest of the dust grouped itself into high cheekbones and a wide-open mouth. The face moved and convulsed as if in the throes of passion. The men all chuckled nervously.

Kim was impressed. The likeness of Le Le was quite convincing. He supposed it was just as well he had not known she was here; assassins could not afford to mix business with pleasure. He took the opportunity to move across the path onto the grass next to the porch.

"We heard a noise out back," Rhan said.

The sergeant let the dirt resume its normal association with the general guidelines of physics. "So why don't you like nights like this."

"Bad things happen," Rhan said, "the night is full of bad omens."

"What kind of bad things?"

"Just bad things; the Eye of the Divine is open and the damned walk the land."

"The Eye of the Divine?"

"He means the moon," said the other man, "it's a superstition he picked up somewhere. You can't shake a stick anymore without some people throwing salt on you."

The sergeant just shook his head, muttered something soft, and then barked, "Shut it, both of you. I'll go take a look. You two keep your eyes open and your mouths shut."

Kim squatted down and counted softly. When he reached thirty, he brought out a small leather pouch. He untied the cord and released the contents.

The two were both slouching again. One reached out and punched the other in the arm.

"Rhan you are a filthy son of a wh–" He stopped mid curse. There was something scrabbling at his foot with tiny claws.

"Rat," he hissed.

"Huh? Whore maybe, sure, but a rat?" Rhan asked.

"On my foot."

"Huh? Where'd you get that from?"

"Idiot." He shook his foot, and the rat bit his ankle. "Ah shit!"

Rhan took the butt end of his pike and jammed it down at the rat's head. It missed.

Kim climbed up the bronze statue. He stood with one foot on the tiger's head and stepped across onto the thick beams that angled down to the corners. Just as he pushed off and shifted his weight onto the roof, a giant boom came from beneath him. Startled, he stepped onto a terracotta tile and broke it. Silence then, below and above, save for the sound of running on gravel.

"Ahh-tend!" The sergeant shouted as he came back around to the front. "What the Fallen is going on here?"

Kim watched him disappear underneath his feet.

"Explain yourselves."

Kim lifted his foot gently and moved it to the wooden beam. The cracked tile stayed where it was. He concentrated on the conversation below.

"A rat sir," Rhan said.

"A rat?"

"Yes, sir."

"A rat just made that noise and that mark on the door?"

"No, sir, I did that?"

"Fighting this rat were you?"

"It was on my foot sir," the other said.

"I am sure that Ra Lee will want to present you with an award for being wounded during valorous combat with an enemy rodent."

Kim could hear the spittle in the man's voice. He heard a door open, and a familiar woman's voice.

"Why are we disturbed? Sergeant?" Le Le asked.

"Do-Hu, blessed Mistress, a thousand pardons, my man was bitten by a rat; he reacted poorly and struck back at it, causing the unfortunate disturbance. I shall have him..."

The window above Kim's head banged open. Divine be damned, Kim thought. Jin Yong, the man he came to kill was leaning out of the window above him, yelling.

"What is this? A rat? What color was it? I must know."

Below, sergeant Du-Ho came down off the porch until he could see Jin Yong's gray head and then bowed. "Honored Ra, A thousand pardons for disturbing your slumber, my man struck at a rat, fearing it was diseased and rabid. Please bless us with–"

"Never mind," Jin interrupted, "What color was this rat? Tell me, quickly."

"Blessed one, the rat was white. It has fled."

"So it was not killed then?"

"No."

"That is good. Still, you must do as I say. Listen to these instructions. You are to take three hairs from the man who struck the rat and burn them with a thumb of sulfur. Carry the smoke from this around this palace three times. You must do this quickly. Do you understand? Tell me, quickly, quickly."

"Yes, honored one, it will be done at once."

Le Le came down off the porch. Kim saw her and his breath quickened. Her pale skin and dark hair were beautiful in the moonlight. Her movements were so graceful; her features so delicate, her ability so deadly; he despaired that she could only love other women.

"Go back to your bed old man," Le Le called out to Jin. "I will see that your instructions are followed." She turned to the sergeant. "See to it." The man moved back up onto the porch. Le Le looked at the grass, the statue and then at the shuttered window, now closed again. "And, sergeant Du-Ho…" she paused, letting the emphasis on his name carry its own implications, "Put two fresh guards on the master's Tse's door and I want patrols around the grounds until dawn."

"Yes, mistress," he said, there was a question in his voice.

"Yes?"

"Our honored guest?"

Le Le snorted, and disappeared up the steps. The door slammed.

Kim looked down at where she had stood. She had frosted the ground around her, and even though the circle of white was rapidly shrinking in the summer heat, he could still make out his footsteps in the grass.

He found the window still unlatched, climbed inside, and sat on the hardwood floor with his back against the wall. He slowed his breath and waited for his heart to calm down. The hallway was dark; the only light came in from the still open window above him. On either side of the hall were various urns, paintings and obscene statuary. He studied the placement of the items, the distance to each and the door that was his destination. Satisfied, he rose and closed the shutters. When he turned, he saw the movement of light coming up the stairs.

A young woman in her nightdress appeared carrying a candle and a steaming mug on a silver tray. She turned and moved up the hallway. Kim followed. He was not surprised when she stopped at Jin Yong's door and knocked.

"Yes, come, come," said a voice inside. The woman knelt and placed the tray on the floor to her side. With both hands, she gently slid the door open and bowed. She twisted her body and picked up the tray. As she did so, Kim moved past her into Jin's dimly lit apartment. She stepped across the threshold, knelt, put down the tray, closed the door, picked up the tray, rose and turned to see Jin Yong scowling at her.

"Bring me warmed goat's milk," he said, "and be quick about it."

The girl lifted the tray of milk towards him. Jin stared at it for a second before realizing what it was.

"Well don't just stand there. Place it next to my bed."

As she bent over, Jin came up behind her and cupped her breast. As she stood up, he pulled her against him. She did not protest. Jin pulled at the cord around his robes and worked them open. The woman slipped the straps of her nightdress off her shoulders and let it fall. Her skin was as pale as the milk she had carried. Jin moved them to the bed.

The girl was pretty, but Kim had gotten his fill of voyeurism shortly after he had heired. He hoped it would not take long.

Jin collapsed onto the bed and pulled the blankets over his skinny, naked body. "I'll want a bath in the morning."

"Yes, Honored one." The girl moved around the room and blew out all but the single candle she had brought, dressed quickly, and retrieved her tray. Jin was already snoring. She moved back to his bed, bent over, dribbled spit into his milk and left.

After a few minutes, Kim lowered himself to the floor and waited. He could hear the sound of boots on gravel and smell the stink of sulfur creeping into the room.

§

Slowly the dawn's rays found their way through the cracks in the shutters and announced the new day. Kim rose, stretched, and moved slowly through a series of positions and exercises meant to keep him limber. When they were completed, he moved to Jin's bed and gave a quick tug on the bell pull. He returned to his corner and waited. After a few minutes, the door opened, and a servant entered. Jin woke with a start.

"You requested a bath honored guest?"

Jin thought a moment. "Yes, yes, just the thing for old bones."

Servants came in with buckets of hot soapy water. Jin relieved himself while they filled the tub. Then he climbed in and gingerly lowered himself down. "Now go away." Jin closed his eyes and sighed.

After the servants had left, Kim reached into his tunic and removed a sharp, curvy dagger. He moved quietly over to the tub and stabbed Jin in the heart. Just before the blade struck, Jin opened his eyes and looked up at his killer.

He looked disappointed, thought Kim.

§

Kim watched a lone donkey cart wander down the rough dirt road in front of the palace, an early riser, eager to beat the others to market. As it rode over another ubiquitous pothole, Kim jumped up onto its open back.

"Good hunting?" the man asked no one in particular.

"Good hunting," Kim replied. It was none of the man's business; he had been instructed to say nothing. Those two words might get him killed, or they might mean nothing. Either way, Kim considered, he would be far away.

The road turned and took them out of site of the palace. Kim relaxed his ability and allowed himself to be seen again. He was tired.

"Wake me at the docks," he instructed.

§

Le Le woke to the call from outside her door. The voice was young and urgent.

"Mistress, mistress," the girl repeated.

Kim, Le Le thought. "Enter!"

The girl pushed the door open only enough to let her skinny body through. She bowed quickly without making eye contact, closed the door and scurried to the side of the bed.

Le Le grabbed the girl's arm. "Tell me."

"It's Master Jin," the girl cried. "He's dead."

"Jin you say?"

"Yes, mistress."

"Divine blessed, thank you." Le Le pushed her away and slid out of the bed. She lifted her pajama top off, threw it on the floor, and hurried over to her wardrobe. "Who found him? Who else knows this?"

"I found him mistress; I came straight to you and told no one."

Le Le gave her a sharp look, and then turned back to her clothes, selected a robe and threw it on the bed. "Help me dress, Quickly!"

The girl moved to Le Le's dresser and started pulling open drawers.

"How did you find him?"

"He called for a bath, but when he did not call again, I was sent to see about him."

"No, these." Le Le grabbed a pair of silk pants and stepped into them.

"Go back to the kitchen and fetch his breakfast. Tell them, no. Wait. Yes, get his breakfast and I will meet you there."

The girl hesitated.

"Now," Le Le hissed.

§

Jin Yong's apartment door was open; Le Le stepped in and pushed it shut. Jin was laying with his eyes and mouth open. The hilt of an ornate dagger protruded out of the red water. The round pommel was inlaid with a golden sun. She touched the water; it was still warm.

"You warned me the council was making plans." Le Le looked around the room. "Did you wait here all night?" There was no answer. She closed the door and waited.

Soon a light knock came on the paneled door. Le Le slid it open and admitted the servant. "Good, can you count?"

"Yes, mistress."

"Count to ten, slowly, three times, then drop the tray, scream and run back to the kitchen. Understood?"

"Count to ten, three times slowly."

"Yes."

§

Le Le pushed her way past the two men outside of Tse Lee's door and entered her employer's apartments. Drayton, his manservant rose to greet her.

"Mistress, he is not risen."

"I am aware of that. I have news that cannot wait."

Drayton hesitated. "He is with one of your girls."

"Then she can hide in there and you can send him out here."

69

Drayton bowed and disappeared. A few moments later, an angry Tse Lee emerged. "We've had this talk before—"

"Jin is dead," Le Le said. She didn't care about the girl, not yet.

"Oh. Did you do it? I will be very angry with you." He shook his finger at her. "You did not have my permission."

"It was an assassin, just not me. It happened this morning, while he was in his bath. There was an incident last night. A distraction was created to allow the assassin entry."

"How do you know this?"

"There was a disturbance last night, this morning Jin is dead."

"A disturbance? Then what did you do to protect my person?"

"I posted extra guards at your door."

Tse walked to the door, opened it, looked at the men and closed the door. "Good, I will expect your full report tomorrow morning."

"Tomorrow?"

"Yes, I will be too distraught with grief at the death of my friend before then, and you will need time to torture the witnesses."

§

Military executions took place at sunrise, though technically Du-Ho was taking his own life to avoid dishonor. This would allow his wife to sell their possessions and return with her children to her family.

Sixteen men in parade dress of fancy red vest and pleated black trousers escorted the prisoner from the barracks onto the grassy field between the canal and the eastern wall of the palace. They were accompanied by their captain Pinan, an obese man with beady eyes who always smelled of spiced sausages.

Four people waited by the canal in dark peasant clothing; Du-Ho's wife, two of her brothers, and a man—with a donkey and a skiff—to tow the sergeant's body north.

Tse and Le Lee waited in the field. Tse sat on a plain dark-wood bench, set on a small stage. To his side, Le Le stood in black skirt and red jacket, her hair braided and wrapped in a black scarf.

The captain stopped his men short of the platform, and re-formed them into double lines behind the prisoner—whom he commanded to kneel. "Honorable Ra-ken Tse Lee, presenting prisoner, Mo-ken Du-Ho, Lord!"

"Thank you Captain." Tse rose from his bench and stepped down into the dew-moistened grass. "Mo Du-Ho, you have failed me, as you failed to protect my dear friend Jin Yong." He felt deep disappointment. It was a deep soul-wrenching disappointment. He called upon his divine ability and allowed the others to share his anguish.

"Forgive me, lord," Du-Ho said.

"I do forgive you," Tse said. "Le Le."

Le Le crouched and opened a small lacquered case at her feet. She extracted the dagger Kim had left buried in Jin Yong's chest, now cleaned. She rose and handed the knife to Tse.

Tse felt shame, and willed the emotion into Du-Ho. "Do you feel my shame?"

"I do, my lord."

"You must erase this shame and this stain upon the honor of your family."

"Yes, lord."

Tse felt calmness mixed with a sense of duty and purpose. He felt a longing for peace. He wasn't sure the emotions translated exactly, but he had worked out the procedure through trial and error and it seemed effective. Tse handed the dagger to his sergeant.

Du-Ho examined it briefly, turned it so that he held the grip with both hands, and placed its tip against his solar plexus.

Tse imagined determination, pride, joy, and these emotions engulfed the man before him.

Du-Ho smiled and looked up into Tse's face where he saw forgiveness. He pulled the dagger up quickly, rolled his eyes, and pitched forward onto grass.

Tse returned to his chair and waited. The men, handpicked for this opportunity, began wishing for the ability to create caricatures with dirt and grass. Time passed, and the men continued to wish, looking more and more confused.

"Well?" Tse asked.

Le Le bit her lip. Abilities, even minor ones such as this were scarce, and it would be a shame if it were lost. Tse had always believed it best to surround oneself with those already in possession of minor abilities; people who had little to gain by your death. Only fools like the Council

Ra-ken surrounded themselves with unpowered sycophants who call themselves priests.

"Examine him," Le Le said.

Pinan stepped forward, lifted Du-Ho's head and grunted in understanding. Du-Ho's resolve had been strong, but not strong enough. He was in shock and dying, albeit slowly. Pinan reached down and jammed the dagger in hard.

Immediately, one of the guards shouted and stepped forward. Pinan held up his hand, halting the man.

"Proceed," Tse said.

The guard bent down, gathered some dirt in his hand, and threw it into the air. The debris swirled around and flowed into an oblong disk as if it were a trained circus of gnats. Bits of grass came together and formed two eyes. Darker bits gathered above to make hair and eyebrows. A wide grin split the whirling particles. The face was crude and amateurish, but proved the point.

"Very good," Tse declared. "I shall retire now. Le Le, walk beside me." Tse and Le Le returned to the palace while Pinan and his men remained at attention.

"It has been three days," Tse said. "What have you accomplished?"

She handed him a loop of silk cord. He took a moment to examine it.

"Where was this found?"

"It was found in Jin Yong's laundry."

"When?" The statement was both a question and an accusation. Le Le was ready with her answer. "This morning, by the staff, the head laundress thought it was mine."

This brought a wry smile to Tse's lips. He wrapped the cord around his wrists to make a garrote, and pulled sharply. The cord was supple and strong. "For all I know, it is yours," Tse said, taunting her. He twisted his hands in the cord until his wrists were bound.

"Three nights ago," Le Le said, "Jin Yong, your guest, opened that shutter at the end of the second floor hall, and shouted down at the sergeant to ask what color the rat was." She let this information sink in. He already knew this; she needed him to start thinking in a new direction. If she simply presented the conclusion, he would deny it out of habit. "Then, he instructed your men to burn sulfur and to carry it around the yard three times."

"Hmmm, what do you think this means?"

"I cannot say," Le Le replied, meaning those words literally, "Jin Yong was murdered in the morning, not in the evening, and with a dagger, not with this cord."

"I will tell you," Tse said, "that Jin Yong let in his own assassin. I was the true target of course." He held up the cord. "It is possible he meant to strangle me himself, but lost his nerve. To think, I invited this viper into my home."

Le Le put on her best shocked look.

"Yes, I am too kind sometimes," Tse continued, "Jin had many debts, and no doubt he sought to pay them off with my death. When he found he could not strangle me, he let an assassin into my home. But when morning came, and I was still alive, the assassin would have had new orders to follow. If Jin could not pay off his debts with my life, then he was to pay them off with his own."

"You are most wise my lord," Le Le said.

Tse snorted, dismissing the flattery and handed her the cord. "See that this is found on some assassin's body, with a bag of Suns with Ra Diaten's face on them."

"Lord?"

"You are so innocent of politics Le Le. The river Tresk lies thirty miles off my western flank, and with it I can move spices and silks far into the north without paying Casta's exorbitant tariffs."

"So you seek to invade."

"This abhorrent and unprovoked attempt on my life is a clear act of war that cannot go unanswered. Besides, what better way to celebrate the year's turn, eh? Can I trust you to find this assassin for me? Or should I have you replaced?"

"I will not fail you lord. I like war. Interesting things happen during war."

"Good, you are dismissed."

# Eight.

*And the Lord answered. Zaloth, first and wisest of my Angels, ask now, and I will deliver unto you the gift of Destruction, so that in your immortal self it shall reside and so be denied to man for all of time.*

*Book of the Divine.*

**2 Kehep, Y.O.D. 745**

## Xialin farm, Tra en Nor, Unaligned Territories

The sun was not yet up, but Haddam and his eldest son Esmund were already out working in the fields. They'd lost most of yesterday to drinking and dancing, not that he minded, but by a planter's reckoning, Year's Turn was six weeks ago when he'd put the seed in, at the balance of night and day. Now they risk losing crops to a day's neglect or be called fools and heretics.

The rain had been light last night, good, but not sufficient. His daughter Marina was down near the river, driving the ox that turned the wheel, pumping water into the irrigation channel. Later when the day turned hot, she would leave the river and join them. A cloud of small red insects had blown over the crops and small brown dots began to appear on the leaves. The three of them moved from plant to plant inspecting every leaf, crushing any bugs they found. Adam knew they couldn't hope to kill them all but they still had to try to save as many plants as they could. They certainly wouldn't stand idly by while their crops died. There was no FarSpeaker in the village with which to ask for help or advice. They were on their own, and if that meant back-breaking labor in the hot sun, then that's what they did. A friendly captain who plied a barge up and down the river had promised to take a message downriver to the city. He had not given them much hope, for his barge ran high and empty in the water when it should have been low with grain.

"It's much worse up north," the captain had said. The barge had docked at the village for one day. During that time, they traded soy and oats for tobacco. They had wanted barley for their stills but could not afford his price. The captain apologized, but they must understand he would get that much, and more, downriver.

Up north, as here, there had been little rain. What crops could be saved by irrigation had been fodder for great swarms of insects. Their lord, Ra-ken Casta Diaten, Divinely blessed and shunned by the jealous Council, held no power over the weather or pests. It would be a tough year and there would be no help from any so-called Uppers. The only advice the river captain had to offer was to be on the lookout for the round red insects. He had said that the real crop killers were tiny and green. They sucked the moisture right out of the plants. The red insects ate the green ones. Haddam had not believed the man. What would a river rider know about farming? The man barely ever set foot on soil, let alone stoop as low as to plant in it. Still, they kept an eye out for little green insects too.

"I wish I had the ability to just crush all insects," Esmund said. He had muttered it under his breath, his head down, as he had looked under the leaves of yet another soy plant.

Even so, his father heard him. Haddam stepped between the rows that separated him from his son and cuffed the boy along the head with his open hand. "You know what I said about wishin'."

Still he had waited just a moment, in case the boy had been struck Divine. He turned around to return where he had been working. He was a little slower than the boy was, not so far along in his row. No, he thought, more careful, not slower. It certainly wasn't because of the ache that had settled into his hip this last month. He saw Marina running towards him and frowned. The ox stood idle by the wheel, the channel already draining. She was running with one hand shielding her eyes and the other pointing. He turned to see what had distracted the girl.

The sun had not yet made an appearance, but the sky in the east was proudly announcing its imminent arrival. As if they were heralds of the morning, a long line of figures had crested the hill into this valley just ahead of the first rays. Haddam saw the line of dark silhouettes and felt fear sink into him. He knew the rhythm of soldiers, and saw it now descending towards his farm and the village that lay further on.

§

The smoke billowed tall in the light breeze and drifted east. Most of the crop fires had died down without wind to fan them, but the pile of bedding and miscellaneous items still smoldered thickly. It had gone well, Tse thought. There were a few casualties: overzealous town-folk who had insisted on defending their meager belongings to no good purpose. The soldiers had orders to avoid killing as many people as they could. Tse wanted refugees, not bodies, but soldiers did what soldiers do.

Tonight they would camp on the river. Tomorrow they would head north and cross over. A small party would chase the fleeing villagers south toward the port city of Britarn. The news of the attack would reach there regardless, but Tse wanted sensation, not rumor or stories. He wanted the kind of impact a tired, ragged stream of people would make.

Le Le rode beside Tse, she interrupted his thoughts. "This is a dangerous game you play."

"The council will not stir for the sake of a few burned huts and villagers. Nor will they come to Ra Diaton's aid."

She shrugged. "As you say, but I must consider all threats a possibility."

"Yes, of course, but tomorrow you will see. Casta will muster some small force against us, and I will send them running with their tails between their legs."

"As you say." She enjoyed baiting him.

Tse opened his mouth to reply, and inhaled a bug. He coughed and spat. "Damn. You would think the smoke would drive these bugs away

"Damnation is it?" Le Le asked, "Are we damned?"

"Forsaken by the Divine and cursed our souls will wander the Earth forever unable to rejoin with the Divine. Did you ever hear of such nonsense? And you wonder why I persecute the clergy."

Le Le laughed; Tse expected her to. She gagged suddenly, and then spat.

"I told you they were damned. Did you swallow any?"

"No," Le Le cleared her throat and spat again, then wiped her mouth. "But I see what you mean."

"I'm afraid my power doesn't work on insects," Tse observed.

"Mine does." She held her right hand up in the air, keeping the reins in her left. She spread her fingers wide and turned it into the breeze. A light frost formed between her fingers and spread, like a thin lace glove. She waved it gently, gathering moisture, making it thicker, until a delicate mitten of frost covered her hand. Tse watched, not sure what she was doing. She passed her hand through the cloud of gnats; those it touched became trapped in the growing snowball. She maneuvered her horse in small circles, clearing the insects from around them. Satisfied, she lowered her arm and let go her power. "It's too thick." She showed her hand to Tse.

"I'm sorry?"

"I can't bend my fingers, I need something to break the ice before my hand freezes."

"I thought your blood already was frozen." He found the sight of this beautiful woman with a pale delicate face, jet-black hair and a huge snowball of a hand waving around incredibly comical.

She brought her horse up alongside Tse and swung her hand at the back of his decorated armor. The ice shattered in a spray of water and bugs. Tse only laughed harder, Le Le, flexed her fingers, and rode off.

§

The men sat on rugs and cushions in a large circle inside Tse's main tent, with skins of wine and trays of shredded goat and curried lentils scattered around the floor around them. Most had a woman on their lap. They were some of the cleaner camp followers, but also two of Le Le's girls had been invited to the celebration. Two dark-skinned women— mummers from the south, wearing finger chimes—danced in slow sinuous movements in front of the low fire. They kissed and rubbed against each other, occasionally discarding a fringed wrap of cloth to the catcalls of the men, only to reveal a smaller piece concealed beneath.

Le Le stood outside their circle, near the back of the tent, and watched impassively. The women were well practiced, professionals, and would earn good wages.

Those men without women to grope were stroking themselves in anticipation. They disgusted her.

"I feel a draft."

Le Le turned to see the pudgy face of captain Pinan squinting up at her. She blew a cold breath at him.

"Le Le," Tse chided. "Behave."

"Maybe she's jealous," Pinan said. "Would you like to dance?"

"I don't dance."

For some reason, all the men in the tent thought this comment was wildly amusing.

"Did I miss something?" Another of Tse's numerous generals, Jo Din Gur, stood in the entrance to the tent with a small girl over his shoulder with her skinny legs kicking wildly, which caused her plain gray dress to fly up and give the room glimpses of a bare bottom.

"Le Le was going to dance for us." Pinan said.

"No need for that," Din Gur said. "Look what I found."

"We have enough girls." Le Le said.

"This one's a spy. The boys found her trying to steal turnips."

"She's too young."

Din Gur pulled the girl off his shoulder and tried to set her down and turn her around but she kept kicking and trying to bite him. He pulled her arms up to her face, and then used his ability to control the hair of others to bind her wrists with her own tresses, but she refused to stop kicking and he was forced to hold onto her. "Could I ask my lord to help a bit here please?"

"Is that little sparrow too much for you Jo?" Pinan called out. Again the men all laughed. Suddenly the girl ceased her struggles.

"Thank you, Lord." Din Gur turned his captive to face the others and lifted up the front of her dress.

"She's old enough," Tse said.

§

Tara heard voices and commotion outside of the tent. She rose and waited, head bowed. Le Le stormed in and slapped her. "I hate war."

"Yes, Mistress." Her face stung, but not badly. Le Le had done worse.

"I hate having to do without."

"Yes, Mistress."

"I hate those stupid swaggering men."

"Yes, Mistress." Tara knew where this was leading.

"You will be more fortunate tonight than your sisters. You know we are celebrating a great victory."

"Ra Lee is a great general mistress."

"Prepare me for bed, and save your tongue for better purposes than useless praise of arrogant men."

Tara helped her mistress out of her clothes and into a thin nightgown.

"In the morning, you will fetch your sisters. They may be tired, but that is not my concern." Le Le referred to all her servants as sisters though they bore no relation. It was another way of degrading them Tara supposed, even though they did come to regard each other as sisters under her harsh rule.

The flapping of wings and a soft caw came from above the tent. Tara looked up, and immediately received another slap. Le Le moved to a corner of the tent and squatted over her chamber pot. She finished pissing and stood up. "Empty this. When you return, wait outside until you are summoned."

§

Tara returned with the chamber pot and waited outside as instructed. She did not understand the reason for the orders, but she knew better than to disobey, ask questions, or look like she was thinking of questions. Questions brought pain.

She heard whispered voices within, her mistresses', and another, odd and slightly shrill. She stepped back and turned away. She would stand guard until her mistress called for her. With her back turned she would avoid seeing the man leave. Le Le didn't care for men—everyone knew it—even though sometimes she did. It was best not to notice.

She stood in the cool air of the night, not yet shivering, and watched with some alarm as a soldier approached.

"Left you out here all by yourself are you?" The man was of too low rank to be in this area, and possibly drunk. "Pretty little thing you are, waiting for someone? Well here I am."

She stood her ground, bared her teeth, and hissed at him. He made a quick grab and pulled her into his arms.

"You're Le Le's girl." He glanced over at the tent. "Sounds like your lady already has herself a man then, leaving you all by yourself. My lucky day. Now you've got a man too. I got just the thing for you, pretty little one."

Tara sympathized with her mistress's views on the male species.

"All you got to do is say no," He said feigning seriousness. he pulled her in for a kiss.

"Wouldn't you rather have the real thing?" Le Le asked. She stood in the opening of her tent, the flap held aside with one arm, her other on her hip. The light from the lamps inside was low, but her nightgown was thin and gauzy. The combined look was that of a naked woman covered in spider webs. Her breasts seemed to glow around the edges. The darkness of her hips, deep and absolute, was contrasted by the thin line of light that spilled between her slightly spread legs.

The soldier licked his lips; a slightly puzzled look crossed his face. He had not seen anyone leave the tent and wondered where the other man had gone. Tara broke from his grasp; he seemed to have forgotten her. She bowed low to her mistress. Le Le waved her inside and approached the soldier.

Tara stopped inside the tent, and peered out through a gap.

The man looked confused, a little frightened, but confident in the attraction he held for women. Le Le moved in close and rubbed her breasts against him. She put her hand around to the back of his neck and kissed him.

Tara looked away. She noticed one of the side flaps was up and the netting pulled back. Le Le would be mad if bugs got into the tent and would blame her. She hurried over and put the netting back into place.

Le Le returned with her mood improved. Tara sat patiently waiting.

"You should have watched," Le Le said. "You would have enjoyed seeing his eyes frost over."

Tara looked away.

Le Le sighed. "Dress and go outside. Wait for the guard. Tell them, oh tell them anything you want, I am not to be disturbed. When they are gone you may go to your bed, I have no need of you tonight."

"Yes, Mistress."

The dead guard and the chamber pot were still both outside. Tara knelt down beside the man and gently stroked his hair, crying softly.

# Nine.

*And the Lord answered. Yeywah, second of the Angels, you are also wise, ask now and I will deliver unto you the gift of Creation, so that in your immortal self it shall reside and so be denied to man for all of time.*

*Book of the Divine.*

## 4 Kehep, Y.O.D. 745

### Raceridge field, Tra en Nor, Unaligned Territories

It was a fine day to be on horseback riding to war, Tse thought. The day was warm, the sun just above zenith in a cloudless sky. A light breeze kept his banners unfurled all along the western road. They had made good progress, and his scouts reported no resistance so far, though he did believe that Casta Diaten wouldn't leave them unchallenged for long.

In the meantime, he had another problem to deal with: Le Le.

There had been words between them earlier about last night's incident. She was in a foul mood, and barely spoke to him.

"We will make many good miles today," Tse said. "Perhaps we will come on a farmhouse or two."

Le Le said nothing.

"Come now. The generals are all complaining about you usurping power, and have warned me of your bare ambition. You should not have killed that soldier; it was a military matter and not a security matter."

"She was my favorite."

"You shouldn't have favorites then. They rarely last much past womanhood anyway, so why the concern?"

"It's my affair what I do with my servants, and she was my servant."

"And he was my soldier. So we're even. But you can get new servants out here. I can't get new soldiers. Besides, where were your guards?"

"I gave them the night off. It was only fitting they should celebrate your victory as well."

"Were you celebrating?"

"I was, privately."

"Then what was the girl doing outside your tent?"

"I told you. I was celebrating privately. You don't normally require me to ask your permission to punish a soldier."

"Yes, but we're not normally thirty miles into enemy territory." Tse stopped; one of his men, Captain Pinan, was galloping toward them. Tse looked back and saw that General Din Gur, who had discretely given him and Le Le some distance, was already coming forward.

Pinan reigned up in front of them and saluted. His horse looked like it was about to die.

"Speak," Tse said.

"We have encountered a wall, Lord. It blocks the road."

"A wall?" Din Gur asked, "What kind of wall? Where? Why didn't you knock it down?"

Pinan looked panicked. "It's ahead about a half mile, I just rode back from it. It's made of earth and it's very big, yet it is hidden by the trees until you are almost on top of it."

"You're not making any sense. How big is this wall?"

"I have riders following it in both directions. I have not had word back from them yet."

"We should go see," Le Le said. "Is there anyone guarding it?"

"No, lady."

"Then we might be able to just dig through it. Does it look old?"

"No, my lady, it looks new. Grass and shrubs stick out from the wall, as if it was raised from the ground recently."

"General," Tse commanded, "Have your captains halt the troops while we go look at this wall."

"Sir." Din Gur rode off to give orders.

Le Le and Tse followed Captain Pinan to the wall where the advance soldiers were already trying to dig through. It was as he had described; the road ran up to the wall, and then up the wall until it reached the top some six feet above their heads, as if a giant plow had passed through the earth, curling it upward.

"The Council–" Le Le began.

"The Council be damned," Tse said. "This is old. Captain, where are your scouts?"

"I sent two riders out in each direction. One was to return when he had gone no more than a mile. The other was to find the end. Neither has returned."

"This is a trap," Le Le said. "We should flee."

"Stop your prattling. I am not going to be stopped by a mound of dirt."

"The Council warned you not to take action."

"It is not your place to correct me."

"Sir, look," a man shouted. At the top edge of the wall, several crows had landed and were watching the men below. As the moments passed, more and more swooped in and joined them until they formed a long black line. "Die Die Die," they called.

"Does your ability work on crows?" Le Le asked.

Tse paused a few seconds. "No, apparently not, but my arrows will. Archers!"

Captain Pinan looked around, wondering if he had missed something. "Lord, the archers are still in formation."

The birds launched themselves down as a single convulsive black mass. At the same time, the trees in the immediate area erupted with great flocks of their own and hundreds of the deadly creatures filled the air.

The first wave dropped—winged daggers with unerring aim—and drove pointed beaks into the flanks of Tse's horse, the stallion reared and Tse fell with the loud crack of breaking wood. Le Le was ready. She slid quickly off her horse and fell on top of Tse and covered his body with hers.

A black cloud descended. The birds hovered, dodging blades, shields or shovels and then swooped in for a quick peck or claw at any exposed flesh.

In the eye of this chaos, Le Le's hand found the back of Tse's neck. "Die you fool," she said softly, and Tse screamed in exquisite pain as the ice clawed into his brain.

Then it was over. The crows returned to the air, retreated to the edge of the wall and the surrounding trees, while their dead littered the ground like ebony leaves. Men stood panting, red lines crisscrossing their faces and hands. Several men held bloodied hand over bloody face. One lay dying, a victim of another's sword, a great wound open in his neck.

"Lord," someone yelled.

"Your Lord is dead," Le Le said. She rose to her feet and stood over Tse's body, then dusted the dirt and grass from her pants.

Captain Pinan, cut and bleeding, sword drawn, stomped towards her screaming, "I will have your head on a pike you evil bitch." He pushed the tip of his sword up under her jaw.

"Aren't you forgetting something?" she asked.

Around them, the other men were quickly wishing for Tse's ability.

"Well?" shouted Pinan. "Which of you has it?" He turned to look at the men, to see if any. When he looked back, Le Le had hold of his blade. He jerked his arm back, and then thrust it forward. He heard a snap, saw the weapon and his hand fall to the ground. A ring of frost formed where it fell.

She could see the hate in his eyes, the anger, the thoughts passing through his mind as he looked at the stump of his right arm, and then made a fist of his left hand and drew it back to strike her.

There was nothing more in her, nothing she could do. She could barely stand. People just didn't understand how hard it was to freeze things.

Captain Pinan staggered then, his left arm cocked, the cold in his right creeping upward, freezing his blood, cooling his heart and stealing his breath. His eyes rolled up into his head. He fell down and died.

Le Le looked to see if any of the others would challenge her, but they had discarded their weapons and dropped to their knees.

"What?"

"Behind you," a man said.

Le Le turned. The earthen wall was rolling back, lying down, like a wave breaking in reverse. Not far away, Cordain Leighland, Master of Earth, sat on the head of a giant hump-backed beast fashioned of stone and mud, with long wavy grass for fur, granite-gray rocks for eyes and toenails and denuded tree trunks, ground to points, for tusks.

Sitting on the back, in a kind of sedan with velvet seats and a fringed canopy, were a young boy and his twin sister, looking as if they were out for a country ride. On the back, the head, and anywhere there was space on the mighty creature, a crow perched, their eyes, all focused on Le Le.

"Just a moment, Le Le," Cordain said. "Dharyl, Sharyl, I want the soldiers to hear my words.

"Yes, sir," the twins said. Immediately the birds leapt into the air and flew out over Le Le and Tse's army. They did not attack, but flew in tight, double-looped patterns over everyone's heads.

"It is time for you to leave," Cordain said. The birds echoed these words in their own cracked voices. Le Le moved up to the beast and observed the twins. The girl seemed entranced, and the boy moved his own lips as the crows spoke

"Your Lord has paid for his crimes," the crows said. "Return to your homes and wage war no more. I am Ra-ken Cordain Leighland, Master of Earth. I speak for the Council Ra-ken, this is their law." As he spoke, the earth shook and boomed three times.

"You may let them go," Cordain said. The girl opened her eyes. The crows wheeled, turned east and flew away.

Cordain stood then, and addressed Tse's men directly. "Generals, take your men home, and confine them to their barracks until further notice. A steward will be appointed by the Council to rule in Tse Lee's place and he will arrive in a few days. He will hold you accountable for any further acts of looting, violence or rape. The ability to control the emotions of others has been removed from this land and will not return. You have a new master, and that is the Council Ra-ken. Now go home, all of you." He looked to Le Le. "You should return with us. I will make stairs that you might climb up."

"Thank you, but I must find my own refuge. Do you know where my horse went?"

Sharyl leaned over the side and pointed towards the north. "A bunch of horses ran up that way. They're not too far."

"Thank you."

Cordain sat back down on the beast's head, and it started shaking, as if it needed to wake sleeping limbs before it could move.

Le Le pulled back. "Wait, Cordain, I don't understand what happened here."

"The Council is thankful for your assistance; you can forgive us if we keep our secrets."

"You knew no one here would claim it didn't you?"

"The ability to control the emotions of others is not a power you will need to concern yourself with again. A word of caution though."

"Do I need your warnings?"

"You do. The Council does not look upon you favorably. Tse may have tolerated your foul ways but we will not. You have our pardon for your past crimes, but should we hear of more children's deaths by your hand we will come for you."

Le Le said nothing. She had already figured out that if the Council Raken were going around killing the powered, then she didn't want to be any place where they could find her.

Tse's army was already moving back up the road the way they had come, their banners, pikes, or anything heavy already thrown to the side of the road.

"You should bury them," Le Le said.

The ground shuddered and she staggered before finding her balance again. When she looked, the bodies were gone.

Then Cordain's giant shaggy boar turned and headed north, back towards Imtraud, and soon the field was empty. She removed her jacket and threw it away.

She found her horse grazing in a field beyond the trees, found a knife in her bag and cut away all its trappings and ornaments. She headed west, where she would sell the mare and buy passage south on the river.

# Ten.

*And the Lord answered. They that I have blessed with the gift of Life must also have the gift of Death. I give to you instead, the gift of heraldry, that you shall announce my presence to men, that they might know me, and love me above all others.*

*Book of the Divine*

### 24 Tobeth, Y.O.D. 745

## Kherlestra, North Seleton

"Kim," the man to Kim's right said out of nowhere. "Why are you traveling to Kherlestra, if you don't mind my asking?"

Kim did mind, but he could not say so, nor could he give his real reason "I am looking for work my friend."

"What do you do?"

Kim had expected this line of questioning and was ready with his answers. "I am an engineer and an architect. I build bridges, roads, fountains; I go wherever stone is being laid."

The man and his wife smiled at him with renewed respect, professional men were in short supply in Kherlestra. "Really?" he asked, "that is most fortunate, my brother's family live there. He has told so many wonderful tales that I decided I must see for myself, and when I told him I would visit, he said 'No, you cannot visit; it would pain you so much to leave again, you must gather your possessions and move here.' So here we are. But my brother knows a man at the palace, I would be happy to introduce you."

"Don't tell such lies," the man's wife said, giving her husband a dirty look. She had spoken in her native language, not the Colovencia they had been using. Kim pretended not to know what she said.

"My wife asks if you are married."

"I am not yet so blessed."

"Perhaps then you will find a beautiful woman and settle down with us," he said, "Are you orthodox?"

"I'm sorry?"

"Do you know who the Divine Lord of Kherlestra is?" the man asked, apparently concerned.

"Yes, Ra Timèatteo."

"Divinely touched with the ability to destroy those who offend with his eyes," the man said.

Kim thought this a novel description of Kherlos's power. "Yes, I hear he is a harsh lord."

"He is fair and just and strict in the teaching of the Divine. Only those who fall from grace need fear him. You will find no thieves lurking in the shadows, or beggars crowding you on the streets. The Divine Kherlos makes sure that they know they are not welcome in his city."

Kim was disappointed with this news; he often made use of beggars and other low people. They were the best spies. "But certainly, men of good character have nothing to fear?"

"My brother tells me that a strict orthodox devotion to the Divine Kherlos and the Divine Creator are observed. There are clergy aplenty to instruct those who would seek their guidance."

"Perhaps I will need to seek them out before my introduction to the palace. Would that not be wise?"

"I could instruct you."

"Are beards required by law then?"

"Ah, a fine point I believe." The man stroked his own long beard. "I am told Kherlos himself shaves, and so the clergy relax their... vigilance on that matter some. Who can tell a Divine what is and is not law?" the man joked. Kim nodded in solemn agreement.

"Please, could you instruct me while we ride? We appear to have time."

"It would be my pleasure, I can tell you what I know, but of course, I am not an expert on all matters of protocol, but I know enough to get by."

"Of course," Kim said," but I would love to hear your thoughts."

"Well, I am certainly happy to be of service where I may. Do you know the prescribed times and manner of devotion?"

Kim looked blank. The man took this as a "No."

"Well then, in the morning, you may have observed my wife and me..."

Kim let the man drone on, keeping him tuned in only enough to be able to nod at what seemed to be the right places. It suited him to let the man talk. It kept the questions away.

The road they followed wound back and forth lazily along the bank of a twisting river that flowed through a high mountain gap. A stone bridge crested the rushing waters; here travelers paused to catch the first glimpse of their new home before tackling the steep switchbacks down to the valley floor.

"You can see the palace," the man said.

Kim looked over the city. The man pointed, and Kim caught the one building close to the lake, larger and taller than the others. "I see it."

"It gets plenty steep here," the man said, "you should go on ahead." He tied the reins loosely to a hook by his seat. "I'd best walk these girls down, arrive safely you know."

Kim nodded. "I am most thankful for your instructions."

"Oh, it's a pleasure for me to talk, Divine knows I do enough of it for three, I thank you for the opportunity." Kim had nothing to say to this, he longed to be parted from the man.

"You have a place to stay?" the man asked.

Kim dreaded this moment. "I will be looking for an Inn, I hear they are expensive, but rooms are available."

"Well, you heard partly right, expensive yes, available doubtful. I would offer you a room with us, but we will be living with my brother until our own place is built, and he has no rooms to spare."

"You are very kind," answered Kim, relieved that he would not have to fumble for some excuse.

"You might want to ask after Fat Arlond. It is said he keeps a room available, but at a dear price. He might know if there is another room to be had."

"Thank you, again, tell me the name of your brother, and I will come visit when I have found lodging."

The man brightened considerably at this, he had found a good listener and regretted the thought of parting his company. He and Kim continued to exchange pleasantries, until finally assured that he would indeed visit with them at first chance, Kim was allowed to leave.

§

Kim marveled at the growing city as he walked its straight and regular streets. It was a clean city; the people were friendly and open. There were parks, or, areas designated to be parks, as the decorative masonry in many had yet to be completed. Stone streets ended abruptly in uncut grass, yet surveyor's stakes ran on, marking phantom intersections yet to be. It was clear from the amount of construction still going on that there was work for all. There had been work available in Linnaton, but that had been no deterrent to the beggars. There were always plenty of people willing to take the path of least effort, but apparently not in Kherlestra. The usual cadre of beggars, prostitutes and street cons were missing. Kherlos kept a tight leash. This did not please Kim. He was here to do a job that would require the anonymity of faceless strangers, people willing to look the wrong way at the right time, and people who can do odd tasks without asking questions. This town didn't seem to have any of those people so ubiquitous throughout the rest of the world. In order to blend in, Kim could adopt the orthodox customs of this town, but he had not seen any others that shared his eastern descent, nor any of his own people. He felt out of place, vulnerable and exposed, in spite of so many people trying to make him feel welcome.

§

"Welcome traveler," Arlond said to Kim as he rode up, "just arrived?"

"You must be Fat Arlond," Kim said, "Yes, just this morning."

The man looked Kim up and down but said nothing.

"I am told you have a room."

"And who would be telling such a thing?"

Kim recognized the opening salvo of a tough negotiation. "Ernic, brother of Merrick the Tanner, he said I should inquire with you."

"Well, now there's a man who's been known to say much, and half of it believable." Fat Arlond laughed at his own joke, just in case Kim might think he meant the words in offense.

Kim smiled back. "So true my good man, my right ear is still numb, it hangs limp and useless, exhausted from this long morning's ride along side the man. It is a wonder his family is not all deaf." Fat Arlond roared and shook. At the sound of the commotion, a shutter opened. A plump woman's face poked out of the window. Kim smiled, as she carefully looked him over. Apparently, Kim's purse looked adequate. She gave a sharp nod at her husband and disappeared back inside.

"My wife," Arlond said. "Fifty Suns."

"I'll rent a room at the palace for that sum."

"A week," Arlond countered, looking apologetic for the misunderstanding.

"Ten, and a hot dinner and bath."

"For ten, you can have a patch of straw, a bowl of gruel and the cold waters of the lake." Arlond folded his arms and straightened his spine.

Kim understood; he had seen the men sitting on their straw beds underneath a canvas tent, eating their morning porridge, though the sign had read three silver Moons a day, not ten Suns a week. "Fifteen, any more and I would have to claim robbery." Kim regretted these words; Fat Arlond was visibly offended.

"Do not speak lightly of robbery good sir; fifteen is my price for honored guests who have been blessed with the touch of the Divine. If you are so blessed, perhaps a small demonstration so that I may prostrate myself in your presence and honor you with my most lavish room that I keep unoccupied at my own financial loss for those of divine grace that may bless my humble household with their presences."

"Peace good sir, I meant no offense. It is I who must beg your humble forgiveness. I wield no such blessing. I am but a modest architect looking to establish myself in a new land. I would be honored to reside within your home at the fair and just sum of twenty five Suns a week."

At the mention of the price, the sound of rattling pans could be heard coming from inside. Arlond relaxed. "First week in advance."

"Breakfast and dinner," Kim said.

"Agreed, but..." Kim's eyebrows rose. "It is but a small matter. Should a traveler arrive seeking lodging that is blessed with an ability, however minor, I am afraid I would be required to ask you to defer and seek your lodging at some other more convenient location."

Kim frowned.

"I'm just saying..."

"Agreed." Kim climbed down off his horse. It was unlikely he would be here a week.

"Excellent," Arlond exclaimed and clapped his hands twice. A young boy came running out. "Twenty five Suns and seven Moons please," Arlond said, holding out his hand. "For your horse."

Kim grinned; it was his own fault for being outfoxed. He counted the money into the man's palm.

"This is my wife Elvina," Arlond said. Kim turned to see Elvina coming out to greet him, wiping her hands on her apron. She was every bit as plump as her face had led him to believe. "Let me show you to your room, my boys will tend to your horse and fetch your things." She produced a key from some hidden pocket. "I didn't catch your name." She smiled and waited.

"Kim."

"Well, Mr. Kim, it's a pleasure to have such a nice young man staying with us. We're all excited, an architect did I hear?"

"Yes." Kim started to wonder if his actions were wise.

"Bless me, how exciting. Have you visited the palace yet? Oh what am I thinking, you just arrived. No matter, time enough for that later, I'm sure you're hungry."

"Mr. Kim," the young boy interrupted his mother.

"Yes?"

"What's his name? Your horse sir?

"Swiftness of the Night. Swift, for short."

"Thank you sir, C'mon Swift" the boy said. He led Kim's horse away.

§

For Kim, life became an ordeal. He was accustomed to being invisible, unnoticed in a crowd. This, along with his ability made him the perfect assassin, but here he was never left alone. Whenever he ventured out, Arlond's wife Elvina had some urgent errand, just remembered, that coincidently was right along the way. And when he was able to sneak out, everyone he met wanted to know who he was and where he was staying and everything about his business it seemed.

Kim put away his charcoals, wiped his hands clean, and put on the silk vest Elvina had helped him purchase. He left his room, descended the stairs, and found Elvina waiting for him in ambush.

"Oh! Mr. Kim, how fortunate; I was just mentioning you to my niece. Have you met Anya? Anya, this is Mr. Kim, our new architect."

The girl, probably no more than fifteen, was already showing signs of womanhood and of being well fed. She wore a plain green blouse, a darker green wool skirt, and a fancy vest laced up the front and her hair wrapped in a green and white striped scarf.

"Pleased to meet you," Kim said. He bowed. The girl had not offered her hand, and Kim suspected he was not allowed to touch her.

"Are you going out Mr. Kim? Auntie and I were just on our way to the palace."

"How very nice, I was on my way out to get some dinner and inspect the site of the wells."

"Splendid," Elvina said, "Anya's Uncle, on her mother's side, is off duty, he's a guard at the palace you see, that is, he has offered to give Anya a tour of the palace, and we'd be most delighted if you would join us."

"That is a very kind offer, but I could not impose upon you in such a way. It would make me feel impolite."

Elvina looked sad, as if he was refusing her honey-laden pastries. "Nonsense Mr. Kim, I can assure you, it would be no imposition. I would feel safer having the company of a well-mannered man along."

Kim knew a trap when the saw one. "Perhaps I could accompany you to the front steps. I'm afraid I haven't even had the courage to go that far uninvited."

Elvina smiled like a viper. "Mr. Kim, you have nothing to fear from our Lord. While it is true that he has a Divine power, he is wise and good and only uses his ability upon the wicked."

"Oh Auntie, be so good. Mr. Kim is a stranger here. I am sure he has heard terrible lies about our lord. He will see how he loves his people." Anya stepped up and hooked her elbow into Kim's "Please do come along."

"How could I refuse such an offer?"

§

Kherlos and Takoda stood behind the glass patio doors in his office and watched traffic in the plaza in front of the palace. Normally Takoda observed the comings and goings of their own citizens, but today there was someone he wanted Kherlos to see. "There, walking with young woman in green. Is that Fat Arlond's wife with them?"

Kherlos moved to get a better look. "Yes, Elvina. I see the man. What of him?"

"He intends to kill you. His name is Kim."

"Kim?" Kherlos asked.

"Just Kim. That is what I am told."

"His power?"

"The ability to make others believe they do not see him."

"Impressive, and clever, and I mean both of you. What made you suspicious?"

Takoda looked embarrassed.

"You're a voyeur, aren't you?"

"Habit," Takoda insisted. "I protected the Butcher too, if you recall."

"And of the worst and most intimate kind," Kherlos ignored the interruption. "You know every foul and indecent thing everyone might think to do."

"No."

"No?" Kherlos looked amused.

"That woman down there, Elvina, with her wits and sharp eyes, knows as much about people's intentions as any. It doesn't take a gift from the Divine to know when a young couple desire to sneak off and make love."

"You're avoiding my question."

"I was suspicious because he was suspicious, if you watch him, you will see that he is constantly looking around, always making sure of his surroundings."

"Don't most people?"

"Not here, not in your city. Those two women he's with aren't afraid of being attacked, or robbed, but he sticks out like a rat looking for a sewer."

"So when does he intend to kill me?"

"Tomorrow night or the next, later than that and people will begin to wonder why he does no work. Shall I have him arrested?"

"No, that could go badly very easily, and I need to know who sent him."

"Isn't that obvious?"

Kherlos watched as the two women dragged their captive into the palace. "No, it might not be the council. I've made more than a few enemies since I've heired."

"I like your idea," Takoda said.

"Damn you, that's very annoying. Why didn't the Butcher ever kill you?"

"Because I'm useful, and he wasn't as clever as you."

"So you'll…"

"Yes."

"Be careful Takoda, I'm guessing this Kim can be very dangerous."

Takoda grinned and bowed low. "I'm touched by your concern."

# Eleven.

*And Uumvault spoke unto the men he had gathered there. The Divine is your Lord, His gifts are as waves upon the ocean, Endless, and in all proportion. You may ask upon them, and they shall be received.*

*Book of the Divine*

**27 Tobeth, Y.O.D. 745**

## Kherlestra, North Seleton

Kim rose when the house was quiet and settled for the night. Fat Arlond rarely stayed up much past dark because his wife loved to fuss. She loved to lecture about the evil of waste and virtues of frugality. She particularly liked to fuss about the over use of candles and expense of lamp oil. They were running a hotel and not a liquor mongery, in case no one had noticed. Any tenant daring enough to ask for candles or extra oil earned themselves a sharp look and a surcharge on their bill when it came due. This suited Kim, few guests lingered late after sundown. Kim had oiled and cleaned his window earlier in preparation for this night. He eased the lower pane up, just enough to let his slim frame through. He lowered himself; hand over hand, touching the wall with his feet as little as possible. When he was almost down, he reached up, cut the dark cord, and dropped the remaining distance. Yes, the cord would be found, but not be in time to raise an alarm.

It was a perfect night; the moon sat high and full and there was no wind. Two guards lounged at the entrance to Kherlos's courtyard, half of the gate stood open. Normally this would indicate some kind of clandestine activity, but Kim had learned that in this city, even the most furtive nighttime rendezvous would prove to be mundane.

The two men huddled together off to one side talking in low voices. Kim slipped past them and then paused inside the gates, listening to their conversation. They discussed how one should deal with a son who was starting to act disrespectful towards his mother. Kim shook his head in amusement, and moved on.

On one side of the palace, scaffolding had been erected where workers were finishing the decorative cornice along the roof. He would have to be most careful. Not only was the scaffolding in the shadow of the building, but it could easily sway under his weight and give a signal. A third guard walked lazily around the compound. Kim timed his assent so that the guard was on the opposite side of the palace. He reached the first floor with no incident, and moved onto the stone ledge that ran the circumference. There were several windows and balconies around the second floor of the palace. He moved from one to the next. At the front of the palace, the window directly over the main entrance was not shuttered.

He thought back to his incursion into Tse Lee's palace. If this string of contracts continued, word would eventually spread amongst the powered to keep their shutters tightly locked. No power could stop an assassin while you slept.

Kim slipped inside the palace and looked around. The room was sparsely furnished with a couple couches and a low table. It looked like a small waiting room where guests could be served tea. The doorway was an open arch with a beaded curtain across it. He frowned. The curtain went most of the way to the floor. He looked out through the curtain. The hall was empty. Kim carefully squeezed through, disturbing as little as possible, and then waited until the beads were still. Although he could not be seen, the effect he had on objects could.

Kherlos's apartments were on the fourth floor. Most Ra-ken took wives later in life rather than trust to the patience of their offspring, but this did not mean Kherlos would sleep alone.

Kim made his way up easily. Each floor was patrolled, though the guards, as they are prone to do all over the world, lounged and chatted with each other in the places where they could see before being seen. No one knew as well as Kim how people's behavior changed while they were not being observed, and how they relied upon their eyes alone for safety.

Kim found the steps to the fourth floor. A uniformed man stood guard at the steps. The hallway was well lit, giving him a good view in either direction. The man stood at attention, alert. This meant that a superior officer was making rounds. Slowly Kim lowered himself onto his hands and feet like some giant bug. He moved one limb at a time until he was past the guard and up the steps.

The entrance to the apartments was an arched doorway with another beaded curtain. They looked new. They led into an outer foyer, where guests would wait until announced. He paused outside the curtain and peered in. The room inside had little light and the shutters were closed. He waited for his eyes to adjust. Light from behind revealed the dim shapes of couches, and a dark doorway at the far end. That door would probably be locked, but Kim had tools and oil with him.

He pressed slowly through the curtain, easing himself between the beads. Then he turned back and started moving towards the far door, a light cough came from his right. He turned to look in that direction. A bright light filled his vision, then darkness. He crouched and listened for footsteps approaching. None did. He waited, knowing what the flash meant, knowing that his sight was lost, and with it his life, but also knowing this man Kherlos might now become careless.

"So the man who can't be seen now can no longer see," Kherlos said.

This was the reason for the many long hours of training. Kim ducked low and rolled over his shoulder. As he came up again, he reached inside his tunic, pulled out his serpentine dagger and lunged at where Kherlos's voice had been.

Having missed his target, Kim crouched low and made quick dart like lunges of the dagger into the surrounding space, while at the same probing his flank with his left hand. He did a quick spin, sidestepped, and then repeated the procedure.

Kim's fingertips brushed against the cloth of a stuffed chair. In an instant, he was upon it with the dagger and slashed it in a wide sweep of his arm. There was no spray of blood, no cry of pain; he had missed again. Kim made another fast slash though the air around him, and then followed that with a roundhouse kick just in case. Satisfied he was not in immediate danger, Kim continued his search, feeling his way around the chair as it silently bled woolen stuffing.

Kherlos coughed again, and Kim knew he was being baited. He moved quickly to the side, but a hard edge caught his leg. Kim fell onto what had stuck him, a wooden chair, pushed, with weight behind it. He pushed back onto his feet and stabbed at the space and followed up with a high spinning kick.

Breath! He had felt breath on his ankle; the kick had been close somewhere along its path. He turned, deliberately facing the wrong direction. Kherlos should be close, off to his right. He crouched, tensed; he felt the air in front of him with his left hand, hoping to catch Kherlos off guard, then quickly lunged to his right in a tight thrust.

His right arm vanished. It disappeared from that sixth sense that lets you know where your limbs are, that lets you feel the shape of your body. He heard the knife strike something soft, heard a grunt, and felt a piece of meat—his right arm—strike against his side. He turned and leapt, left leg out straight, right leg cocked and ready to strike.

§

Kherlos killed Kim mid-leap, but even dead, Kim's body refused to yield. In a parody of an old school yard trick, Kim's lifeless form slammed into Kherlos's chest, toppling him over the low footrest crouching down behind his knees. Kherlos toppled over and slammed his head into the floor.

§

When Kherlos woke, the brightness forced his eyes shut tight. There was stiffness in his side, and the room refused to lay still.

"Leave us," someone said. Footsteps then, echoing, loud and close, retreated, faded.

"The healer said you'd have a headache when you woke," Takoda said as way of greeting.

Kherlos sat up slowly, groaned, rubbed his eyes and looked at his friend. He felt the back of his head; it was still tender.

Takoda offered a goblet. "Drink. When I found you, the guards were standing around wishing for your power."

"Typical. I'm surprised one of them didn't finish the job."

"Ah, that's an interesting problem. If the one that kills you doesn't get the ability, then he has committed murder but hasn't become Divine. It's too risky."

"What is this?" Kherlos peered into the cup.

"Water."

Kherlos poured it out onto the floor. More of the room started to come into focus and he noticed Travia standing nearby. "Get me wine."

"So what happened, Takoda?"

"I was hoping to ask you the same thing. We found you and the other man lying on the floor looking dead."

"Is he?"

"Yes."

Kherlos snorted, "I was right about my ability."

"You could see him then?"

"Yes, I could see his life, but not him. More grist for your philosophical debates I suppose."

"You fought though."

"First I blinded him. I expected that to take the fight out of him, but it didn't even slow him down. He came right at me. Next I killed his arm, to make him drop the dagger, but the next thing I see is his foot flying into my face. I killed him just before he hit me."

"Travia," Takoda shouted.

"Yes?" Travia stood at the doorway, holding a skin of wine.

"Both of you," Kherlos said, "help me up into a chair."

Takoda helped Kherlos while Travia brought a padded chair.

"Travia, what do you know of this attempt on my life?"

"Nothing, my lord," he handed over the wine. "We serve the Divine. We do not meddle in the politics of men."

"So, now what?" Takoda asked.

Kherlos took a long drink of wine, and then nudged Kim's body with his foot. "Dispose of this, search his room, ask around. I smell the Council behind this, but I doubt we'll find anything with their mark on it."

"We could probably torture a few things out of baldy here," Takoda suggested.

Travia stiffened. "Yes, why not? I'm privy to all of the Council's secrets. Ra Vernault has personally informed me he plans to have quail stuffed with figs for dinner tonight."

"Stop it, both of you. What time is it?"

"Ra Timèatteo," Travia said. "It is just before sunrise."

"See what you've done Takoda. Now go search Kim's room before someone tidies it up. Have Arlond pack his possessions and send them here. We can trust him to keep his mouth shut. Travia."

"Yes, Lord?"

"Do you know someone we can trust to quietly dispose of this man's corpse?"

"I believe I do."

"Then please see to it."

"Then what?" Takoda asked.

"Then we act as if nothing happened, and wait for them to try again."

§

A fancy carriage, top-loaded with trunks, arrived at the front of the palace. Passers-by stopped to watch, not many dignitaries called upon their lord with luggage. The driver jumped down, readied a stepping stool and then opened the door. A young woman in a long, satiny dress emerged into the summer heat.

"Serrah." Kherlos was already running along the flagstone path toward the front gate. The two embraced with a quick hug.

"You are as beautiful as always." Kherlos hooked her arm. "Welcome to your new home."

"Thank you, tell me dear friend, what is so urgent? Are you in danger? Your message was most unsatisfactory!" She struck at him playfully. "And they tell me I missed your Divine Day by over a month. How dare you not invite me?"

"Please, please. I am sorry. I know I have much to answer for, but all is well for the moment. Come, I have rooms ready for you. I know you must be exhausted. I want you to get refreshed and meet my friend Takoda, he's such a bore; all he wants to talk about is philosophy."

"Are you two lovers then? Your letter didn't mention him."

"Sadly, no, but he vexes me just as much. And you can blame him for the oversight. He keeps my social calendar and I have no say in the matter."

"But I can trust him?"

Kherlos took her arm and walked her towards the door where Travia and other priests were waiting. "Of course, like you, he is more useful than one can imagine. It's the only reason I keep him around."

# Twelve.

*And Keavon asked upon Uumvault, that he might have the gift to fly as if a bird. And Leo asked upon Uumvault, that he might have the gift of the strength of a thousand men. And Jessa asked upon Uumvault, that he might have the gift of command over other men. And Uumvault answered yes, and these gifts were given.*

*Book of the Divine*

**16 Veena, Y.O.D. 745**

## Kherlestra, North Seleton

Kherlos could see the cloud of dust raised by a fast horse long before the rider would reach the city. Soon he would hear the first cries of alarm. He had hoped for more time. He had hoped to be wrong. Now he hoped it wasn't Cordain.

They had searched the assassin Kim's room and possessions but they held few clues to his identity, only his purpose. His dagger was made of folded steel, rare and expensive, with rubies in the pommel. He carried tools to slip locks, black silk garments, garrote cords, an ability only a very few people knew existed, and gold Suns.

The list of people who would want him dead was endless, if for no other reason than to claim his ability for their own, but the list of those who could afford a man such as Kim was short indeed. The council, certainly, but they had no reason to kill him. The Yellow Guard, perhaps, they certainly had the motive, but Takoda had assured him they were resolved to simply wait him out. Ra-ken were never known for their longevity.

"Guard," Kherlos called.

"Sir?"

"There is a man riding and shouting in the streets. See what he is about, and find Merridon."

"Yes, Lord, and Travia?"

"Yes, him too."

In a few moments, there was a commotion outside of his office, a knock on his door, and then Travia entered, followed by the captain of his guard, and Takoda.

Travia spoke, apparently already briefed on the situation. "Forgive me lord, soldiers approach from the north. They are half a day's march away, maybe as many as three hundred men with spears. The rider you saw came with the news."

"Under whose banner do they march?"

"They march under three banners my lord, the rising sun, the crossed sword fish, and the banner of the black stallion."

"You can always count on Cordain to be subtle," Takoda said.

"I see he finally got your invitation then," Kherlos said with a wry smile. "Travia, send riders to get the people indoors. Then get a few men ready to join me, we will ride out to meet these invaders."

Travia sent the commander on his mission. "I must remind you, my Lord, the clergy will always remain neutral in these matters."

"Whereas, I will not," Takoda said.

"I appreciate your show of loyalty, both of you, but this is Cordain we are dealing with. This show of force is just to get my attention."

"The way Kim was?"

"That was unkind."

"No one knows more about the nature of good intentions than I do," Takoda reminded him.

"You speak true. But there is nothing to be done except to ride out and see what he wants with me now."

"Will you kill him?" Takoda raised the critical issue.

"You know I cannot."

"Yes, Kherlos, you are such a man of principle. Now you know what reward is given to men of principle."

"Don't be bitter, the day is not yet over."

§

Kherlos and his men—six regular guards on horseback, six infantry with spear and shield, one commander, a sergeant, Travia and two other priests, and Takoda—rode past the last of the houses that marked the city's edge. He considered if perhaps a city wall would not have been a bad idea after all.

A couple of miles further on, they met Cordain's army. It had formed a line along a low ridge over an open field. Two rows of men stood with tall shields and long pikes with their banners flying high behind them.

"This certainly doesn't look good," Takoda said.

"They're not moving," Kherlos said.

"What is that behind them? Over to the right?" Takoda asked.

Kherlos looked through his spyglass; Takoda did the same. Both men saw what appeared to be some sort of giant beast with a large dark box on its back. Out of the top of the box, flags waved rapidly back and forth.

"I believe they're signaling to their commanders out of the box on its back," Takoda said.

"Hmmm," Kherlos mused, "New tactics. He always said we had gotten lucky with the Butcher." He surveyed the soldier's front line. "They're hiding behind their shields and cloth hoods. Do you think maybe they were expecting me?"

"Lord?" Takoda asked.

"My beams don't work through cloth, even cloth you can see through. Keep that in mind if you need to revenge me."

Kherlos signaled them forward. They moved to where the road met the field, and then halted. When he and Cordain had ambushed the Butcher—about two and a half years ago—they had put the sun at their front. This allowed their men to use their shields to reflect the sun into the Butcher's eyes; to hinder the use of his power.

Today, Cordain had adopted a neutral stance and placed the sun at their flank. It was a message only Kherlos would understand.

"Good news," Kherlos said.

"I don't see any," Takoda replied.

"I'm not meant to die today. Dismount and form up, let's draw him out."

The infantrymen formed a small line behind Kherlos and Takoda, while six others stood on either side. Travia and his priests stayed mounted, to the rear.

"What's that?" Takoda said, pointing skyward.

"Where?" Kherlos asked.

"Above, high above the birds there is something else, something larger."

"Good eyes. Getting anything?"

"No, sorry, my power is line of sight too."

"Keep an eye on those soldiers, I'm going to look." Kherlos put his spyglass to his eye. After a few moments, he spotted the figure in the air. He lowered the glass and squinted upwards.

"Signals are coming from the beast. Flags," Takoda said.

Kherlos waved a hand at him without looking down. "Got Him." A thin bright line shot out from his eyes. Takoda looked towards where the beams had pointed. A small dot against the blue sky could be seen, growing larger.

"Arrows!" shouted the commander. The guards around Kherlos and Takoda raised their shields and made an umbrella over the two men.

"Shields down, I need to see," Kherlos shouted.

The captain scanned the sky and gave the command. Kherlos examined the ranks in front of him. They were shielding archers who were firing blind. The arrows had landed some thirty yards short.

"More signals are coming from the beast, Lord," his commander said.

Kherlos ignored him. "Get our men wishing, ask the Divine for the ability... Damn, too late." One of Cordain's soldiers, presumably one of the smarter ones, rose into the air. Almost immediately, a line of crows dived towards the flying soldier, but Kherlos could not think of why this might be important.

The airborne enemy drew his legs up as if he was riding an invisible steed and charged while the birds chased him.

Kherlos waited, his men formed a protective flank around him, but he shoved them back.

The flying soldier yelled. It was all Kherlos needed, twin beams punched out and met the exposed flesh inside the man's mouth. He fell, twitched on the ground, and was still.

"Nice," Takoda said, "How could he see where he was going?"

"You can see through cloth. Us or them?"

Takoda looked back; one of his soldiers was twirling around just above the heads of the others. "Us, get that man down, and tell him he's now Ra-ken."

The man released his ability and landed with a jarring thump on his backside. A huge boyish grin spread across his face.

"Arrows," shouted the commander. Another volley arced in, landing closer, with several arrows striking the ground around them.

"They're firing blind, but let's withdraw before their next volley," Kherlos commanded. "I don't think the death of a council member was part of their strategy. This is going to buy us some time and give us bargaining power." Kherlos could already see the signals from the beast.

The lucky soldier flew back up into the air, wobbled forward and then made a successful but awkward landing on his horse. There was jealousy and awe in the faces of the soldiers around him.

"Enough, let's go," Kherlos said. They returned to their mounts and began their retreat. Kherlos looked back, but they were not being pursued.

§

Cordain's army marched to the edge of the city and stopped; the warning was clear. Most of the citizens were already hiding indoors. Few had been seen fleeing, and they were mostly the transients that constantly flowed in and out anyway. Overall, Kherlos was pleased; his citizens had faith in him, he wished he had as much optimism, but at least he did have a plan, of sorts.

"What do we do now?" Takoda asked.

"We wait," Kherlos said, "the next move is his. Where did that soldier go?"

"Ra Bramer? He's flying around the palace I think."

Kherlos stepped out onto his balcony, and waved the man down.

The Freman Bramer dropped onto the balcony with a clumsy landing. Kherlos ushered him into his office.

"My Lord," Fremen said, "I was just coming, I saw two riders approach under a flag of peace."

"Fremen, you are Ra-ken now. We are equals and I am no longer your lord. In fact, this may be about you."

"Me, lord?" Fremen asked, still not sure about his change of status from common soldier.

"Yes, Fremen, you," Kherlos said. He clasped Fremen on the shoulder. "The man I killed, whose power you now claim, was a member of the Council Ra-ken. They rule the Union of Colovencia. The position is allotted to the power, not the family, which the Vernault's will be quite upset about. However, you are now the Lord of Arbadorium, Grand Marshal of the Northern Ranks, and probably several other titles I am unaware of."

"I'm a lord now? That's right funny. Do they expect me to fly home?"

"Oh no, if you fell asleep while flying, you would plummet to your death." Kherlos said. "If you fly for long periods you will become tired. Your power may simply stop of its own accord. That's usually fatal. Powers are tricky, they mostly work the way you think they should, but often work in ways that will astound and surprise you. Not always pleasantly."

"How does your power work then? If you don't mind me asking?"

"Sorry, but I do. It's considered rude to ask people about their powers. You see, the more other people know about your power, the more they can take advantage of its weaknesses, as Cordain is taking advantage of mine."

"But you seem to know so much about mine."

"Yes, it's also considered essential to know as much as you can about others at the same time. Now that you're Ra-ken, a big part of your education will be learning not only politics, but everything you can about every other Ra-ken, Mo-ken or Ra-fel on the planet."

"Damnation. Sorry, my lord," Fremen apologized for his profanity, and then sort of realized he didn't have to. "I mean Kherlos, I mean, all because I can fly now? I mean, it's not anything like your power and I don't feel any more Divine."

"Powers are what you make of them Fremen, no more, no less. They are a manifestation of the Divine. However, we have little time for philosophy. You might talk with Takoda though; he loves that topic. But for now, we should go see what these men want."

Fremen headed for the window, Kherlos grabbed his arm. "Let's take the stairs, it's safer."

Three of Cordain's men waited in the entrance hall of the palace, flanked by his own men. A few priests hovered about, but Travia was conspicuously absent.

"Mekos!" Kherlos cried out, recognizing his old friend. "Welcome, it seems like only yesterday that you were helping me defeat the Butcher. Are you a Captain now?"

Kherlos held open his arms, and the two men embraced briefly.

"I am. Those were exciting times, sir. I wish I could say I was here on a more pleasant errand."

"You're a loyal soldier Mekos, you always were, and never afraid of anything. I bear you no ill will."

"Thank you sir, that means a lot to me, but I am here on another matter. As the duly sworn representative of Ra-ken Cordain Leighland, and the High Council of Colovencia, I am here to command that you release Council member Able to Fly Unassisted to our custody."

Kherlos smiled and spread his hands. "Ra-ken Fremen Bramer, Able to Fly Unassisted, is not mine to release; he is a free citizen and may come and go as he pleases. I cannot release what I do not have."

Mekos's face became emotionless. "I am instructed to inform you, that if you release this man to us, my Lord will hold no warrants against the citizens of this town. They will be free to go about their business."

"Your lord is most generous, especially with other people's lives. What do you think of this offer Fremen?"

"I think it reeks of dung."

"Are you Divinely blessed with the Ability to Fly Unassisted?" Mekos asked.

"He is," Kherlos said.

"Lord Cordain Leighland, extends to you the invitation to join him on the Council Ra-ken, in Colovencia. He wishes that you should return with us."

Kherlos spotted movement at one of the circular windows high above the front entrance, a crow, perched on the sill, peered inside. Kherlos lashed out, his bright beams killed the bird and startled the people in the room. Mekos was visibly angry.

"Crows are dirty animals," Kherlos said. "They carry disease and are bad omens." Perhaps he should kill more of the crows. They seemed to be everywhere all of a sudden. "Does your Lord Cordain not wish for my surrender?"

"I have no instructions to that regard. My purpose here is to return with this man."

"What if I don't want to go?" Fremen asked. "I like it here."

Mekos looked confused. The situation was clearly outside the scope of his instruction. Kherlos came to his rescue. "What guarantee do I have of this man's safety?"

"You have the word of Cordain Leighland, honored member of the Council Ra-ken"

"The same man who is here to kill me?" He could see the truth in Mekos's face. It wasn't that he was a poor liar; it was his pride. They were proud to be here doing the Council's bidding. To them, he had become just another version of the Butcher.

"I know nothing of that," Mekos said.

"Tell your lord I will meet with him under truce tomorrow to discuss the terms of my surrender, and the transfer of the prisoner."

"I will."

"And also tell him that I will kill any crows or other flying objects that I see."

"I am sure he will not be pleased to know that." Mekos saluted towards Fremen, hesitated, as if he were about to salute Kherlos as well, but instead, turned and retreated.

Kherlos waited until the men had ridden away. "Arrest Fremen Bramer and charge him with treason."

"What? Treason? Me?"

"Sorry but it can't be helped. Please give up your sword. I promise you'll be treated well."

"But why? I've served you loyally. Everyone knows you're a good man." Kherlos felt sorry for him; he was honestly hurt.

"Fremen," Takoda said, "they think you were taken prisoner. They see Kherlos as a Fallen, evil, to use the old word. They assume he threatened to kill you if you didn't surrender, which I guess is what has just happened."

Fremen handed over his sword to the other guards.

"Fremen," Takoda said, "suppose I wanted to be a Ra-ken. If I wanted to fly unassisted, call myself the Lord of Arbadorium, sit on the Council and dine on fattened goose liver, how could I make that happen?"

"Well, first you'd have to kill me I suppose."

"Precisely," Kherlos said. "Cordain has permission from the Council to kill me. But, he doesn't have permission to kill you. You came by the power honestly and you are its rightful vessel— by tradition and decree of the council. If they killed you, they would all be putting their own lives at greater risk."

"But if you stay here," Takoda said.

"Then you are their enemy," Kherlos continued. He put his hand on Fremen's shoulders as a sign of affection. "There are many who would be quite happy to take your life and your power. Even under Cordain's protection, you will still have many enemies, and they can always arrange an accident. You must watch your back. I thank you for your many years of service." Kherlos stepped back. His face became stern. "You are now a member of the Council Ra-ken, and for reasons I don't yet understand, my enemy. You are under arrest for treason and spying. Take him away."

The look of betrayal on Fremen's face is what hurt Kherlos the most. He spoke to the commander. "See that he is clothed simply, he is no longer a soldier in our guard. He needs a few bruises about the face, but don't close his eyes or hurt him otherwise. With luck, he will soon be better off than the rest of us. Apologize to him first and show respect."

"Yes, Lord."

"I seem to recall the word surrender somewhere," Takoda inquired.

"Yes, it will throw them off. I want you to be able to meet Cordain; we need to know his full intentions."

"You mean other than killing you?" Takoda asked.

"Yes. Divine knows why they are going to all this trouble."

"An old vendetta perhaps?" Takoda asked.

"Possibly, maybe we're on top of a mountain of gold and don't know it," Kherlos said with little humor.

§

The next morning, with the sun barely above the horizon, and a high moon hanging in the sky, Kherlos, Takoda, Fremen and a few guards rode out of the palace displaying the white banner of treaty through empty streets. Travia, and two more of his priests brought up the rear.

Fremen rode in civilian clothing, white pants and shirt with gold needlework on the hem, a gift from Kherlos. His mouth was swollen and one eye bruised. A leather cord ran around his neck, which was attached to his horse to keep him from flying away.

They found Cordain and his men waiting at a level clearing setup for the negotiations. Ornamental rugs had been laid down over the soft grass, with a table with a white tablecloth and velvet padded chairs. Cordain stood at the table facing the oncoming party, his lieutenant standing to his right and a handful of guards behind holding his banner of a rearing black stallion.

Cordain's army, Kherlos observed, was stationed further along the road, within sight, safe from his ability behind their hoods and leather. He halted his own party and dismounted. Fremen was helped down from his horse and had the tether removed, though two men continued to hold him.

"Wait here," Kherlos said to his men. "Travia, Takoda."

As the three men approached, Cordain stepped from behind the table and opened his arms. Kherlos accepted the invitation and the two men hugged.

"I see no birds," Kherlos said by way of greeting.

"They are otherwise occupied today."

"How are you? Is that bitch Tawnya now in charge? That makes what four more?" Kherlos asked grinning.

"Well enough, and yes, she is, and it makes three, but who's counting? Your city has grown most impressive."

"I am proud of what my people have done. But you, three chairs away from head of the council? And yet here you are out running errands. You always were a risk taker."

Cordain sighed, and gave his friend a pained look. "Why must you vex me so? Come, let us sit, this is a sad day for both of us. Have some wine."

The two men sat down. Cordain's guard took a position behind him. Takoda stood on Kherlos's right, Travia on his left.

"Thank you for sending Mekos," Kherlos said. "I was most pleased to see him again." He accepted a goblet of wine and took a long drink. "But your threat against my people was cruel."

"We all do what we must, but first," Cordain spread his hands, "are you are prepared to release the prisoner?"

"Yes, you are prepared to leave?"

"No, that is not the offer. If you release your prisoner then we will not harm your citizens, those that offer no resistance."

"So first I release Ra Bramer, and then we discuss my death?"

"Yes."

"That is acceptable," Kherlos said, and offered his hand. Cordain shook it. "We should talk of old times then. Did you bring bread?"

"Fetch bread," Cordain commanded.

"Release the prisoner and send him forward," Kherlos said.

When Fremen crossed an imaginary line between the two sides Cordain spoke. "Take the Divine Fremen Bramer and escort him to the healer's tent. Treat him with dignity and respect as an honored guest. See that he comes to no harm." A section of Cordain's guards surrounded Fremen and led him away. He waited until Fremen reached his troops before continuing. "I am hoping to hear how you managed to foil the assassin."

Kherlos grinned, wondering what that information might be worth when Takoda, standing just behind him to his right, yelled and lunged sideways across the table. There was snap and the sound of a spring being released. Takoda landed flat on his back, a steel bolt protruding from his chest.

Kherlos's eyes blazed; the assassin along with all of Cordain's other men fell where they stood. Travia screamed, ran, tripped, and skidded in the grass and mud. Kherlos's soldiers drew their swords and rushed forward. The ground shook.

Kherlos jumped up, vaulted across the table smashed his knees into Cordain and drove him over backwards. Kherlos's momentum carried him off the edge of the table, onto his friend and the edge of the heavy chair. He rolled off into the grass onto his hands and knees. He felt a sharp pain in his side that made it hard to breath.

Cordain lay his side, curled into a ball shouting "I surrender."

Kherlos struggled to his feet. His side hurt and felt like it was bleeding, but he kept his eyes fixed on Cordain.

"Let me up," Cordain said. "You must, or kill me and take the consequences."

"Get up then, coward." Kherlos backed away, but it hurt to move. He looked toward the hill. Cordain's men were advancing.

"Stop your men or you die." Kherlos used his hip and pushed the table, somehow still upright, over on to its side. There was a hole in carpet where Cordain had placed his feet. "You bastard."

"I can explain."

Kherlos threw the blood soaked tablecloth over the hole. "Sit on that."

Cordain did as he was instructed.

Kherlos quickly assessed the situation; his men were thigh-deep in the earth, struggling to free themselves. Cordain's army was advancing.

"Stop your men," Kherlos said.

"I need to stand."

"Do it."

Cordain stood, then waved his arms in a flapping motion. "Crows will come, don't kill them, or I can't halt my troops."

"Fine."

Several crows launched themselves from trees in the distance and beat their way over. They circled as Cordain spoke. "Halt, reform the line, await further orders."

"And send your healer," Kherlos shouted.

The birds sped off and intercepted the advancing troops, which stopped, and then slowly retreated.

Cordain looked over at the dead man.

"The healer is for me." Kherlos said.

"I'm sorry, but you know this changes nothing," Cordain said.

Kherlos stepped up and slapped him. "Free my men. Use your hand, no tricks."

Cordain knelt down, moved the cloth aside and touched the bare earth. Kherlos's men rose out of the ground until they lost their balance and fell over.

"Whoops," Cordain said. He covered the hole and stood.

"Leave us," Kherlos shouted at his men.

"Sir?"

"Leave us! Find that stupid priest and wait at the horses."

"Sir!"

Kherlos looked around, located his chair, righted it and sat down. "That man who saved my life had the ability to know the intentions of others." He read the doubt on Cordain's face. "Yes. You did not know of such a power, but then I had not heard of the ability to not be seen either."

At the mention of Kim, Cordain's face brightened, as if to ask, "Yes, just how did you survive him?"

Kherlos ignored the question. "I know you've come to take my life. I agreed to meet with you to understand why. So tell me, or I'll carve my name in your forehead."

Cordain brought his hand to his face, and then ran his fingers through his hair, as if that had been the reason for the movement all along. "The council wants your power."

"I know that much, but what will they do with it? They all have powers of their own and no one can have two."

"They want it under their control, in someone very far away."

"How much further away is there?" Kherlos asked.

"Under their control," Cordain said.

"Everyone in Kherlestra is probably wishing for my ability right now, what chance does some knave of the council have? Do you intend to kill everyone here then?"

"Don't be a fool."

Kherlos leaned back, unsure. "It seems a little late to be giving me that advice, but please, elucidate."

"I grieve for you my friend, but the council will kill you and destroy what you have built here. It's complicated, but you must accept it for what it is."

"Must I? You seem pretty confident that I will keep my promise."

"To not kill me? I don't know, time changes people, but I was willing to take that risk. I did not know my man would try to kill you."

"I know that. If this had been a trap, Takoda would have known it when we arrived. I can only guess that your man did not intend to kill me at first either. Yet your intention is plainly to see me dead."

Cordain forced the anger out of his voice. "My intention is to offer you a choice. The Council doesn't care about you, your city, or your people. They just want your ability. I came here to save lives, to offer you the opportunity to be the only casualty."

"It is too late for me to be the only casualty my friend."

"True."

"So you go around with a hole in your boot?"

Cordain turned his ankle to show how his toes could touch the ground.

"Gets cold in the snow I bet."

Cordain looked like he was about to say something, then thought better.

"Oh, that's right; snow is water, isn't it."

"Yes."

"There's a man coming down the slope dragging a chair." Kherlos said.

"That would be the healer."

"I hope he has more wine."

"He does."

"Why did you surrender?"

"Why didn't you kill me?" Cordain countered.

"You had that look of 'what the fuck just happened' on your face."

The healer arrived; Cordain took the chair and wine from him. "Heal my friend over there."

"Are you hurt lord?"

"No, Aggar, thank you."

The healer lifted Kherlos's shirt and placed his hand over the wound.

Kherlos felt the heat burn in his side as bone and flesh re-knit. "That will do, you may go, but first help your lord with the table."

They righted the furniture and sat down to drink. Cordain smashed the top of the bottle open and emptied the contents into their cups.

Kherlos took a long drink, wiped his mouth and spoke. "What will you do if I release you?"

Cordain looked sad. "I will return to my men and march on your city until your body is brought before me."

"And if I kill you?"

"Then my men will march on your city until your body is brought before them, but they will use cannon."

The last word caught Kherlos by surprise. "The forbidden weapon?"

"Yes. I know how stubborn you can be sometimes."

"So you brought cannon against me. I am honored." Kherlos looked up, ravens circled.

"Don't" Cordain said. "You have no idea how much it hurts when you kill one."

Kherlos considered this. Neither man enjoyed the pain of others. "So answer me this. You could have brought the Master of Abilities."

"Jessa? You know better. As simple as that answer might be, the council would never authorize her release, nor would the priests. Not even to me. Besides, she hates me."

"And with good reason, but you don't need me telling you that. But let's play a little game of 'let's pretend.'"

Cordain looked at Kherlos with suspicion. "Imagine I surrender my power; give the council what they want. Will they leave us alone?"

"I don't follow, what do you mean us?"

"I mean me and my people. Plural."

"I told you, the council won't allow it. You're too dangerous and too smart and Jessa is too treacherous. She'd fake removing your power just to spite us."

"What you say is true, but you and your priests have been played for fools many years now. Jessa nulled her own ability out long ago rather than let you keep it and her hostage."

Cordain frowned. His day was not going well, and this was grave news.

Kherlos yelled over to his men over. "Has anyone wished for the ability to know the intentions of others?"

"Yes, my lord, but to no avail."

"Divine Indeed!" Kherlos exclaimed. The loss of that ability frustrated him almost as much as the loss of his friend. "Will you take my offer Cordain?" He watched as the impact of his words registered.

"Oh dear Divine, you have her here? You mean to take my ability?"

Kherlos grabbed Cordain's shirt and pulled him close, stretching him across the table. "I will keep my promise, but know this; the life you leave with today is the price I pay. You will keep your power, and I will keep my life." He pushed Cordain back down into his chair. "My debt to you is paid. What you once gave me you now take away. That cancels our bond."

"You still are the man I love," Cordain said.

Kherlos spat. "Get a couple of your soldiers down here and clear out these bodies." He signaled his captain over. "We are under truce. They will gather their fallen. Prepare a litter for Ra Merridon, and return him to the palace. We will bury him tomorrow with honors. Also, send a man to town. He is to bring me Serrah Elroy and Nillas Tibble, they are both guests at the palace. And more wine. Skins, no bottles."

"Yes, lord."

"Travia!"

The priest scurried over. "Lord, Lord. How may I be of service?"

"Leave."

"My lord?"

"Take your priests and go back to the palace."

"I assure you, the Priests of the Divine are neutral in all matters of the Ra-ken, our vows of impotency and non-interference are sacrosanct."

Kherlos's eyes blazed and burned the ground at Travia's feet.

Travia screamed like a little girl, and fled.

"You'll regret that later."

"If there is a later," Kherlos replied. "But honestly, I've been wanting to do that for a long time."

§

"Lord," Serrah cried when she saw the blood on Kherlos. She jumped off her horse even before it had settled and ran to him.

"I am healed," he said, but she patted his chest and arms before she accepted his embrace. Nillas came forward and bowed to both men.

"Serrah," Kherlos said, "Nillas, this is Cordain, Master of Earth. Cordain, Nillas Tibble, able to breathe smoke from his mouth, and Serrah Elroy, the Master of Abilities."

"No," Nillas said, "wait, Lord?" He turned to Serrah, eyes wide, "You're the Nuller?"

Kherlos touched his arm. "I am asking you to take a small risk with your power Nillas; it is to save my life and our city."

Nillas kneeled. "My life and my ability are yours, my lord."

"Stand man, if all goes well you will walk away with your power intact. Please, demonstrate your power for our guest."

Nillas cupped his hands over his mouth, and blew gently though them. From his hands issued a dense stream of black smoke.

"That is sufficient, thank you."

Cordain stepped forward. "Let me see your hands."

Nillas's hands were empty. "I breathe the smoke from my mouth," Nillas said, "My hands keep it from getting into my eyes."

"Serrah," Kherlos said, "please understand that I do not ask this lightly, but I need to you remove my ability."

"But I thought…No. Why?"

"The council means to have my power. I mean to have my life."

"Together we could defeat the council."

He touched her cheek gently. "I am sure that is true. But many people would die and suffer, and for what? Would our city survive? Please, this is hard for me too."

"Will we get you a new power?" she asked.

He sighed. "Yes, eventually, but not today; do this now, and then Nillas."

Serrah hugged Kherlos tight and then kissed him on the lips. "It is done."

Kherlos looked at Cordain. He willed the man dead but nothing happened. He felt naked and impotent without his power, but he had always believed it was the man and not the divinity that really mattered. Now it was his chance to prove it.

"Now Nillas."

Nillas held out his hands for a hug, Serrah reached up and touched his forehead lightly, then nodded at Kherlos.

"I wish I had the ability to breathe smoke from my mouth," Kherlos said. As soon as he had finished the words, smoke came out of his mouth. It stung his eyes, and he coughed.

"Don't inhale," Nillas said. "Just breathe out slowly. The smoke will keep coming out all on its own."

Kherlos cupped his hands the way Nillas had done and breathed out slowly. He could feel the air coming out, but his chest was not deflating. He cut his new power off. "Satisfied?" he asked Cordain.

"I wish I had the ability to shoot beams of death from my eyes," Nillas said while looking at Cordain.

"It would seem that power is no longer available," Serrah said.

"Cordain?" Kherlos asked. "Serrah, give Nillas his power back." She kissed him again, long, sweet and tender. Nillas wished for his power, and a cloud of black smoke puffed out of his mouth. He leaned forward and blew a jet-black stream at Cordain.

"Enough," Cordain said, "Yes. Yes stop, I am satisfied. I will keep my word and withdraw."

"When we meet again, I will kill you," Kherlos said.

"I'm sure you will, friend, but until then, be careful. Word will spread quickly that your city has lost its lord and protector." Cordain stepped away from the rugs, kneeled and touched the ground. A bulge in the earth formed under his hand and rose. The grass around him shook violently.

Under Cordain's touch, the mound split open. From it came the head of a jet-black horse. The head shook and snorted dust from its nostrils then opened two shining quartz eyes. Cordain laughed with delight. The ground heaved again, split wider, and the shoulders appeared. The horse shook, tensed, and struggled upward as if forcing its own birth from an earthen womb. With each effort, more of its body came forth. The rich topsoil that was its flesh hardened and dried to the consistency of obsidian. Cordain rose with the horse and spread his legs over its back as it came up beneath him. With a final flourish, the horse leapt out of the ground and onto the grass beside them. The magnificent black stallion stood over all their heads. It shook its head and mane. Cordain's attention to detail bordered on Divine. He patted its neck as it pawed the ground from which it had been born. The muscles rippled under his touch. The beast reared on its hind legs and beat at the air.

Cordain looked down at them. Exhilarated to be alive, he turned his steed and galloped away.

# Thirteen.

*And Keavon flew up as a bird, and cried in joyous alarm.*

*Book of the Divine.*

**1 Rasee, Y.O.D. 745**

## Blazer-Canter Farm, Colovencia, Alasta

"Mommy," Liam asked, Is daddy Ra-ken? Is he an Upper?" Clea laid aside her embroidery and looked down at her son Liam. He was sitting at her feet on a rug her mother had made, playing with little painted-wood animals that had belonged to his grandfather. She smoothed her skirts and moved a cup of tea that Jarod had prepared for her slightly further away on a little end table next to where she sat. "Come here, dear."

Liam rose and held out his hands. Clea lifted her son and placed him on her lap. I'll not be able to do that much longer, she thought. "No, dear, he's Mo-ken. He's still blessed by the Divine, but in a lesser way."

He laid his head against her bosom, and seemed to think this over. "What's the difference?"

Clea laughed and stroked his wavy brown hair. "A Ra-ken is very powerful. Usually someone who can use their ability to hurt others, but the nice ones like our Ra Brawley, don't do that. A Mo-ken usually makes you wish you could hurt them."

"Okay." Liam squirmed and sat up a little. "Did daddy kill Pop-pop?"

Clea's eyes moistened, she dabbed at them with a hanky, and then looked at the enamel portrait of her father-in-law she kept on her tea-green sewing cabinet. "No, dear, Pop-pop was called up to the Divine by the Angels. Okay?"

"Okay."

"Be a good boy now, go outside and play."

"Can I have a cookie?" Liam scooted back down onto the floor, knowing it was always best to ask for a cookie while standing still and looking well behaved.

"Yes, you may. Tell Nunna and then run outside."

Liam scampered away, his curiosity momentarily abated. Clea sat there, tears slowly dripping onto the white brocade of her blouse, breathless.

# Fourteen.

*And Leo, in sport, struck a blow unto Jessa that felled the man as if he were but a sparrow.*

*Book of the Divine.*

**13 Huptun, Y.O.D. 745**

## Kherlestra, North Seleton

Kherlos sat in his office with nothing to do. He had tried writing to his sister, but what could he tell her? That her divinely blessed brother was just another Ur-non? He supposed she would find out anyway, and that should be from him, yet still, he could not bring himself to write such sad tidings. He had started and discarded a dozen or more letters and now they no longer brought him paper.

And there were no documents to sign. Although they still called him "Lord," it was only because there was no one else to give that title to. Yes, at first, they had kept up the ruse, but the priests were very good at what they did, and what they did was run things while everyone else waited for a new Ra-ken to show up.

Travia knocked, and then entered, not waiting to be asked, his way of giving insult, Kherlos supposed.

"Ah Travia, do come in." Kherlos tried to sound positive. "I was just about to call for you, we need to discuss the upcoming justice day."

Travia looked like someone just farted in his oatmeal. "Yes, that time is fast approaching. I believe we do need to discuss a solution. Most people are confused; they see you are alive, so they assume you must have your ability. Yet the rumors persist."

"And how is Serrah?" Kherlos asked. Anything Travia actually wanted to discuss—he didn't.

"She is well, and being cared for with every courtesy," Travia replied with no trace of irritation. The priests had "escorted" the new Master of Abilities, as they called her, and placed her in apartments somewhere in Linnaton.

"Why don't you just let her go, there is no point in keeping her," Kherlos said.

"That is being discussed," Travia replied, "But getting back to your pressing issues; the usual cadre of beggars and whores have not appeared at your gates demanding entry, but they will come eventually. In the meantime, we have been quietly dealing with minor issues, but eventually our hand will be forced."

"I could just pardon everybody, lecture them sternly."

"I think we may already be past that point. Your guards have wasted little time in appointing generals, and are now recruiting. No one can deny that Cordain's army was dispatched, but we cannot hide the facts forever. Already there are doubters among the citizens."

"And I'm sure you're handling them sternly. Why did you really bother me, I was seriously contemplating getting drunk."

Travia stiffened at the brusque tone in Kherlos's voice.

"Well, Lord, officially, as you have noticed, we no longer require your signature on documents, as you are no longer the true heir to this city."

"The true heir," Kherlos added, "being Divine knows where, but clearly, not here."

"Exactly. When this situation occurs, it generally falls upon the clergy, us, to step in and maintain the government until the new Ra-ken arrives to make his, or her, claim, as per the treaty of Colovencia."

"I wasn't aware it stipulated the Priests of the Divine as the designated bureaucratic functionaries."

Travia gave a conciliatory nod of his head.

"Indeed, it does not, but this too has become, a tradition of sorts."

"But in this case?" Kherlos asked.

"Well, you're still alive; there is no precedent on how we should proceed. People are not yet voicing the opinion that you should be killed, but I suspect that is because they fear you are...if you will pardon this insult."

"What?"

"Some fear you are simply faking."

"It would be far better for me if I were."

"Forgive me, my lord, it is painful to explain this. Sometimes the transition is swift, and sometimes the transition is of a much longer duration. But during that time, taxes still need collecting, soldiers need to be paid, and obligations must still be met. The faithful of course continue to serve your divine self, but there is a growing schism in the community."

"So you're telling me I would be better off dead."

"We were thinking more along the possibility of an absence, but yes, your death would suit our purposes."

"Three weeks ago, such an offense would have been fatal."

"But things have changed." That he could make such remarks now was exactly his point. Soon Kherlos's enemies would become bolder.

"So what you're telling me is that at some unknown time, a new lord is going to show up here?"

"Yes."

"Well, I wouldn't saddle the horses just yet."

"I'm sorry?"

"It means things might take a lot longer than you expect."

"Ahh, I see."

"Oh get out. I want no more visitors; I'm in a foul mood."

Travia inclined his head slightly, he used to give full, deep, bend at the waist bows, but times had indeed changed, and would probably continue to do so.

Kherlos opened his cabinet and poured a glass of wine, drained it, poured another, and walked out onto his balcony that overlooked the front courtyard. People came to the palace for their business just as always. Whether to worship, seek the blessings at his statue, negotiate a contract, bribe a priest, or to kill him, he didn't know, but still they came and went. It was still a favorite place for women to negotiate engagements for their nieces, and for businessmen to seal the terms of contracts as if the proximity to their Divine Lord lent authority to their dealings.

Below, the people began to notice their lord was observing them. Some bowed, or kissed their fingers and raised them to him. One man, leading on a donkey, sneered and made a rude gesture.

He was immediately accosted. "Get down and beg forgiveness," a woman shouted. "How dare you insult your lord?"

"He's not my lord, he's nobody's lord now." The man stepped away from his accuser. "Now let me be."

"He will strike you down." Evidently, not everyone had heard the good news yet.

"Let him try."

The woman gasped, shocked by the remark. "Lord?" She looked up and pleaded.

Kherlos moved back inside. He grabbed his bottle and slumped down his chair. He could hear the sound of shouting outside as the two fought and a crowd gathered.

Moments later, a houseboy entered looking distraught.

"What?"

"Pardon me Lord, I am very sorry, but there is a stranger who demands to see you."

"I wish to see no one, send him to my generals."

"I am most sorry, my lord, but he is most insistent that you see him. We are quite unable to, to dissuade him."

"Do the guards not have swords? Has everyone suddenly gone useless?"

"My lord, I'm sorry, but they tried, the guards that is. The man took their swords away and told them they could have them back after he has seen you. Then he sent me after you." The boy paused again. Kherlos wondered now if he had misjudged the boy's fear. A younger Kherlos could have dealt with any threat; now bullies are able barge into the palace and order people around with impunity.

"He told me to tell you his name was Kim, and you would see him."

Kherlos sat up. "What else?"

"That he means no harm. Do you know him?"

"Fetch him in then, and tell him to stop annoying my soldiers."

"Yes, lord."

Presently a young man with brown skin, short black hair, and elaborately embroidered red and black silk pajamas entered, followed by two sheepish guards.

"Alone," Kim said.

The guards tried to look gruff, but Kherlos waived them off. "Leave us." He looked at the new Kim. He had the same general skin color and hair color as the former. Perhaps they had been brothers. "Do you inherit the name as well as the power?" Kherlos asked, ignoring any pretense of cordiality, or the courtesy of inviting him to sit first.

Kim smiled. "Yes, that is the tradition."

"Aren't you lucky then, to have kept the power in your family?"

"Our power, like ourselves, is not what we appear to be. Most see a small man who could be no great threat. But you know this is not so."

"Yes, I am lucky to be alive. I think. He almost bested me even after I blinded him." This news didn't seem to shake the present Kim at all. In fact, it seemed to Kherlos that the man showed pride.

"The Divine ability that we hand down from brother to brother is not a simple wish, nor easy to guess. We have held the power for many generations in succession."

"The ability to not be seen by others?" Kherlos asked.

"That is a generalization. We do not believe that power actually exists for humans. Our power is different. I am sorry that I cannot reveal its nature."

"That is quite all right, I believe I already had a demonstration, but that's what you're here about isn't it?"

"Yes."

"You want to know how I managed to kill him, to learn from his mistakes?"

"Yes, we wish to offer you information in return."

"Such as?"

"The names of those who purchased our services for you."

"Oh I already know that, it was the Council Ra-ken." This news seemed to disappoint Kim. "However, I believe we can still help each other. You know my power was taken."

"Yes, we are sorry for your loss."

Kherlos felt the statement was genuine. "I hope to get it back. Maybe you can help me with that, for my cooperation."

Kim took some time considering this. "We do not know where the power is; but your offer intrigues. I very much want to know about your conflict with my brother. We are not often thwarted."

"Yes, I imagine that must sting a bit."

"What is your offer?"

"If you and your brothers will help me get my power back then I will tell you everything I know about it and how I killed your brother."

"This would require us to find the new owner, unless you already know where it is."

Kherlos looked away. "I have not been able to obtain that information."

"Perhaps we can manage that, but how will we liberate the ability."

"I believe I have something on that regard that could be of use. Of course, I would have to be present at the time."

"So that we are clear." Kim held up a single finger. "you propose that my brothers locate the ability." He raised a second finger. "And then together we go and help you reclaim it."

"Yes, but this is only because my city suffers. I bear you no ill will. I only wish to recover that which was taken from me, for the sake of my city."

"So you would not seek revenge?"

"No."

"Then I accept your offer on behalf of my brothers and elders. We will provide what assistance we can. We do not know why the council wanted you killed, we never ask. Nor do we know where the power is now, but we will watch." Kim waited while Kherlos took this in.

"I find that acceptable." Really, he thought, what choice did he have?

"Tell me please, how did you defeat my brother?"

"My ability is not random or uncontrolled. It is a two part process, yet sometimes not." Kim listened attentively. "Would you like some tea? Wine? We might as well relax." Kherlos realized that Kim had maintained a fighter's distance and stance the whole time they had been negotiating. Now that an accord had been struck, they could sit down and relax.

Kim bowed. "Tea, please. That would be very kind."

"Perhaps you had best ask for it then," Kherlos said, "You seem to command more respect here than I do."

Kim nodded. He pulled open the door swiftly, startling the guards trying to listen in.

"Bring us tea." The men looked confused. "Your master commands it," he added, meaning himself.

Wish for butter, wish for bread,

Wish your mother, father dead.

Wish for silver, wish for gold,

Wish again to not grow old.

Wish for fortune, wish for fame,

These are answered both the same.

Wish for sorrow, wish for pain,

Wish you had but half a brain.

Finally when your wishing's done,

You'd have wished you'd not begun.

– Skipping rhyme –

# Fifteen.

*The first of men went unto the world and denied the Angel Uumvault. For they told no man nor woman nor child the tidings of the Lord Divine, but kept unto themselves, and made themselves as kings.*

*Book of the Divine*

**10 Raveen, Y.O.D. 745**

## City of Andoline, Colovencia, Alasta

Derek enjoyed the morning's ride to the city of Andoline. At first, the distance from his work had concerned him, and he would have taken a house in the city, but Clea had insisted they live on the land she had inherited, and he had acquiesced. The land had been in her family for generations, and she had told him quite plainly that if he wanted to live in the city he was welcome to do so.

The ride was pleasant enough most of the year. It gave him copious time to compose his stories, or review the day's events. The Andoline Herald was an institution with deep roots. They had so far staunchly withstood the pressure to publish on a daily schedule, and Derek had no doubts that any publisher that tried to do so would soon fold under the burden of its own deadlines. The world rushed by fast enough already and had no call for daily pamphlets. His own Divine day, his fourth, was but a week away, though there would be no celebration other than a solemn pre-dinner visit to his parent's graves at the back of their property.

In sour spirits, Derek entered the city. As with any area so congested with humans and animals, it was filthy, smelly, and majestic. People ebbed and flowed in all directions on unfathomable errands, others loitered conspicuously, demonstrating bizarre abilities to the curious for pennies. Proprietors stood outside their shops and extolled the virtues of their wares. With no rhyme or reason, they crowded together and vied for the attention of the unwary traveler. Derek spied a man holding a fine long dress on the walk in front of his shop. He had the attention of a sharpish woman, dubious of the quality of the item.

"You can see the fineness of the fabric. Cool and light. Please touch." The merchant held the sleeve out for the woman to feel. Derek halted his horse and watched. The woman felt the fabric and showed a brief look of interest, but quickly scowled to cover her mistake.

"The colors are exquisite and you would be the envy of all Andoline."

"How is the stitching?" she demanded.

"See for yourself," he said, turning the sleeve inside out, revealing a well-sewn seam. Derek turned his ability on the man and let him talk. It was childish, but today he didn't care.

"You see, good thread well applied. Here where we show the customer, but certainly not everywhere. We use the cheap thread on the hem within a wash or two the back falls out and is dragging in the filth of the street. You blame the maids and not us. We sympathize of course, and offer a discount on your next purchase. Not to my mistress do I do this. She would not stand for such a thing. She would refuse to see me and has said as much but I think she sees other men. Unfaithful but so willing, what do I care if other men give her gifts? I will tire of her soon. What am I saying?" The woman had stood mouth agape as the man talked, too stunned by what she was hearing to react, too curious about these confessions to interrupt.

Derek turned off his ability and urged his horse on. He loved his gift, but even this brought a touch of melancholy, as he was forbidden by everyone he knew to use it in their presence.

§

It was customary for Clea to inquire about her husband's day in town over dinner. She cared, she knew she cared, but he never seemed to appreciate what a job her day was. Liam had come home late from school and slunk into his room with a sullen look of guilt. Nine-year-old boys weren't hard to read, but if she confronted him, he would learn to hide his emotions just that much faster. Better to wait and give the boy's conscience some time to worry him. She decided to raise the subject after her husband finished blathering about work. He seemed excited about something.

"You know, just my usual argument with Vester; I swear by the Divine that man will print anything if he thinks he can make a coin." Derek punctuated his point by waving a bite of potato at his wife and then stuffed it in his mouth. He paused while chewing, a rule his wife enforced with daggers. Clea looked at her son. Normally he would have blurted out some clever remark, but he was picking quietly at his food and had appeared not to hear his father.

"And when I suggested that he help pay my expenses, he just looked at me blankly, as if I had spoken Archaic. I suppose he wants me to sleep out in the street like an unpowered beggar while I'm penning stories for his rag."

"Did he like your story then?"

"Oh there really wasn't anything there, just another old woman claiming to have seen the Divine."

"Is that a crime?" she asked.

"No, I guess not. The council seems not to think so, and it's not a story either. I could tell right away too, I didn't really need my ability. She just wanted attention. Still, I had to make her babble out a confession in front of her family. I didn't feel right about that, but otherwise they would have pestered us."

"I'm sure you showed restraint."

"Well, yes, I know how you feel. Just a touch, nothing intrusive, but Divine knows that's not why I have an ability in the first place. Making old women confess to petty falsehoods is poor use of Divine intent. I'm sorry, how was your day?"

"Pleasant," she replied, "Thank you for asking. Liam came home late from school, didn't you dear?"

Liam opened his mouth and looked at his mother in fear.

"Young man, account for yourself."

"Teacher held me late," he said.

A knock came at the door. Presently their caretaker, Jarod entered the dining room. "Mrs. Pritchett has come calling. I have invited her into the study."

"Thank you Jarod, please make her comfortable," Derek said.

"Certainly sir."

"Finish your dinner Liam," Clea said. She was fairly certain she knew what this was about.

Clea and Derek rose and moved to the study where Mrs. Pritchett was waiting for them.

"Rose, how kind of you to visit, we are just at supper, may we offer you a place at our table." Clea held out her hands, Rose took them and the two women exchanged kisses on the cheek. Derek stepped forward to offer his hand, but the woman did not wait for the formalities to be over.

"I'll not take much of your time, thank you for your generous offer," she said sternly, putting them on notice that this was not a friendly visit. "My cows were run all over my field a'fore supper this evening, and rocks thrown at my chickens. My man says he chased two boys off and knows that one of them was young master Liam."

"I see," Clea said. "My son claims that he was held late by his teacher after school, I think we should question him further."

"Clea dear, my man knows your boy when he sees him."

"Please, let me call my son." Clea walked out of the room.

"May I offer you a drink, water? Tea perhaps?" Derek had never been comfortable with their neighbor from down the road.

"No, thank you kind sir. I know you be blessed with the Divine and all, but that's got nothing to do with my livestock."

Derek was taken aback. "No, of course not, I'm sure we'll have this sorted out right away." She didn't seem much assured.

Clea entered the room with Liam in tow. She stood behind her boy and had him face their guest. "Liam, Mrs. Pritchett says you were bothering her cattle and chickens."

Liam remained silent, a mixture of panic and fear showed on his face.

"Did you?" she asked.

"No, Ma'am," Liam said. "Mrs. Rosewood kept me late to help clean. I came straight home."

"My man says he saw you running away, he's a good man, not one given to lying."

"I was running home."

"I can get to the bottom of this real quick and simple," Derek said.

"That will not be necessary dear, I am quite sure." Clea's words were ice, a promise of consequences to come.

Derek ignored the warning, winked at her, placed his fingertips along his temple with his thumbs against his jaw and began massaging his temple.

"I'm sure that is not called for—" began Rose.

"Josh made me do it," Liam shouted.

Clea glared at her husband.

"See, simple."

"Thank you Liam," Clea said, "You will spend the next two weekends helping Mrs. Pritchett clean her barn and hen house and whatever other chores she might find to teach a young man his manners."

"Is that acceptable Rose?"

"Perfectly, thank you," she turned to Liam. "My man is up before dawn, I will expect to see you then."

"Yes, Ma'am" Liam said, eyes down.

"Thank you Rose, has Derek offered to make you comfortable?"

"He has, thank you, but I must be back to attend my supper. I'm sure you understand."

"Yes, of course, give our love to Lester." Clea moved Liam and herself aside so that the woman could leave. Rose took the hint. After she left Clea turned on Liam. "Young man, we will find a suitable punishment for you for lying to us, in the mean time you are to go straight to bed."

"But," Liam tried.

"No buts, I am very angry at you." She kneeled down and gave Liam a hug and a kiss on the cheek.

"Now off to bed young man." She closed the door behind her son.

"I didn't," Derek said.

Clea crossed her arms. "We had an agreement."

"I didn't, I just pretended. If I had used my ability he would still be talking."

Clea frowned, she didn't believe her husband, but she couldn't call him a liar either. "Your ability doesn't give you the right to just do whatever you want. Not in my house."

The reminder stung. "I know. I know, I'm sorry, I just thought that the threat would be enough. We could both tell he got caught and was just digging himself deeper into the muck."

"I'm not happy with you," she said, softening slightly.

"Well, you should be. I have a new assignment." He put his hands on her shoulders and tried to look pleased.

"You didn't mention that at dinner."

"Sorry, I was waiting for the right moment. It's all very mysterious. All that Vester would tell me was I had been hand-picked."

"Does it come with a raise?"

"It comes from the Council, but it has nothing to do with her," he said, guessing her thoughts.

Clea raised her voice. "How do I know that?"

"Love, look, I meant for this to be a surprise, a good surprise."

"So out with it then." She hadn't meant for it to sound that harsh. A direct summons from the Council was a high honor. However, she didn't have to like it.

"I don't know all the details yet, I'm meeting with an envoy from the Council tomorrow. It involves travel."

Clea found her eyes moist. She turned and fled the room, leaving her stunned husband behind.

§

Clea kissed her son goodnight. She closed the book and tucked him in. She blew out his lamp, and stood by his bed. She liked to linger in the darkened room. He looked so peaceful. She returned to the library to continue the conversation with her husband.

"How long will you be gone?" As soon as she spoke, she realized she was still angry. She stood in front of his desk and confronted him with arms crossed.

He sat there and pretended to be busy. She waited. He rose from his desk, walked to her and pulled her close, put his face in her hair and kissed her neck. At first, she resisted, felt guilty, and finally accepted the comfort.

"There will be FarSpeakers. You know I won't be completely out of touch."

"That long? That far?" Even after ten years, she still missed him when he traveled.

"About five weeks."

She pushed back so she could look into his face. "You'll be gone over Year's Turn."

"Yes."

"You know it scares me when you're away that long, and you have no idea what the story might be about. I'm always afraid for your safety."

"Of course you are, but Tameria has been—"

"Tameria, Divine's sake."

"—settled for over two hundred years now. They have cities and civilization just as we do. Just not as close together. I'll be traveling under the protection of the Council Ra-ken. I will be safe." He hugged her again.

"Your precious power won't stop a knife thrust."

Derek sighed.

"What the Fel do the Ra-ken want with that Divine forsaken place?"

"I don't know."

"Can't you just ignore this?" Derek shook his head.

"That would not be good for my career."

"When are you leaving? Tonight? Now?"

"No, I'm guessing they're in a hurry. But I won't know until I meet the envoy."

"You're just full of good news."

Derek frowned at the insult.

"I'm sorry," Clea said, "I know you think this is good news, and maybe it is, but you know I don't trust the council. You're asking for a raise when you get back. You hear me?"

"Yes, dear."

"Good, now let's go to bed, I'm tired."

§

Derek's appointment with the envoy came and went, leaving him with little more information than before. Passage to Vesport, the principal city of Tameria, had been booked on Ve Grange, a sailing ship that plied the trade routes out of Trent. Of the Ve Grange, he knew very little beyond its status as a commercial ship. The envoy assured him it was one of the newer, larger ships, less prone to sinking. So he knew when, and where, but that was it.

His co-workers suddenly seemed to be either clueless or overly busy; no one knew anything, had heard any rumors, or had time to chat. Even his editor had been short with him.

Derek despaired. Couldn't anybody just be happy for him?

§

Clea had said little. Her cool demeanor had only melted briefly once his baggage was loaded onto the waiting coach. They had agreed on goodbyes at the door, rather than at the docks. Liam still had lessons and chores, Clea still had a home and farm to run. Hugs, kisses, and promises were given all around. Derek climbed aboard the coach and wished the trip were already over.

§

He watched the land drift by, the farms, crops, animals, people working in fields or herding animals. There were so many ordinary people in the world, just living simple lives and trying to scratch out some brief stretch of happiness before they died. In some ways he envied them and their simple routines; while his ability made him a good newsman, and earned him a decent living, it didn't automatically make him a good husband, and it certainly didn't make him happy. He didn't expect this trip would change much either.

"I wish I had the ability to be happy," he said aloud, to no one in particular, wondering if at least one person somewhere had that ability. If they did, they probably kept it secret.

§

"Sailing is like living in a small cramped hotel with bad service during an unending earthquake." Derek wrote in his journal on the third day of his voyage aboard the Ve Grange, and saw no reason to revise it by the end, save perhaps to fit the word "dull" into it a few more times.

# Sixteen.

*There was born into the family Chochanakea, who was known as EagleEye, in the time of sorrows, a third son, Apachawea, who desired to be a warrior of his people.*

*Myth of the Revelation*

**23 Raveen, Y.O.D. 745**

## City of Vesport, Tameria

Derek carefully navigated the gangplank away from the mobile prison known as Ve Grange. A chill wind blew off the sea, and kept the moss-covered boards damp, forcing him to cling to the guide rope, while the wind whipped his long-coat around his legs. Below him teemed a maelstrom of activity. Animals, people and carts with boxes and barrels of all kinds, rushed back and forth. People in every manner of strange costume milled about and jostled each other like an upturned anthill–except ants didn't wear bright colored hats or curl their hair around their ears.

Now what, Derek thought. He was safely on the pier, but lacked a purpose. According to the plan, he was to be met at the dock, but details were sketchy. He had expected some kind of committee, perhaps a small band with a banner, and a couple young women with skirts above the knee. Okay, he corrected, he had actually expected a man wearing a grungy jacket and no shoes holding a badly painted board with the word "Kenter" on it, or something.

He scanned the sea of people. Everyone looked like they had somewhere better to be. Even the other passengers—a priest herding a flock of acolytes on a missionary expedition—were already boarding an open coach and about to be underway. No one, except for him, looked like they were looking for someone.

One man, Derek noticed, a full head taller than most, wearing a bright red shirt and black headscarf, literally swam through the crowd with an overhand stroke, pushing people aside with his strong arms. He brushed past Derek and headed up the plank, only to be intercepted and halted by the mate.

Good luck, Derek thought. That same mate had stopped Derek from boarding in Trent with repeated shouts of "Geet offen witcha" until the captain intervened and allowed the paying passengers onboard. Derek saw that this man was having no better luck. The mate was repeatedly pointing at the pier while the two shouted at each other. Derek started his way down the pier toward the street. Perhaps, he considered, his welcoming committee was waiting there.

A meaty hand grabbed his shoulder and spun him around; it was attached to the man who had just been trying to board the Ship. "Derek Cantor," his voice boomed, deep as thunder.

"Yes?"

"Ah, most excellent, yes, I am Martsen; I am to be your guide."

"Yes? Yes! Excellent, I was beginning to despair."

"You are black?" Martsen said. He held his arm out to compare skin tones.

"Yes, so are you" Derek looked around, "But I can see this is not unusual here."

"This is so, but where you come from, I am told they are all white as the belly of a grub."

"Some are, some are not, and they are as diverse as those you see here, more or less."

"Oh come now, you know I jest. Tell me, how was your voyage?"

"Dull."

"Excellent, never wish for excitement while at sea. Did you eat well?"

"Nothing I would FarSpeak home about. I fear my teeth are loosening, and I'd kill for a beer."

"Aha, this I can do. I have a coach waiting. Your luggage is being attended to. Please come." Martsen began pushing his way through the throng.

Derek followed behind, grateful for the man's size as he followed in his wake. The two climbed into a waiting coach and sat, waiting for the luggage to be loaded.

"I promised my wife–"

"Of course," Martsen interrupted, "there are FarSpeakers at the hotel. Were there none on the ship?"

"I believe the phrase 'Navigational purposes only,' sums up the captain's sentiment."

"Never mind, tell me, so you are you married, yes?"

"I believe I mentioned a wife, yes."

"And is your beautiful wife as black as the two of us?"

"No, she is as white as the belly of a grub."

Martsen let out a full roaring laugh.

"And my son is golden skinned with bright eyes of copper," Derek added.

"I am sure he is. I would love one day to meet your family."

"We would love to have you as our guest, Clea, my wife, loves to entertain." It was an easy offer to make to a man on a different continent.

The driver rapped on the roof, and the coach rolled forward and bumped its way along slowly.

"Tell me," Martsen asked, "Is your wife also touched by the Divine? I hear that everyone in the fabled city of Andoline has abilities."

"No. She is unpowered. Are you?"

Martsen laughed. "No, no. You have all the powers over in your land. We have so few here." Derek looked skeptical. "No, it is true, we have the FarSpeakers and Healers, Apachawea we call them, or 'Little Foot', but not the Ra-ken that are your blessing and your curse."

"That can change," Derek said.

"Indeed it can my friend, indeed it can." Martsen pulled open a shutter and looked out. Derek caught a glimpse of sooty buildings and crowded streets. Martsen gave a running commentary and history on the city, pointing out statues and buildings whenever he knew some trivial fact and generally talked the entire trip.

When the door opened and Derek climbed down, it looked like a city street from anywhere, with three and four story buildings fronting on a hard packed clay street.

"I see that women wear the hats here, and men favor scarves," Derek said.

Martsen shrugged, "It's what people do, come." He urged Derek towards an ornate glass-decorated door flanked by two men, with elaborately braided headscarves of blue and gold, matching blue jackets, and baggy pants trimmed with gold studs. The men, with synchronized movements, opened the oversized doors and ushered them in.

The interior of the hotel was just as lavish; framed wood panels hung on every wall, each with some kind of shell and ivory inlay, and depicting scenes of conquest and debauchery. Leather furniture with gilded frames sat on a white marbled floor and uniformed attendants stood at strategic locations around the room. A young woman in a brightly colored woolen dress approached and spoke with Martsen briefly. After a moment, a jacketed attendant presented himself.

"This is Pasco," Martsen said, indicating the man. "He will show you to your room and deliver your trunks. A FarSpeaker is being summoned; he will attend to you as soon as he arrives."

"Thank you," Derek said, "What about dinner?"

"All is arranged. Am man will call upon you when dinner is ready. I am sure you will find the food most enjoyable."

"You won't be joining me?"

"Ah, I am so sorry, no, but I assure you, you will be well taken care of here. There is no need for worry. I will meet you again tomorrow morning to start our journey."

"Oh, I thought I was already there."

"No, no my friend, you are here, but not there, not yet, but soon. First you must rest."

"Do they have beds here?" Derek asked. The hammocks on the ship had been quite novel, but he had not yet learned the art of relaxing in one.

"Such questions you ask. Pasco will show you to your room. Do enjoy, I must be off."

Derek shook Martsen's hand, and followed Pasco to his room. It was simple enough with papered walls, gaslights and an inviting bed. He accepted it's invitation.

§

He woke to the sound of knocking on his door. "Yes, what is it?" he felt foolish; no one would be able to understand him. He opened the door. An older man with brown weathered skin came into the room, bowed slightly and spoke.

"Speaker is ready."

Derek paused, replayed the oddly pronounced words, and took a moment to comprehend.

"Oh yes, yes, you're the FarSpeaker to Andoline."

"Yes, I am in Andoline, what is your message please."

Derek spoke. "Message from Derek Canter for Arness Leffane editor of Andoline World News Andoline City, Colovencia, end." he paused to gather his thoughts. "Expected arrival tomorrow or the next day end I have been met and have a guide end I will communicate again when I know more end. Message terminates. Second message follows."

"Speaker is ready."

"Message from Derek Canter for Clea Canter Mistress of Dorrant Farm, south of Andoline City end. Hand deliver end. Clea end all is well end at destination end will return soon with haste and love end. Message terminates. No further messages."

After the FarSpeaker had left, another man appeared. This one pantomimed eating and rubbing his belly. Derek followed the man down into a small dining room, where he was the only guest. As soon as he sat, wine, bread and a bowl of thick paste were set before him. He used the bread to scoop up and taste the paste, which reminded him of licorice. In quick succession, the staff set out plates of pickled vegetables, small fish, pungent sauces, and other delights until he protested that he could eat no more.

Overall, the meal had been excellent, and though he had almost no idea what he had just eaten, he was starting to look forward to the rest of the trip.

When he returned to his room, a young lady waited in his bed. He sighed, he was thousands of miles from home, and who was he to say what customs these people had? What might they consider essential hospitality and what might be an insult? Still, infidelity was not an option. Clea claimed to eschew powers, but Derek secretly believed she had the ability to know when he was doing something he shouldn't. The last thing he wanted was to return home and find his possessions out on the road.

The young woman was quite put off, to be put out, but once she understood, she wouldn't even let Derek watch her dress.

§

He awoke in the morning to the sound of a rapping on his door. He checked to make sure he was wearing pajamas, though he didn't remember putting them on. The rapping came again. He dragged himself out of bed, and opened the door. An old woman pushed past him, chattering with a shrill voice in a language he didn't understand. His lack of understanding either didn't register or didn't matter. She quickly made his bed, and then started rummaging around in his bags. She pulled out a pair of undershorts and laid them on the bed, followed by a pair of trousers and a clean shirt. Derek stepped toward her to intervene, but as soon as he came near, she grabbed his pajama top and pulled it off over his head, and then she pulled the string on his pajama bottoms. He managed to grab them in time to save his dignity.

"Out," Derek said, one hand on his pajamas, the other pointing at the door. The old woman stuck her chin out and folded her arms. She could be stubborn too.

"Out, please?" Derek asked, with more than a little pleading in his voice. The woman relented; shaking her head she walked out, leaving the door open behind her.

§

Derek found Martsen waiting for him in the lobby, idly chatting with the wait staff.

"Good Morning," Martsen announced in his booming voice. Derek decided that his first impression had been wrong; he could not be friends with anyone that cheerful in the morning.

"Would you care for some smoked fish and hard eggs?" Martsen asked.

Derek assumed this was food. "Yes," he said.

"Good, Good, we must eat, it will be a long journey." He showed Derek trays of smoked fish, dark sausages and boiled eggs. "Help yourself. I must see about the packing of your things."

"But I'm already packed," Derek said, confused.

"Ah yes, but we travel by horse from here, I'm afraid they do not do well with heavy trunks. We must move your things into panniers."

"Those big fancy skirts women used to wear?" Derek asked.

"Sorry?"

"Never mind, I'm sure you meant something different."

"You eat," Martsen said, "I will come back and get you when we are ready."

§

Derek and Martsen rode on dappled, black-and-silver native horses, both short and stocky with shaggy hair. A brown-haired mare carried Derek's clothes and notebooks in panniers, which were a kind of saddlebag. Martsen assured him the animals were quite surefooted, and only occasionally bit the rider.

"Occasionally" Derek mused, was clearly meant to be translated into "as often as possible." He decided the new tear in his coat could be attributed to his bravery in fending off some wild mountain cat, and not his carelessness around domesticated beasts.

The coastal valley that nestled Vesport quickly gave way to steep mountains, cut in deep furrows by a snow-fed river that had no time for idle chatter. A narrow trail climbed the sides of the mountains, switching out, and then back, each time revealing the mighty torrent more and more diminutive, until it was naught but a pencil line on a cartographer's page.

Eventually they rounded the final switchback and looked out onto a broad plain swept with tall grass and patches of thin scrub trees. The sun gave a brief appearance, Derek beheld the shimmer of a broad shallow lake, and beyond, mountains piled on top of more mountains their white peaks rising up and merging with the gray skies.

"That is our destination," Martsen pointed, "We will circle to the far North end of the lake where we can cross the river, and reach the base of the mountain by midday."

"Why not go around that way," Derek asked, pointing to the South."

"It has a bit of a sharp drop; a waterfall, that feeds the river into Vesport. If you are in a hurry to get back, you could go for a swim. Do you have the ability to survive falls from a great height?"

"No."

"Ah ha, well if you did, I hear that the trick is to wait to use the ability near the very end." Martsen laughed at his own witticism.

"I'll try and keep that in mind."

As they rode, the trees became taller and closer together. Soon they were on a well-maintained trail through a thick wood of tall pine and spruce. They rode into a clearing, the center square for a small village of stone dwellings with wood-shingled roofs.

"Welcome to Cohote," Martsen announced, "they do not speak your language here, but they are friendly." Dark-skinned people had come out of their houses, or straightened up from in their fields to watch them arrive. Martsen waved and spoke to people as they rode past.

"I'm surprised it merits a name," Derek said. There were no more than a dozen buildings with no roads or fences, just dirt tracks between small vegetable gardens. "Are we here then?"

Martsen laughed again, a sound Derek would be pleased to be rid of. "I am, but no, you are not." He pointed to the far end of the clearing. A high wall marked the end of the village. The break in the wall was capped with a high arch. Beyond the arch, broad stone steps rose up into the thick pine.

"How far do they go up?" Derek asked.

"Far enough, but not too far. You should go now, they are waiting for you. Your things will be sent up."

"I'll need my notebooks."

"Travel lightly my friend. It would be bad protocol to collapse on the steps of this temple."

Derek considered this, dismounted, and started pulling a few notebooks, journals and writing supplies out of his bags while keeping a careful eye on the beast that carried them. "Where are you going to be?"

"Why here, enjoying their hospitality and talking with old friends."

"Waiting for me?"

"Waiting for you," Martsen assured him, grinning broadly as if there were some tremendously funny private joke.

Derek lifted the leather bag he had stuffed with necessities, and headed for the stairs. For the better part of an hour, he climbed a slow steady pace, conserving his energy.

Finally, the steps ended onto a flat bare stone plateau and he knew this was his destination. The mountain rose up from the valley on his left, cut straight across, then straight up, then resumed being a mountain again, as if there were a notch, like those cut out of a tree from the first strokes of an axe. The plateau appeared to be polished white marble, inlaid with two gigantic dark granite crescent moons—the sigil of the Ra-ken, writ large in stone.

In the sides of the steep cliffs to his right, two arched doorways led into tunnels running deep into the earth. At the far end, opposite from where he stood, perched a high stone building with tall arches and steep gables that melded into the sides of the mountain at the back.

Even from a distance, he could tell that this was either a temple or palace, depending on the ego of the man in a light gray robe standing in front of the heavy wooden door.

Derek approached and gave a formal introduction. "I am Derek Duane Canter; able to make others speak without reflection."

Ahten bowed deeply at the waist. "I am the low one Ahten Diao. I welcome you to our humble Temple of the Divine. I will show you to your room, we have guests here from time to time, and I am sure you will find us most hospitable. As you may have guessed, this retreat as we call it, was built by the Council Ra-ken. With each Council member contributing according to their ability." He pointed at the twin doors. "Ra Leighland carved those tunnels, and Ra Leo lifted the stones and built these arches." He indicated the arched stones that formed the massive doorframe. Ahten pulled open the tall oak door, and allowed Derek inside.

"Cordain is able to make stone flow?" Derek asked. This was news all by itself.

"Impressive, isn't it?"

It was impressive, though Derek suspected Ahten meant the building. The main hall had a high arched ceiling supported by a double row of columns. Colored-glass windows, six on each side of the hall, depicted scenes he recognized as the twelve fatal wishes. The first, according to legend, was the ability to visit the moon.

"Were you involved in the construction?" Derek itched to dig out his journal and start taking notes, but he restrained himself.

"Yes, well, I supervised you understand. Most of the designs were—"

"So you can describe how the Ra-ken each contributed their abilities?"

Ahten gave a puzzled look. "Later, for now, you should wash off some of the day's dust; we are having a banquet in your honor tonight."

"Isn't that a little much? I mean, my ability isn't all that impressive."

"You were hand-picked by the Council for this story. We were told to treat you well and to give you every courtesy, and this is what we will do."

Ahten led him through the main hall, and introduced him to several other of the clergy. Try as he might, there was little in the way of distinctive features that would allow him to remember their names. They each shaved their heads except for a single, shoulder-length lock of hair on the side, and each wore a simple gray robe of varying shades. He understood, being a newsman, that the shade of their robe, and the badge clipped to their side braid indicated their status, but he found the particulars escaped him.

Ahten continued the tour, and led him down a stone hallway, clearly inside the mountain, to a plain wooden door.

"You'll find we are quite civilized here. We have faithful, who will bring you heated water, and launder your clothes while you bathe. The fires are tended to regularly, we have indoor commodes with running water, and if you have any needs, you have but to ask, and I apologize for saying this, but I do mean 'ask'. The faithful here are not servants or slaves, please bear that in mind."

"Of course, I am a guest, I shall act accordingly."

"Splendid," Ahten said, "then if you'll forgive me, I have matters to attend to. You will be summoned for dinner."

"Thank you, I am most pleased." Derek nodded lightly, Ahten bowed deeply again and departed.

In spite of Ahten's words, the faithful acted exactly as if they were servants. Derek relaxed in a hot soaking bath drinking a sweet Vesport wine and mused on Ahten's use of the word "Slaves;" an archaic word, long fallen out of common use.

Derek had a thought, and turned to the acolyte waiting patiently for him to finish bathing.

"Who brings the supplies up the mountain?" he asked, indicating the goblet and wine he was enjoying.

"We have a lift," the acolyte replied.

"Really, a lift? How is it run?"

"Umm…" the man paused a moment, "by water, Ra Leighland made these chambers, then designed and built it."

"Interesting."

"Shall I mention to Ahten that you would be interested in seeing it?"

"Yes, of course," Derek replied. The man said nothing further. Derek finished his wine and rose from the bath. The acolyte took the crystal goblet from him and handed him a large soft towel.

"I can dress myself," Derek said, just in case there was a misunderstanding.

"Yes, of course."

"There was this old woman you see." Derek stopped; the man clearly did not want to hear.

"Is there a FarSpeaker here?"

"There is one in the village; I can have him sent for."

"Would you, please?"

"Yes, is there anything else?"

"No, thank you."

146

As soon as the man was gone, Derek donned the soft cotton robe they had provided for him. His room was furnished with a writing desk, a large recumbent bed, chest and armoire. He opened the chest and found his things neatly laid out inside. He extracted a leather-bound volume with loose stitching that could be undone so that new pages could be inserted. Seated at the desk, he carefully opened the book to the page labeled "Cordain Leighland, Master of Earth." He added the date, and a line about Ahten's remark. Then he turned to the back, found a blank page, and wrote the title "Ra-ken Sanctuary, East of Vesport, Tameria." Underneath he added the date, and then started describing what he had seen.

§

Dinner was a simple affair; fish and mushrooms in a clear broth, rice, and cooked greens. Derek ate with Ahten and several other senior clergy. Each took a few minutes to describe their duties. Yves, a little shorter and stouter than the rest was in charge of supplies. Umbra's locket of hair was blond, and he managed staff. Pench had white hair and age-mottled skin. He oversaw the student's education. But after that, they all just blurred together in Derek's mind.

Taken together they described the mid-level managers you would find at any well run traveler's inn, except no one would ever put an inn so far away from everywhere else. The only thing noticeable about them was they were all fair-skinned men.

"I trust your stay so far has been pleasant?" Umbra asked.

"Yes, thank you, everyone has been most pleasant and courteous."

"Helpful?"

"Well no," Derek answered. Umbra looked hurt.

"No one will tell me why I'm here. I mean, it's a nice retreat, certainly remote enough, but no one wants to say why the Ra-ken went to such trouble. They're not here are they?"

"Oh," Umbra seemed relieved. "I thought one of the staff might have been rude to you."

"No," Ahten replied, "There are no Council members here currently, but they do come and visit." He held up his hand to forestall any more questions. "We have a full day planned for you tomorrow; you will get all your answers then. Today is a day of rest and enjoyment; tomorrow you can go back to work." The others chuckled at Ahten's joke.

"Do you play cards? Or shall we be forced to educate you?" Ahten asked.

"I play."

"Excellent. Money here has little meaning. Everything we need is supplied by the Council, or bought on their credit as you might imagine, so we like to amuse ourselves by playing for large sums, but it's all play money really."

"Don't you believe him," Pench said, "he only says that because he owes each of us a large fortune." The men all rose and allowed the younger acolytes to clear the table.

"Nonsense," Ahten said. "We'll stake you 5,000 suns."

"Who will?" Yves asked.

"I will," Ahten said.

"We keep accounts," Yves explained, "but when Ahten runs out of money he makes us pay him tribute."

"I do not," Ahten said, only to be shouted down by a chorus of "Yes, you do."

They moved into a library with a heavy wooden table in the center and decanters of wine placed near each seat.

Derek sat, poured himself a glass of wine, and watched as Ahten unlocked a small cabinet. "Locks?"

"What?" Ahten said.

"You have a lock on the cabinet, who don't you trust?"

"Us mostly," Umbra said. Everyone thought this was funny.

"We keep our gaming supplies in here," Ahten said, as if that explained it.

"He doesn't want one of us changing accounts," Pench said.

"Or examining them," Yves added.

Ahten removed an ornate box, a leather-bound oversized book and a large heavy case. He passed the book to Yves, the box to Umbra, and kept the case, which he opened to reveal rows of brightly colored wooden chips.

"We have a new account to add this evening," announced Yves. There was a smattering of applause. "Derek Duane Cantor, 5,000 Suns; who will make the loan?"

"I will," Ahten said, and pushed a stack of wooden chips to Derek.

"So noted." Yves then read out the accounts of each player while Ahten counted out each man's sum in chips. When they were done, Yves closed the book. It and the extra chips were returned to the cabinet. Meanwhile, Umbra had extracted the deck of cards and had been gently shuffling them.

"What is your ability young man?" Pench asked.

"Useless against you," Ahten said quickly. The others laughed, but the old man just looked confused.

"I can make others talk without reflection," Derek said.

"Oh. I thought you were the one that could sneeze money?"

"I heard about that," Derek said, "what happened to that woman?"

"I sneeze wine out my nose sometimes," Pench said.

"I'm sorry?"

"Ignore him," Ahten said, "I believe the authorities took a very dim view of her economic impact and conscripted her into civil service at the minting ministry"

"Really? I thought only the Divine held the power to create. Did they figure out where the money came from?"

Ahten laughed. "Okay, you caught me. Yes, the money comes from nearby people's purses; it turned out to be a mere translocation ability, albeit of an unusual, and sometimes painful, variety."

"That's too bad," Umbra said, "I wanted to see if you could sneeze one of these." He held up the large chip. Derek just shook his head.

The evening passed quickly. He could see why Ahten was in such debt. He started as a careful player, but after a few glasses of wine, became aggressive and reckless. Derek sipped his wine slowly and played loose until he had the measure of his opponents. In the end, he had over 40,000 suns in his account or about three years' salary if he could ever collect.

§

In the morning, they served a breakfast of oats, honey, dried berries and nuts. Derek found it tasty, but somewhat hard to chew, though sipping tea helped. After pleasantries about the health of his wife and son had been asked and answered, Derek got down to business.

"I am anxious to know why I am here. I can't imagine that I was sent here to document the opening of a summer retreat for snow-tigers."

"I'm sorry?"

"The large cats, black and white stripes, they're supposed to live in the ice-covered Bridge atop the World."

"No, I know all that, why would this be a retreat for them?"

"I mean," Derek said, slightly flustered, "is, why am I here? What's the story?"

"Ahh, I see what you mean, about the tigers, that is, but yes, the story here is a complex one; it will take some time to explain. We are prepared to answer your questions, but first we would like you to know more about us."

"I must warn you," Derek said, "I am sometimes required to ask questions that people don't want to answer."

Ahten shrugged, "Yes, well I sometimes don't answer questions I don't want asked."

Derek didn't seem to know what to say to that. It was at odds with the "...help you in any way possible," he was sure he had heard the night before.

"Perhaps you should come take a walk with me." Ahten led Derek out onto the courtyard. There were several young men and women playing some sort of game with long sticks with nets at the end. They seemed to be chasing a ball around and throwing it to each other with the sticks. Both sexes wore short slacks, and about half of them, boys and girls both, were topless.

"I'm not familiar with the game," Derek said. It seemed total chaos, but he was starting to notice that not everyone chased the ball at the same time.

"The game keeps them active, it helps them bond into teams, they build friendships, and it serves as a test."

"What kind of test?"

"None of these young men or women are touched by the Divine. What usually happens when un-powered children play a game?"

"Usually the losing side finds a wish they can use to help them win."

"A useful ability?" Ahten asked; his face all-innocent.

"No, one that has relevance just for the duration of the game. A wasted wish some might say, unless you never expected to get one anyway."

"Just so," Ahten said. "Put un-powered into any sort of competition, and eventually someone finds a way to have a brief touch of the Divine. Such a pity."

"I notice you're fairly casual about dress."

"Yes. We find it's best to adjust the natives slowly to our more modern ways. They are innocents Derek, in many ways."

"Is that reason for all this then? To see what kind of abilities they can think up. Is this so you can add data to your catalogues, to finally name the nine million aspects of the Divine?"

"No, in fact just the opposite. Do I detect a note of anger in your voice, do you not approve of the clergy prosecuting false claims of Divinity?"

Derek chose not to answer. Ahten continued anyway.

"Those who have a direct relationship to the Divine can be more magnanimous. Those of us who have sworn an oath forsaking Grace for a life of servitude do not see false claims of divinity as harmless, nor do we find temporally limited abilities to be little more than 'renting' the Divine presence, as if the supreme being was some common whore." Derek backed up a step and held up his hands. The game came to an abrupt halt.

Ahten caught his tongue, relaxed a bit, then bowed slightly at Derek.

"My apologies, I become emotional easily." He turned to the children. "Go ahead, continue." He waved at them. The boy with the ball threw it to one of his teammates at the other end of the courtyard who was still distracted. The ball sailed over his head, bounced once, and headed down the mountainside.

Several cries went up. Players dropped their sticks and sat down to wait.

"We have only one ball," Ahten said, "someone must climb—"

One of the boys disappeared. What looked like a part of his face and one hand fell to the ground. Derek raced to where the boy had just been.

"Children, to your rooms," Ahten commanded. He clapped his hands and pointed at the door to their dormitories.

"Go, back to your room now. You will be told when we know more. Now!"

Most of the students obeyed, but two boys stood at the edge of the plateau and shouted "Tarren, Tarren?" down the side of the mountain.

"Go on," Ahten said to them, a little more kindly this time.

"Did you hear his wish?" Derek asked. They shook their heads.

Ahten pulled them gently away from the edge, "Well, if he turns up nearby, we will let you know. And I'll send someone to his village."

Derek picked up what was clearly the boy's hand, now solidified into fresh wood. Sticky sap oozed out like corn syrup blood. The hand extended just past the wrist, which was capped in tree bark.

He turned the oval piece over and saw a face staring back at him, small bits of dirt clinging to its surface. He brushed the debris away, and tiny wooden eyelashes broke off underneath his fingers. Derek showed the freshly minted mask to Ahten. "I think maybe, the boy trans-located. I'm guessing he went after the ball." Trans-location abilities weren't new, and anyplace you could think of going to, already had someone with the ability to go there. The moon was rumored to be littered with the bodies of those who trans-located to it. The problem was that they were one-way. This made it easy for one person to return home from anywhere, which is why these people tended to be thieves. However, this seemed different. The thought that he might have witnessed a new variant of the ability excited him. He really wanted to conceal these artifacts and keep them for his collection.

Acolytes and other priests, alerted to the incident came out from the temple. Ahten ordered two boys to descend the steps down to Cohote. "Organize a search for his body; send a runner to his village."

"Wait, I see something." One of the priests pointed down into the valley where a tree was thrashing. "Tarren? Tarren, are you okay?"

The words, "I'm unhurt," echoed up the mountain.

"Stay where you are, we're coming to get you," shouted Ahten.

"Sevin, go and tell Rasha that Tarren is found and unhurt. Let the word spread he is now powered, though with what, we don't know. Also come get me when he is returned and may be questioned." He turned to Derek. "As I said, it is a test, and this young man has just failed."

"Failed? How? What will happen to him?"

"He is powered now, he will be healed of any injuries, questioned about his ability, possibly trained in its use and then allowed to leave or stay as he wishes."

"Are they allowed congress?" Derek already suspected the answer. There had been clear indications of bonding among the youth playing the game.

152

"Yes, but we discourage pregnancy, we have no nursery here. Otherwise, we share most work equally. Some of it is hard and unpleasant, but we have a simple life here and have many pleasures as well."

"I want to meet him."

Ahten sighed. "He is a distraction, but yes, you can meet him, but first, there is someone already waiting to meet you."

"Me?"

"Yes, please come." He led the way back across the plateau into a tunnel through the mountain. Oil braziers lit their way while a light breeze stirred the air ahead. The tunnel took a sharp turn to the right and then ran on with a slight curve. They passed by two plain doors and stopped at the third. Ahten knocked. Derek heard the sound of splashing and giggling coming from inside. He took a quick glance down the hall; it ran on for another fifteen paces or so and then ended in smooth stone.

"We're a little ahead of schedule, but this will help answer your questions," Ahten said.

"Please, you may enter now," a voice called out from inside.

They entered into an expansive cavern. The far side was lined with glass, which let the morning sun fill the room. The walls were paneled with a dark wood and the high ceiling ornately plastered. "Lavish," Derek spoke the word aloud, stunned by the opulence of the suite. To his right was a large fireplace. In the middle of the room was a circle of couches. Along the other wall, a number of well-stocked bookcases stood sentry. To his left stood a man in a simple white robe, still wet from his swim. The man was laughing at Derek's comment, as were the two young women still idling in the pool.

Ahten straightened himself and spoke in a deep authoritative voice.

"Derek Duane Canter Able to Make Others Speak Without Reflection; I am pleased to introduce you to Ra-ken Seth Vihiate, Able to Shoot Beams of Death From his Eyes."

Two powerful beams of light shot from the man's eyes and swept over Derek's face.

§

Derek figured he was dead. His body must have disintegrated, leaving his shocked spirit in its place. Soon the Divine would come and collect him. He was saddened; his power was still…working? He felt his face with his hands. Nothing felt dead. Then he remembered his protocol, and

153

bowed deeply toward Seth. Ahten put out his hand, and raised him back up.

"Yes," Ahten said, "you are still alive, completely unharmed. This was a little demonstration that Seth and I worked out between ourselves to elucidate how an otherwise fallen ability can actually be turned toward the good. We're quite pleased with the results."

"Although," Seth said, "there are many thousands of tiny animals on your skin that no longer share that status."

"I am most humbly honored to meet you, Ra Vihiate," Derek stammered, unsure of what had just happened, yet at the same time guessing it had been of considerable significance.

"Please, I am just Seth."

"We believed it would be important to demonstrate Seth's power. To make certain you would have no doubts, and yet, not actually harm you."

"Yes, well I appreciate the not harming part; most impressive control." Derek frowned.

"What?" Ahten asked. Derek hesitated. He needed to pick his words carefully.

"I am so sorry, but I have a hobby you see, if I'm guessing right, this would mean Kherlos Timèatteo is dead. And I was unaware of this."

"That is correct," Ahten said.

"But," Derek continued, picking his words carefully. "I've never met anyone with this ability. I've only heard it described. So how do I know this is the real ability?"

"Well," Ahten said, "I can't blame you, you're supposed to be skeptical after all, and most people would consider themselves lucky to never meet any of the Ra-fel. We hope to change all that. But why don't we sit and talk?" Ahten guided Derek to a couch.

"Ladies," Seth said, "it appears I have an honored guest. Could you please excuse us?"

The women climbed out of the pool, unashamed of their nudity. One picked up her robe and put it on; the other walked over to Seth and embraced him before returning to her clothing.

"Yes." Ahten spoke as they all sat down facing each other. "Kherlos Timèatteo the latest incarnation of Beams of Death from his Eyes, is with the Divine. You don't need to know how that happened. Seth is now host of that power."

Derek was actually thinking about the young women, but Ahten's words refocused his attention. "Something makes me think that you didn't run into Seth by accident, and just invited him to visit."

Ahten beamed. "That's correct; Seth has been living here since the project began."

"Project?" echoed Derek. "But even if you knew Ra Timèatteo was going to be killed, there is no way you could have predicted Seth would get the ability."

"My," Ahten beamed, "you do catch on quickly. No, we did not know that Seth specifically, would obtain Kherlos' power, but we were fairly certain that someone on his team would."

"Team? There was a team, wishing for the ability to shoot beams of death?" Derek shook his head. That there should be a multitude of people wishing at any given time for that ability was no surprise, but that there should be an organized team of people, supported by the Council Ra-ken, seemed to be too bizarre to accept.

"Yes, we have teams that take shifts and keep sunrise to sunrise vigils," Ahten explained.

"Nonstop, you mean."

"Yes, we train and drill until our timing is very precise. While the odds of any individual team member acquiring the power are low, our combined effort is highly effective."

That was all very well Derek thought, useless if the current owner of the power had no intention of dying. "So all these young people were wishing for Kherlos's power?"

"No, not all of them, just those specific teams," Ahten said. Derek was becoming somewhat confused.

"I was just the lucky one," Seth said, "but it could have been anyone."

Derek smiled, they were playing him the fool. "Ra Vihate, Will you be establishing a new capital city here? Or maybe in Vesport?"

"I'm sorry?"

"What areas, what lands will you claim?"

"None, why would I do that?"

"Derek, Seth isn't going to conquer anyone."

"Is there a threat then? An invading army? How do you see your role in helping the Council meet this threat?"

"No," Seth looked confused by the questions.

"Derek," Ahten said, "what would you say if I told you Seth wished for the ability just to keep others from using it?"

"I'd say, and please, do forgive me, just in case, but I'd say you were lying."

"But," Seth interjected, "that is exactly the reason."

"Wait," Derek tried to get his mind around the idea. "Are you saying you wished for Kherlos's power, but didn't want it?"

"No, not exactly," Ahten said.

"Yes," Seth said.

"Which?"

"Derek," Ahten said, "What do people with these Divine gifts usually do with them?"

"Well, most have already established a territory, so according to the treaty of Colovencia the new Ra-ken, or Ra-fel, in this case, usually just moves in and assumes control. Which is what Kherlos did initially, I believe."

"And before that?"

"These lands aren't under the treaty, as far as I know, so you would have to gather an army or following, and start subjugating your neighbors. I assumed that's what Seth was doing; establishing a new empire, just like Kherlos was." Derek looked at the two men, some of their words starting to register. "But you were on a team, you knew Kherlos was going to be killed, and everyone here was wishing to see who got his ability."

"Yes," Seth beamed.

"To what end? Why wish for an ability if you aren't going to use it?"

"I believe our news man is starting to catch on."

"You're not the only one with an ability here are you?"

"Ah," Ahten said, his face brightening, "he now understands. We are honored to host Make Others Paralyzed with Fear, Able to Spit Burning Acid, and Able to Control the Emotions of Others."

"Tse Lee! Yes, I knew of his death, but no one had come forward yet and…the Council had appointed a proxy."

"Indeed." Ahten slapped his hands on his knees. "You do know your Ra-ken."

"As I said, it's my hobby. Will I be able to meet them?"

"Of course, and soon, but we should leave Seth to dress. He will gather the others while we visit the wishing chambers."

"The wishing chambers?"

"You will see. It will be easier for you to observe than it would be for me to explain. We are very proud of them in our own humble way of course."

Derek wasn't fooled; Ahten was anything but humble.

As Ahten led the way, Derek took the opportunity to press further. "You have here three others with Fel powers?"

"You seem concerned."

"Would you mind if I asked how you control them."

"We're very nice to them."

"I would imagine."

"We believe that the fall, to use the modern term, lies in the person, not the power. The people here are not Ra-ken, true, but they are not Ra-fel either. We, meaning the Priests of the Divine, along with the Council, are gathering fel powers here, true, but not to conquer, not to hurt others, but instead to remove those threats from the world. You will see." Ahten led Derek to an unmarked door and paused. "We must not speak inside this room. Observe all you want but disturb no one. We will talk outside."

There were twelve men and women seated around what appeared to be a clock, set face up on a pedestal in the floor. A single hand sped around the clock. As the clock-hand passed one of the marks, it gave off a sound. The first sound given off was the kind of tick made by two sticks striking. A single chime of a bell followed this sound, which was then followed by another tick, but of a lower register. That was followed again by a chime, this time of a higher register than before. Alternating tick, chime, tick, chime, in rising and falling registers the clock marked time. Derek studied the clock until Ahten touched his arm, he pointed at the mouths of each of the people seated. They were all saying something, but it was at a whisper. Derek leaned in to listen.

"I wish I had the ability to make people obey my commands."

Ahten tapped Derek's shoulder, and motioned for him to leave. He quietly shut the door behind them.

"Their wishes overlap." It was the first thing that came to Derek's mind.

"Yes. Depending on which theory of divinity you subscribe to, either there is very little time, or none at all, in which some other agent may intercept the ability."

"How long do they sit like that?"

"About four hours at a time, it's quite comfortable, very relaxing, but we find that much more than that and the vocal chords slowly deteriorate. They each take one four hour shift per day, three, sometimes four days out of seven."

"How many teams do you have here?"

"Fifteen at the present, some are backups in case a team member gets sick, or as we just saw, quits the team."

"And this goes on until…"

"Until we succeed," Ahten finished for him, "We haven't missed yet."

"Divine above."

"Indeed, come, the others should be ready by now."

"Wait." Derek had done the math.

"You have over one hundred and forty people here."

"Oh more than that, yes, it's quite a large operation, but many of them prefer to stay with their families when they are not on cycle. Shall we?"

As they walked back to the main temple, they were intercepted by a young man with news of Tarren. "He is all right. He has a few scrapes, bruises and a face full of tree sap, but is otherwise unhurt. He recovered the ball."

"Yes, thank you, and how is his mother then?" Ahten asked this in such a polite manner that Derek almost missed the point entirely.

The man looked sheepish. "He has elevated himself to Able to go to Where the Ball Is."

"Incredible." Derek said.

"I see," Ahten said, now somewhat less annoyed. "So where then is the ball?"

"It is with the boy."

"Ah, yes, you mentioned that, and the pieces of the tree?"

"Also with him. He claimed them as first souvenirs, but he says he knows how to make more."

"He is saying too much. See to it that he rests more and talks less."

"Yes, Ahten." The man departed.

"Later," Ahten said to Derek even before he could ask. He led them to his private chambers. It was as lavish as Derek expected it to be, a stark contrast to the plainer room that he occupied, even as an honored guest.

Seth, along with another young man and woman lounged in padded chairs.

"Excellent!" Ahten exclaimed. "Derek, allow me to introduce Cal Estass, able to spit acid without injury, and Lana Stannis, able to paralyze others with fear." Derek shook hands as each was introduced. "And of course you've met Seth. Lunch will be served shortly, please make yourselves comfortable." There were five plush chairs arranged in a circle around a polished stone table. Derek took a seat between Seth and Lana.

"I fear our guest is still having trouble understanding what we do here," Ahten said.

"What do you think is happening?" Cal asked.

"I believe he thinks we are collecting evil for our own sake," Ahten answered for him. "Derek, have you ever had an infection?"

"Yes, of course I have. I still have the scars."

"No healer available?"

"No, Healers couldn't localize then. There was just the one healer, Janus Colgan; I believe he was the last."

"Do you think that's what we're doing here," Lana asked, "localizing powers?"

"Divine no!" Derek shuddered, "Are you?"

"Of course not, that's not what I was talking about. Look, Seth tells us that we are covered with tiny animals, much too small for the eye to see without power. We understand that when we have an infection, it's because these animals have gotten inside us and are making us sick."

"I don't follow." Derek wasn't sure he believed in animals you couldn't see.

"If Seth uses his power and focuses it on the animals, like he did with you today, then the infection is healed. Is that fel?"

"If Seth saw two people fighting, and he killed one, would the other consider it fel?" Derek asked.

The arrival of food interrupted his thoughts. Plates of fish, seasoned rice, mushrooms, steamed cabbage and a number of pungent condiments were set before them.

"You understand, yet you choose not to understand," Ahten said. "When Seth or any other Ra-ken uses their gift, they always have the choice between good or evil. The person makes the choice, not the power. We are taking peccant abilities and putting them into hosts that will refrain from their use entirely. We have found a way to contain these abhorrent 'gifts', to put them into innocent vessels, to seal them away here, where they are safe."

Derek watched to see how the others ate. There were no eating utensils.

"Show our guest how it's done."

"You take a cabbage leaf," Seth said, picking up a broad leaf, "they are soft, but sturdy." He scooped some of the fish and mushrooms into it, rolled it up, and dipped it into one of the sauces. He handed the roll to Derek who took a small bite; it was spicy, but tasty.

"Good, thank you. Tell me Cal, Lana, how do you feel about being sealed up here?"

Cal looked startled for an instant, and a quick look passed between him and Lana.

"It is a great honor to live here," Lana said," my family has much prestige and honor in my village. They are very proud of me."

"It is the same for both Seth and I," Cal said. "You see how well we are treated. Our families are compensated for us being here."

Derek looked to Ahten for comment.

"You didn't think we kidnapped them did you? These young people would otherwise be hunting, or tending crops, of course we compensate their families for their services here."

"Where are each of you from?" Derek asked. He looked closer at the three. They were brown-skinned, but a lighter shade than his. Seth's nose was thin, Lana's broad. Seth and Cal were thin, Lana was plump, she braided her jet-black hair in tight-curved rows, Cal's was wiry, but Seth's was long, wavy and slightly reddish.

"They each come from villages on the other side of the mountains," Ahten said, "further inland. We take a few children from each village, those who have good reputations, and are from good families. We bring

160

them here and educate them. They attend classes along with their other duties. We teach them to read and write, and to speak Colovencia."

"Do you recruit from Vesport, or along the coast?" Derek found that Ahten's answers gave him plenty of time to chew his food.

"No, we are looking for innocent souls, children who have not become corrupted by the maddened quest for Divinity." Derek looked puzzled. "You see," Ahten continued, "the mountains here keep the villages isolated from the rest of the world. Here the abilities were shrouded in mysticism and superstition. Only a very few knew the secret, the village shaman usually, and they kept that knowledge to themselves. We have acolytes and priests even now traveling from village to village as missionaries, spreading the word of the Divine and educating the heathen. As you might imagine, their work is not always appreciated."

"It's true," Seth chimed in, "I never knew I could have an ability, no one did." The others nodded agreement.

"You see, Derek," Ahten said, "months ago; Kherlos Timèatteo was slaughtering and torturing innocent people. Did you know that he could kill part of a person? For minor offenses, he would kill your ear, or your tongue. That dead part would have to be removed, or it would rot on your body and poison you. Now here sits Beams of Death from the Eyes, who plays games and lives in peace."

"How do you decide which powers to focus on? Do you decide or are you told?"

"We are informed from time to time of events that might transpire. Between such times, we are free to concentrate in whatever direction we choose."

Derek could see this did not sit well with him. Ahten's life may in theory be devoted to serving the Divine, but that didn't mean he liked them telling him what to do.

"Aren't we missing someone? You mentioned Tse Lee's ability."

"Yes," Ahten said, "the young lady who acquired it for us, Briana, is off visiting her family. I understand her uncle passed away."

"Oh, I'm sorry." What he meant was he was sorry he wouldn't be able to talk with her and have her sign his book, but the remark worked the other way as well.

When they had finished eating, Derek spoke. "I'd like to speak with Tarren if you don't mind."

"That would be fine," Ahten said, though his tone seemed to indicate it would be anything but. He led them to a small room with two beds and a number of wood cabinets. On one of the beds lay the young man. Ahten made the introductions.

"I wanted to ask you a few questions," Derek said to the young man. "I hope you don't mind."

"No, sir, I don't mind at all. I'm not hurt badly, just a few cuts and scrapes."

Derek smiled; that wasn't the question. "Can you tell me what happened when you first made your wish?" The young man looked sheepish, as if he had been caught playing some foolish prank.

"The ball was bouncing down the mountain, and before... well, I didn't know I was speaking out loud. I just wasn't thinking."

"No need to apologize," Derek said. "You have a power now, maybe even a good one. Where I live, people would want very much to have such a power."

"I guess," Tarren said. For him, this was an opportunity lost, yet Seth, Call and Lana all seemed jealous.

It was an odd contrast, Derek thought. The cities were teaming with people looking for powers, any power. Eventually news of this boy's power would get out and people would wish for every variation that could possibly be imagined.

"So what was the tree all about?" Lana asked.

"My friends brought the pieces to me. When I made the wish, the ball was just bouncing down the mountain, and all of a sudden, I could feel it. It just appeared in my hand. But as soon as that happened, everything went dark. I pulled back. I could feel something sticky on my face and it was getting in my eyes. I managed to get my face free, but my left hand was stuck inside a tree."

"So how did you get out?"

"I figured out pretty quick what had happened. I could feel the ball in my right hand. I thought if I could throw the ball away from the trees, I could go to it again and not be stuck in any of them. So I threw it up into the air."

Ahten laughed at this. "So that is why we heard you crashing down."

"Yes" the boy admitted. "I went up into the air with the ball and fell to the ground. My breath was knocked away, but I held onto the ball."

"What would happen if you went to the ball and the ball was just sitting on the ground?"

"Oh, that's okay now." He seemed excited. "I know the ball is always going to end up in my right hand, and I can sort of feel where the ball is, and what's around it. I don't know how to explain, but I would know. I could bend down and end up on top of the ground, or I could hold my hand up and end up inside the rock or ground if I wanted. I would know before I went. The exciting part is that the rock or whatever would end up back where I was. I could make really neat statues that way."

"You might find it hard to get out. Someone would have to move the ball for you, and then you might hurt them. Remember you can't breathe inside rock, and it might be under great pressure."

"Yes, Ahten, I understand."

"Good, rest now, we will speak more tomorrow." Derek suspected Ahten meant him and the boy, not the three of them. Derek wanted to ask a few more questions, but it was okay if the interview was over. There was some experimenting he could accomplish back in Andoline easily enough to satisfy his curiosity.

Outside, Tarren's friends were waiting to see him.

"You may go in," Ahten instructed. "But only for a few minutes. Then leave him, he needs time to adjust to his new status and think about the consequences of his actions." The kids muttered agreement and went inside.

"You seem quite angry at the boy," Derek mentioned.

Ahten sighed. "Walk with me." Derek followed him down the hall. Seth, Cal and Lana returned to talk more with Tarren.

"The training takes time, but beyond that, we can't just take every young man or woman we see. You can understand that we have to be able to trust the students we train here. The teams all train together, and the loss of one member means the loss of the whole team. Now we may lose more to this foolishness. There is no cause here for me to celebrate."

"I can see your point."

This seemed to mollify Ahten somewhat. "Let us retire where we can talk and enjoy wine in comfort." They walked back to his private suites.

"You realize that we can't collect every fel ability on this planet." Derek nodded agreement. "Nor would the council want us to. By rights, these children here are the heirs and lords of domains thousands of miles away, of which they are totally unaware."

"And currently without a ruler," Derek added.

"Not exactly, but the point of this project is not to change the name of the ruler; that happens often enough on its own. No, the point is to accomplish the opposite, to bring stability to those regions, and to free those people from that constant upheaval."

"So who controls Epe Tianore now?"

"I am afraid I am not kept informed on those matters," Ahten said somewhat testily. "This isn't about land either, Kherlestra has not been made a province of the Council, and not every ability we intend to capture has a corresponding territory or income associated with it."

"Do they know about their rights? Are they allowed travel?"

"Yes, and Yes," Ahten replied, "They know, but it doesn't matter, to them, this is paradise, they told you, their families gain stature and fortune. They know nothing of politics, hunger for power, avarice, greed, or the need to hurt others for their own pleasure. They are innocent vessels holding fel powers. They bring peace to thousands who have known only conflict."

"Doesn't it scare you that four terrible destructive powers are all right here in one place?"

"No, not at all," Ahten said, "it scares me more to think of them out there, being used."

§

Derek paused outside of Seth's door to clear his mind. He needed to focus on two larger questions: "Are you safe?" and "Are we safe?" Then a third question crowded in: "When are you going to stop pretending you're not Ra-ken?"

He knocked, entered, and bowed deeply.

"Ra Vihiate, thank you for seeing me."

"Please, just call me Seth. I'm sorry about this morning."

"Seth it is. You know you don't have to apologize, but I must admit it is kind of refreshing."

"That stunt yesterday was rude; it's not how I was taught to treat guests." Seth indicated a chair and Derek sat. He examined the massive tome Seth was reading, "Layton Vernault Sr. – an autobiography."

"It's really good," Seth offered. "Have you read it?"

"For professional reasons, yes, but never before a meal."

"Sorry?"

"Never mind, who picks your reading material?"

"Ahten has books brought in from Vesport. What do you mean picks?"

"Well, there are maybe, thousands of books available to choose from, and possibly many more printed in Vesport and other cities."

"Oh, I had no idea. Reading is pretty new to us; most of the people in my village don't read."

"I'm not surprised, the Council Ra-ken is still arguing over whether a hand operated ink-press is against Divine law." Derek's face went blank for a moment, then he frowned.

"What?" Seth asked.

"You have a lift."

"Yes, Cordain installed it."

"Operated by men?"

"Umm, no, there's a pool a short ways up the mountain, water flows down a channel and turns a wheel."

"Well, I don't think they'll want me printing that in our pamphlets."

"What, about the lift?"

"There shall be no machine, that man gives, nor builds, nor creates, that derives, nor demonstrates any ability that is the province of the Divine."

"Ah, yes, from the Book of the Divine," Seth said.

"Exactly, and that's always meant, that water-driven machines, such as your lift, are forbidden."

"Are you going to argue the point with the Council Ra-ken?"

"Ahh, no. Anyway, do you get our news pamphlets here?"

"We get the Vesport News and transcripts from others through the FarSpeakers. But I find them too depressing to read."

"Really? How so?"

"They are mostly about people dying."

"Yes, but there are other stories as well." Derek felt the need to defend his profession.

"I guess." Seth shrugged.

"Ahten seems to be in charge here." It was a start, a gentle nudge in the direction of the second question.

"Does that seem wrong to you?"

"Have you thought about being in charge?"

Seth looked away. "No, that's not something I would want."

*Too direct, of course he has.*

"Do you think Ahten does a good job?" *Better.*

"I do. He is strict, but I think he has to be."

Derek let silence ask the next question.

"This is a very important project. He has to think about the safety of all these people. People who break the rules, even a little, can bring trouble to all of us."

"Do you trust him?"

"I do."

"And I take it he trusts you."

"I guess."

*He misunderstands.* "Ahten has to trust that you won't abuse your power. I mean, not in the obvious way, but suppose…I mean, people get used to having their every desire fulfilled. Do you follow?"

"You mean if I ask for something and don't get it, do I get angry and start making threats?"

"Yes, but you understand that you don't really have to threaten."

"So far, I guess I still get what I want."

*Leave it for now.* "Do you get to go out much?"

"Outside?"

"No, down the mountain, back to your village, into Vesport."

Seth brightened. "Oh, yes, not Vesport though, but yes, I visit my family and friends, and they come up here sometimes. My family is very important now in my village."

"How so?"

"They're building a house for them, out of stone, and land to plant on, and even a goat."

*Ahten spares no expense.* "Don't most of the villagers here live in stone buildings?"

"No, only the important families. We lived very simply here until the priests came."

"But you're not allowed into Vesport? Why do you think that is? Do you know what our cities are like?"

"Oh yes, we get visitors, dignitaries and Ra-ken here. He says it is too dangerous, that we cannot risk losing my power."

*No, he doesn't trust you.* "Do you know who had this ability before you?"

"Kherlos somebody."

"Timèatteo," Derek offered, "you understand that he had to die for you to get your ability?"

"Yes, we all know that, but these are people who hurt others. We really do know the consequences of our actions here. Besides, wasn't he setting himself up as some kind of evil god? Making his followers worship him?"

*Evil God, I haven't heard that term in a long time.* "That's pretty much the standard history of that ability, but we call them 'Fallen Divine' these days. Gods were idols, small statues really, that people carved and worshiped before anyone knew about abilities and the Divine."

"And now men are worshiped instead. Is this an improvement?"

"Well, gods didn't really do anything. They just sat around and took the blame for anything bad that happened. You couldn't reason with them, but then you can't reason with most Ra-ken either, so I guess not much has changed there. Have you heard of the legend Abareth?"

"No, was he a God?"

"He was supposed to be the first person to claim the beams of death power, and yes, he was worshiped as a God. He set a standard of abuse that thankfully, no one, not even Bouchard, has managed to equal. He is a tooth-knocker we tell children who wish too much."

"What's a tooth-knocker?" Seth asked.

"An imp that hides under the bed at night and knocks loose the teeth of children who misbehave."

"What an awful thing to tell children."

"I didn't make it up. The Point is, Abareth is supposed to have killed tens of thousands, if not millions before he was stopped."

"But I control the power, so that's not going to happen anymore, is it?"

*He's excited, change the topic.* "I'm sorry; I didn't mean to offend you. You understand that it might take a while before people stop being afraid."

"Yes, no, you're right. I just want people to see me, as Seth, and not just as my ability."

"There's nothing wrong with that. So tell me, what do you usually do with your time now that you're not spending all your days in the wishing wells?"

"Reading mostly." Seth thought about his days. "It's true I don't have as much to keep me occupied, but I can play games of draughts, talk with my friends, take walks, though the priests don't like that."

"Oh? Why?"

"Someone has to come with me, and I walk pretty fast sometimes."

Derek looked around the room again. "Do you want to have a family?"

"Yes, of course, I mean, sure. Not right now though."

"Do people treat you differently? Not just here, but back in your village?"

Seth sighed.

*Ah, something's up.*

"Yes, it's like they're all afraid of me. I know, I know, I understand why, but…"

"It makes relationships difficult?"

"It's like everyone wants to be my friend," he said, "but they don't act the same."

"I'm sure they don't. Could they be afraid of you?"

"No, it's not that. We all hunt, still, even though we can buy food from Vesport now, but most people prefer the old ways."

Derek wasn't sure he believed him. "You enjoy the sport."

"No, we hunt for food, but we won't starve if we don't I'm not allowed to hunt anymore, but I was just happy to go along, to be with my friends."

Derek guessed where this was heading. "They want to see you use your ability."

"Yes, we go into the woods in one big group. Normally we divide into teams. But everyone wants to see, even though I told them I was not allowed. So this scares all the deer away, and no one is loosing arrows anyway. So finally we agree to split up.. Then two of my friends come fetch me. I followed them back with everyone else trying to stay quiet until we see a large buck wandering along one of the trails."

"Did you kill it for them?"

"I told them I was not allowed to use my power, but of course, they taunted me. You know how other boys can get."

"I do."

"So I killed the deer. It was a mistake; it just fell over. At first, they were jubilant, dancing and whooping, but there was no arrow, you know, to claim the kill. So it was my duty to clean it, to um…have you ever hunted?"

"Yes, we call it dressing, so you just take the meat."

"It was my kill, but I didn't want it. I couldn't take the meat back; people would ask if I had used my ability. In the end, we just left it, a wasted kill."

"I guess they left you alone after that."

"I haven't been back."

"You aren't allowed to use your power? Without permission I mean."

"Those are the rules. Can you imagine what it would be like if we all started using our abilities anytime we wanted?"

*That's what worries me – I can.* "Do you have a girlfriend up here?"

"All of them," Seth replied, "and none."

"I'm sorry, I didn't mean to depress you."

Seth shook his head. "It's Okay; I know I will find a girl. Are you married?"

"Yes, her name is Clea, and my son Liam is nine."

"Does your wife have an ability too?"

"No. She's like a priest; she says she is happier without one."

"Does she shave her head?"

"Oh Divine no. She has very long beautiful hair."

"She is pretty then?"

"Yes. We are both very happy."

"How does your ability work? Do you mind if I ask?"

"Not at all, it makes people say whatever they are thinking. It doesn't work as well as you would think though. It's only good for short periods of time."

"I don't understand, would you show me."

"No, you really don't want that, but I know what you mean when you say people change. Getting back to you, have you talked with Ahten about long-term plans? Are you going to sit up on this mountain and read for the rest of your life?"

"I guess we haven't really discussed it."

Derek stood and stretched. "Do you mind if I look around?"

"Not at all, I have nothing to hide."

"Pity, they were cute." Derek peeked behind the screen at Seth's pool, just in case. He walked over to the window. Beyond the glass lay a sunlit valley thick and green, an unending carpet of treetops that fell away, and then rose again like a series of forested waves, each higher than the last. In the distance, Derek could make out the white breakers of snow-capped mountains. He let out a low whistle.

"That is some beautiful view." Seth joined him. "So this room is on the other side of the mountain?"

"Yes, it took quite a lot of work to build."

"I don't doubt it."

"My village is down there. The mountains have kept us isolated, and it is said a great, cold plain, stretches out forever past those mountains, but no one I know has ever been there."

"Interesting, I've heard that too, that if you go far enough north, you end up going south again on the other side. I can't imagine how that could be, but anyway, I wish I could draw. This is an extraordinary view."

"You don't have mountains where you live?"

"Not like these, so you've never seen a city?"

"I'm told they're not much to look at, a lot of people, animals and buildings all crowded together, everything is ugly and stinks."

"Pretty much, but I live outside the city, low rolling hills of grass, dotted with white flecks of sheep, long racing rivers that drain into deep lakes filled with fish the color of rainbows."

"You make it sound very beautiful; I think I would like to see these things. Where do you live?"

"Andoline, in Colovencia."

"The center of the universe, or so I am told."

Derek laughed. "Yes, well some people think so. Seth it's been a pleasure talking to you. I was wondering if I could ask a favor of you.

"Yes?"

"Oh, wait, can you make your letters? Your name?"

"Yes."

Derek pulled out his scrapbook and turned it to a new page labeled "Seth Vihiate." Could you write your name on here for me? It's a little hobby I have."

After Seth signed the book, Derek carefully blotted the ink and put it away. "I want to thank you for taking the time to talk with me." He held out his hand to the young man.

"You're welcome, have you spoken with the others?"

"Not yet, but I will."

"You will see they share the same feelings and ideas that I do. We all do."

"I have no doubt of that. Seth, I think I understand what you and the council are doing here. And I really do mean that I hope it succeeds. Thank you so much for talking with me."

"It was my pleasure Derek. Please come back and visit any time."

Derek chuckled. "And if you're ever on my side of the ocean, please look me up. You can always reach me through the Andoline Herald."

"Well I'll try. But I'm not sure the Council will let me."

Derek was pretty sure they wouldn't. "Ask. I think you will be surprised how much persuasive power you can exert over people if you try."

This made Seth laugh. "Perhaps we will meet again Derek, I certainly hope so."

"So do I Ra Vihiate, so do I."

# Seventeen.

*In the morning, Apachawea did marvel at the whiteness of his toes, that they were as the color of frost. And in seven days, he did marvel at the blackness of his toes, that they were as the color of soot.*

*Myth of the Revelation*

**11 Kehep, Y.O.D. 745**

## Derek Cantor's article for the Andoline Herald.

It is hard for those of us who live in crowded cities to imagine an idyllic land of virgin beauty where men and women live in harmony to the primeval land the Divine Creator bequeathed us. There are not just small patches on this planet that have been untouched by the spoils of progress, but entire countries where people live as if time had never touched our fair globe. In these provinces live a people innocent of the ways of the Divine. Within these lands and amongst these people our low brothers of the Divine have found a new purpose and plan posterity will one day come to view as the turning point in our history. For it is within these pure and simple souls that our priests have found incorruptible vessels in which to house the fel abilities that so plague our lives.

Months ago, the Divine Council Ra-ken reported the death of Kherlos Timèatteo. Since that time, no person has come forth to claim the heired rights to Kherlestra. Not from our lands, nor from across the seas has any news been heard of a new lord forging war and death with this ability. Save your breath, waste not your time believing this ability has passed beyond mortal men into the realm of the angels. The ability is claimed, yet silenced, held within the heart of a pure and simple man who needs no lands, lusts for no new conquest and cherishes every living creature that our Divine has so created. For his companions, he keeps Able to Spit Acid, and Able to Control the Emotions of Others. Soon Able to Make People Obey my Commands will join them.

They live together peacefully, reading, learning, and enjoying a simple life of luxury. Held in great esteem by their peers, and doted on by a devoted clergy they enjoy every comfort and want for nothing. They are living vessels, sealing off abilities that others would seek to use to do harm. In so doing, they liberate the rest of humanity from fear, worry, war and death. There will be no new tyrants to take the place of the likes of Tse Lee.

From this day forward, The Council will claim jurisdiction over the province of Epe Tianore, the rightful heir being an underage ward of the council. The Council is expected to appoint a governor by the end of the month. Peacekeeping clergy have already been dispatched to quell the civil unrest that erupted since Tse Lee's demise. Tawnya Brawly, head of the Council Raken issued the following statement.

"It is with great pleasure that I am here to announce to all of our beloved citizens, that those who use the abilities of the Divine against their fellow man will no longer find haven, or succor, or peace, or rest, or protection from our wrath. Those who would wage war, imprison, or impoverish their fellow beings will not be suffered. They will be given but one choice, yield, or die. Those who do not yield will find no comfort in knowing that another will rise to replace them. The undying abilities that have forever caused us grief shall plague us no more. We are unfailing in our capacity to seek, acquire and contain abilities that others would cherish, but we do not seek these abilities for ourselves, nor do we seek them for greed, nor gain, nor spite nor wickedness.

A fair trial and lenient sentences will be given to those who surrender to the Council. Those who do not will perish and their legacy of terror and oppression will perish with them."

It is the Council's wish that there shall be one impartial witness who can testify that their claims are honest and true. I am that witness. I have traveled across the sea and then many days over land to meet firsthand those who could demonstrate unique and undeniable abilities. I have met and interviewed people who could wield devastating powers, but who are graceful and kind, and wish only to help others.

Those of us who already live under the protection offered by the Council will not see a change in our daily lives. The benefit reaped by this bold move will be to those who now live in fear at the mercy of a harsh and erratic dictator. Then, once peace has spread and the specter of war is no more, it is through trade, new markets, intercourse with new peoples and the exchange of cultures that we will reap our gains. The Andoline Herald Editorial staff petitions the Council Ra-ken to declare a new Holy Day, celebrating this historical dawn of a new age.

# Eighteen.

*So it was, that upon his name-day, the lame boy Apachawea, denied by Divine intervention the path of warrior, chose then the way of the Shaymen. The way of the healer.*

*Myth of the Revelation*

**19 Kehep, Y.O.D. 746**

## Anonymous article published in the Andoline Herald.

If you travel east from Vesport, on the continent of Tameria, and know the way, you will come across an idyllic village nestled between two mountains with a sparkling stream that runs down through the virgin woods. The villagers for their remoteness are surprisingly in touch with current events and even boast their own Andoline FarSpeaker. Noticeably absent if you stay long enough to notice, is the sound of children at play. You will see infants and young children but no adolescents. It will be as if a generation of youth has disappeared, for this is exactly what has happened. This is not a great mystery. They are all living high on the mountain where a small community has been carved into the slopes. These children have heard the call of the Divine and have dedicated their lives to following the priests that have established a temple there. A sweeter story in a more beautiful exotic location with a nobler purpose you won't find. Or so it seems, but we know that things are often not as they seem to be.

It is typical of our lot in life to bear witness to events in which we cannot participate. People who have known misfortune bear witness to the great tragedies throughout our history. Floods, fires, earthquakes and great storms have all brought suffering, but we know that the plan of the Divine is hidden from us and that we are strengthened through the trials of life and nature. We also know misfortune through the fall of man. With us constantly are the powers that harm. Even so, we are blessed with balance. For every storm there is a rainbow, for every power that harms there is a power that lends comfort.

The priests have gathered up the unpowered from the surrounding villages, and have them living in dormitories on the grounds. There they work, play, pray and are educated. Their life is a happy well-structured one with no room for doubts or restlessness. For four hours a day, each person joins his or her brethren in prayer. Not a "Divine we exalt you" prayer one would expect of the faithful, but the "I wish I had the power" prayer. Mechanical devices, forbidden machines, time their prayers such that at any moment you might choose one of them is starting the wish for a power. Each group has its own power that they target, and the wish for the power is maintained day and night, nonstop. It is not for an individual to choose their wish, for the play is well scripted. It is instead a kind of lottery, where they all try their luck at heiring a power.

These acolytes are not trying to discover new dimensions to the Divine's greatness; they are singularly focused on capturing powers that are currently incarnate. Like most of us, they wish to become Ra-ken. Unlike the rest of us, they have help. They are not investing in powers we consider good. They are investing in powers of death and destruction. They seek to become Fallen, and they are succeeding.

This is the work of the Council Ra-ken, sworn to protect and watch over us. Their justification is perhaps valid, but their means are not, and the results will be horrific. They justify their actions thusly: Evil men wish for powers that harm, that they might do harm. If good men wish for those powers, they need not use them towards evil ends.

They have trained themselves and their servants to love and respect each other, to honor those who are blessed by the Divine, and to strive for that blessing themselves. The successful heirs are given lavish apartments with gifts and arts and servants, and there they are held imprisoned. There they plan to hold the power, removed from mankind until the natural end of the vessel, only to be recaptured again and thus held for all time. Four abilities have the council captured and sequestered in gilded cages, and still they seek more.

While the treaty of Colovencia does not encompass the lands of the fallen, it has been observed to become their standard practice as well, which has lent stability to our borders and lands distant. The heirs to those lands, titles and incomes are distant and unaware of their stature and inheritance. Meantime the people are leaderless, and civil war looms where once there was peace. Will the Council intervene? Will they place puppets to fill the vacancies? Is it their plan that over time, these territories will be absorbed and our great union expanded? Who could argue the wrongfulness of this?

Perhaps this is a noble purpose, but it is also a flawed purpose, for there is no sanity in their method. Their selection of prayer is purposeful not random, not chance. They are told what they will pray for, and that the deliverance of that prayer will be nearby. It is not the hand of the Divine that guides their works, but the hand of man, and that hand bears the blood of its victims.

This is all speculations, but until now, we have always been blessed that evil has been dilute, blessed that the powers that harm have been spread thin and have never come together. We are no longer so fortunate. These Fel abilities are now concentrated, and though the distance is great, so also is it's reach. Somewhere in the east, a storm is brewing that will scatter the Ra-ken like leaves. There is a lesson here for us all – a lesson about actions and consequences, a lesson about playing with fire and getting burned. Even the Council Ra-ken must come to regret wishing the moon.

# Nineteen.

*On the third day came the death of Chochanakea. Then did EagleSon speak the words given unto them by the angel Uumvault, and so claimed the gift. And he broke then out of the Maupau, and covered with chalky-dust, proclaimed himself EagleEye. There was much celebrating, with dancing, acrobatics, boasting and the drinking of fermented milk.*

*Myth of the Revelation*

**7 Ahmat, Y.O.D. 746**

## City of Kherlestra, North Seleton

Kherlos rose from bed. The sun was up and lit the room with its soft glow. Still in his pajamas, he walked out onto his balcony to bless the divine and salute the morning. He spoke the ritual words, kissed his fingers and raised them to the sky. The people in the street below, who had once gathered to share his morning blessings, now ignored him. Kherlos sighed and returned to his apartments.

"I see your heart is heavy." The voice spoke from an empty chair across the room.

He had not heard Kim enter, but then few men could. Kim faded into view, standing behind the chair wearing light brown pants and shirt. Kherlos gave a brief smile. He had assumed Kim would be seated in the chair, and Kim had known this and caught him up. He brushed aside his annoyance with his own mistake. He was glad to see Kim, for this meant some news and any news was welcome.

"How did you like it?" Kim had been working on exploring the range of his powers. Though neither of them could fathom a practical use for partial invisibility, they both found this new aspect of Kim's power fascinating.

"It was very well done, very smooth." Kherlos said.

"I am glad, next I wish to isolate parts of my body. Perhaps one day I can show only my smile."

Kherlos laughed at this. What a picture that would make, a floating deadly smile of death.

"It is good to see you in such spirits, but it is time for you to leave here. Perhaps you already know that."

He did know this. This was a city without a leader, without his power to protect and claim it. No heir to his power had surfaced. He was now a liability and an embarrassment. The rumor was that that Travia was preparing to negotiate with Mo DuKirk in Linnaton. Many of the people Kherlos had executed came from that city, and probably had family there. If this alliance with Linnaton came, he would be arrested and tried as a murderer. It was time to leave.

"I had been thinking just such a thing," Kherlos said. "I figured I would saddle up and ride out some morning, just to see how far I would make it on the road."

"That would be sad. For then I would lose my chance at a re-match."

"Yes, that would be sad. I have built a home here." Kherlos picked up a pair of small portraits and showed it to Kim. "My mother and father, my mother is still alive. She lives with my sister in Bellaniss. I was thinking of paying them a visit."

A knock on the door interrupted Kim's thoughts. He vanished.

"Yes?"

A uniformed man stepped into the room and saluted, one of the old guard, one still loyal. "Letter for you, Lord."

Kherlos leaned across the desk, and opened a small chest. He selected a gold sun from the contents, and handed it to the man, taking the letter.

"Thank you, Lord."

"Thank you, sergeant."

Kim winked back into view after the man left. They waited a few moments before speaking.

"It is a letter from my sister," Kherlos said, "and we were just speaking of her." He placed it on the desk. "I will read it later. Tell me, what is the reason for your visit here today?"

"I have my own news to share with you, but I must ask you, are you really ready to leave?"

Kherlos snorted. "Yes, I have been ready."

Kim reached into his shirt and removed a folded yellow paper. He opened it and handed it to Kherlos.

Kherlos read the article. "Very interesting, but this does not tell us where the sanctuary is. I assume you know something." He handed the paper back to Kim, who folded it carefully and put it back.

"Yes, I know where we can find the man who wrote this.

"You know who he is?"

"We have his name; we know the city, and that is sufficient. He will know where your power has gone."

"And you can make him tell us?"

"I can be very persuasive."

"So you will go and find this man, and then send for me?" Kherlos asked.

"No, we will go and find this man. It is time for you to leave here, but this must be done in secret. You cannot be seen traveling." Kherlos considered this. Something bothered him.

"What's in this for you? Why are you helping me?"

"I have been thinking on that matter," Kim said. "There is no animosity between us; I do not believe that if I allowed you to get your ability back, that you would turn it on me. Therefore, we have no reason to deny you your ability. We also appreciate the importance of keeping our word."

Kherlos frowned. This didn't seem right. The Kim's were mercenaries, not merchants.

"I see you doubt me. We have come to believe that our interests are served by traveling to this sanctuary. Understand that normally we do not ask why one person wants another person dead. Reasons are complications, and complications are dangerous. But now that we know the reason, it intrigues us."

"I don't follow, but hold on, would you care for some wine?"

"Yes, thank you."

Kherlos looked around, wandered off into his bedroom, and came back with two glasses and a bottle of wine under his arm. He took a penknife and dug out the cork, poured the first glass for himself and a somewhat less "corked" glass for Kim.

"To life," he saluted.

"Ah delicious," Kim said. "Where was I? Yes, income. The province of Epe Tianore was traditionally a rich source of income, as are most of the domains of the fallen."

Kherlos smiled wryly, but made no comment.

"So the inclusion of this land into the fold of the Council means a loss of opportunity for my family. However, this concentration of abilities at their hidden retreat may be an opportunity to regain this lost income. But only if I am able to make contact with the new heirs of those abilities."

"So this is about money," Kherlos said.

"It's always about money, and I tell you this so that you have no illusions. The heir of your ability has little reason to engage my particular services, and we have historically shied away from taking contracts against the ability. So not only was the contract substantial, but I believe my brother was both curious, and overconfident. Visionary maybe, time will tell. Never mind, the point is simple. Don't become a liability."

"I'll try and keep that in mind," Kherlos said, "So how will we do this?" Kim reached into his tunic again, and produced a small glass vial. He handed it over to Kherlos, who held it up to the light. It contained a dark brown liquid.

"You will take that tonight before you sleep. Do not forget this, or your life will be over before morning." Kherlos gave him a careful look but said nothing. "Void your bowels and bladder well, eat and drink little…else today, claim you are unwell. Leave your balcony unlocked, but not open. We are taking you from here tonight."

"And all my art, my pictures, my vast fortune?" Kherlos waved his arm around the room.

"Are these things not already lost to you?"

"So they are." Kherlos looked around the room, his eyes rested on the letter on his desk. "I guess then I should write my sister a letter tonight. You know they will search for me."

"Yes, but you will be on board a ship that has left the harbor this morning." Kherlos laughed.

"I would be disappointed had you not thought of everything."

"As would I. Please remember your instructions. Now I must go. There is much to do."

"Can't you stay? Chat a while?"

"We will have much time for discussion as we travel. You and I will find this man, and he will take us to where your ability is. This may take many months."

"Men are not mountains," Kherlos mused.

"Yes, exactly."

"Stairs or balcony?"

"Balcony if you please," Kim said, and then faded out of sight. Kherlos strode to the balcony doors and opened them wide. Then he stepped back. He considered just a moment randomly swinging an arm or leg to see if he could catch Kim unaware, then thought better. After a few minutes, he assumed that Kim had gone and so closed them again. He left them unlocked.

§

The night was black; the air lightly held the fragrance of wood and coal smoke from the now dying fires of the evening meal. Four figures dressed in black moved silently across the open courtyard towards the palace. Two more advanced further along the wall and disappeared into the darkness around the building. In the morning, four guards were found to be sleeping at their posts, and Kherlos was gone.

# Twenty.

*In the morning, EagleEye awoke his brother Apachawea, who languished in the sorrows of his cups, and bade him to join him in his inaugural hunt of fish from the deep pool, as an honor, and in sympathy for his woes.*

*Myth of the Revelation*

**7 Ahmat, Y.O.D. 746**

## Council Monastery, East of Vesport, Tameria

Cal, Seth and Lana stood before an obviously angry Ahten waving a sheaf of paper at them.

"Who told him?" he shouted. The other priests in the room flinched. He may have forgotten whom he was yelling at, but they hadn't. The three of them stared back with blank looks of puzzlement.

Ahten sat back down in his chair and composed himself. Perhaps he was not sure how far he should push them either.

"Derek Cantor, that idiot newsman. Who told him we had Briana imprisoned?" Their eyes gave him his answer; they had not known.

"Yes, but I can see it wasn't one of you." He thought for a few seconds.

"Well there's no putting the salt back in the grinder, somehow he found out, and now I have to deal with the consequences." He said this more to him to himself than to them.

Seth stepped forward. "What did you do with Briana?"

"Well, yes, she was using her ability, against the same explicit instructions I gave each of you." Ahten looked at them each in turn. "As punishment, I had Cordain seal her up in her room. And that same punishment can be applied to you three too, don't forget." He shook his finger at them.

"Is she dead?" Lana asked.

"No, of course not, we lower food and supplies down to her windows. After a suitable time I will release her," Ahten seemed lost in thought, as if the matter of Briana hardly concerned him.

"Is she alone? Can we visit her?" Cal asked.

"She's not alone," Ahten seemed to focus, "when I say she used her ability, I don't mean casually, I mean she made men fall in love with her, and then made them fight for her affections. She was seen going back to her room with two other men, and so I instructed Cordain to seal her away." This was a lie, but it would serve. "And someone told that nosey newsman." He glared at the priests around him, but no one replied. He looked back at his charges. "The three of you are dismissed; go back to your rooms."

No one moved.

"Understand," He tried to sound more conciliatory. "She's in no harm. I saved her life. My instructions—and I didn't want to have to tell you this—but my instructions are that when one of you disobeys our most important rule, that I am to move the ability to another student, one who more fully understands our purpose here. I'm, sorry; I argued that would send the wrong signal to the rest of you. We aren't murderers here, I said, but now it's my brisket in the brazier if this happens again." He let his words sink in; he could see they were worried. The threat that they were replaceable wasn't one he wanted to make often, but it had the desired effect.

"Now leave me," he commanded "but if I find out it was any of you who embarrassed this sanctuary you will regret having done so!"

# Twenty One.

*In its youth, the other trees had taunted and bullied it, thinking to crush its spirit. Instead, Old Man Chestnut had grown thick and strong and spread its leaves over the others. The pines became jealous. In their anger, they pushed and beat it towards the river until they forced it down the slope, hoping to topple it into the pool and drown it. There it clung, hanging out over the banks where no other trees would dare. It found peace. The soil was good, the water fresh. The fish would grace its shade, and boys found sport on its back. On this day, it held the proud figure of a man, standing bravely with bow and arrow. Its back was strong and its feet were thick in the earth. It would hold this man, and many more; though it cared not for their lives.*

*Myth of the Revelation*

## 35 Ahmat, Y.O.D. 746

## City of Andoline, Colovencia, Alasta

Seth waited as the gangplank lowered. The regular crew of the ship was busy on deck, all hands regardless of watch worked to put in. They had said their goodbyes earlier, knowing Seth would need to disembark quickly when they landed. A hand grabbed his shoulder.

"Not so fast, Seth," the Captain said, "let the 'spector on deck, mind the law."

"Cap'n" Seth said. In the weeks on board, he had dropped his pretense as a priest and adopted the habits of the seamen he lived with. He had worked hard, pulled his weight without complaint. They had taken to him, and even found clothes to fit him.

"You're a good man Seth, Ye' worked hard and gave no cause, ye' can stay on board ye' know."

"I know sir, but I think it's best if I go."

"'Tis so, I saw ye' be goin' but I came t' tell, you'll be welcome aboard any ship at these waters, I'll see t' it," the captain promised.

"Thank you, Sir, that's very kind."

"Mind your step and your backside, 'tis a foul place with low men where you be goin'. The boys threw t'gether for ye, 'tain't much, but it'll see you through a spell." The captain handed over a small purse with a few coins in it.

"I don't know what to say." He took the gift.

"Don't say it then, just get off my ship ye' damned boatswain."

"Aye Aye Cap'n."

The captain watched him move down the plank and along the dock until he disappeared in the crowds on shore. He shook his head, and then shouted at his men, who'd all stopped to watch as well.

Prostitutes called out as he passed, a sailor and his kit meant shore leave; which meant money combined with certain urges demanding attention. Seth pushed on through the streets. He needed a place to shave and change. Fewer people bothered the clergy, they were not known for either their purses or personalities.

"Excuse me mate, could I have but a word with you?" A thin reedy voice said as a hand touched his elbow. Seth whirled. A small man, dressed like a dandy, but with bad teeth and a scarred face, took a hold of Seth's sleeve. "I know just the place for you mate, clean sheets and clean women, high class mind you, food fit for an Upper, and I know what ships grub is like mind you."

Seth looked down at the man. "Leave me alone, let go of me."

"Ah yes, I assure I will mind you, but just across the street here, you won't mind looking, C'mon what?" He tugged at Seth's sleeve.

A low male voice spoke from behind. "I believe he asked you to release him."

"Bugger off, I got here first."

A strong hand grabbed the man by the back of his jacket, lifted him up and threw him into the street. He hit the ground like a rat and was up on his feet in an instant with a thin blade in his right hand. The man who threw him was well dressed, tall and strongly built.

"Are you all right Seth?" Cordain asked.

Seth sighed. "Yes, I suppose." He waited for Cordain to make the first move.

"I had heard that you were traveling. I felt it would be unbecoming if we did not give you a proper welcome."

"I ain't done with the two of you'se" the little man spat, hurting more from being ignored than being thrown. He waved his little knife in their direction. Cordain turned, stomped his foot down onto the street and sent a shockwave in the man's direction. He and everyone else around fell on their asses. Horses reared and windows shook in buildings around them. Those not knocked down quickly moved back, while everyone else came out to witness the commotion.

"Are you done with me now?"

"Ye, Ye, Yes Ra, beg Ra-ken's pardon I do."

"A wise choice." Cordain turned to Seth, "I have my carriage nearby, I thought I might give you a lift and share a meal. Have you eaten? We need to leave."

"Why?"

"Because I don't have all day to stand around shaking hands and touching babies." Cordain eyed the gathering crowd. "Oh come on, I know you're not going to kill me, and I'm certainly not going to kill you, I think it's wonderful that you're finally getting out and visiting new places."

"You're serious?"

"Absolutely."

Seth didn't know what to say, Cordain seemed genuine, but he couldn't shake the feeling that it was an elaborate means of capturing him.

Meanwhile people were starting to edge closer.

"I need an answer."

Seth's antagonist, now all smiles, his hands held open and empty, stepped into the shrinking circle of space around the two men. "Ra ku ketti mah. Ra Leighland, might I interest you—" He lunged, the knife making a sudden appearance in his hand again. Cordain leapt back as the blade punctured him just below his left ribs and then withdrew. The man cursed and made to lunge again, but his feet were stuck firmly in dirt.

Cordain, just out of reach of the man's slashes, took the time to examine his wounds. The crowd of people moved back, but not very far.

"Leave him to me, Seth." Cordain said. He held his left hand against his wound, which was seeping blood.

"Beg your Uppers' pardon," the man said, "I was just trying my luck. Healer will fix you up right nicely." He threw the knife to the ground, and it instantly sank from sight. The man swallowed nervously.

"Put your hands at your sides," Cordain said.

"Kill him," Someone shouted.

"Not today," Cordain replied. The ground around the man began to bubble and soften. The man sank rapidly into the street until only his head was showing.

"Clear way! Clear way." A man in a coachman's uniform, brandishing a coiled whip was calling and pushing his way through the crowd. "Lord Cordain, You're hurt!"

"Reese, thank you. Help me and Master Seth here to the coach."

"Are you hurt as well?"

"No," Seth said.

"Then lend a hand here young man." Reese put Cordain's right arm across his shoulders. "And be gentle."

"What do we do with this fellow then?" someone shouted.

"Anything you want," Cordain called back.

"I should have killed him," Seth said once they were in Cordain's coach and on their way. The crack of Reese's whip punctuated his words.

"I'm glad you didn't. That would have complicated things."

§

The coach rolled to a stop at the entrance to the largest house Seth had ever seen. The doors on both sides instantly opened and fancily dressed men with little red caps came in and spirited Cordain away.

Reese had been yelling instructions from the top of the cab since they had started, and word of Cordain's injury must have already reached here. Another man in a red cap, and vest with gold fringe addressed him. "Ra Vihate, welcome, I have been instructed to show you to a waiting room and provide for you every convenience while Ra Leighland is looked after."

The man led Seth to a large room with a fireplace at each end, numerous tables and well-padded chairs and paintings of men riding horses adorning the walls. "Do you prefer beer or wine?"

"Just water, thank you." The man bowed and left. Shortly a girl came in, set a crystal pitcher of water on a table, along with a bowl of steaming broth, bread, and a plate of thinly-sliced smoked fish. Seth picked at the fish, and waited.

After a while, Cordain entered wearing fresh clothes and limping slightly. With him came a thin man, balding, wearing dark blue trousers, a white shirt and a green tasseled armband around his right bicep.

"Are you healed?" Seth asked.

"Yes, thank you. I asked Benito to examine you, while he was here."

"I am not... I'm fine."

"Were you not just three weeks on a sea vessel?" Benito asked.

"Yes."

"Then I should examine you, have you been healed before?"

"Yes."

"Excellent, then please take a seat."

Benito lowered Seth's long stockings and felt around his ankles, then slipped his hand inside his shirt and felt around his abdomen, chest and then groin. Then Benito touched the back of Seth's neck and forehead. "He is well."

"What about you?" Seth asked Cordain.

"He will be sore for a few days, but that is normal."

"Thank you Benito." Cordain lowered gently into the chair beside Seth and tore off a piece of bread. "Are you hungry?"

"No, thank you."

"I am to eat only broth and soft foods for the next three days. May I?" Cordain pointed at Seth's untouched bowl.

"Please." Seth pushed the bowl towards Cordain. "Where am I?"

"You're in a private residence, reserved for visiting Ra-ken."

"Will I be allowed to leave?"

"You are a guest, you may leave whenever you like, but I was hoping you help me get a few matters sorted. The Council was quite concerned about your disappearance."

He didn't like the distrustful look Seth was giving him. "Ahten was quite fearful, he was afraid you had somehow been kidnapped, and spirited away. When you frightened off his priests, he became even more concerned."

Seth remained silent.

"You don't believe me," Cordain said.

"No, he told us what you did."

"I'm sorry?"

"To Briana." Seth's anger was plain.

"I know Briana, she heired the ability to control emotions. Is she okay?"

"No, she is not, and I don't intend to go back"

"Seth, I don't know what's bothering you, but I am not here to send or take you back. Yes, I came to meet you because we are concerned for your safety, but while I...might be capable of killing you, I am not capable of capturing you. It is a subtle difference, but the point is, I can't make you go, and I see no reason that you should." Seth looked unconvinced. He also looked sleepy.

"I'm sorry. You don't trust me."

"No, sorry."

"Well I'm not your mother, so I'll not keep you from wherever you're going. Do you need money? I can lend you a few suns."

"I have money."

"Well, good, I'll take my leave then." Cordain paused, trying to judge Seth's reaction. "When you are ready to go, tell my man here, and he'll get you a coach. A city coach, not one of mine." He added in response to Seth's doubtful look. "Good luck," Cordain stood and offered his hand. Seth didn't take it.

"Well then." He turned to his waiter, who had appeared at the sound of a chair scraping. "See that this young man gets anything he asks for."

"Yes, Ra." He gave a curt bow.

"Good luck Seth."

"Wait." Cordain turned, and waited.

"Ahten didn't send you?"

"Ah, as to that; I am Cordain Leighland. Member of the Council Raken. Able to shape and command earth to my will. Blessed vessel of the Divine Creator, source of all light and life. And you my divine friend. Are Seth Vihiate, master of death, able to extinguish the life force of all and any through your will, also a blessed vessel of the Divine creator, source of all light and life. And neither you, nor I, are 'sent' by anyone."

Seth stood up, his eyes flashing angrily. "So why did you seal Briana up in her room?"

Cordain looked puzzled for a second. "Oh, damn...That wasn't what happened. That is, I mean yes I sealed the room. It seemed an odd request; Ahten claiming something about water and mildew, and they had moved her to another chamber. I remember we were escorting his Patriarch around, showing him what we'd accomplished."

"You didn't even check?"

Cordain walked back to the table and sat down. "Divine, is she dead?"

"I don't think so." Seth calmed a little. "Ahten said they lower food to her and the other two men."

"Other two men?"

"Ahten said she had used her power, which was forbidden, so he instructed you to seal her up as punishment. She had made two men fall in love with her and taken them back to her chamber. You sealed all three of them in there."

"Do you know who the men were?"

"No, we were never told."

"It has to be Xavier – I thought it strange he left without me, or without saying anything, but then, we do what we want don't we? I figured he'd turn up somewhere eventually with some wild story. He usually does." Seth shrugged; he wasn't familiar enough with that side of a Ra-ken's life to comment.

"Yes, well Ahten has some questions to answer."

"He threatened to do the same to us."

"You and Cal and Lana?"

"Yes." Seth sat back down.

"So you ran, and the last person in the world you wanted to see was me."

"Exactly. Ahten has a way of getting what he wants, even from the Council."

"Where were you headed? I mean, who do you know here?"

"That newsman, Derek, the one who wrote the stories."

"Why him?"

"Because he said I could visit him if I needed to, and he wrote that second story, the one that made Ahten so mad and threaten us, I thought maybe if he knew, he could write another story and force you to let us go."

Cordain wasn't sure he followed that logic. "Do you know where this man lives?"

"No, but he said I could find him at the Andoline Herald, I thought I would come disguised as a priest."

"You're dressed as a sailor."

"Yes, the crew knew right away I wasn't a priest— and they made me work for my passage—but they were really nice. The captain even gave me some money."

Cordain considered this. "I think your plan is a good one. Emmund"

"Sir?"

"Get this man a barber and some priest's robes; he's going to convert to the clergy."

"Very good, straight away." Emmund bowed to Cordain and Seth, and then departed.

Cordain paced, thinking. "I need you to hide. This journalist fellow sounds like as good as place as any. Andoline isn't safe, and you can't go wandering around by yourself either. Go to him, and have him hide you for a couple weeks. I have to go find out what's going on but I can't risk taking you with me."

Seth looked confused.

"Seth, it's the Council I want you to hide from, I don't know what's going on here, Ahten could be acting on his own, or acting under someone else's orders. My home is too far away, and if this newsman doesn't like the Council then he's likely to help you. What did he say in the article?"

"He said the sanctuary was a mistake, that you were wishing the moon."

Cordain considered this, shrugged, and stood back up. He dropped a purse onto the table. "Take this. Money has a way of coming in handy. I have to go see a man about a boat." He offered his hand again, this time Seth took it.

"Emmund won't be long, make yourself comfortable. And one last thought. If another Council member is behind all of this, then you can't tell anyone where I'm headed."

"If they capture me, you mean."

"Yes."

# Twenty Two.

*EagleEye stood upon Old Man Chestnut and touched within himself
that which was of the Divine, and revealed to him were the spirits that
were the lives of the fishes. He thanked then, the father-spirit, that
was the Divine, and thanked then the spirit of the fish for the gift of
its life, and loosed his arrow into his prey.*

*Myth of the Revelation*

**2 Tobeth, Y.O.D. 746**

## City of Avaria, Lisitar Island South of Epa Tianore

The man lay sleeping, untroubled, in a splendid room, on a soft
down mattress, smooth and cool cotton sheets, a young and
beautiful woman pressed up against him. Beside the bed, two sleek and
powerful dogs lay snuffling and shifting with troubled dreams. Outside,
two guards sprawled on the floor, snoring loudly in their rumpled
uniforms, their swords, undrawn. Beside the bed stood two intruders;
Eslanda, slender and graceful, with long gray hair, and Billix, a large,
powerful man, skilled at not asking questions.

Eslanda carefully removed the covers from the sleeping couple;
exposing their naked forms. Sensing the cold air, the woman pressed
closer into her companion's warmth. Billix leaned over and fondled the
sleeping woman's breast, and then slid his hand down along her body.

"Don't play," Eslanda said softly. Billix frowned; she never let him
have any fun. He took the pillow from beneath the man's head, turned
him so that he was laying on his back, then pushed the pillow down hard
onto his face. The man jerked and struggled in his sleep. The dogs also
jerked and twitched, snapping at imaginary foes. Then it was done.

"He's dead," Billix said.

"Come," she said.

Billix gave the naked woman another quick squeeze. With what he
was being paid, he could buy two just like her, but he was never one to
pass up something for free.

"We're done here, go."

When they were away from the bed, and not in danger of falling on the dogs, Eslanda extended her will onto Billix and put him to sleep as well. He might wake before anyone else and affect his escape. That was his chance, but she doubted it. The dogs would likely wake as soon as her influence waned. They could already sense something was wrong.

She stepped over him, then dropped a small pouch with his share of the payment onto the floor beside him, and then walked out into the night.

# Twenty Three.

*Into the shallows of the river came the fish, well pierced by EagleEye's arrow. Such was the size and magnificence of the creature that Apachawea lifted the prize up as in display, but found then that his brother had quitted the tree.*

*Myth of the Revelation*

**3 Tobeth, Y.O.D. 746**

## Council Monastery, East of Vesport, Tameria

The air in the wishing chambers was chill. Dharla could see the mist of her breath and that of the other team members. They shivered and hugged themselves against the cold; warm garments were not permitted. Ahten believed that the cold kept them alert and focused. Silently she wished for warmth and comfort and knew she was not alone. From time to time she would hear the brazen vocalization of desires other than those they had been assigned. Ahten would deal with such acts of mutiny harshly, but the wishing chambers had infrequent visitors so boldness and indifference had crept into their spirits. They sat huddled around the wheel, making their endless pleas to the Divine. They had trained hard and learned their lessons well, but long hours of discomfort, combined with the rumors about Briana, had worked their discord upon the mountain. Ernic made no pretense of diligence and left the wishing wholly to others, though he did nothing to interfere. Rasha could not be so bold, and subtly shifted the wish. Perhaps he feared they were spied upon, and as such, he would give the appearance of wishing earnestly, though his efforts provided no more substance than Ernic's silence.

Secretly Dharla was pleased, but still her chances of heiring the power were slim. Even with team members abandoning their task, her odds increased only a small amount. Seth, Cal and Briana had all been on morning shift when they heired, and she had learned this is because it had been nighttime in the land far away where the people were killed. She didn't understand how this could be, but hoped it would help. But, if it didn't, even if someone else here got the ability, there was always a more direct, brutal way to take it. In the meantime, she wished, over and over to the chiming of the wheel, until finally, cold, shivering, sore and near despair, she felt a new presence within her mind, a surge of energy, a need, an urgent need to speak, to impress her will upon others, the first rush of power that manifests when the desire is granted.

"Stop," Dharla said. The others stopped. The command was vague, but she bore no malice, no desire for harm, and as such, her team members ceased all activity, but remained capable of breathing and blinking. They neither spoke nor moved, but waited, still. Had they been standing they would have become unbalanced and fallen, but they were sitting and so it was a few seconds before their lack of motion became something real and substantial, apparent. They waited while Dharla gathered her thoughts.

"Get back to wishing." She said, and then added, "as if I didn't have any power."

They understood. With the command went the will, and the will was that they resume normal activity. Normal was what she expected of them, meaning idle chatter, not the diligence of their training. After some thought Dharla spoke again, using the will of her power.

"Forget that I have commanded you." She did not know if this would work. She knew very little of her new ability. They had been warned that whoever should come by the power must resist the temptation to use it, and that their first and only command should be for the others to rest. Ahten had spoken sternly and warned that while the heir to the power would be treated as Ra-ken, he had also mentioned that the power required a voice with which to issue the commands, and deceit would not be tolerated. Dharla didn't care about that; they all knew what had happened to Briana, and now Seth was gone too, she would not make the same mistakes they did.

"Dharla?" Brandy asked, "Why did you stop wishing?" Her tone was not gentle. "One of us has to keep up the pretense. We thought you wanted this power."

Seir held his cup out to her. "Here, drink mine if yours is empty."

Dharla took the cup and drank, "Thanks."

"Keep it," he said as she made to pass it back. "I don't need it." This was true, for he did no wishing and his throat did not dry like hers. She lowered her eyes, listened for the rhythm of the wheel, and resumed her wishing.

§

Dharla woke to the sound of a pounding on her door. A man's voice called, "Dharla, Brandy, Rise and attend Ahten, you and your team are summoned to his presence."

A cold fear passed through her, she readied her will, and held ready a command for when they entered and grabbed her. They would cover her mouth, but she was sure she could stop them.

The knock came again. "Dharla, Brandy?"

"Coming," Dharla replied. She relaxed, the doors had no latches, they served only to provide a modicum of privacy and block drafts and they did both poorly. Students, such as herself and her teammates, slept in dorms, two to a room, which were in fact just cold, damp caves carved out of the mountain by the Ra-ken years before. They might have been cozy once, dry and well lit, with fresh bed coverings and new rugs on the floor, now they were just damp and drafty with mildewed rugs and thin blankets.

Dharla sat up and slid her feet into her slippers. When she opened the door, whomever had knocked was now gone. She could see it was morning by the light from the portcullis holes in the hallway ceiling. She propped the door open. There was just enough light to dress by, and to notice that Brandy's bed was empty.

She returned to the gloom, lifted her nightdress over her head and dropped it onto her bed. Her locker-box contained a variety of clothes; dresses and bright patterned skirts from her family, soft woolen sweaters that would keep her warm, and a fine cotton blouse for special occasions, but Ahten would want them dressed as students, so she selected a fresh set of dull-gray shirt and pants.

As she dressed, Brandy came darting into the room, naked except for her underpants and clutching a nightshirt to her chest. "You won't tell will you?"

"About what?" Dharla asked.

"You know, about me and Rasha?"

"I don't think Ahten cares about that."

"Yeah well maybe somebody else does, okay, just don't tell, ok?" Brandy tried to look both tough and hurt at the same time.

Dharla was relieved. "No, I won't tell, don't worry about that."

Brandy said nothing, as if her smile were thanks enough. She hurried to her own locker and started hunting for clothes.

Dharla finished dressing, put on slippers, and went to the door. "I'll wait with the others."

Outside three of the other team members had gathered in the hall, behind them, one of the acolytes paced restlessly as he waited for everyone to assemble. Seir looked sheepish; Ihrim and Rasha stood close together and looked guilty. The other team members came out, but said nothing, and avoided eye contact. Brandy was last out.

The acolyte led them, as if they didn't already know the way, across the plateau to the main hall, and then into one of the small meeting rooms inside the main building, where Ahten waited in a raised chair with Pench, Umbra and Yves standing behind.

He allowed his face to display his displeasure while the team stood and waited with their heads and eyes lowered.

"I have been informed, that the power we seek was liberated yesterday morning." He paused to accentuate their discomfort. "Yet your shift and the two after claimed no power."

They shuffled and waited, offering no confessions.

"There is no mistake that it was liberated, yet we have not claimed it here, and that is a great loss. This is a major setback for us, and I must personally inform the council of this disappointing news.

"Did you think I would not know of your laziness? That you scoffed at your duty and forsook wishing?" Now he had their attention.

"I cannot conceive why this should be so; that you would not desire desperately this honor we have offered to you. Yet you wasted it and there shall not be another. Is this how I am to be repaid for my trust and for the gift that has been offered to you? If so, I shall not have you. I am done with you.

"Your team is done, disbanded. You are to take what belongings you have and depart from this mountain, save Dharla."

They turned their narrowed eyes upon her, each with their own suspicion.

"I am very sore with all of you," Ahten said, "and your team leader Padra especially, for it was his duty to report your actions to me before the chance had passed us by. It is his fault as much as it is yours that this power has escaped us. That does not excuse you, but he did tell me that at least one of you—Dharla—held faith and kept vigil, though she too failed in allowing the rest of you your leisure.

"I cannot banish her for failing to act as a spy on her teammates, however poor their behavior. It is indeed sad that your efforts were in vain, but perhaps the reckoning of time is in err, and there was naught any of you could have done. Still we have failed where we should not have.

"Dharla, your punishment is to be accepted back as a student. You will start training afresh, and if luck serves you, you may find yourself on a more disciplined team with another acquisition before you. If this does not please you, then you may leave with the others. Choose now, what is your answer."

"It pleases me sir, I will accept this most gracious—"

"Enough. It is done. Be gone." Ahten rose and left.

Pench stepped forward and spoke. "You will all be escorted back to your rooms. Gather what you wish to carry, the rest will be sent down on the lift. Dharla, remain here."

They filed out, each accompanied out by a member of the clergy.

"I will help you gather your belongings and will show you to your new room," the Pench said. "But we will wait here, until the others have departed." Dharla didn't care. All she needed was to remain on the mountain.

"You're lucky to be given a second chance young lady," Pench said after a few minutes had passed. "He's been nastier than a drooling raccoon."

"A what?"

"Trust me, you don't want to know. Let's just say he's had a lot of bad news in a short amount of time, and when he's unhappy, we're miserable."

§

Dharla settled in with her new team. It was rough at first, re-learning the vocal exercises, and enduring the endless practice sessions, but soon life became routine again.

One evening, Dharla and her new friend Emit, snuck out onto the plateau. The thin moon just peeking up above the mountaintops grinned mischievously at their late night tryst. She led him over to the edge of the wood, to the path that led up to the pool. She stopped; she wouldn't take him up there unless she had to.

"I should have brought a blanket," he said. Dharla handed him a walking stick.

"I'm okay, I can see the path. You should keep it." He made to give it back.

"Hit yourself with it," she said.

"Why?"

"Just do it." Emit looked at the stick and hit himself lightly on the leg.

"No, on your foot, hard."

"No."

She lifted her head, pulled back her shoulders and let her breasts press forward underneath her thin shift. They caught and held his eyes.

"Please?"

"No, sorry, this is stupid, besides, it's too cold." He held the stick out to her.

Dharla summoned her will and her power. Her intent had been only to will him to hit himself, but the words that formed in her mind came out of her mouth unbidden. Though she spoke in a flat voice, it was a voice of command.

"Take your foot out of your slipper and hit it hard with the stick."

Emit did as he was told, his face showed his annoyance. "There," he said, "pleased?"

"Yes. Why did you do that?"

"Because you told me to?" He was clearly puzzled by the question.

"Did I make you do that?"

"No, you didn't make me, can we go in?"

"No, do it again," she said this without using her power, but tried to make her voice have the same tone as before.

"Forget that." He threw the stick down at her feet, careful though not to hit her with it. "This is too cold; I'm going back in."

"Pick up the stick and hit your foot hard with it." Again with the will came the flat command. He picked up the stick and hit his foot with it once more. He had two red welts across the tops of his toes and several small scratches that were damp with blood. He looked down at his foot, disbelieving that he had struck himself twice and then threw the stick away towards the edge of the plateau.

"Please don't make me do that again."

"Did I make you do that?" She no longer felt the cold; now all she felt was the heat of her power and the urge to make him do more.

"Yes, no, I don't know. I feel stupid and I want to go in. Please?"

"Take me in and love me then." Her test had gone well, and sex would cloud his mind.

# Twenty Four.

*There, on the rocky banks of the lazy river, EagleEye lay broken. His life, his spirit and his secret slowly leaking into the water.*

*Myth of the Revelation*

**3 Tobeth, Y.O.D. 746**

## City of Andoline, Colovencia, Alasta

Gray skies and intermittent drizzle accompanied Derek on his trip to Andoline. Accusations of false divinity were rare, he thought. He looked at the clouds. If the Divine was pleased, why didn't he provide us with sunshine for the upcoming trial?

Tents had been erected in the city square for the Ra-ken and the priests. Some seating had been set up and roped off for guests, while the large crowd of onlookers was left to stand in the drizzle. Those that had them huddled together under umbrellas or crowded under the awnings and ledges of nearby buildings, and there were those who were content to get soaked and shiver if it meant a closer look.

The official proceedings would begin at noon. Derek could see by the tower clock that he still had an hour and a half. Plenty of time to interview the accused and see who would preside, though he already had his suspicions. He made his way to the courthouse at the north end of the square. The woman would be in a holding cell, already fed and ready. The Ra-ken in charge would be having breakfast in the upper apartments with the mayor. He would interview the accused first. Technically, no one was allowed access to the accused, but the clerks and guards knew Derek, and a Sun or two crossing palms would be sufficient for his needs.

Derek hurried through the wide double doors into the main foyer, a short marble hall led into the grand entrance to the court. He looked up and found the entrance blocked by two unfamiliar guards.

"I'm sorry sir; the court is closed for the day."

"I'm Derek Cantor, I'm with the Andoline Herald, and I'm here to interview the accused."

"I'm sorry sir, orders, I'm afraid your name has not been given to me."

Derek considered this. It was difficult to bribe two guards at the same time. "Perhaps that is an oversight. I'm a newsman, with the Andoline Herald. We routinely interview suspects and publicize trials."

"No doubt you are correct sir, but your name is not one I have been informed of. I'm afraid I'll have to ask you to wait outside."

"Can you tell me which Ra-ken is presiding over the trial?"

"Ra Echliesties, Master of Water, now please wait outside sir."

Derek realized he wasn't getting in. He stepped back out and looked at the sky. The rain was thinning. That at least would be an improvement on the day. He made his way back to the square.

A stage had been constructed for the trial at one end with tents for the clergy set to the back. Off to one side was a small section with a few tables that had been set aside for newsmen. Although the Herald was the only local pamphlet, some journalists from other cities kept a presence in the capital and filed their stories via FarSpeaker. Derek knew most of them, and was comforted in some small part by learning no one else had gained access to the courthouse.

Already seated at a table was a young man with his drawing tablet. Derek recognized him from the Herald, though he didn't remember his name. The man had finished making a quick layout of the stage and was adding faces from the crowd. Derek watched the man work. He studied the man's drawing, and then looked around, recognizing some of the faces the man had captured.

"You work for the Herald?" Derek asked.

"Yes, I've seen you there, you're Derek aren't you?" the man replied without pausing from his work.

"Yes, I'm sorry; I forget your name,"

"Randal," the man said without offering his hand.

"I didn't know you were powered." It was a rude comment, but Derek was feeling put off and rude.

"I'm not." He paused from his work, looked at Derek and waited, hoping the interruption would end.

Derek didn't know how to respond. He had heard of people doing incredible work without powers, but had assumed the stories to be exaggerated. "Nice to meet you."

"Likewise," Randal said.

Derek took a seat next to Randal, and waited.

A barrier had been set up in front of the stage and was guarded by cudgel-wielding clergy of the stouter variety. As always, capitalism thrived in such venues. There was a man selling onions; and another offering salted potato slices. Across the street, a local tavern had set up a makeshift bar and was selling beer at outrageous prices, though neither the weather nor the prices seemed to slow business any.

Eventually the Magistrate clergy came out on stage in formal attire and rapped his staff for quiet. When the crowd had settled, he announced in a loud voice:

"I will now lead in our devotion to the Divinity." What the clergy lacked in power they made up for in pageantry. Several local children in white robes trimmed in gold, ascended the steps, and formed a line. Two older boys, probably around twelve in age, dressed in the dark gray robes reserved for the first year priest initiates, their heads half shaved in the back, stepped forward carrying the massive Book of the Divine. Together they opened the weighty tome to the marked page, and stood shoulder to shoulder, each holding their half so the book rested just underneath their chins.

Prayers were offered and the children were anointed with water that had been touched by Ra-ken, which in this case, was a slightly more significant gesture than normal. When the formalities were over and the children departed, the Magistrate came out and rapped his staff of office on the stage.

"Today we conduct the trial of elder Lewellen Illitary of the village of Glyvia, Widow of Mascus Illitary of whom she took his name; mother of Javon, Eldrith and Ilsa Illitary. The charges against her are of the heresy of false Divinity."

The crowd hissed and booed. Derek shook his head; they had all known what the charges would be. Did they think they were seeing an mummer's play? The Magistrate rapped his staff again and continued.

"Presiding over today's trial and conducting the investigation is the Divine Master of Water, Council member Ra-ken, Vellenia Echliesties." As he spoke these words, the magistrate swept his hand out and bowed. Coming up the back steps onto the stage was a slender woman in a gauzy pale blue gown that shimmered as the breeze swirled around her. On her brow rested the double moon sigil of the Ra-ken, held in place by a gold chain woven into her auburn hair.

Derek held his breath as she ascended to the stage and took her place in the chair. She was as beautiful as he had ever seen her. He looked to his left and saw Randal adding her into the sketch of the stage. He leaned in to the man's ear.

"Do a portrait of her, it's for me, and I'll pay you out of my own pocket." The artist gave no indication that he had even heard. Derek was about to repeat himself when he heard the young man speak a number softly. It was a larger number than Derek had expected. It was an arrogant number, possibly inflated to compensate for earlier rudeness. He looked at the image taking form underneath the man's quickly moving fingers.

"Done."

Vellenia carried herself as one touched directly by the Divine. Her manner, her poise, her confidence all left no doubt that this was a formal proceeding, and as such, required a formal demonstration before sentence could be passed. She stepped up to a clear bowl of water set on a small pedestal.

She reached into the bowl with her left hand and touched the water. A snake of pure glimmer and moistness crawled up and circled up her arm. The crowd in front gasped, the people behind pushed forward. The serpent circled her arm until all of the water had been withdrawn from the bowl. It moved across her shoulders and onto her outstretched right hand, where it curled into a translucent globe. She held this up for all to witness, gave her hand a little dip and snapped it back up again quickly. It was a little trick illusionists use, to hide the motion of their fingers. The ball of water shattered and reformed. Wings spouted and flapped, a head emerged and the form of an owl appeared to hatch into full adult life. The watery owl flapped its wings, shook its crystal feathers, and settled down into her hand. Its large, glassy eyes blinked at the crowd. They clapped appreciatively. Having satisfied all that she was indeed the Master of Water, Vellenia transferred the bird from her hand onto her left shoulder and moved to her seat. "You may begin the proceedings."

The magistrate strode forward once again. "Who will bring charges today?" A man walked forward from the wings of the stage.

"Please state your name sir," the magistrate said.

"Tucker Moyer, I am a tavern keeper from Glyvia."

"What charges do you bring to recount to the Divine Master of Water."

"I bring charges of false divinity."

The crowd gasped then, as if this was news, and not the reason they had all gathered there.

"On whom are these charges brought?" The magistrate asked.

"On elder Lewellen Illitary, also of Glyvia."

"Please name the nature of the offense."

"She lays false claim to the power of knowing the evil intentions of others."

Vellenia interrupted. "The issue of false claim is not settled. She lays claim, not false claim."

The magistrate turned to face Vellenia. He bowed and thanked her, and turned back to the tavern keeper. "State again your claim please."

"She lays claim to the ability to know the evil intentions of others."

"Thank you, bow to the Master of Waters and you may go." The tavern keep did as he was instructed, smug with his performance.

"I call upon the Keeper of the Register." An older man struggled up the stage.

"Keeper, have you researched the aforementioned claim of power?"

"I have."

"What is your finding?"

"There is no such power registered."

Really? Derek thought. If the power had been registered, then there wouldn't be a trial.

"We shall now call forward witnesses." The magistrate said. With his role now complete, he and the old man bowed to Vellenia and departed while the lesser clergy came up and conducted the questioning of witnesses. They came and told their stories, one by one.

Derek let his mind wander,preferring his memories of simpler times to the prattling of coached witnesses and only occasionally took notes of what they said.

§

"I didn't trust the man, so I sent payment to her, and received the answer that he was good and honest. The next morning he had run off without payment, stolen a horse, and several days' worth of dried meat."

"Did you ask her about this?"

"She said he must have taken advantage of the opportunity, but my own good sense told me otherwise. I demanded payment for what he took from her but she would not repay me."

§

"The boys didn't take nothing, but they didn't work like they were told to either. They threw rocks at my livestock and wandered off into my fields to sleep. She had told me they would be good workers and I lost a day's harvest because of her."

§

"I carried a letter of credit from the Magistrate of Kiana, but she told them I meant to have their young daughters. I was tired and in need of rest, but they chased me out of the town. I was forced to camp by myself in the woods between here."

§

"She just whirled around and pointed her finger at my brother and started shouting about how he would see us all starve. Well we all jumped him and held him down. When we searched his pockets, he had a few apples he'd taken from Darrow's orchard. He claimed they had fallen and rolled outside the fence, and that he hadn't stolen them. Maybe he had and maybe he hadn't, but even so taking a couple apples isn't evil."

§

The last witness was always the accused, so that all might hear the answers to the testimony and judge.

Vellenia rose, took the woman gently in her hands and turned her to face the audience. "You have heard the testimony against you. Now if it pleases you, you may answer the charges."

"I know the Evil of all of you." She pointed out various faces in the crowd. "I know what you mean to do, but you hide yourselves. You scurry like rats and once revealed, slink away like cowards." She faced Vellenia.

"They asked me and I told them. I know the evil of men, but when revealed they set their ways aside. They bide their time and wait for me to forget, but I know. I always know."

"What about the man who stole from the tavern keeper."

"He hid his thoughts! I felt his change, but it was too late to warn them. It wasn't my fault!"

Vellenia soothed the woman. "I believe you." She raised her left arm. The owl on her shoulder shrank slightly as a stream of water flowed away from it and formed into a ball in her upturned hand.

"Ra ku Kellsee, Drink," she said.

"Dannu see, Ra ku Kellsee, auch." The woman put her lips to the water and drank.

To the audience, the transition was as miraculous as it was instantaneous. The old woman's clothes fell away into a pile—hiding her shriveled corpse—while the woman herself appeared to be transformed into a crystalline beauty of shimmering fluid. Years too had fallen away. Slim with straight back and firm breasts, the woman who was once the elder Lewellen Illitary was now a radiant youth sculpted in living water. Vellenia moved her right hand to the woman's back and kept it there. The transparent face smiled at the audience. The woman tilted her head back and gazed upward. She held her hands out palm upwards in supplication to the Divine. Thin tendrils of steam started rising from her face. Little wisps appeared around her body and rose in the slight breeze.

Like the morning mist rising from the lakes in cold months, the woman slowly became enshrouded in fog, which then thickened and rose until not a feature of woman could otherwise be discerned. The audience witnessed the birth of a cloud, gray against the gray background of the sky. The water that had recently been a living woman rose in the cool breeze. It drifted away to join the other low clouds gathered over the city.

"Let no others make false claim to the divinity, or this too shall be their reward."

The show was over. Vellenia retreated off stage to her tent. The chief clergy came out and proclaimed the court adjourned. Some people started moving away, but others came forward to touch the mummified remains of the old woman before it was covered with a cloth.

Derek paid for his sketch and placed it carefully inside his own notes. He wandered over to the side of the stage and approached a beefy man with a mostly shaved head.

"Hey Jode, long time," Derek said in his best casual tone.

"She's not seeing anybody," Jode replied, letting Derek know that he would be leading this dance.

"I'm hurt, can't a guy come over and talk to old friends?"

"I'm just letting you know."

"She and I go way back, c'mon, it wouldn't hurt to ask now would it?"

"In the mood she's in it just might."

"Nah, she's had her kill for the day, calms her down, makes her into a pussy cat."

"So why am I sticking my neck out for you?" Jode was a man of business, coming right to the point. Derek showed him two Suns, the usual payment for minor services and information. Jode didn't budge. A third sun slid out from behind the other two. He grunted appreciation at the minor sleight of hand.

"That's right, prices have gone up," he said.

Derek shrugged, bribes were part of the business and rates always went up. It just meant it was time to find another friend in the clergy.

"Stay here," Jode said, "Don't let anyone past."

For less than three suns, Derek thought. He almost said it aloud, but he had learned that expensive lesson already. Derek tried to think of what he might say if questioned. Fortunately, Jode returned before any other clergy came to find out why he was missing.

"Go on," he said, tossing his head back. He resumed his post at the entrance and Derek slipped past. The clergy had erected a small camp in the square behind the stage, but there was no mistaking Vellenia's sky blue tent set in among the dingy gray ones. He stood outside trying to figure out how to knock when the tent flap opened.

His heart still quickened every time he saw her, and each time he reminded himself how lucky he was, how good Clea was to him, how strong their marriage was. It helped, some.

"Come on in, I can't say I haven't been expecting you," she said. He went inside. The tent held a small sofa, a washbowl and a mirror stand. It was a simple way station, a place to hide from the crowd until it was convenient to depart. Vellenia let the tent flap close, stepped back to the little sofa and sat down. She stared up at him, holding his gaze while she remembered other simpler times when that face had meant so much more, or held the promise of more, which might have been the same thing.

"Paying bribes to see me? I'm flattered. But is that wise?"

"I do what I have to do."

"Don't we all? I assume you want me to write my name in that book of yours again?"

"No, that's not why I'm here."

She changed the subject. "My condolences on the loss. I'm sorry I wasn't able to attend your father's funeral. How is your mother?"

"She is well thank you. Jacob and Rissanne have moved in with Ella, It's still a little awkward, but it seems it will work out."

"That seems fair, considering."

"Yes, but I'm not sure which one of us got the better end of the donkey on that one."

"Oh you newsmen, you sure know how to turn a phrase."

"I take my job seriously."

"No doubt, and how is Clea?"

Just for an instant, he felt a little panic.

"Come," she offered, "sit down beside me. Care for a drink of water?" She waved at a pitcher on the small washstand.

"No...not thirsty, thank you, I'll pass if you don't mind." He sat on the small sofa, keeping a small distance between them. She made no move to press herself against him, so he relaxed a little.

"Derek, you're a damned fool, but you seem to be happy, so I guess that's more than most people manage. You know I can't stay mad at you."

"Thank you, I guess. It's good to see you again, and you're looking well. I just wish it was under better circumstances."

She looked away. "I had hoped this was to be a social visit, but you're here to ask about my verdict, aren't you?"

"I'm only asking for myself, you understand," he said, picking his words carefully, trying to judge her reaction as he went. "That woman was not making a false claim."

Even frowning, he thought, she still looked beautiful.

"But you killed her anyway."

She sighed. "Did you come here to discuss philosophy with me?"

"No."

"Good, because I'm not in the mood. Go argue with my priests if you want to, they don't charge."

Derek looked away, and then started to rise.

"Sit damn you, how long has it been? And you come here to tell me something I already know, and you think you have to pay someone to see me. Me?"

"He said—"

"Yes, I'm sure he did," she said. Derek blushed.

"Yes, the old woman's ability will show up somewhere, but it won't show up here, so it will be someone else's problem, which is just fine by me, and besides, she was dead anyway."

"Because she was old?" he asked.

She rolled her eyes at the question. "Lover, let me be blunt," Derek wondered what being blunt meant to her, given her earlier comments. "You and I are Divinely blessed, and were both still fairly young. We're lucky in that regard. However, I'm a Ra-ken and you're not. Derek nobody wants your power. Your son sure, probably, but you don't go around looking over your back all the time." This was true, though he didn't often think about it.

"I don't have that luxury and neither does anyone else at our level, good or bad. Everyone wants to be an Upper, and all it takes is a careless moment on my part for someone else to get their wish."

"So how does that apply? She was no Ra-ken." He refused to use the slang.

"Do you think I enjoyed what I did? I didn't, but I gave her a quick, painless death. If I had found her innocent what would happen? Would she have made it home alive? And after that? Would a few months of training repair her reputation? Do you think she even had a few months more left to live? Derek, the only reason she made it here alive was because no one took her seriously."

Her cheeks were flushed with emotion. Derek felt like a heel for having asked.

"You're not dumb, mostly, but you misunderstand a lot for a journalist."

"You're referring to the Monastery?"

"That and our relationship and just about everything it seems. You caused me considerable embarrassment with your article. You know I personally recommended you for that job."

"I think what you're doing there is a mistake."

"Well some opinions are best kept to themselves."

There was no point in continuing. He had the answer to at least one of his questions and there was not going to be a resolution of any of the others. He knew Ra-ken were often cruel, but she seemed to have developed a talent for it.

One more question came to mind. "Why you, and not Tawnya? You're a little far from home."

"I'm on an errand, and she asked me as a favor. You can see why."

"Much less messy, yes, how is the old dear?" He was fishing for something, but he wasn't sure what.

"Covered in dog hair mostly," she said, "and if you print that I'll teach you the true meaning of the word 'enema'." Derek shivered at the mental imagery.

"I'd best be going."

She didn't argue. "Give my love to Clea."

He stood. "Thank you, I will."

"Hold old is Liam now?"

"He's almost nine."

"Bring him to see me at Carnival. I'd like to meet him."

"I'll do that. He'd very much like to meet you."

He waited then, to see if there was more, some other kindness she wanted to offer, but all he saw in her face was regret.

§

Derek had plenty of time to think on the trip home. He rode along the country road at a leisurely pace, mulling the events of the day. It had been suggested he move into the city to be closer to the paper, but he had come to prefer the distance between his home and the raucous city. He had written and filed his story before he left. It was a dutiful piece about the justness of the Ra-ken, and the fate that awaits those who would profane the Divine. Derek had no illusions that the story would appease the Council, but it might divert them for a while. He felt sure that he would be revisiting this story and setting the record straight, but not now. He had no doubt that the woman had discovered an unregistered power of some significance. Someone in that crowd must have made that wish— only to be surprised when it was granted. What evil intention was revealed must have been enough to silence that lucky person, for there was no cry of foul; No joyous soul came forth to claim elevated status, to add their name and ability to the registry, or to prove Vellenia a murderess. One day, he might hope to track that person down, but for now, he must let it lie.

It was nearing dusk when Derek rounded the hill above where his home lay. Jarod's daughter Meary, a girl of eleven, waved when she saw him and ran up the road to meet him.

"Hello Meary," Derek said when she reached him.

She curtsied. "Welcome home, sir, Ra ku Kellsee." She skipped alongside, always eager to greet the horse.

"I see your archaic is improving."

"Dannu see," she said.

"You're welcome."

They stopped at the gate. Derek climbed down and stretched, happy to be home. He opened one saddlebag while she held the reins and pulled out a cloth, which he opened to reveal several sticks of rock candy.

"Take one," he said.

"Thank you, may I share it with Beauty?"

"Of course, I'm sure she'll be happy to help you eat it." He closed the cloth and secured the saddlebag. "Have the rest of my things sent in."

"Yes, sir." She curtsied again and led the horse away, telling it she had a treat to share.

Clea and Jarod met him at the door; Jarod took Derek's jacket, helped him out of his boots and into indoor sandals, Clea waited and then received her husband home with a hug and quick kiss.

"Welcome home, sweetheart."

Derek handed her the cloth. "Candy for Liam. I'm starved, have you eaten?"

"No, dear, I have been waiting for you, but Liam has been fed."

Of course, he thought.

"You have a guest, a visitor from the east," she announced.

"Oh?" This could not be good news, "Man or woman?"

"Man," said the voice from behind Clea.

Derek looked past his wife's face to see a dark skinned visitor with the shaved head and gray robes of the Priests of the divine. The face was somehow familiar. "I'm afraid you have me at a loss."

Clea moved back so that the two men might shake hands. "Derek, this is Seth, from Vesport."

Derek hesitated, protocol required him to bow to Ra-ken, but he was dressed as a priest, someone who eschews the touch of the Divine. Clearly, Derek thought, Seth was traveling in disguise, but this made no sense, and then it came to him.

"Seth, are you here to kill me?"

"Derek," Clea admonished.

"No," Seth said, "please. I'm here to visit."

Derek held up his hand. "Oh, good. Umm, well then, welcome, Seth Vihiate. Mana nyum ku ana nyum."

"My place is your place?" Seth asked, slightly puzzled.

"Yes, my home is now yours." Derek shook hands with his friend.

Clea, smiling again, ushered the men into the dining room. "Wonderful, Seth, we get very few visitors from all the way across the world. We're ready to eat now. You're welcome in our home as long as you would like. I want to hear all about your adventures."

"Yes," Derek said, "I have a thousand questions myself."

§

Jarod wrapped the shoulder cut of pork with a plain oilcloth, tied it into a neat package, and bound it with twine. "Meary" he called out.

The girl came running. "Yes, Papa."

He handed her the package. "Take this on over to Mrs. Pritchett, and don't dally girl. Your chores still need tending."

"Yes, Papa."

"And take the road mind you, any more tears in your skirt and there'll be a tanning on your hide."

"Yes, Papa."

"Good girl, now hurry along." He looked at his blood stained hands. "I'll have a kiss for you when you're back." Meary gave a quick curtsy and hurried down the road.

§

"Do come right in Meary." Mrs. Pritchett opened her door for the little girl.

214

"I saw you coming down the lane I did. You do your father right proud."

"Thank you Mrs. Pritchett."

"Just take that right into the kitchen and set to the table. Mind the cats." The cats could smell the meat, and swarmed around Meary's legs and arched their backs against her shins. She made it into the kitchen and set the package down.

"There's a ladle of milk and a fresh cookie there for you." Rose indicated a plate and cup set at the far end.

"Thank you Mrs. Pritchett."

Meary sat down at the table and waited for permission to eat. The woman pulled a long knife out of a block and slit the twine. "Go ahead girl," she said. Meary picked up the cookie and took a small bite. Mrs Pritchett cut a thin steak off the end, and slid the rest into a large pot of simmering water. She wrapped the steak back in the cloth and put it up. "Meary."

"Yes'm" She made to get up.

"No sit, finish your treat." Rose busied herself at the stove. "I hear tell you have a guest at your master's house."

"Yes'm"

She saw the look of worry on the girl's face. "Oh, never mind, it's just something your father mentioned. I'll bet you're excited about carnival aren't you."

Meary nodded her head vigorously.

Rose walked over and plucked at the sleeves and sides of the girl's dress. "Yes, I can see you've filled out this thing about as much as can be; 'bout time for a new one." The idea of a new dress brought a big smile to Meary's face.

"Yes, well I suppose we'll have strangers wandering through here day and night soon enough. Your father did warn you about strangers did he?"

"Yes'm"

"Well that's good, best to keep an eye out, finish your milk now, that's a good girl. Now I'd have guests in my own house a' fore long but it's just me and my cats here. I could use an extra penny or two you know, I fancy a new dress myself." She handed the girl a towel. "That's good, wipe your nose. Sit a bit; I'll fetch another cookie for you to eat as you walk back." She rummaged around in her cupboards.

"Do you think it's safe for me to have travelers in my house? I could use a boarder."

"I guess," Meary said.

"Well, that man, staying with Mr. Cantor, he's a kind man?"

Meary nodded. "He's a priest."

"Oh well, dear me, is that so. I saw three of them just the other day. Was that him?" Meary gave a puzzled shrug.

"Oh of course dear, you wouldn't know." She found the cookie she'd been holding and gave it to the girl.

"Here you go dear, say how would I recognize Mr. Cantor's guest, if I had some questions about the Divine that is?" Meary turned her cookie over and pointed at the well-baked bottom.

§

"Ah Seth, there you are." Derek found Seth reading in the library, lounging in some of his old clothes Clea had loaned him. "Not teaching today?"

Seth had taken to his role as a member of the clergy with amazing zeal. Those who could afford it sent their children to private schools, as was the case with Liam. Those who could not, received their education from traveling clergy wherever and whenever the opportunity presented itself. Often, a wealthier neighbor would sponsor a priest to tutor the locals for a week or two, and as the only powered individual in this area, that duty had mostly fallen to Derek and Clea. Seth had not only given lessons to Jarod's children, but also visited several other families.

Seth looked up from his book, a history of the false religions. "Not today, Jarod made it clear he needs Meary to help clean, something about making hay while the sun shines."

"Ah yes, Clea took Liam into Andoline early this morning. I think his teeth were bothering him again. I remember being scolded about giving him too many sweets."

"I must confess; I find them irresistible myself. Wait, she went to Andoline for a healer?"

"It's a long story, he's an old friend, and she says the merchants there have better goods, so the two of them go off for a day and it's a treat for both of them."

216

Seth marked his place and closed the book. "Can I ask you something, personal?"

"I suppose." Derek took this to be an invitation to a long conversation, and took a seat.

"I notice, and forgive me if this is too intrusive, but where I come from, families tend to be much larger."

"Yes, our private little shame, I'm not surprised you weren't told. The clergy are not fond, to put it mildly of certain abilities."

"I'm sorry, I don't follow you."

"Well, you know how theoretically, everyone could have an ability. For instance, we could all be FarSpeakers. Yet most people don't."

"Yes, I find that fascinating," Seth stood up and shelved the book. "That some people believe that no one should have abilities."

"Clea, for instance."

"Yes, so I understand, but…"

"Well there's no delicate way to put this. Some people believe that the Divine is not beneficent, but is in fact an evil presence, a curse on humanity for their sins."

"I hadn't heard this."

"It's not a point of view the clergy, as you might understand, want widely spread."

Seth automatically ran his hand over the top of his head, felt the stubble, and then entwined his tassel around his finger.

Derek continued. "Most of the controversy surrounds a particular ability, one of the first to be localized, according to some legends."

"What?"

"The ability to end a pregnancy."

"Divine no!" Seth almost shouted. "That's murder."

Derek held his hands up defensively. "They claim, and I'm certainly no expert, but those who have this ability claim that the child has not quickened until the third week. Before that time, it's not a person yet, the child to be has not received its soul, and later than that, they refuse, though I am inclined to believe, that instead the price just goes up."

"But why? Is this what you do?"

"No. I'm sorry, I know this is news to you, but there are many sexually based abilities. And yes, the clergy find all of them offensive."

Seth thought about this for a second. "No doubt, but that seems at odds with their teachings; they venerate the divine and all of his aspects."

"Oh, you mean you've noticed that what they teach and what they practice are different. Isn't that why you're here? Anyway, I'm glad Clea's not here, she's pretty touchy on this subject."

Seth nodded, understanding. "She would never let someone use an ability like that on her body."

"No, and she doesn't like healers much either, so you know Liam had to be in a lot of pain."

Seth made a face of sudden understanding. "Which means you did!"

"No. We use other methods of contraception, and it's considered impolite to ask."

"You're blushing."

Derek folded his arms and tried to look offended. "Well now I don't feel so bad about asking you for a favor."

"What kind of favor."

"I want you to kill something for me."

"Something?"

"Can you ride a horse?"

"I'm not liking this already."

"I'll take that as a no, good, I have some weeding I thought you could help with, and with Clea and Liam gone this is a good opportunity."

"I don't understand."

"I want you to kill some plants for me."

"Can I do that?"

§

"Here is that vine that's giving us so much trouble." Derek pointed out a thick greasy vine that was invading his fields from the adjacent woods. "We cut it back all the time, but it grows divinely fast. Careful not to touch it or you'll get a nasty rash. We have to wear gloves and heavy coveralls."

Seth dismounted and examined a small section of the vine, looking at it thoughtfully. He turned to Derek. "The life in plants is very slow compared to animals. I see life as bright colors. Plant life is darker, harder to distinguish. It's like trying to see a painting by a low burning candle."

Derek wondered idly if all the heirs of a power experienced it the same way. "You're sure you don't mind?"

"No, I've been thinking about what you said." Seth let the words hang.

"Which part?"

"That I have a duty to know about my ability. That expecting me to ignore the Divine, which is now a part of who I am, is folly."

"Well, you're the first. To think about something I've said, that is."

Seth focused on the greasy vine he had agreed to kill for Derek. "First I must let my eyes adjust to the hues of the plants and then start sorting them out. I'm going to try one small section first." Twin beams of light shot from Seth's eyes and traced up and down a short length of the stalk. "How did that look?"

"Impressive, scary. How long do we have to wait?"

Seth studied the vine again. "This section is dead. I now see it as a blackness surrounded by grays."

"It doesn't look any different."

"No, it doesn't, but it should dry up in a couple days."

"Can you get the rest of it?"

"I don't think so. Some of it goes pretty high up, and it looks as if it feeds off the trees. I take it you don't want me to kill the trees too?"

"No. The trees are not on my property, and the owner would be offended. The vine however is fair game."

"I can only kill what I can see. I can't make out the vine high in the tree but I can do a lot of damage to it near the ground."

"Do what you can please. Maybe we'll get lucky."

Seth obliged. He carefully stepped through the thicket, beams lashing out from time to time. "Okay, that should do it."

"Do you feel any different? I mean, after you kill something?"

"Only once. And I never want to feel that again."

Derek understood. He had probably asked as many questions as he could get away with for now.

"I think I did a fairly good job on most of it, but I could also see that it extends much further back into the forest. I think you will be rid of it for a while, but don't get too hopeful."

"I sure appreciate this. Could this be a new profession for you?"

"You are most welcome Derek, but I don't think so." Seth managed his way back up onto his horse.

Derek guided them out of the field. "What will you do if you don't hear from Cordain?"

"I haven't thought that far ahead yet."

"I hear Kherlestra is looking for a new leader."

Seth shook his head. "And I could settle down and start a family."

"I guess I've made this argument before?"

"Once or twice."

Derek led Seth around the perimeter of his land, coming at last back out to the road. They turned back to his home. The front yard was deserted, but the barn and house were both closed. Derek dismounted and called for Meary. There was no answer. Seth dismounted and drew closer.

"Where is everyone?" Seth asked.

Water jetted up around them and drove hard into their faces. Derek clamped his hands over his face and turned away, but the water was everywhere, following his every move. Seth cried out, but it quickly turned into a gurgle. The two men twisted and stumbled about while the horses fled.

The attack on Derek ended; soaked and doubled over, the water boiled away from him, leaving him disoriented, but dry.

A circular curtain of water leapt up around Seth, foaming and swirling around him it encircled him in a shimmering, light distorting wall—a liquid oubliette.

"Vellenia!" Derek cried. He stepped toward Seth and received a quick, wet, slap in the face, like an errant cat.

From inside his prison of water, Seth called out. "Ra-ken Vellenia Echliesties, Divine master of water, I am your humble servant. I mean you no harm."

Vellenia stepped into view from around the side of the house and moved quickly but quietly towards Derek. Motioning him to silence, she

220

moved behind him, put her arm around his waist, raised her chin up onto his shoulder and spoke gently into his ear. "You've been naughty again."

She gave a quick squeeze, stepped back with one hand still on his arm, and shouted at Seth. "Seth, you've been a bad boy, Ahten is very concerned."

"Vellenia? I meant no harm."

"Then why did you leave?"

"I don't care what you do to me."

"That's not an answer, why did you leave?"

"To find Derek," his voice trembled, "to escape, to get help, all of those, I don't know."

"I find it hard to believe that someone with your ability should need much help," she said.

"I don't use my ability Vellenia, that why we were chosen."

"They why did you leave?"

"Because he killed a deer, and my article." Derek said.

"What?" She punched him playfully in the back, "What do you know of this? Stay facing away from us Seth, if you turn your head, you die. I knew you wrote that."

"Ahten's gone power crazed," Derek said, "He had Cordain seal that girl…"

"Briana," Seth offered.

"Briana," Derek said, "the one who controls emotions, he had Cordain seal up her room with her inside, and then threatened to do the same to anyone else who started using their powers."

"How do you know those weren't his instructions? Besides, why didn't he just kill her?"

Derek turned and glared at her, "Is killing your answer to every problem?"

"It's a good answer, it leaves few loose ends."

"So kill me then," Seth yelled, "just get it over with."

"Ahten says you used your ability on his priests."

"I didn't hurt them, I just scared them."

Vellenia leaned in close again. "Did you know Bouchard was Vernault's bastard?"

"No, really?"

"Before he figured out his own little method of birth control."

"Which was?"

"He liked to drop his lovers after he was done with them, from five hundred feet up. Maybe someday I'll let you print that."

"Really?"

"No, but you can write it in that stupid book of yours. I saw flashes earlier, what were you two doing?"

"Weeding," Derek answered flatly. Inside the wall of water, he saw Seth jerk his hands up to the sides of his head, and then a flash of light. Vellenia shivered against him, as if shocked. The wall of water collapsed. Seth doubled over, fell, and lay still on the grass curled in a tight ball.

Derek felt Vellenia clinging to him, using him for support. "Is he dead?"

"No, but Divine, that was tiring. You know Derek, it saddens me that you believe that I kill so casually. No one has died here. I may have actually saved your lives."

He pushed away from her and hurried over to Seth, and was able to pick him up as easily as a small child; his skin was dry and leathery.

"I sent for a healer."

"What did you do to him?"

"I also waited. He's dehydrated."

"Waited for what?" He whirled upon her, wanting only that she should leave.

She stood there, her shoulders slumped, her blouse and brow wet with perspiration, exhausted, and as always, impatient with him. "I would have preferred to take him alone. So there would be no hostages. Now take him inside, we all need water."

Derek took Seth into the house, carried him upstairs and laid him out on the bed. Jarod's wife Nunna met him at the door and followed him up. The woman laid a wet cloth across Seth's eyes, dribbled a spoonful of water into his mouth, and started washing down his skin. "My man has the wagon ready sir, with a tarp across the top to keep the sun off."

"What?" Derek asked, "How did you know?"

"Well, I hadn't seen Elly in years, but I knew her soon as I set eyes upon her I did. Master Echliesties' little girl, and right pretty and grown up. Didn't I hear you used to have a fancy for her?"

"That was long ago."

Nunna continued to sponge pungent water from a basin onto Seth's skin. "Just a liniment, and bag balm, good for the skin, and don't worry, I won't be speaking my mind none to Mistress Clea, I know you have a good love for her and all. You should go down and catch up on old times while we get Mr. Seth here ready to travel, there's tea and fresh cakes in the kitchen. It's not much to set out when Ra-ken come calling, but it's all I could do what with no notice and all."

Derek looked at Seth, his skin was the color of ash, his breathing was slow, labored, and his body twitched with tiny spasms.

"I'm sure it's fine."

"Please sir," she pleaded, "She's waiting for you. I know you cared a great deal for this young man, but it's not ours to say, and the best you can do for him is to see that Elly don't get on one of her tempers."

It was true, the Ra-ken did what they wanted, and the best anyone else could hope for was to stay out of their way, beneath their notice. Vellenia was taking Seth, and he could no more stop that than stop the sun or turn back the days, or unwish his ability. All he could do, of any value, was to see them off before Clea returned. "Goodbye Seth," he whispered, and went downstairs.

# Twenty Five.

*And then EagleEye revealed unto his brother the words of power and
the secret of the gift of the Spirit Father, who is the Divine, and of the
angel Uulvault. And Apachawea spoke then the words and asked for
the gift of the Divine, but received no answer, for the life was still
within his brother.*

*Myth of the Revelation*

**26 Imbro, Y.O.D. 746**

### Council Monastery, East of Vesport, Tameria

"Cordain," Ahten exclaimed, "come in, come in, I was just in the
bath when they told me you had arrived."

Cordain wasn't quite sure how you could manage to make a robe look
hastily put on, but Ahten had succeeded. The combination of a white
towel still wrapped around his head, his pink, still moist skin, and the
smell of fragrant soap gave Cordain the impression of a woman fresh
from her bath, or in this case, a jowl-cheeked, bald woman with tiny black
eyes.

He surveyed the room—Ahten's apartment was well furnished—and
then flopped down into one corner of a candy-striped couch, where he
could more easily affect disdain than in the straight-backed chairs.

"Wine, and cheese, and bread," Ahten shouted into the hallway,
presuming someone would obey, and then added, "the red, not the white.
Forgive my manners. Ra ku Kellsee, Ra Leighland, how may I be of
service?"

"Kelst tu auch."

Ahten dried off his head, ran his hand over the stubble, gathered up
the strands at the side and affixed a small gold clasp to the end. "Did you
really threaten to shake apart the sanctuary?"

"I was told you were unavailable."

"That is…unfortunate, I must clear up those instructions as soon as
we're done here. What brings you here with such urgency? Do you have
news of Seth? Is he with you?"

"I'm here to discuss Briana."

Ahten's face remained calm. "I see, you understand she is being punished."

"Is that what you call it?"

"I gather," Ahten stiffened as he spoke, "that you have been in contact with Seth. I don't know what he told you, and I might be so bold as to say I don't care. I have a difficult assignment here, it's not easy keeping these children disciplined, and even more so when they are Ra-fel."

"You manipulated me in order to seal her up."

"Oh, so that's what this is about."

Ahten moved to the door and held it open so that one of his priests could enter with a tray of bread, wine and a pot of honey-butter. He waited until the wine was poured and the man had departed, then sat opposite Cordain and tore off a chunk of bread. "Where were we? Oh yes, Briana is well cared for, but we could not allow her to have her liberty until she understood the consequences of her actions. I do love the dear girl, and I understand the impertinence of youth, but I must be firm with them or I'll lose their respect entirely."

"Why didn't you consult with me?"

"There are twelve council members, and while I am a humble and obedient servant to you all, I answer directly only to Ra Brawley. This job is delicate and difficult enough without having twelve masters. Am I to report every decision to the council and let it debate the issue before I choose ham or sausage for my breakfast? Or was I entrusted with this position and expected to act with some autonomy?"

"You were left instructions."

"Yes and those instructions were to kill any student who started to use their ability, as if we were common murderers. Am I expected to FarSpeak a message to the council and then wait two months for one of you to drop by? Perhaps you thought to leave an assassin at our disposal for such contingencies. And how would I expect the other students to react to her death? Killing Briana would only make the situation here chaotic, which it is already."

The man was bold, Cordain admitted; He was not often spoken to in such a manner. "Those are your concerns, but I see your point. Still, it is never wise to manipulate a Ra-ken, we tend to react violently."

"I apologize if you felt I did not treat you with respect. Please, tell me, is Seth with you?"

"No, I came alone."

"But you met with him." Ahten accused.

"He warned me of your treachery. I thought it best for him to hide out until I settled this matter."

"My treachery? Has my punishment of this girl been inappropriate? Have I deceived the council by not telling you of the day-to-day problems that we face? I told you when Seth left the mountain; I did not hide that from you. The small problems I can handle, like when credit is delayed, or corrupt city men demand bribes. You would consider me incompetent should I not be able to handle such trifles. Yet you admonish me for failing to mention that I had a recalcitrant teenage girl."

"She is with two other men."

Ahten shook his head. "No. She was the only one in the room when you sealed it. Yes, it was probably poor judgment on my part not to tell you. I admit some fear that you might feel I could not handle such simple problems, so yes; I kept it a secret from you. Is that why you are here, to free her?"

"Seth seemed to think Xavier and another boy is in there with her."

"Well, we never heard them cry out, and we converse with her daily. I dare say we could investigate and settle this in the morning."

"Why not now?"

"Caution, of course. If she does have two men in there with her, then surely they must be dead. Don't you agree? If we open the wall, she would assume then we were there to kill her, which of course would be true. No, let us open the wall in the morning, while she sleeps. Then if she is alone, we can welcome her back, and move her to a new apartment. If not, then you could deal with her harshly, but that would be difficult were she awake. Do you not agree?"

Cordain rubbed his chin. What Ahten said did make sense.

Ahten eased back and spoke with a softer, conciliatory tone in his voice. "I didn't tell you, because I didn't have time to debate the issue. I meant no offense, but you have the luxury of time and ability that I don't. I don't really know what I would have done if you had not visited. She was toying with other people's emotions, and I felt I had to act before she turned this sanctuary into her own little territory. They don't really know what they can do, and I needed a solution before she figured that out, and not, as you might imagine; a debate."

"Fine." Cordain finished his wine and quickly set the glass down. "I will investigate in the morning, and if she is alone, I will leave the room open. But if my friend Xavier is in there with her, then it's you I'm going to come after."

"I am always your humble and faithful servant."

Cordain snorted, he believed no such thing.

§

Cordain scratched another line off the page, the draft of his report progressing as poorly as had his arguments with Ahten. Autonomy, he had conceded, was essential, the tipping point, and his demise. The man was a master of logic, irritatingly so. His meal sat untouched, scraps of paper littered the floor. Somehow, he knew Ahten was at fault, he just needed to find the right words to convince the council, though honestly, he wasn't sure what he wanted them to do. A knock interrupted his thoughts.

"Yes, what is it?"

A young man, some acolyte or other servant entered. "My apologies, Ra-ken, there is a young woman who wishes to see you."

"Send her away." The man bowed and left. Cordain returned to his papers. He heard whispering outside the door, and the man appeared again. "Ra Cordain?" The acolyte interrupted, a young woman followed him in.

"I'm sorry miss," Cordain started, "I left orders…"

The young girl stepped into the light of his lamp. She was quite pretty; her skin was a soft, creamy brown, her long black hair was tightly braided and hung forward over her left shoulder, framing her pleasant oval face, small nose, and large brown eyes. She wore a thin, white cotton night-shirt. He could see the darkness of her nipples as two small shadows under her shirt.

"Leave us," Cordain said to the young man. They understood each other, the situation old and familiar. The acolyte had been promised some future favor for interrupting his master a second time, the girl had known what the effect of her appearance would be, and Cordain had been Ra-ken long enough to know the aphrodisiac nature of power.

The young man left and closed the door. Cordain rose, came around the desk, and kissed the girl lightly, his hand rested on her shoulder.

"Do not speak or make noise," Dharla commanded. "Do not use your power in any way that I do not command." Her power forced compliance.

I am a fool, Cordain thought, I should have anticipated this.

"I'm not going to kill you," she said. "I need your powers, do nothing that will harm me."

He declined to believe her, but there was cleverness in that command, and inexperience as well. There was much he could do that would not harm her, yet still be unanticipated.

"Do you understand?" she asked. He nodded. "Before we go, I need to know, you sealed the room Briana is in?"

Cordain nodded again.

"Did you know she was in there?"

He shook his head no.

"That's what you and Ahten were fighting about?"

Nod.

"Is he your boss?"

Shake.

"You're his boss?"

Nod.

"Follow me." No power compelled him, but he followed regardless. She led him out of the great hall, onto the main platform, and across to the other apartments, where Seth, Cal and Briana lived. They came to the end of the corridor, smooth and round.

"Open it."

He placed his hand on the smooth stone, paused.

"Open it!"

The stone melted. The odor that greated them was that of a beast caged and forgotten, but not yet dead and it held forth the promise of despair.

Dharla stepped through the opening, into the hallway and motioned Cordain to follow. "Seal it up behind us."

Cordain complied, but made the seal dust-thin, easily penetrated, just in case.

"Stay," she commanded.

§

Dharla didn't know how long Cordain would stay and she didn't care. Her power was stronger than his anyway.

The door to Briana's room was ajar, forgotten in its uselessness. She gently pushed it open and looked inside, and even by the little light of her lamp, she could see the room had been destroyed. Against the far wall was a canopy bed with one post broken off and the canopy shredded. No other furnishings survived intact. Strewn across the floor were the remains of a wooden chair, books, torn bits of cloth, matting, brown pine branches, and debris of every conceivable type. Near the foot of the bed she made out the shape of a pale white hand, connected it to an arm, and followed that to a body lying face up, intermingled with the trash, a man, though she couldn't see his face.

She stepped gingerly over to where he lay and found a second man, dark skinned, younger, a boy really, lying face down next to the first. Both were dirty, thin to the point of starvation, mostly naked and asleep.

"I try to feed them, but I don't think it's working," Briana said.

Dharla looked up and saw Briana sitting up in the bed, sleepy eyed, naked, her hair matted and unkempt.

Dharla stood mute, her plan and prepared words of comfort vanished from her mind.

Briana slid out of the bed, pulled a sheet around her body into a kind of sarong, then slipped her feet into a pair of sandals and shuffled over. "I missed you."

Briana set down her lamp, then stepped forward, put her arms around her lover and kissed her. They stood there, hugging, crying, gently at first, and then in earnest, great heaving sobs that slowly quieted to low tremors.

"Can we go?" Briana asked.

Dharla brushed the hair from her friends face. "I have a power of my own now. I am able to make others obey my commands."

"What?" Briana's eyes went wide, "Did Ahten put you in here with me too?"

"No, listen. You have to promise not to use your power on me."

"Sure, but why? Are you afraid of me?"

"Even if you're angry with me, promise."

"I promise. What's happened?"

"I have the ability to make other people obey my commands."

Briana seemed puzzled.

"I can make anybody do what I tell them, even the other Ra-ken."

"Wow, anything?" Briana looked over at the two bodies at the floor. "They would do what I asked, but only if I made them love me, and I kept having to do that all the time. That one," she pointed at the one further away, "The fire guy, he begged me not to, you know, use my ability all the time, but I had to, right? Didn't I?"

"Are they dead?"

"I don't think they are. Can you make them get up? Can you do that?"

"What happened to them?" Dharla asked.

"Can you make them get up?"

"Sure, but are they asleep? They have to hear me to obey me, I think, who are they?"

"The younger guy, over there, is Emit, he was always trying to be friends, and the other guy is Xavier, I think, the fire guy. Make them get up; I can't get them to do anything anymore."

Dharla looked at the two men, both lay on their backs, staring up as if some cosmic pageant was playing out on the ceiling.

Of the two, Emit looked a little stronger. Dharla focused her will upon him and spoke the words "Get Up." There was no response; no indication that he had heard, that her will was upon him, or that his mind was sufficient to comprehend words any longer. But then, slowly, he moved.

His body twisted, his arms reached out to the side and flailed spastically until he rolled over onto his stomach and was once again, still.

"Stand Up! Stand all the way up."

He moved, perhaps a little faster this time. Joints popped, spasms shook his frame, but he pushed onto his hands and knees, then crouched, then, finally, he stood; unsteady, blank faced and drooling. His mouth hung open, revealing rows of missing teeth. His face and hands were covered with sores. Briana poked him lightly in his chest with one finger. He staggered back, stumbled, then regained his balance.

"What are we going to do with him?" Dharla asked. "Should I make him eat?"

Briana stepped close, and brought her knee up sharply into the boy's groin. He rocked back from the blow, but showed no other reaction, but then, a little at a time, his body started shaking, first with a small tremor in his side, a twitch at the neck and then his arms. His left side sagged, then his knees buckled and he collapsed like a corpse cut free from the noose, and his head hit the stone with the hollow sound of death.

"Why did you do that?" Dharla asked.

"I had my reasons."

"What about him?" She pointed at Xavier.

"No, he was nice to me. I fed him when I could, but he's still pretty weak."

"Do you have any food?" Dharla asked. Briana wandered away and shortly came back with an apple, bruised and spotted.

"Disgusting."

Briana shrugged. "Make him eat this anyway. I won't kick him if that's what you're thinking."

"Okay," Dharla replied, then willing her ability; "Xavier, sit up and eat this apple." As before, the reaction was slow. he pushed himself up into a sitting position, upright with his legs sticking out in front, uncomfortable and awkward. He made no effort to reach for the apple so Briana put it in his hand.

"Eat the Apple," she commanded. Xavier raised the apple to his mouth without looking at it. When he took his first bite, two of his teeth fell out into his lap. Blood from his gums mixed with juice from the apple and ran down his face. He didn't notice. He bit, chewed and swallowed with no trace of humanity.

The girls giggled as he bit into the core and got a mouth full of seeds. He ate the apple from one side through to the other without turning it. He ate until there were no more pieces of apple in his hand, and then he simply stopped.

"Lay down now and sleep." This time her voice held some compassion. She could hear his stomach growling at the unaccustomed food.

"That was amazing," Briana said, then "I want to go. I want to get out of here."

"We can't, not yet."

"I don't want to stay in here another fallen moment. Why can't we go? You know I can make you take me out of here."

"And I can make you swallow your own tongue," Dharla flung back. They stood there, face to face, each daring the other to make the first move.

Briana giggled. "Can you really?"

"Yes, well, I think I can, I haven't tried yet."

"I bet that would be fun, what have you made people do? You're not trapped in here are you? Like I am?"

Dharla saw Briana was afraid again. She stepped forward and hugged her. "I haven't really used my power much. No one knows I have it. Not yet, anyway, look, you have to know what's been going on out there. This is serious, besides, I have a plan, I think."

"What kind of plan?" Briana looked dubious and impatient.

"The kind of plan where we make everyone do what we say."

"I like it. I missed you."

"I missed you too."

"Love me?" Briana asked.

"Here? Now?"

"Is the hall still sealed?"

"Yes."

"But you can open it?"

"Yes."

"Then yes, here, now."

§

"So tell me of this plan." Briana said.

Dharla was lying on her back with eyes closed, her dark hair moist with sweat, and her breath still heavy from their lovemaking. She opened her eyes and looked at her lover. "We must trust each other." She spoke softly but with certainty.

Briana looked away, but she lifted Dharla's hand and kissed it. "I trust you."

"Briana, I made Cordain let me in here. That's how I got in."

"I am going to kill that man."

"No." Dharla stated, "Sorry, but we need him. He can't hurt us, not together. None of them can hurt us if we stick together." She met Briana's

232

stare with one of her own, the command to "stop" held in her mind, her will ready.

Briana blinked, turned away. "I guess you know what you're doing."

"Thank you, you should get dressed."

Briana leaned over the side of the bed and looked around for some clothing. She found a shirt and put it on. "When we get out of here I'm going to make a lot of people suffer."

"I agree, but you have to understand, we can't use our abilities on each other, no matter what."

Briana thought this over. "If I make you love me, you will do what I tell you to."

"I already love you Briana, you can't make me love you more. If you try, I will have to tell you to stop using your power. Then we will fight, and they will win. Don't you have any clothes?"

Briana looked down, giggled, hunted around, found a pair of men's pants. "Hey, where's that guy?"

Dharla sat up and looked around. Xavier was gone; a cleared path ran from where he had lain to the exit. "Cordain," she commanded, "Come back in here now." She climbed off the bed and ran to the doorway. She stood there naked, shivering lightly and looked at the empty hallway. "They're gone."

"Can we get out?" Briana asked.

"Yes."

"Then put some clothes on."

§

They found a stone grate blocking the exit and Cordain waiting on the other side. Xavier lay on some sort of black stone slab, raised up and supported by thousands of undulating legs. A thin rod extended up from the platform and ended in a round knob on which Cordain rested his hand.

"Before you do anything rash," he warned the girls. "Look up." Above them, the ceiling had grown sharp spikes.

"If you attempt to use your abilities on me, or if I relax my ability for any reason, that ceiling will fall and kill you both."

"What do you want?" Dharla called out. She grabbed Briana by the waist. "Shh, it's okay."

"There is much I should tell you, but I do not have the time, and there is no one else on the mountain who can, but this much I must say. You are Ra-ken now, both of you. You have lands, titles and incomes due to you both. You should travel to Vesport and speak to the Mayor there."

"We will." Dharla said.

"Seth is well, living in Andoline and hiding from the council until I contact him. He sends you both his love."

"You killed him." Briana called out.

"No, It's not my way. He is alive and well. I was tricked into sealing you up Briana, and I would go deal with Ahten personally if I were not in a hurry to get Xavier to a healer. Ra-ken must not fight each other, for the world weeps when we do. I will release you as soon as I reach the steps." Cordain stepped up onto his platform, and then made it slither away.

After a few seconds, the bars thinned and withdrew.

The girls emerged into the night. The doors of the monastery were wide open, the light from inside spilled out onto the marble plateau. Ahten was standing outside in his night-robe and cap, arms folded, staring toward the steps, acolytes and priests behind him crowding the doorway.

"Ahten," Dharla called.

Ahten turned, scowled, and then stamped over towards them, pointing his finger and shaking it at them.

"Young ladies, get to bed this instant. What are you doing out—"

"Calm him a bit, please." Dharla said.

Briana willed this so.

Ahten stopped, looked around, and seemed to forget what he was about to say.

"More, and them too." Dharla indicated the others approaching as well.

Briana closed her eyes, gave a little humming sound, and waved her hands in little circles in front of herself. Everyone came to a stop, looked around, seemingly curious as to where they were, and why they were there.

"What's that?" Dharla asked.

"What?"

"That hand thing you did."

"It's just something I do, it helps me."

"Oh, I guess that's okay then." Dharla walked up to Ahten and waved her hand in front of his face. He looked at her with a little smile.

She punched him in the face. "Ow, crap, that hurt."

Briana walked up and kneed Ahten in the groin. This seemed to confuse him.

"Is that all you know how to do?" Dharla asked.

"Well what do you suggest?"

"We can't spend all night trying to kick his nuts off. Besides, that stupid robe gets in the way."

"So make him take it off. Let me see you use your ability."

"Punch yourself," Dharla commanded. Ahten took a swing at his own face, but he lacked enthusiasm.

"How about them?" Briana pointed at the others.

"All of you," Dharla cried. "Beat Ahten to death."

The others surged forward, and started punching Ahten. They punched hard, but they got in each other's way, and all though they landed several strong blows, they still lacked the initiative to accomplish much damage.

"Stop."

"Hey!" Briana cried, getting into the spirit. "Make them eat him."

"No, no, that's a good idea, but I think I have a better one. Make them all calm again."

"Done."

"Ahten, sit down."

Ahten tucked up his robe, lowered himself, cross-legged, onto the plateau, and smiled up at the two girls.

"Ahten," Dharla commanded. "Eat your fingers."

A wish I may, a wish I might,
Can I have my wish tonight?
And if I do, because I've spent it,
Can I have it, as I meant it?

– Anonymous doggerel –

# Twenty Six.

*At once, did the angel Uumvault appear to the two brothers and spoke unto Apachawea so that he too might know the gifts of the Father-Spirit, who is the Divine. And Apachawea asked then for the gift of the Shaymin, that is a healer. And the gift was given.*

*Myth of the Revelation*

## 32 Nebut, Y.O.D. 746

### City of Nivska, Torvask, Alasta

As the first rays of the sun brushed the tops of the brick buildings that lined the streets of Nivska, two black carriages rolled through the mist and gloom, each with a single passenger. They passed through the city unnoticed save by the rats. The clatter of hooves and wheels were muted by the steam that rose from the gutters to greet them. That mist, bereft of form, clutched at the curtained windows, peered into the dim interior, and wept against the glass for the man inside.

Today the two men traveled quietly, without fanfare or circumstance to mark their passage, one friend bringing another friend home. In a few days' time they would travel this road again, and the crowds would fill the sidewalks and alleys to curse, cheer, celebrate, lament, and, Cordain thought sadly, to steal and whore, and finally, to see a man burn.

Abruptly the city fell away from view. Long pastures of summer grass dotted with the thick coats of sheep replaced the dark sooty walls of the city. The countryside held such peace and serenity one could almost imagine that there was good in the world. Soon the pastures gave way to orchards of apple trees thick with green fruit. Finally they reached a lane off the main road flanked by tall pines, the roots of which had been spiked with dye, so that the tips of the needles turned bright red near the base, but faded to orange and then to yellow at the crest. The carriages slowed, and turned.

They arrived at a stone fence with a massive wrought iron gate. On either side, gas-fed braziers issued eternal jets of flame fed from pipes that ran far back into the black hills. The gates were pulled aside and the coaches rolled through. On either side stood servants bearing torches, useless in the morning sun, but symbolic, a tribute to the return of their master.

Xavier Whiste's family waited outside their home; his two sons stood quietly, his daughter, only five, sobbed into her mother's shoulder, looked tearfully at the horses, and put her head back into her mother's neck. They were dressed in black, with trim of bright red at the cuffs and hems, the traditional mourning dress of the Whiste family. A servant opened the door of the first carriage, and Cordain Leighland climbed out.

"Cordain, it is good to see you," Dienne said. She curtsied as best she could, while her sons bowed.

Cordain stepped forward and held out his hands to her. "Dienne, I am so sorry for you and your family."

"Xinia, look who's here," Dienne said to her daughter. "It's Uncle Cordain, You remember him don't you?"

"Xinny! Would you like to pet my horses?"

Xinia nodded enthusiastically.

"That's a good girl." Cordain picked her up, and then leaned forward to kiss Dienne on the cheek.

"Thank you," she said "Thank you for returning him."

Cordain looked at the eldest son, Ezekiel, and offered his hand. "I trust you have…"

"I have," the young man said, "thank you for that. We have kept it quiet, as you have asked."

"Good, that is very good. Where is your wife? And new baby I understand? Congratulations."

"Thank you, she is inside resting I am afraid. The birth was difficult, and the healer says she must rest for a few days before she regains her strength."

"And the child?"

"A girl, Jessia, beautiful with the reddest hair you've ever seen."

"Well congratulations again. You must take me to see her." Cordain turned to the younger son. "Zachary, I hope all is well with you."

"Yes, Ra."

"Are your studies coming along then?"

"Yes, Ra, my teachers give me high praise."

"I am sure they do," Cordain patted the young man on the shoulder, but there wasn't much to be said. Zachary was not the eldest; he might covet his brother's ability, as Xavier's brother and sisters had, but there was little else.

Cordain walked over to the head of his carriage and let Xinia pet the horse's nose.

"Where's my daddy?" she asked.

"He's over there." He pointed to the rear carriage where men waited to remove the coffin.

"Can I see him?"

"Oh, darling, no," her mother said.

Cordain looked at Dienne. "It's okay."

"Are you sure? I guess."

Cordain turned back and nodded at the men at the back of the hearse. They opened the doors and pulled out the ornately carved box, leaving the last part still resting on the back. The driver hurried around, and with a little key, unlocked the top portion of the casket and then lifted it open. The man lying inside was dressed in a suit and jacket, the cloth printed in bright red and yellow flames, a symbol of who he was, and what was to come.

"Say goodbye."

"Goodbye daddy." Xinia waved at her father.

"Goodbye my friend," Cordain said. He carried the girl back to her mother. The casket was closed and carried into the house.

"We will pay our respects to your father in a moment," Dienne said to Ezekiel, "Please, take your brother and sister inside."

"Yes, mother."

Cordain and Dienne waited until the children had left. He moved closer to Dienne.

"Don't," she said softly. He paused, offered her his arm, and then escorted her inside.

Cordain looked around his old friend's study. His eyes lingered on the portraits around the room. The ability had been in the family for seven generations, though not consecutively. Out of respect, the portraits of Torovitch and Schumann remained, but the Whistes had eradicated most other traces of those families when they resumed control—save one. The Torovitches had introduced the city of Nivska to the distillation of beer into a wretched whisky known as Vetch, but it was Xavier's grandfather who had discovered the storage shed crammed with old oak casks full of the stuff, and for that, both the powered of Nivska and Cordain were eternally grateful. He raised his glass of the smoky brown liquid to the portraits on the wall and took another sip.

"Ah, I see you've found my father's private bottle," Ezekiel said, entering the room.

"I hope you don't mind." He didn't really care if the boy minded, but he did prefer to be polite.

"Not at all, our home is your home." Ezekiel walked over to his father's desk and poured himself a small taste. "To my father," he toasted.

"Your father," Cordain agreed, and took a sip. "Have you been practicing?"

"Yes, but I tire quickly, and I've not had good results."

"Hmm, well, I guess that's to be expected, perhaps we can fix that, come then." Cordain opened the glass patio doors and led Ezekiel outside onto a broad porch. There stood a small brazier with a coal fire, a pile of faggots, and a table with candles, oil and tapers. Cordain laughed.

"I see you prepared for my visit. Very well, first, I will explain. When you draw upon your ability, you can will it into action, or will it into readiness, but without action." Cordain looked for understanding. "I know that sounds strange, but you can call upon your ability as if you were feeling it, passively. For me, this means I become aware of the earth that I touch, I can sense it; feel its texture, know it, as if it was a part of my body. Try that, call upon your ability, but don't do anything with it, just feel the fire. Can you feel it?"

"Yes, I can," Ezekiel replied.

Xavier had said he could sense the fires that existed within people, and sometimes animals. Cordain understood this, Vellenia claimed to be able to sense the water in people, but he had little luck sensing the earth in them, though he knew it must be there. Perhaps his definition of earth was too specific. In any case, this information would only distract the boy, and was a lesson for another time.

"Now, quiet it, you can feel it feed, will it to be still," the flames before him flickered. "Gently" he said, "don't force it, invite the fire to die, imagine the fuel spent, the embers fading." As he spoke these words, the flames in front of him lowered, hesitated, and then ceased.

"Excellent. Now hold your hand above the brazier." Cordain held out his own hand to demonstrate.

"Feel the heat?" Ezekiel nodded. "Remember, you can be burned, you are not immune from fire, even while your ability is present. Now I'm going to teach you how to make it move." He took a match and struck it against the iron brazier, careful not to ignite the fumes. He touched the match to a taper and shook out the match.

"Now, here's what you do, when you control fire, it consumes its fuel much more rapidly than normal. You encourage this. You make the fire hungry, make it feed and then bend it to your will. Force it to consume the taper all the way down to my fingertips, and then command it to leap from there onto the brazier. Do it."

Ezekiel obeyed, the taper flared, and the fire raced down its length. Then a ball of fire leapt off the stick and lunged for the brazier, but choked off from its fuel, the fire quickly extinguished before it reached the coals.

"Not bad," Cordain said and showed Ezekiel the short stub of wood ending just above his fingertips. "This time, don't make the flame leave the stick, try and get it to arc over, bend the flame, and lick at the coals." He lit another taper, and held it lower, closer to the coals. This time Ezekiel got it right. The wood flared, a tall jet of flame shot up, and then gracefully arced over and touched the coals. Instantly they ignited. Cordain dropped the stick and put his fingers into his mouth.

"Oh, I'm sorry, did I burn you? Let me see?"

"No, it's okay, a little singed, not to worry," Cordain looked at his fingers. They stung, but there were no blisters. He showed them to Ezekiel, who continued to apologize. Cordain waved him to silence.

"Believe me, I've had worse. Okay, now for the hard part, I'm going to add oil to the fire, I need you to calm it; don't let the fire burn the oil, okay?"

"Sure, go ahead" Ezekiel said. Ezekiel spread out his hands, closed his eyes, and then put his fingers to his temples. Cordain smiled, the powered often developed idiosyncratic gestures to help them focus, it was hard not to.

"I'm adding the oil." He poured the liquid into the brazier. At first, the fire flared, but then it subsided. The oil boiled and hissed.

"Now, remember your father's face, imagine your father's head with flaming red hair, dark pools for eyes, white hot teeth and golden skin. Make the fire obey and let it drink."

The results were spectacular. A fireball erupted from the brazier. The heat of it forced them both back. Ezekiel opened his eyes and lost control; the fire ballooned up and singed the roof of the porch above. Coughing from inhaling hot air, Cordain stepped over to Ezekiel and pointed at the roof.

"Could you put that out please?" Ezekiel looked up; a small flame was peeling the paint and spreading. With a thought, the flame quenched.

"Not bad for your first try. You have the form right, but I think you need to keep your eyes open."

"Oh, okay." Ezekiel's voice was soft, uncertain.

"Don't worry, it's a lot to learn, but like anything, you get better with practice." Cordain picked up another flask of oil. "Ready?"

"Ready." Ezekiel spread his hands and then placed his fingers against his temples. He kept his eyes open. Cordain poured the oil. This time the results were much better. The fire burned into the shape of a head. All one could see was the general shape, and two darker spots for eyes. Then, slowly the features became clearer. A nose formed, colors shifted, lighter for skin, darker where hair should be and red again for the mouth. It was still crude, like a child's drawing with colored wax, but still a good start.

"Hold that a little longer," Cordain said. He looked around and found his glass of Vetch, and raised it to the flame.

"To you old friend, I will miss you."

# Twenty Seven.

*Apachawea healed EagleEye. Apachawea healed the sores and aches
of his people. Apachawea became a great man of power, but he denied
the angel Uumvault and proclaimed to all, a falsehood upon his
Divination. And he was believed, and made himself as if a king.*

*Myth of the Revelation*

**35 Nebut, Y.O.D. 746**

## Town of Jedsburg, Southern Colovencia, Nilikas

The stirring breeze carried the smell of drying hay, wild flowers,
and livestock. Two riders guided their horses along a worn dirt
track and smelled the distinct perfume of a country town. Something odd
also was carried on that breeze, something that left a metallic taste in the
mouth. The riders and their horses were covered in a fine layer of dust.
Both horses carried packs and bedrolls and all four looked as if they had
been traveling for an eternity.

The road they followed wound down from a high pass through rocky
barricades; steep forbidding walls that dropped stray stones upon
traveler's heads for their own amusement. The road and river crossed, the
river plunging steeply to the east, the road opting for the safer course
along the edges of the hills to the west. Low rolling hills covered in green,
flecked with brown and white dots spread out below. At the far end of the
valley lay a cancerous growth of gray buildings with rusted tin roofs
scattering the late afternoon sun.

Kim and Kherlos both noted the town in mutual silence. They might
stop there, they might not, and Kim would decide and let Kherlos know
at the appropriate time. Kherlos had never been one to ask pointless
questions, and Kim had never been one to answer them. The two men
had little in common save for a faint dislike of the other and a mutual
goal. They didn't ride together in a comfortable silence, the kind shared by
close friends who can be together and not need to speak, but rather a
thankful silence, each grateful for the lack of conversation.

The town seemed fair enough. It was a mining town. Looking back
up toward the hills one could see the black mouths of deep shafts
scattered among them. There were plenty of people about on the streets.
They had passed a blacksmith shop, stables, a bank and several supply
stores. The town even had enough business for two hotels that sat across

the street from each other. Whether or not they would stop would depend on what Kim saw, or didn't see, or smelled, or didn't smell, or however he decided. Some nights they slept in beds and some nights in bedrolls.

"We will stop here." Kherlos nodded in silence, not in agreement, but simply acknowledging that he had heard.

Kim looked at the two hotels and picked one, possibly at random. They tied up their horses and went inside. It was crowded and noisy. Kim split off to find the proprietor. Kherlos stood near the entrance and looked around, ignored by the people going about their business of drinking, gambling or whoring. He could hear their voices, but didn't understand their words.

Most of the people inside were clean, which meant they weren't the laborers who worked the mines, but the supervisors, managers and professional class. Well-dressed women in pleated skirts and ruffled bodices hung on the arms of a few at the gaming tables or milled about waiting for a customer. The hotel looked passably clean and dignified enough to change the sheets every third patron or so.

Two men began arguing, their voices starting to rise above the din. The crowds quieted, people stared, something was happening. Kherlos followed their eyes, but he already knew what he would see.

Kim was arguing with a tall heavy-set man with tattooed arms. The man repeatedly pointed towards the door as he spoke. There was anger in both men's faces and people started giving them room. Kherlos looked around to see if anyone was taking bets.

Abruptly, Kim backed down, and headed for the door. "We will stay at the other hotel." Kherlos shrugged and followed him. He didn't care what the argument had been about and didn't ask. It was likely Kim would not tell him anyway. The other hotel was directly across the street. They untied their horses, walked them across the road and tied them back up. Kherlos hoped the accommodations would be more to Kim's liking. He didn't relish sleeping outside. As he turned to speak to him, he saw that Kim's attention was focused in the distance. Following his gaze, Kherlos saw a young man look away.

This hotel was much less crowded than its competitor. It had a bar, and tables where people ate and played cards, but lacked the prostitutes and professional gamblers. Kim talked briefly with the man behind the bar, passed over a couple Moons and came back to Kherlos. He handed over one of two room keys.

"Dinner first," Kherlos said, "then a healer."

"I will not be dinning with you tonight, and you don't need a healer."

"We've been over this before."

"We'll see."

"Just tell me the word," Kherlos said.

Kim considered this. "Techa, the word you want is techa. Now wait here. I will be back later."

A man wearing an apron came up to Kherlos and spoke to him. Kherlos smiled and shook his head. The man motioned towards a table and Kherlos sat. The man left, and after a short while, a plain looking woman in a simple brown dress brought out a beer and placed it in front of Kherlos. She spoke, but he only smiled, shrugged, and took a sip of the warm beer. When dinner came, it was some sort of game bird stuffed with brown rice and served with vegetables and buttered bread. Kherlos raised his beer and toasted Kim, then finished in silence. The woman returned, cleared away the pewter plates, and brought a fresh beer. Kherlos touched her sleeve as she turned to leave. When he had her attention, he spoke his word.

"Techa," he said with a polite smile. The woman's face darkened. She pulled her arm away and fled into the kitchen. Almost instantly, the man with the apron returned. He did not look friendly and spoke roughly.

Kherlos smiled, and spread his hands palms upward. The man in the apron motioned for Kherlos to rise and follow. They went to the door. The man pointed across the street to the other hotel and gave Kherlos a gentle nudge in the back.

Kherlos got the joke and started laughing. Kim had tricked him, but he knew another way to get a healer. "No, no, no techa. No techa," Kherlos said. The man grunted, shook his head and walked away. Kherlos walked back toward his table, groaned loudly and sank to his knees, and then rolled to the floor clutching his stomach. For good measure, he even shook a little.

Two men helped him struggle up the steps while the barman opened his room. They laid him gently down onto the bed, and then backed out of the room, making "stay" motions with their hands.

The room was clean but spare. The bed was covered with a brown woolen blanket without any large holes. There was a dresser and a basin, above which hung a mirror. It pleased him that he would be able to get a decent shave in the morning.

§

Two men entered the room, the barkeep, and another, wearing a white shift with a silver moon embroidered over the breast, and tasseled leather wristbands.

"Who is he?" the healer asked.

"Don't know, came in with some cootie from out of town."

"Don't use that word."

"Sorry."

"Tell me what happened."

The barkeep recounted what he knew, which wasn't much.

The healer started with the legs so that there would be no misunderstanding. He summoned his power and directed it at the man's ankles. There was some minor swelling in one ankle, which he soothed. This helped his patient relax a bit, so he waived the barman back. Slowly he worked his way up the legs. They were strong and healthy. Above the right knee, he found the remains of an old wound. A sharp instrument, probably a knife had penetrated there and nicked the thighbone. A small chip of the bone still rested in the healed muscle. It would ache from time to time, but to heal it correctly would require cutting into the thigh and removing the chip. The healer that had done this job had rushed his work, but this was not the cause of his patient's pain.

He gave a perfunctory check of the bladder, penis and testicles, which checked out fine, and moved to the bowels. His patient had moved his bowels recently and had no more than the usual amount of gas. He moved his hands carefully around the patient's sides and lower abdomen. There was no hernia, muscle spasms, no blocked intestines, no sign of any problem. He moved to organs. The liver was in good shape, the man was not a heavy drinker. The kidneys gave no indication of trouble; there were no stones.

"You say he fell off his chair."

"No, walking back from the door." The healer gave a quizzical look.

"He was asking for a whore, I pointed him across the street. He thought it was funny and changed his mind, I guess. Then he fell to the floor and started shaking."

"Did he hit his head?" He examined Kherlos's scalp.

"Nope, he sort of sank to his knees."

The healer put his hands onto Kherlos's knees and let his power examine the skin. He found the slight irritation of the skin he had missed while concentrating on the bones and ligaments. Returning his attention to his patient's midsection, he began to gently poke and massage Kherlos's stomach. Finally, he poked his forefinger deep into Kherlos's side. Kherlos yelped in surprise.

"We'll talk outside."

"What's going on you think?"

"Outside, I'm done here."

§

It was never hard to find home. Kim walked the dusty streets seemingly at random, but in truth, he simply followed the signs. Little marks, little symbols, woven into the daily fabric of any moderately sized city, made by his fellow countrymen so his kind would know where they could find solace and sanctuary. Even without the marks, he could have found his way by the smell alone. The fragrant spices of his native cooking saturated the air in the narrow alleys between the closely packed shacks that littered the ground.

Kim walked up to the first door he saw and knocked. A little girl opened the door and looked up at him with dark brown eyes. She wore a simple gray shirt and trousers; patched and worn, around her waist was an orange streaked apron. The little girl's fingertips bore the same tint of color, the mark of a spice grinder.

"Who is there?" called an older woman's voice from inside.

"Mama, it is a friend," the girl replied, and bowed low. The girl's mother came into view, bowed respectfully. Kim bowed back.

"Go, now."

The girl disappeared. The woman bowed again and motioned for Kim to follow. She led him to a tiny room with a low round table of plain wood. Kim pulled a quarter-moon stool out from under the table and sat. The girl returned with a porcelain bowl of hot broth and placed it in front of him, and a pewter plate of pungent fish soon followed. The two women watched as he ate from a polite distance.

Kim ate quickly, enjoying the familiar flavors of home, and took in the surroundings. In one corner stood a small but dignified statue of the Divine, a bowl of oil burning slowly through a slender wick. A stylized sketch of a craggy mountain on handmade paper hung from a rod next to the shrine. The rest of the walls were given over to shelving, which held jars of pickled vegetables, fruits and fish, wooden bowls, tins of oil and a dark wooden box, which bore the pictogram for a game of tiles. Kim completed his accounting of the family's belongings, and closed his eyes to listen. He could hear the grinding of Caymen spice—the preservative in the fish—and hear the soft whispers of two females and one male. He could also hear feet approaching from outside, those of two people walking quickly.

The woman spoke as her husband entered the room. "Friend, my mother has asked to be entertained. My husband will assist you."

"Thank you, I am honored. I will mention your kindness."

"This way, please," the man said.

Kim followed his guide back out into the street and then immediately into a narrow space between two houses. The path shifted and twisted between buildings and dead-ended at a door, which his guide opened and entered. They walked through the home, past a room where many people were seated around a large table, eating and talking all at the same time, and through another door that exited back out into the night. Finally, they arrived at another featureless, unmarked door, which his guide opened and held. "Please."

Kim entered into a narrow hallway. The inside contrasted starkly with the plain exterior. The walls were paneled in a deep rust hardwood; painted tapestries hung on the walls, depicting scenes of the Divine and the twelve forbidden wishes. Small oil lamps cleverly placed in hidden niches provided ambient light. There were multiple doors along the hallway. They were all closed save one at the far end.

"Welcome friend," an ancient voice called, "please enter and introduce yourself."

Kim followed the voice, and discovered an old woman wearing a bright green robe with yellow brocade down the center and on the hem, seated in a high-backed chair, with several men squatting on low stools around her, but in much plainer, coarse clothing, that spoke of hard times.

"Greetings Mother," Kim said with a low formal bow. "May all your children prosper."

"Thank you young man, please tell us who you are and of your travels. Do I hear in your voice that you are from the South?"

"Yes, Mother," Kim bowed low again, then straightened and stood proud so that they might know the truth of his words, "I am Kim."

The others in the room stood then, and bowed, as was their duty. The eldest remained sitting, as was her right. It was the normal custom for travelers to accept the hospitality of the community in exchange for gossip and labor. You were family, certainly, but on which side and by what linage? These things take time to sort out, until then you were

248

housed and fed, and in return you became the personal slave of the eldest until your debt was paid off, but first, you answered questions, that is, unless you were Kim.

"Bring tea. Come, Kim, let me look at you then." The old woman cupped her hand underneath Kim's chin and turned his head back and forth. She wanted to see if his face held the marks of honesty and courage, and to check closely the signs of his birth and parentage. Old men wanted to know that your arms were strong, that your back was straight, and that your form and technique were clean. Old women wanted to know who your mother was, and if you honored her well. So it always was with his people, so it always would be.

"We are troubled here, my sons are maltreated. How will you help this?" she asked.

"I will speak with my brothers, I will not be here long, but they may come and be of service."

"May come?" the woman asked, reproachfully.

"Will come," Kim corrected himself.

"You will not stay then?"

"I am sorry, my time is not my own." This meant he was under contract or obligation. It excused him from yielding to this woman's wishes.

They served tea. Kim waited until the old woman sipped, then he sipped, then the others sipped.

"Your tea is strong and bold; it gives strength like the mountains of your home."

"You have a pretty tongue," she said, "You honor your mother well. It is sad that you cannot tarry on your travels. We will miss your voice amongst us. It would please us if you were to return here upon your leisure."

"I would be honored to sit at your feet and spin glorious tales of your son's adventures."

"Yes, well, we shall see. Our FarSpeaker's partner is in Tzusan, if I read your intentions correctly."

"You do, Mother."

"Then I shall retire. These men shall see to your needs, such as our meager stores may provide. May your industry be rewarded," she said. A young girl appeared at her side and helped her down from the chair.

"May your children prosper," Kim replied. The occupants of the room bowed as the old woman was helped away.

When she was gone, Kim turned to the eldest male. "Stupidity and bigotry sprout here like gnarlweed."

"So you have talked with locals then. Perhaps you know of an ability that will become available soon?" Eyes brightened around the room at this suggestion. They had little to be happy for; Kim was not their savior and would only strain their already thin resources.

"Sadly that is not the case, my duty this time does not involve separating a soul from its connection to the Divine." The men looked away, disappointed.

"Are there abilities here I should liberate?"

"None to speak of or we'd of sorted matters out for ourselves," the eldest said. Kim nodded; the bullied usually found the simplest solution.

"I will speak with my brothers then. FarSpeaker, is your partner listening?" The man bowed to Kim.

"No, I am sorry Master Kim; we will listen for each other in about two hours."

Kim nodded and took a sip of tea. It was to be expected. "Tiles anyone?"

§

The results of his meeting were mixed. The families could only supply dried meats and some tobacco. This they packed into a worn saddlebag. They had no money to loan. Their FarSpeaker had been hard of hearing, and conversing with home had been tedious, but there the news had been better. His village would send four of his cousins to this backwards excuse of a town and teach that equality and respect for each other is truly the will of the Divine.

Good news had come from his sister. She had born a son, and honored Kim by giving the boy his own birth name of Shin-Cho. If Kim's career proves to be long and prosperous, Shin-Cho would receive much honor, and favored chances at becoming Kim himself one day. It was a strong vote of confidence for him at a time when the elders were not fully pleased with his actions.

Time passed and the evening grew long. They were eager for gossip and stories and he was less than eager to return to Kherlos. No doubt, he could have stayed the night or the week and bedded many beautiful women. But the longer he stayed, the more egregious the mess Kherlos would make. In the end, he settled for walking back to his hotel late into the evening.

The streets were dark and deserted. The moon was neither high nor full, there was light enough to navigate, and shadows deep enough to conceal. Most windows along the narrow street were dark and shuttered, a few let loose a stray beam of weak lamp glow, but the dark swallowed them with an easy contempt. It was a perfect night for trouble and Kim was delighted to have found some.

Two men had picked up Kim's trail and were following him along the street. The men behind him were decoys, meant to spook him and distract him from the real threat. They were clumsy and stupid. They whispered and guffawed while casually keeping pace with him, making sure he knew he was their mark. They were supposed to be acting drunk; instead, they really were drunk. This tempered Kim's enthusiasm. Dealing with them would be little more than spanking children. If he was lucky, the person, or persons waiting in ambush would be more of a challenge, but he had his doubts.

There came a short snort of laughter from the two men behind Kim, one slapped the other on the back. This was their cue. Kim stopped and turned to look at them. They grinned and started forward as if to give chase. Kim was supposed to flee. The two men were so certain he would flee, that they didn't even bother to notice that he in fact, had not. They made a mock lunge, and that was all. When Kim failed to turn and run, they thought this was funny.

"Run you little man," one said, "and we'll give you a head start."

The other man looked over Kim's head, letting him know that the rest of the gang was in place.

Kim counted the footsteps of two men coming up behind him.

"That bag appears a might heavy for you, cootie. Perhaps we should help lighten that burdensome." The voice had come from over his left shoulder

"Yes, I agree," Kim said. He turned around to face the new assailants, picked the bag off his shoulder and threw it at the man on his left. The hands of the two men behind him had been empty. The hands of the man catching the bag were also empty. This left assailant number four; he had his left hand out and his right hand slightly back, hidden. Kim shifted his weight and thrust his left foot out at the head of the man who he now considered the leader. The foot missed. It had been meant to miss.

"Watch out Slim, this cootie knows some chop-chop." The voice came from behind on his right, and Slim's eyes briefly flicked to the man who had spoken. This betrayal of intention made Kim consider closing his eyes and fighting blind, just for practice's sake. Instead, he rocked slightly and drove his right elbow backwards into a man's stomach. He had been aiming for the solar plexus but had struck low. His teachers would have given him marks off for the mistake, and while he too was disappointed with his own error, it had however had been sufficient to the task, as the man collapsed behind him.

The man they called Slim brought the knife around from behind his back and drove the point towards Kim's side. He wasn't even holding it correctly, it probably wasn't sharp, or even particularly good steel. Kim faded his right leg from view, shifted his weight forward onto his left, and then drove the ball of his right foot into Slim's groin.

The knife dropped. Slim dropped.

Two down, two up, one in front, one behind; he took a quick glance back, turned and drove his right heel up into the jaw of the man behind and popped him up into the air. He reached forward, and caught the saddlebag as it fell, put it over his shoulder and turned back towards the final assailant. "Your turn."

"I have no fear of you," the man said. This actually impressed Kim; he looked down at the knife lying on the ground. He pushed it towards the man with his foot, and took a step back.

"My brothers will be here in three days."

"I have no fear of them either."

The man he had elbowed was recovering, but hiding it, hoping to spring up at Kim from the side. Kim snapped a sidekick off into the man's jaw, sending teeth and blood flying.

"Stay," Kim said.

"I assure you, that I and my friends, will kill you little cootie."

"That is fine, I have four brothers coming, but I am leaving. You fetch your friends and your brothers, and fight with my brothers. If you win, then they deserved to die for being weak, I will not come back for revenge."

"I sure wish I had the ability to kill little fuckers like you," the man said.

"Don't we all," Kim replied, and walked away. He was disappointed with the fight. He had missed with one blow, and wasn't sure that using his power to make his leg invisible had made any difference in delivering the kick to the groin. In the end, he concluded the exercise had been worthwhile but it had not improved his mood. When he arrived at the hotel, the manager was waiting for him.

"Your friend called for a healer," the man said, "but I don't think he was sick. Mo Pearson, that's the healer in this town, came down muttering and speaking ill of your friend, said he was soaping the bacon."

"Yes, he does that. I try to discourage him, yet he always seems to find a way. You say he called, I did not teach him the word for healer. He does not speak this language."

"Well, I wasn't here at the time, so I don't know what happened; I'm supposed to let you know that it would be best if you were to move on in the morning." Kim nodded at this request.

"Yes," he said. "It would be best."

# Twenty Eight.

*Therefore, it was that the message of the Gifts of the Spirit-Father,
who is the Divine, again was withheld from the knowledge of men.
But Uumvault had the patience of the Angels, for the Revelation had
been foretold, and he was the Herald.*

*Myth of the Revelation*

**4 Shabin, Y.O.D. 746**

## Blazer-Canter Farm, Colovencia, Nilakas

Derek sat on the back porch of his home and looked out over the
long rows of corn waving gently in the fragrant spring breeze.
The warm sunlight and cool air made a perfect combination for an
afternoon nap. It was days like this that made him appreciate owning a
country home. Technically, he only lived there, Clea owned the property,
but that was a minor issue. Running a farm was a lot of work; fortunately,
he had a competent man doing it. The point was that it was a good time
and a good place for an afternoon nap, and he had better get started. If
you want something done right, his father had always told him, you had to
do it yourself, and Derek definitely wanted this nap done right. The back
of the chair was set back to the fourth peg, exactly the correct position for
comfort. The chair was positioned to put his head in the shade of the
porch, which would continue to lengthen over his body, giving him
maximum exposure before any chill could creep in. He had his favorite
pillow behind his head, and a glass of sweetened tea on the table within
easy reach.

Derek closed his eyes and relaxed. Jarod coughed lightly from the
door, to announce his presence.

"Yes," Derek asked, not opening his eyes.

"There are two gentlemen to see you sir."

"Send them away."

"Very good, sir." Jarod left, Derek started to relax, and then heard his
servant's footsteps return.

"They are quite insistent sir; they say they have traveled many weeks
to find you."

Derek sighed, opened his eyes and sat up. "Did you get their names?" Derek of course knew that Jarod had gotten their names, but he couldn't help but ask.

"A Mr. Kim and A Mr. Timèatteo I believe were the gentlemen's names. I showed them into your library and had their horses placed in our stables. Do you expect them to be staying for dinner?"

"I was expecting them to not stay at all, Kherlos Timèatteo did you say?"

"I cannot say sir, only Mr. Kim spoke, and he did not offer further information."

"Must be his brother then," Derek mused, "Kherlos is dead."

"If you say so sir. Should I send them away again?"

"No, no," Derek came back into focus and rose from his chair. "Do we still have ice?"

"No, sir, I am afraid I have instructions to tell you we are out until the next delivery," Jarod waited. Derek gave him a knowing look. It would do no good to argue.

"Fine then, would you please bring us some cheese and bread, and a bottle of Andoline red?"

"Of course, sir."

Derek found the men looking at his moderate collection of books. "Gentlemen? Which of you is Mr. Timèatteo?"

Kim strode forward and nodded slightly. "My most humble apologies. I am Kim; this is my friend and traveling companion, Kherlos Timèatteo." Kim let his words hang in the air. At the mention of his name, Kherlos nodded in Derek's direction but then resumed his perusal of the shelves

"Horseshit," Derek said.

"I am sorry?"

"You heard me. Kherlos Timèatteo is dead. I am sorry if you didn't know this, but I am certain of it. This man is an imposter."

"I assure you, this is the man who was formally able to shoot beams from his eyes of death."

"I believe it was the other way around," Derek said.

Jarod entered with his tray of food, glasses and a bottle of wine. He set the tray down, uncorked the wine and poured them each a glass.

"Gentlemen, please, sit, doesn't Kherlos speak Colovencia?" Derek asked.

Kim spoke quickly to Kherlos and the two of them pulled chairs up to the table. Derek took his seat at the other end.

"No, and that is a blessing, but never mind, yes, beams of death from his eyes. This is Ra-ken Kherlos Timèatteo."

Kherlos heard his name, pointed to his eyes, and thumped his chest.

"Thank you Jarod," Derek said.

"Excuse me sir," Jarod replied, "Should I instruct Master Liam to wish for your ability?"

"No, Jarod, but thank you for asking. I don't think I will be dying just yet."

"Very good." Jarod bowed, first to Derek, then to the other men, and backed out of the room. Kherlos started nibbling on the cheese, sampled the wine, and then raised his glass to Derek.

"I have eaten, thank you," Kim said. "May I inquire as to the nature of your gift?"

"I have the ability to make people talkative." He watched for Kim's reaction, some trace of amusement.

"Interesting, I suppose that would make sense given your occupation. If you don't mind, I would prefer to leave away the demonstration."

"As you wish," Derek replied. "But, speaking of which, if this is Kherlos, as you suggest, perhaps a simple demonstration might be in order?"

"He can't" Kim replied. "He no longer has his power."

"Really, that's very interesting. Has he come here looking for it?" Derek looked around the room furtively. "Well, sorry, I don't think I have any beams of death here, at the moment anyway."

Kim shook his head. "You do know who does have his power though. We know you met him."

"Yes, as a matter of fact, I do know who currently has the power of beams of death, and it isn't Kherlos any longer, which means Kherlos is dead. I don't know what kind of poke you might be selling here, but I'm not making a purchase."

Kherlos tapped Kim on the arm. The two spoke back and forth for a few moments.

"Kherlos wishes to convince in his own words, with me translating," Kim said in answer to Derek's unspoken look of concern.

"He's welcome to try," Derek said.

Kherlos spoke, Kim translated. "The council sent an assassin against me. This was almost a full year ago now. The assassin failed, but it was only through sheer stupid luck that this happened, and no indication at all of incompetence on the part of my brother. After this…failure, the council sent Cordain Leighland, the Master of Earth against me. Cordain brought a well-trained army that knew how to protect themselves against my powers."

Derek raised his eyebrows, asking the obvious question.

"Yes, it's true, there are ways to block my powers, we were once friends. Together we defeated the Butcher, and I acquired the eyes that kill. Then, we both shared a dream of using it for the good of people instead of enslaving them. I founded the city of Kherlestra on North Seleton. I invited people to come live with me, who wished to live free from crime, jealousy, heresy, and the vile corruption that is your Council Ra-ken. Kherlestra flourished and grew under my guidance. My people were happy and we had none of the filth that pervades all other cities."

"Why did Ra Leighland come to kill you then, if he helped set you up in the first place?" Derek conceded, at least for the moment, the possibility of truth in the story.

"Cordain knew he could not stop the Council from defeating me, all he could do was to save lives. He is a strange man, he believes we are all equal, ken and non, alike. He came to offer me a chance to commit suicide, that my city might be saved, and that my people could carry on in my name."

"But?"

"Much happened, but in the end I knew I was defeated. I offered to allow my ability to be removed, to spare my city and my people."

"But you're not dead."

"We're getting to that," Kim replied.

"I made a deal with Cordain; I would relinquish my power if Cordain would spare my people. I knew that even if I won that battle, more would come, and eventually my people and I would be overwhelmed. In the end I sacrificed my power in the hope that I could convince the new owner to take over what I had started."

"That's very noble of you, but aren't you leaving something out?"

"Do you know of the Master of Abilities?" Kim asked.

"Yes, Mo-ken Jessa…wait…Millote. That's it. I remember some controversy over her. I heard she had escaped from the clergy."

"Not exactly, she removed her own power. Another woman claimed it and moved south with Kherlos."

Derek hadn't heard this, and it was newsworthy all by itself. He would press them for more details later. "I have heard that people who lose their abilities don't do well."

"So I am learning," Kim replied, "but so far he is managing. He does keep seeking healers though."

"Does that help?"

"No."

"What is it you want?" Derek felt it was time to call their bluff and end this game.

"We want to hire you as a guide."

"You want me to hire you as a guide to where?"

"No, you will guide us? We will pay you."

"I'm confused. I don't know where anything is."

"We are seeking to return Kherlos's power."

"I'm not going to help you find Seth," Derek replied.

"We do not expect you to help us kill this 'Seth', only to help us find him."

Before Derek could protest, Clea knocked and entered. "Jarod said something about checking to see if you were still alive, and something about dinner."

"These gentlemen were just leaving."

"We would be delighted to stay for dinner," Kim replied

"Then it's settled," Clea said, "I'll have Jarod set you up with rooms and a bath. I'm sure you gentlemen are in need of refreshment."

"You are most kind."

"Not at all, please, this is Meary, my housekeeper's daughter; she will show you gentlemen to your rooms."

Kim looked to Derek for confirmation.

"Yes," Derek poured himself another glass of wine, "Kherlos, Kim, I'll see you both at dinner."

§

"Are you Ra-ken?" Liam blurted out almost as soon as the meal of roasted pheasant, corn, peas, fresh bread, and potatoes from the farm had been served.

"Liam, mind your manners," Clea said, "forgive him, he's wound up about carnival and is excited about seeing Ra-ken."

"I don't blame him," Kim said, "I'm very interested to see someone myself."

"I take it your friend does not speak Colovencia?" Clea asked, nodding at Kherlos who was wolfing down the meal.

Kim looked at Kherlos. *"Manners."* He then replied to Clea. "No, he does not."

"Will you be staying until Carnival? Is that where you're headed?"

"I am not familiar, what is Carnival?"

Clea hushed her son, and then answered for him. "Once a year, but in a different city, the Council call for Carnival, a kind of weeklong celebration, and those who are touched by the Divine, are allowed to freely demonstrate their powers.".

"Please, explain."

"This year it's being held in Andoline. It's almost upon us now, which is why Liam is so excited. It's one big fair really, merchants come from all over the Unified Territories, often members of the Council Ra-ken demonstrate their abilities, and that's what has Liam all excited."

Kim looked at Liam, who was almost bouncing in his seat.

"I will show you something amazing." He held up a single Sun coin in his left hand, held with his thumb and index finger. He grabbed the coin in his right hand, and then put his closed fist in front of the boy's face. "Blow on it."

Liam blew on the hand and Kim unfurled his fingers to show that it was empty. Kim then reached out and tugged on the boy's ear. He brought his hand back and revealed the coin. It was an ancient trick, invented, perfected and passed on secretly from generation to generation from a time long before abilities had been discovered.

"Did you steal that from my daddy?"

"No," Kim said, "I pulled it out of your ear."

"My daddy says that there is a woman who steals money from other people by pulling it out of her nose."

"No, it was mine; I showed it to you first."

Kherlos nudged Kim; Kim related the incident.

"Here," Derek said, and handed Kim a beaten copper coin. It had been pounded thin and given a fluted edge.

"What is this?"

Kherlos looked at the coin and began to laugh.

"He understands," Clea said.

"It's for that woman," Liam exclaimed, "to make her nose hurt."

"The woman with the ability to sneeze money from her nose has become well known in Andoline," Derek said, "people have taken to carrying coins that will cause considerable pain in an effort to discourage her particular brand of larceny."

"You would think she could select which coins to extract, some translocation powers give the owner the opportunity to think about the act before hand," Kim said, and then translated for Kherlos before he could be nudged again.

"I haven't heard exactly, but that's not a subtlety we'd want her to learn."

*"I have a story,"* Kherlos said, *"translate."*

"Kherlos says he has a story. Would you all care to hear it?"

They all agreed, and so Kherlos began his tale.

"I have heard a story, told to me as a boy, of a man who could urinate gold. People did not know where the gold came from. They thought that the Divine created the gold because it matched the color of urine, but the ability was difficult to control. Sometimes his power worked well, sometimes not at all. The man lived in a poor fishing village, near the mouth of a river that emptied into the sea. They knew how to fish, but not how to sail, so they traded smoked fish, and sometimes, blue polished rocks that washed down from the mountain each spring. They had no gold of their own, so even the little amounts he made were treasured, and carefully hoarded for when the traders came with their axes, pans, and other items of metal.

"The man came to learn that his ability worked better the closer he was to the river, but that he had to keep moving around, for if he tried his ability too many times in one place, it stopped working again. In this way, he learned to travel up river carrying three water skins. He would drink the water as he walked, and then urinate into each empty skin. When he returned the skins would be drained and would be full of fine flakes of gold. This worked very well, and the village prospered, but each time, he would have to travel further and further.

"One day the man came back, after many days of being away. He could barely walk, and was in much pain, and had none of the water skins with him."

"'Where is the gold?' the people asked. 'Were you robbed?' 'No,' replied the man, 'I have no use for them, because I can't pee anymore.' And it was true, with or without his ability, he could produce no more urine, and he was in great pain because of that.

"Why didn't they heal him?" Liam asked.

"This was before we knew how to let many people share an ability," Kim said.

"Each day," Kherlos continued, "his pain got worse and on the third day, the man died, but no one wished for the ability, because they were all afraid. For two more days, the elders and his family argued if they should bury him whole or cut him open. Finally, the elders sent for a surgeon, who came and cut open the man's bladder. When he did, a fistful of gold nuggets fell out. They kept the gold, for they were a practical people, but no one has ever had the courage to wish for that ability again."

"That's funny," Liam said.

"Thank you for that story, I think," Clea said, "Liam dear, it's time for your bath." Liam made a sad face. "Don't pout at me young man, say good night and thank Mr. Kim for showing you his trick." Liam got up from his chair.

"Thank you Mr. Kim, Thank you Mr. Kherlos."

"You're most welcome," Kim said. Kherlos smiled and nodded at the boy. Liam slouched out of the room and then broke into a run. They heard his feet pound up the stairs.

"You should go to Carnival," Derek said, "the man you seek might be there."

"You would meet us there, and make introductions?"

"Of course we would," Clea said, "I understand you will not be staying with us long?"

"I am afraid we must move on. I have obligations in Andoline, and I feel we might wear out our welcome."

"Nonsense," Clea said.

"That is such a shame," Derek said.

This earned him a steely look from his wife. "My husband works for the Andoline Herald, which prints some pamphlets. You may leave word for us there on how to contact you."

"That would be most excellent," Kim said.

# Twenty Nine.

*Then, in his thirty-seventh year, resplendent and comfortable with his second wife and many children, Apachawea had occasion to visit upon the site of his divination, and to recount the true and accurate story to his family of the matter of how he became a Man of Power.*

*Myth of the Revelation*

**12 Shabin, Y.O.D. 746**

## City of Vesport, Tameria

The Ve Donduan sat at anchor among a dozen or more other ships, in a harbor dug deep by glacier fed rivers, resting a harpoon's throw short of its destination. For three days it had tarried here, waiting to be lashed to the docks and its cargo unloaded.

In three days, weather and fair winds permitting, the Pristine Ray would sail out of the only berth long enough to accommodate another of the newest ships to ply the Colovencia trade, and then, with the Harbor Captain at the helm, tenders would come and tow the ship in. All of this was well known and understood by all parties involved save one, and that one, like the sea herself, was a bitch.

"You are telling me I cannot leave this wretched, vermin-infested ship for three more days?" In fact, Vellenia had gotten quite skilled at killing rats over the first week of the voyage, but it so unnerved the crew to find the dehydrated bodies that the captain had eventually asked her to stop.

"No, Lady, I would not dare, you are free to leave at any time," Captain Epstein said.

"Do you expect me and my charge to just walk across the water to the docks?" Vellenia asked, and saw the question in his face.

"Yes, in fact, I could, but that is not how Ra-ken behave. Indeed, even if that was my design, my ward is blind and could not scale the ladder, or have you forgotten the level of the sea."

"No, lady."

"Would you have me raise up the seas until they flowed over their banks so that I might stroll across them to shore?"

"No, Lady, I know that you are not destructive or cruel."

"Well I won't be tendered in some open longboat, and be forced to climb up some slimy ladder, am I clear?"

"Yes, Lady, but it cannot be helped. I have bribed the officials and even sent word to the palace, but it is the longshoremen who hold us all hostages here."

"Who are these longshoremen, and why can't they be beaten then."

"They load and unload the ships, and it is their captain, blessed by the Divine who orders his men, and he will not budge."

"You told him who I was."

"I did, your Lady."

"And he still refused."

"He did, my Lady, in so many words."

"Well then captain, if I am stuck here, then so are you. If you value the blood in your veins you will not step foot off this ship before I do." Vellenia raised her eyebrows to ask if he understood.

"Yes, my Lady."

Vellenia stomped back to her tiny cabin where Seth lay on the single bed, his nurse Tabitha sat at his feet, reading aloud softly. When she entered, Tabitha stopped and stood.

"Three more days," Vellenia spat.

"Don't they know who you are?" Seth asked.

Vellenia looked at the poor boy with sympathy and pity. He had hardly spoken to her at all during the trip and she didn't blame him. He didn't seem to harbor resentment, only sadness. The nurse she had hired to accompany them had grown quite close to Seth, and she had encouraged her to become his lover as well.

"Yes," she said, "and no. Your situation is an embarrassment to the council, no offense, but because of that, I'm not officially traveling as the Duchess of Imtroud. Am I boring you?"

"No," Seth replied, "I find your politics fascinating."

"It means there is no official welcome from the Mayor, or anyone else for that matter, so there is no band to play for us as we disembark, and the ship has no priority in the port, so we sit on our asses and wait."

§

From Vellenia's point of view at the rail, it was not clear that either side had the advantage. It was all she, Seth and Tabitha could do to keep from falling as the ship lurched. Around them men struggled with massive rope and winches, but all their effort did not seem to tame the ship, but rather to enrage it only further. The captain watched the struggle from his vantage above with calm detachment. Slowly, with the steady application of cunning the ship was brought to heel and secured against the bulwarks of the Vesport pier. Men appeared from nowhere and started moving the gangplank into position.

The captain descended the rail and approached Vellenia. "It will be but another moment of your time and you will be rid of me, my lady."

"Thank you, captain, you are most kind." She said this with no trace of irony in her voice, but her face made her true feelings quite clear.

Three men stood waiting to board at the pier. They dressed in dark gray pants with matching jackets over white shirts with large frilled sleeves and collars, the universal dress of civil servants. The one with the most elaborate frills was clearly most senior. When the walkway was in place, he started up with his subordinates in tow. "Permission to come aboard Captain."

"Ah Mikael, good to see you, come aboard. My guests are anxious to depart."

The men came up, and the Captain clasped hands with them affectionately.

"Well, we mustn't keep them waiting any longer." The customs official turned to Vellenia. "Lady, may I check your visas?"

Vellenia thrust out the documents. Mikael took them, studied them carefully and then passed them to his subordinates who also made a great show of reading them diligently. "I see only papers for two of you," Mikael said, "but none for this unfortunate young man?" He indicated Seth.

"He is a citizen of Vesport," Vellenia said.

"Is he? May I see his documents please."

"I don't have any," Seth said.

"I'm sorry?"

"He doesn't have papers, you fool."

"Oh dear, this is most irregular. Of course, my lady you and your nurse are quite welcome to come ashore, but I'm afraid—"

"Afraid what?"

"Well," he said, raising himself up slightly, "That he can't come ashore without official papers."

"Are you aware, of who I am?"

"Yes, my lady, quite aware."

"Then you have no authority over me, do you?"

"Lady, I am acting on the authority of—" He stopped. Vellenia's face was covered with fine spidery lines that shifted and swirled underneath her skin, but she seemed completely unaware of them.

"Very well everything seems in order I see no reason to hold you any longer." He snatched their papers from his subordinates and thrust them back at Vellenia.

"Much better," she said, and then, addressing the captain, "May we leave now?"

"As you wish."

Vellenia led the way down onto the end of a long pier jutting out from the main road. This was relatively un-crowded; men and wagons moved back and forth, hauling a seemingly endless supply of barrels out of one ship, while at the same time moving an almost identical load into another. The street however, was a different matter. Traffic surged in both directions chaotically, with no regards for courtesy, decency, or safety.

"Damn," Vellenia swore, "I don't see our carriage." Seth's nurse looked about. They were to have been met by official carriages of the Mayor. They were to be his guests this evening. Vellenia started towards the road, dodging people, animals and obstacles as she went. Seth and his guide followed as best they could. They caught up with her at the street that ran along the wharf.

"This will never do, we can't wander back and forth like blind beggars, here, give me your hand." Vellenia grabbed the girl's wrist and assayed her water. Seth apparently liked the young lady, and his cooperation was possibly dependant upon her continued presence. She could not arbitrarily kill the girl, at least not in front of Seth. She pulled the water out the girl's bladder. It wasn't enough for her purposes, but there was ample water nearby. The girl gasped as the water flowed out of her body, across her skin and into Vellenia's hand.

"I've not killed you," she said, "I just needed a little bit." Seth turned towards Vellenia, his body tense.

"I'm alright," Tabitha said, "it startled me. That's all."

Vellenia concentrated and made a thin thread of the water she had taken. The thread arced away from her hand down onto the boards of the pier. There was a great sucking sound. The pier and the connected boardwalk shuddered. Traffic around them didn't pause for a second. Vellenia smiled; it would clear soon enough.

A great wet hand reached up and slapped itself down on the embankment next to the road. Spray flew from where it landed, wetting the people nearby. No one seemed to notice other than those who were splashed, and they barely registered even that. A second hand reached up and joined the first, and then a giant watery head pulled itself up and surveyed the scene. It was a crude work with a giant slash of a mouth and bulging eyes. It lacked the finesse and detail one would associate with a seasoned master of the ability to shape water, it looked like a tooth-knocker drawn by a child come to life. It was effective however.

Traffic around it came to an abrupt stop. The beast pulled up massive haunches and shambled into the road. There it turned, swinging its massive arms back and forth to clear a path. Vellenia smiled, pleased with herself and her creation. The thin line of water that connected her to the beast thickened and became a leash. A studded collar took shape around its thick neck. People close to the beast struggled to get away while curious onlookers fought to get a better view.

She couldn't really march the beast up and down the docks looking for her carriage; her power would tire her quickly controlling this much water. She considered her options. She could have the creature shamble back into the sea, or let it dissolve, possibly even turn it into a wave and have it wash people away. She was distracted from her thoughts by yelps of pain coming from the onlookers.

A slender woman wearing an ornate silk dress appeared and examined Vellenia's creation.

"Crude," the woman observed, "I heard you could do much better than this."

"Who are you?"

The woman ignored her.

Vellenia had a thought. The water responded and flowed. The mouth grew teeth, then fangs, long pointed shafts of water protruding outward at bizarre angles. A face formed, eyes pulled back and nestled under a bulging forehead. Spikes extruded from the spine, toes and fingers grew claws, muscles took on definition and a long tail pulled itself out of the creature's backside. The new beast shook, and a fine mist of water droplets flew off. It snarled, and lowered its head, mouth agape, to bite this foolish woman.

"Perfect." Reaching up the woman touched the menacing figure on its face. Instantly a transformation began. A shock wave pulsed away from point of contact, raced through its head, down the neck, through its body and ending at the tips of its extremities. The water turned crystalline solid, frozen. The transformation from water to ice consumed the creature and moved down the leash of water towards Vellenia's hand. Vellenia released her power and broke the link before the ice could reach her. The woman pulled her hand free of the creature's face and turned.

"Hello Vellenia," she said, "there were rumors that you were in town."

"Hello Le Le, you can't trust rumors."

"True, but I think I can trust this one. I also heard you intend on meeting with the mayor."

"I might."

"Well, a girl could get a lift?"

§

They sat at a long dining table, capable of seating at least forty guests. Le Le, Vellenia and the Mayor Johan sat at one end, and Seth at the other. Tabitha sat next to Seth, helping him eat. She did not officially sit at the table, but was allowed to taste Seth's food, to make certain it was of a palatable temperature.

Johan focused his attention on the two lovely women dining at his end. "The situation on the mountain is grave, grave indeed, I can't stress enough how nervous this makes me."

"Johan," Vellenia said, "you know how important this project is to me personally. That's why I'm here. It's clear Ahten was not quite the capable administrator we thought that he should be."

"Clearly."

"Yes, clearly, we are after all, still human in addition to whatever other gifts we may possess. The point is, we move forward. I believe deeply in this project. I'm not just saying that."

"Well what assurances can you give me? You told me there would be no risk, yet here I sit with beams of death eating at my table with his eyes torn out."

"Please, some sympathy for the young man, he's been through quite an ordeal."

"Ordeal or not, he is completely unable to defend himself, how can he protect his ability from predators? How can you protect his ability or that of any of the others?"

"That's where I come in Mayor," Le Le said, "I have many years of experience as the head of security for Tse Le.

The mayor let his face explain what he thought of Le Le's experience. "Aren't you on their list?"

"Le Le turned out to be sympathetic to our cause."

"I don't own any lands or titles, is what she means."

The mayor pretended not to hear this insult.

"Some people choose to see this struggle in the baser frame of financial gain," Vellenia explained. "They claim the council is making a 'land grab'. Foolish prattling is really all that is, a caretaker is appointed, much like you, to steward the lands held by the fallen."

"I see," he said, glancing over at Seth.

"Seth is well aware of his rights and claims over Kherlestra, aren't you Seth?"

"Yes, Vellenia," Seth answered, "I am aware."

"He's hardly in any shape to make that claim stick."

"Nor are any of the other children who have heired here," Vellenia snapped, "The point of this project was not to change the names in the book of registered powers."

"So what you're really telling me, Vellenia my dear, is that you and your Council want more credit."

"Exactly."

# Thirty.

*He was not believed, and scorned by his youngest daughter.*

*Myth of the Revelation*

**12 Shabin, Y.O.D. 746**

## City of Andoline, Colovencia, Nilakas

Carnival was everywhere. Chaotic and untamed it sprawled through the city. Every side street and open lot was filled with tents, lean-tos, and sit-a-bouts. Hawkers of strange wares cried their goods and services in different languages from every corner. There were sweets decorated to be exotic animals, spiced meats roasting over open flames, braided breads with jars of jam to dip them into, beer in tall glasses and harder liquors dispensed in thimbles.

Wherever you turned someone or something cried out for your attention and money. Faux Ra-ken, seers, charlatans and mystics preened and pranced for the attention of the wandering throngs. Women in bright skirts packed with red crinoline, twirled about with bare arms held aloft and heads that seemed disconnected from their bodies, while men in beaded vests kicked and jumped from leg to leg.

Making their way through this throng were three men, a woman and a young boy.

"Is that an Upper?" Liam asked, pointing at a man in red tights and a cape.

"No, dear," Clea answered, "He's not Ra-ken, that's an actor, just pretending."

"He looks like an Upper." Liam was disappointed. Derek picked his son up and held him, turning to look where the man was standing.

"Is that what they look like?" Derek asked. His son nodded vigorously.

Kim and Derek both laughed. The man in question looked like a farce, a fool pretending to be unable to speak, pantomiming that he could fly and had super strength—as if Leo or Vernault ever wore capes.

Kim translated the joke to Kherlos. Kherlos stepped up to Liam, looked up into the young boy's eyes and said, "Me Upper." Then he dramatically thumped his chest.

270

Liam, with a grave look of seriousness shook his head at Kherlos. Derek looked at Clea. He was smiling, but she was not.

"Me Upper, yes" Kherlos said reassuringly to Liam. When this failed to convince the boy, Kherlos raised his arms and pointed them straight out. With his shoulders hunched, his head tucked slightly and his fingers pointed it gave a comical mimic of his former power. He made zapping noises and gently poked his fingers into Liam's soft belly, making the boy giggle.

"Stop that, please." Clea placed herself between Kherlos and her son.

"Clea dear, he was only playing." She did not look convinced. "He wasn't hurting the boy. He was only trying to show that Ra-ken look just like ordinary people, mostly."

"My friend makes his apologies," Kim said.

Clea's look left no doubt about her thoughts on Kherlos's attempt at being friendly.

"I will tell him to be more careful," Kim said.

"*We should get moving,*" Kherlos said.

"*I agree,*" answered Kim, and then switching tongues, "We need to keep moving, the square is not far, but time I believe is short before the first performance."

"I want to see an Upper, mommy."

"Ra-ken dear, Upper is impolite, and you will see one soon, I promise."

They passed a young woman on a low platform crying "Rhymes for a copper." Her dress was a patchwork of rags, her hair was wild and matted, but bright bangles of silver and copper covered her arms from wrist to elbow. A small crowd had gathered around her. A man in dark work clothes held a copper up to one of the two burly guards that flanked her.

"Keep it in your in trousers, sir." The woman closed the man's hand and pushed it away as the crowd laughed. "For copper one, I'll shake my bum, and shine your master's shoes. For copper's three I'll squat and…"

"Really," Clea said.

"See... if the buckles have come lose."

As the crowd hooted with pleasure, the woman laid one finger against her nose, and snorted a copper coin into a hat held just below her chin. "Who's next? Don't be shy." The woman scanned the crowd. Her eyes rested briefly on Derek.

"I know that woman," he said. "Well, not personally."

"Perhaps she can sign your book for you," Clea suggested.

The woman glanced at Kim. A look of fear flashed on her face. She pointed at a man on the other side of crowd. "How about you sir?"

"We should go," Kim said. He frowned; Derek's dark skin would make him easy to follow. "Go, I will catch up, watch out for children."

Not more than twenty steps on, five or more grubby children holding our dirty hands and begging for coins accosted Derek. Kherlos cursed and swatted at them but they darted easily beneath his arms and popped back up with their own little hands reaching for his pockets. Clea grabbed Liam and lifted him up in case their intent was to spirit her son away, but they ignored her and concentrated instead on Derek and Kherlos. There came a shrill whistle, and the children darted away like ferrets. In a moment, Kim returned.

"What was that all about?" Derek asked.

"They were after your purse." Kim held up a small velvet bag and jingled it.

Derek jammed his hand into the pocket of his jacket and it came out through a slit someone had made.

"I suggested they give it back," Kim said. "The woman who sneezes money."

"Oh." Derek thought for a moment. "Oh! She senses it first. Very clever."

"Yes."

Clea lowered Liam to the ground. "Put that in your book."

"What book?" Kim asked.

"I have this hobby—"

"Never mind."

§

The center square was packed; walking in a straight line for more than two steps seemed impossible. The square was a public park devoted to the worship of the Divine. Most of the park was shaded grass with walkways demarked with elevated gardens. At the center was a fountain with a figure of the Divine, surrounded by the statues representing the twelve deadly wishes. The north end of the park sloped down toward the river with the amphitheater at the edge. The public seating was full; the grass edges around the seating were full. Families camped out on blankets, one

272

overlapping with another so that squabbles about space were frequently breaking out. People wishing to move to or from their claimed space did so at their own peril. Rules of easement, right-of-way, courtesy and consideration had clearly been abandoned. Beyond this people stood where they could, and climbed anything that didn't immediately fall down.

"Divine touch me," Clea exclaimed when she took stock of the situation.

"Not to worry dear, we have seats."

"How is this possible?" Kim asked.

"We need to get to the center steps; we have seats reserved for press, one of the few benefits of my profession."

"Because of your power?" Kim asked, somewhat incredulously.

Derek decided to ignore the jibe. "Try and move in that direction." He pointed towards the steps. All Kim could see were the backs of other people, but he got the idea. Soon they were moving through the crowd and reached the top of the steps, which under normal circumstances would be thick with people sitting on them, but an efficient team of white robed acolytes was busy keeping them clear through ceaseless vigilance and stern faces. A man standing at the top stopped them as soon as they approached. "You will not be allowed to sit on the steps."

"I'm a newsman. I am with the Andoline Herald and these people are with me."

The acolyte looked over the group with distaste, and then gave his grudging approval for them to descend.

It was clear there were no seats available. Clea moved back and forth, asking people if they could shift, or put a child on their lap. Most either ignored her, or explained why they were saving the space. Meanwhile, Derek saw two large women sitting in a reserved area, who in his judgment didn't belong, and even better, that if they left, there would be plenty of room for the four them to sit, as long as Liam sat on Clea's lap. He focused his ability on first one, then the other and let each suddenly— and to them—inexplicably, speak their mind, and within seconds, they were both quite agitated with the other. For good measure, he let a few people around them add their thoughts to the fracas, and soon the women were laboring their way up the steps, sniping at one another quite heatedly, without the benefit of his talent.

Clea glared at him with suspicion, but he feigned ignorance, and they were now able to sit.

§

The opening act was a comedian. He made lewd jokes about the kinds of powers he'd like to possess. They were the usual dirty jokes they had all heard as kids. Few people laughed, they had not come here to see a clown. The man gave his best but the audience wanted no part of him. Next, he tried a few impressions and they fell as flat as his jokes. The audience had enough and started booing at the poor man. Exasperated he slunk off stage while a slightly bemused woman walked on. When they saw her, the crowd gave its approval.

She was a slight woman, not much more than five feet tall. Hazel eyes flashed full of life from a weathered face capped with curly gray hair and the silver half-moons of the Ra-ken. Her dress was light brown trimmed with green. The sleeves were long with large cuffs, as was the normal fashion of formal attire. She raised her hands in an open benediction and smiled warmly at the crowd.

"That is Shenna DeCort, able to…"

Kim held up his hand and replied, "We know who she is."

Two men wheeled onto a stage a large set of tubular bells. Shenna touched the longest tube. The sound that filled the air was low, sweet and clear. She had laid but a single finger on the tube, when she lifted it, the sound ceased.

Touching the metal tubes with both hands moving briskly, she played out a simple tune. It was a popular ballad, easily recognizable by most. She stopped after a few bars and let the crowd show its appreciation. Then she played in earnest, with both hands running quickly over the bars. The notes sang out in a complex melody of surprising beauty no other human could reproduce.

"Does she give concerts?" Kim asked during the applause.

"Not that I know of," Derek said.

"Pity."

The instrument was wheeled off and small table brought out and set down on one side of the stage. A crystal goblet was carried out and placed on the table. Shenna held aloft a small metal rod. She tapped it against the goblet, once, then again, so the audience could hear its note. Then she raised the rod again, and willed it to life. It rang with the same note. She walked to the opposite end the stage and pointed the rod at the glass.

Sound erupted from her hand. People in the front clasped hands to their ears, babies cried and birds erupted into flight. At the other end of the stage, the goblet shattered under the onslaught of the sound.

After the mess was cleaned up, Shenna held aloft a very thin and short brass rod. She let it emit its high piercing note just long enough to irritate. She smiled sweetly, and put the metal down.

Next a large brass cymbal was wheeled on stage.

A shirtless, well-muscled man strode out onto the stage. He carried a large mallet with a soft cloth end. He raised the mallet and struck gently and a deep mellow sound echoed through the amphitheater. The man bowed to the audience and walked off. She raised her right hand and gently laid her index finger against the cymbal. Softly at first, a low sweet note started building. As she held her finger against the edge of the disk, the sound grew until it filled the air as if it were coming from everywhere at once. She jerked the hand into a fist and silence rushed in to fill the void.

The crowd responded with moderate applause. She stepped forward and pantomimed that they should applaud more. This brought the expected response, and she continued to pantomime for more applause. Obviously not pleased with the appreciation shown by the audience, she put her hands on her hips and glared out at the crowd. Feigning anger now, she strode back beside the disk and slapped her hand against it.

It shrieked. The metal screamed and buzzed. The disk shook and warped as it was made to emit frequencies it would never naturally choose. The audience joined in with their own cries. They ducked their heads and covered their ears while yelling. Shenna pulled her hand away from the disk and waited for the audience to recover. She pantomimed for applause, and got it.

*"I see they will let anybody wear the sigil of Ra-ken these days,"* Kherlos said.

Derek looked at Kim who translated, "Kherlos is disappointed with the performance."

"I guess we should be thankful it wasn't Tawnya trying her magic act." Kim stared at him blankly for a second then spoke to Kherlos.

*"He believes something is wrong, he will go speak with this woman and ask where the others are."* Then he spoke to Derek, "Perhaps you should ask where the rest of the Council members are."

"Yes, that might be a good idea. I can always claim I want to interview her. They love doing interviews." Kim nodded.

"Well, Liam? What did you think?" Derek asked. The boy pouted. Derek laughed at his son. "Yes, I think everyone else here agrees with you."

Liam looked away.

"I need to talk to her," Derek said to Clea.

"That's fine dear; we won't be going anywhere very quickly."

§

Derek returned from his interview to find his family and new friends watching the street performance of a fire-eater. They were all eating shaved ices. Clea held an extra, which she handed over along with a kiss.

"Look daddy, we found an Upper." Liam exclaimed through his red stained mouth. Derek looked where the boy was pointing. The man was doing an impressive job of twirling a flaming stick in each hand.

"Liam, that man's not an Upper; he doesn't even have a power. What he has is called a skill," Derek replied.

"What's a skill daddy?" Liam asked.

Clea interjected. "Something you accomplish on your own dear, not something you get for free," and then just barely audible, "or by killing your father."

The boy looked confused. Derek interjected. "The woman we saw on stage was Ra-ken, Liam. She was the master of vibrations."

"You mean the one that made all that noise?"

"Yes."

"Uhn uh," Liam insisted, "I saw that man breathe fire. He's way more better than she is." Derek and Clea laughed.

Kim took this as an opening. "What did you learn?"

"Nothing of value, she thought I wanted to ask her about her music. She wouldn't say where Vellenia was."

"That is unfortunate. How else might we obtain this information?"

"Well there is good news and bad news, I ran into a friend of mine from the paper. He says Vellenia is rumored to have booked passage to Vesport."

"Then they are all at the mountain?" Clea asked.

"I believe this is most likely. We should be on our way soon," remarked Kim, "When did she leave?"

"They weren't sure, possibly as much as month ago."

Conversation came to a halt as the fire breather started his finale. Both torches had been thrown spinning high into the air. The man reached out and caught them both, one in front and the other a split

276

second later behind his back. He spun them at his sides briefly and then brought the flaming ends to a stop underneath his mouth, and completed the act with a huge fireball. The man extinguished the torches in a pile of sand at his feet and bowed, while his lovely assistant, a young woman dressed in less clothing than Clea's undergarments, began prancing around the circle of watchers holding out a small brown leather cap. Liam had clearly enjoyed the show. Derek gave the young woman a few coins.

Kim spoke with Kherlos at length, and then turned to Derek.

"You have been most resourceful. We will need you to help us find this retreat."

"Could we please find someplace out of this sun?" Clea asked.

"Yes, I know a place where we can get food and talk in peace. It will not be too crowded."

"Please," Derek said, "lead on," Kim spoke again to Kherlos and then started back the way they had come. Derek picked up Liam. Clea stepped close and together they followed behind.

Kim led them unerringly through the twisted streets as if he had grown up in them, and within a few blocks, they were in a part of town that looked like it was in a different country. The buildings huddled together like refugees with little regards for where the actual street might be. Few had glass windows, and those few were broken. The smells of harsh chemicals and dead animals drifted around them and threatened to attack without provocation. Clea's eyes danced furtively everywhere, but more and more frequently shot looks of distress in Derek's direction, while Kherlos, Kim and Liam seemed completely at ease.

Kim stopped at the entrance to a narrow, inexplicably clean alley between two greasy, gray-walled buildings.

"Wait here," he said and walked into the alley alone. He stopped in front of an unmarked door and knocked.

"I don't like this." Clea said. "You don't know this man."

Someone opened the door and spoke briefly with Kim. Kim turned and waved at them. "Come please," Kim said.

Clea grabbed Derek's arm, and hesitated.

Kim returned. "Clea, you are safe here, it is a place of peace, of refuge, for those who are trodden upon, a place where people like me can forget that they are far from home."

The inside was a single large poorly lit room, that smelled of odd flavors and spices. People were sitting on long benches at rows of low tables. Most of them appeared to be hunched over steaming bowls of some unknown stew. The smell of broth and meat was strong and made them all hungry. Towards the back, Derek could see men in bloodstained aprons at long tables chopping meat, while white-haired women stirred large iron pots and fussed at the men.

Kim led the others over to a clear bench before a rough wooden table. As soon as they sat down, two girls in gray aprons and with their black hair pulled back in tight buns, set steaming bowls of clear broth onto the table.

"Please, eat," Kim said, "We can talk here, no one will disturb us."

"What is this place?" Derek asked.

"It is a place where people can relax without being asked unwanted questions." Kim's tone suggested that Derek's question was exactly the one that people here wished to avoid. Clea was eyeing the broth suspiciously.

"It is chicken broth with vegetable, spice and onion," Kim said. She took a tentative sip, gave Kim a reassuring smile and set the bowl down. Kherlos had already finished his bowl and pointed at Clea's with an expectant look. She nodded. Kherlos took the bowl, and lifted it to his lips.

"Tell them what you know," Clea prompted Derek.

"I already have. They know the mountain is east of Vestport, north of the lake."

"Yes, but there are many mountains there. I suspect they did not take you directly, so that you could not tell of its location. You must guide us."

"He will do no such thing," Clea said.

"I am afraid that he will have little choice; only he can direct us to this mountain retreat where Kherlos may regain his power."

"His power is not my concern. I need him at home. You aren't Raken, and you can't order us around as if you were. My husband will remain at home with me."

Kim stood and bowed, deep at the waist, to Clea. "Of course, you are right, and I am on a fool's errand. I have been away from my duties too long. It is time to end this. Thank you for the help you have given us. We will go now." Kim indicated to Kherlos that he get up.

"How will you find them?" Derek asked. "The mountain I mean?"

"We will not. Our journey ends here. Please, you may go." He motioned again for Kherlos to rise and tugged on his sleeve, but Kherlos just sat, looking confused.

"What will happen to Kherlos?" Derek asked.

"I will kill him tonight and throw his body into the river."

Kherlos turned to Kim.

*"I told them I would kill you and throw your body in the river."*

*"Did they ask you to do that?"*

*"No, she told me that we cannot have her husband to help us,"* Kim said, choosing his words to avoid using any names.

*"Will you?"*

*"I make no promises."*

Kherlos's shrugged, and then motioned for someone to bring him more soup.

"You told him," Derek said.

"Yes."

"Could I get his sigil? I assume he still has it."

"Derek!" Clea chided. "Mr. Kim, this isn't our problem, and threatening to kill Kherlos won't help your cause. And you're upsetting Liam." The boy in fact seemed fascinated by everything around him, and not upset in the least.

"Mrs. Cantor, I am sorry that you perceived my words as a threat, it is simply our arrangement, he has ceased being useful to me."

Kherlos, as if suspecting the tide was against him, attacked his latest bowl of soup with vigor.

"We aren't wealthy," Clea conceded "Derek's gift is our only source of income. He was being paid by the council on his last venture."

Kim sat back down, pleased that negotiations had begun. "I am of course, prepared to pay for your husband's services."

"I understand that you will be traveling across an open ocean."

"And dense jungle," Kim added.

"And," Clea paused slightly as she took in Kim's words, "the possibility, no, probability that none of you will return."

"Much is unknown."

"How will you make payments in a timely manner?"

"I believe that there are FarSpeakers…" Her reaction ended that line of negotiation quickly. "Perhaps a large sum left in trust here in Andoline."

"Paid out monthly."

Kim nodded. "Until all principle and interest are depleted. Payments to cease upon our successful return, of course."

"Of course," Clea said. "And of course there would be a deposit in my name against his death."

"Very well, tell me, what value do you place upon your husband's life?" Kim asked.

"Privately," Derek said quickly, that figure was something he did not want to know.

# Thirty One

*Apachawea in his wrath, did then break the promise to his brother EagleEye, and revealed unto his family the secret of the Gifts of the Spirit-Father, who is the Divine, and the deceits of MauPau, which was naught but smoke and feathers. And he was not believed, and twice scorned by his daughter.*

*Myth of the Revelation*

**14 Shabin, Y.O.D. 746**

## Council Monastery, East of Vesport, Tameria

"I hate these fucking steps," Le Le said. She turned around and sat on the cold stone. She looked up at Vellenia standing over her, and then down towards where Seth and Tabitha were struggling along slowly.

"Give me a drink," Le Le said, holding her hand up for the water skin Vellenia carried.

Vellenia hefted the skin. "You drink too much, it's light, I might need it."

"Well you can have it back when I'm done with it."

"I'm not thirsty," Vellenia said.

"I meant my piss."

Vellenia glared at her shrewish companion and handed over the water skin, then looked to the top of the steps. "There's someone up there."

"Waiting for us?"

"So it would seem. Whoever it is isn't moving much."

"That's fine by me."

"I think it's Ahten, I'm going up."

"Suit yourself; I think I'll wait for the next coach." Le Le looked back down at the seemingly endless steps they had been climbing. The steps had been Cordain's idea, to make the sanctuary inaccessible and if need be, defendable. Trust a man to do it wrong, she thought. Below Tabitha and Seth continued to labor their way up. She held on to him while he lifted one foot, moved it up onto the next step, and then moved up with him. Sometimes he would wobble a little and threaten to tip them both over backwards.

They looked comical. She hoped they would fall and roll all the way back down. If they caught up with her though, the girl would ask for help, which meant she would be forced to help or kill her for the affront. She stood up and resumed her climb already angry with the two of them for being a burden.

Ahten was waiting for them, or at least, she reconsidered, waiting. He was wet and cold, his robe soiled, snot dripped from his nose unnoticed, the only signs of life were his shivering and the occasional blink of his eyes.

Vellenia stood in front of him, arms folded and puzzled.

"What's wrong?" Le Le asked.

"He's filthy."

"He's also fingerless."

Le Le poked him in the shoulder with her finger. He stumbled back a step, regained his balance, and then coughed; a sudden burst of phlegm. He bent forward, moving downward with each successive retort, until he was hunched over and spraying the ground with mucus and blood. When the fit passed, he slowly stood back up.

Le Le touched his cheek, from the side, out of harm's way, and froze a small patch of his skin. He gave no reaction.

"No one's home."

"So it would seem," Vellenia said. "Give me the water skin please."

"Well, since you said please."

Vellenia squeezed the neck of the skin and let a trickle of water into her hand, and then raised it to Ahten's mouth. The water in her hand swirled around, formed a little bridge, parted Ahten's lips and forced its way inside, and then a torrent of liquid gushed out of his mouth and into the water skin.

His shrunken corpse collapsed at their feet.

"Remind me not to drink out of that," Le Le said.

"Why not?" Vellenia hefted the full skin. "It's as pure water as the Divine can create. Only the water obeys me, everything else is left behind."

"Perhaps, but I'll still pass if it's all the same." She prodded Ahten's body with her foot.

Seth and Tabitha crested the steps. "Only four more," Tabitha said. Once Seth was up, she guided him over to where they stood.

"What happened here Seth?" Vellenia asked.

"What do you mean?" Seth asked. "When, now? I don't hear anybody. We should find Ahten."

"We've already found him." Le Le said, "He was waiting for us, I think."

"Where did he go? Ahten, Ahten," Seth noticed something wrong. "What?"

Vellenia touched his arm gently. "Ahten's body was waiting for us; his mind was not...present. Have you seen that before?"

"Briana. I think she can do that."

"Fascinating," Vellenia said.

"Who's Briana," Le Le asked.

"One of us, Me, Cal, Lana, Briana, we called ourselves the winners, like it was a game."

"Who was this Ahten?"

"He was in charge." Vellenia said.

Le Le snorted. "Were you friends?"

"Yes," Seth said.

"No," Vellenia said.

"I think she's in charge now. We should go pay our respects."

"I'm in charge now," Vellenia said, "and I expect your help if there's trouble."

"Yes, of course."

"Vellenia?"

"Yes, Seth?"

"She's not going to be happy to see you."

"No one ever is."

§

It took the combined strength of Vellenia and Le Le to pry open one of the large oak doors at the main entrance of the grand hall. The four visitors entered. Le Le found a rock and propped the door open to provide light. Past the immediate foyer was the main hall, empty of people, but littered with overturned chairs, tables set askew, pewter goblets, and cloth napkins scattered about the room. Oil lamps had burned dry, candles had exsanguinated into broad pools of wax. It had the look of sudden abandonment.

"I suppose no one thought to bring matches," Vellenia said.

No one answered.

"Fine, wait here."

Vellenia disappeared into a side alcove. After a few moments there came a loud snap, and then a low rumbling, like machinery being forced into action. Vellenia re-appeared but said nothing. She walked from lamp to lamp, located one with oil, adjusted the wick, and struck a match to it.

"I found matches, and started the lift; our belongings are on their way up."

"So it wasn't broken," Le Le said.

"Why bring it up if no one's here?" Tabitha asked. They all looked at her.

"We're here, and we're staying, so let's find out who else is still on this stupid mountain."

§

Le Le woke and stretched. The bed and blankets were soft and comfortable. Not, of course, as fine as those she had in Tse Lee's employ, but still, adequate in their own sort of way. There was something wrong with the mattress. She sat up. "Oh."

A young woman with dark brown skin lay next to her. She shook the girl's hip.

"Huh?" Dharla rolled over and snuggled against Le Le. "Mmmm, good morning."

"Get up. Go, before your girlfriend finds out."

Dharla pushed herself up, and held her arm out, comparing it to Le Le's. "Your skin, It's so pale and creamy. You're really beautiful, you know that?"

"Stop that. You must leave."

"She already knows," Dharla leaned over for a kiss, but Le Le moved away. "Come back."

Le Le slid out of the bed, her skinny, naked body almost glowing in the morning light. "There will be trouble if we are found together, even if Brianna doesn't care."

"Oh she cares," Dharla teased. "She makes me tell. Look, we want to know something."

Le Le found a robe and put it on, then gathered up Dharla's clothes and tossed them onto the bed.

"No, wait," Dharla protested. "This is serious."

"What? What is so important?"

"How did Seth really lose his sight?"

Le Le's eyes narrowed. "What did he tell you?"

"He wouldn't say."

Le Le sat back down on the bed and stroked Dharla's hair. If she were to kill the girl, she would need to be close. "You think I did that?"

"Maybe, I don't know. It wasn't very nice."

There was a light knock on the door. Le Le moved her hand around to the back of Dharla's neck.

"It's Briana," Dharla said. "Come on in."

Briana entered, dressed in a nightshirt and robe. She undressed, lifted the covers and slid into the bed next to her lover. "Did you two have fun?"

"She won't tell." Dharla said.

Le Le lowered her hand. Her powers alone weren't going to solve this problem. "She will kill me if I tell."

"I hate that bitch," Briana said, "all of them."

"You do?"

"They act like they own the world." Dharla said. "And blinding Seth just proves it."

"We are all Ra-ken," Le Le said, "We can leave anytime we want."

"This is our home," Dharla said. "My uncle owned these lands before they came here and drove him off."

"Really?"

"It's true, and no one can hunt without their permission."

"I see, but what do you two propose to do?"

"We want to kill her," Briana said.

"You realize, her power would just go to someone else, and the council would come take all of our lives?"

"Le Le!" Dharla chided, "You're so dense. What do you think the wishing wells are for?"

Le Le smiled as if this thought had never before occurred to her. "She is not easy to kill," she said suddenly. "Did you not see Ahten's body; all dried up like a prune? That is what she can do; even from across the room she can attack you. You two would be no match for her."

"What do we do?"

"If we kill her," Le Le purred, "then someone here must get her power. Agreed?"

"Yes!" the said together.

"But we must be ready. If we capture her power, then the Council cannot hurt us."

"So how do we do it?"

"Wait," Briana asked, "why do you, you know, want her dead?"

Le Le leaned in and put her arms around the girl's shoulders. "I have my own reasons to hate Vellenia. I too have been cheated by the Council Ra-ken. We must wait until we are ready, and then I will set a trap for her. I will lure her into attacking me. My cold can stop her water long enough for you two to catch her unawares."

"When?"

"I don't know, first I must find out where other people's loyalties lie. Now get dressed and go, we should not be seen together."

"Maybe I could come and visit?" Briana asked.

"We'll see."

# Thirty Two.

*And then did Uumvault appear to Apachawea and his family and spoke upon the truth of his word. Thereupon Apachawea was revered, and believed and honored. And his son asked of the Spirit-Father, who is the Divine, that he, as Keavon before, might have the gift of flight and soar as a bird. And the gift was denied.*

*Myth of the Revelation*

**28 Shabin, Y.O.D. 746**

### En Route to City of Vesport, Tameria

Derek joined Kim up on deck. The two of them looked out over the railing as the ship rolled in the still heavy swells. A quick storm had gathered and buffeted the ship. Below decks, Derek had been sick while Kherlos snored and Kim read. Now with the winds calmer Derek and Kim had opted for fresher air and better company. Around them, the crew busied readying the sails to catch the fresh breeze that chased the few clouds. A few other passengers were about. Derek had traveled on a newsman's budget, while Kim traveled on an assassin's budget. There were a few differences between the trips; one of the most amazing was that he could actually order food to be eaten in his room, though Kim forbade this.

Before them, a rainbow made a hesitant appearance and then gathered its courage for a bolder presentation. The shipmen started whistling at the display, and he could see the sails starting to unfurl on the two sister ships that accompanied them. He had made this crossing twice before, once each way. He did not believe that either Kim or Kherlos had spent much time at sea, yet they showed none of the concerns or ill effects that currently plagued him. As ever, they were calm, aloof and inscrutable. Kim started the inevitable conversation.

"You have much you want to ask me." Kim spoke without looking at him.

"Yes, but I'm not sure I want to hear the answers." This was a casual conversation, not one to be elevated to the seriousness of eye contact and facial expressions. "Your name isn't really Kim is it?"

"No, well yes, it is now, but it was not. Kim is a title that we pass along with the power."

"What does it mean?" He'd get around to that admission of power in a bit.

"It means 'Giver of Death' in my language."

"I thought that was Kherlos. Did you get his power then?"

"No, my skills allow me to give death to others, skills that I and many other men from my family train for. It is the power that we conceal that gives us the edge."

"A power that few know of, and one that certainly isn't on the registry."

"Isn't that the best kind?"

Derek wasn't surprised. Kim had always acted as if he had a power others would envy. "So when you die, there are very few who can wish for the power, and it stays within your family."

"It is how we earn our way in the world. There are always people who will pay to have others killed."

"You mean the Council of Ra-ken," Derek said.

"This year the Council, next year, someone else, we have allegiance only to the contract."

"So I'm guiding you to your next victim."

"In a manner of speaking, yes, but it is not as you think. It is complex."

"Why didn't you kill Kherlos? I don't understand that. I can see why the council would want him dead, and they might even think that he is, but why isn't he?"

Kim glanced around. There were sailors shouting in the rigging above them, and a few hurried by from time to time. A few officers were on deck, but they were busy giving orders.

"I answer this so that you may one day write this story. Even my family has the need for careful publicity to feed the legends and insure continued employment. Kherlos killed my older brother. I do not fault Kherlos for this, but when something like this occurs, we must know why. After I acquired my brother's power and finished my training, I went to see Kherlos to learn what I could of the former Kim's fate. By the time I reached him, he had already given up his power to save the city that he had founded. There is much irony there, for the man who helped Kherlos gain his power has taken it away again."

"And that would be?"

"You must get that story from Kherlos, later, if you both survive, and it is my intent that you shall."

"I'm glad to hear it." Then Kim's words dawned on him. "Both of us? Survive that is?"

"We'll see. At some point Kherlos will be on his own, but to answer your question, no, killing Kherlos is not required to fulfill the contract, though again, that would be up to him."

"Let me see if I have this correct. You read my article about what the council was doing, and since you, your family, was involved, you sought me out so I could lead you to the sanctuary, where you can get Kherlos his power back, but not so you can fight him?"

"Yes, essentially correct. My contract is to kill the wielder of eyes of death. Perhaps that will be Kherlos, but I suspect it might be this Seth that you know, or perhaps some other person by the time we arrive."

Derek waited while a sailor hustled by. "I kind of liked Seth, I can't say I'm too happy to be leading you to him. But isn't the power the ability to shoot beams of death from your eyes?"

"Perhaps it translates differently from language to language. The words are a formality; the trick is to know in your mind what you are wishing for."

"The council could have used some of your advice."

"Sadly it is not our advice that is most often sought. Perhaps you can write a story about what great advice my family gives. We are always looking to improve our services and broaden our product portfolio."

Derek laughed. "Well, what advice would you give me then, not to get mixed up with the Council?"

"I would advise you to write about travel."

"Travel?" Derek looked at Kim; he was serious. "Why travel?"

"Am I not correct that you are on your third voyage across this sea? Most people live and die within a few miles of where they are born. You on the other hand are making your second paid excursion to a different land. Few people who are not Ra-ken can make such a claim."

"But people don't want to read about things that can't matter to them. People want to know what the weather will be like next week, and what the Council is wearing. They don't care about beasts with shaggy manes or biting insects in hot jungles. Besides, I thought you wanted me to write your story."

Kim sighed. "It has been suggested that we should follow up the advice we give with death threats, but that would make us rulers, and we do not wish to be rulers. First, you must write about travel. To write about it, you must do it, is that not so? That is a good thing. Then when you are famous and near death, you must write my story. You will be killed of course, that is why you must wait until you are near death, and famous already."

"I always thought the key to good advice was to tell people what they wanted to hear," Derek said, choosing to ignore the part about being killed.

"Most often, people who are smart enough to heed good advice don't really need it. The Council live in their own world and are often told only what they want to hear, and very little of that is ever good advice."

Derek didn't know what to think of this, and apparently, Kim had said all he wanted to on the subject. Kim left the rail and wandered off. Derek watched the waves and the scattered clouds. There was a certain peace of mind, a calmness, that came from watching the ocean without trying to understand it or guess its motives.

"Excuse me sir." Derek turned to look at the voice, thick with a sailor's brogue. One of the ship's officers had approached and was now addressing him. The decorations on the man's uniform were a complete mystery to Derek, but they looked impressive nonetheless.

"Yes, err, I'm sorry, I can't quite get the hang of your uniforms yet."

"L'tenant, Senior Grade Emmerson, sir," he offered helpfully.

"Thank you Lieutenant, how can I help you," Derek inquired, wondering if perhaps this man had overheard their conversation. The lieutenant neither offered to shake hands nor saluted. Derek stood and fidgeted, unsure of protocol.

"Oh aye, as I am sure y'know; tomorrow is the feast of the martyr of Ignatius. It is the tradition of the Cap'n to invite all those blessed with the presence of the Divine to attend dinner with him on this occasion." The lieutenant paused, and coughed, "um, ye're so blessed are ye not?"

"Yes, I am registered with the ability to make others talkative," Derek said with some formality and annoyance. They could have checked for themselves, perhaps they had.

"Oh aye, thank you, we don't always travel with the latest volumes of the registry as ye might imagine."

Derek was not sure if this was an insult or not. He had been in the registry for several years and his father before that. He figured that either the lieutenant meant was that a sailing ship had no such need for a registry of powers, or that the registry was just so much pompous crap to begin with, or both.

"Are there many other powered on this ship Lieutenant?"

"Aye, we have a few spread amongst these ships, will you be joining us then?"

"I would love to," Derek replied, knowing it would insult Kherlos and Kim.

"Oh Excellent, I will add your name to the list. Dinner is at seven bells, formal attire please, and the use of your abilities is strongly discouraged."

"Just mine or everybody's?"

"Oh everybody's," the lieutenant answered, "but everyone talks all at the same time anyway, so feel free, Aye?" The lieutenant turned to leave. Derek couldn't decide if he was being mocked or not. He let it pass.

"Lieutenant."

"Aye?"

"I've heard rumors of pirates, is that true?"

"Oh aye, it is, privateers really, but they don't bother us much anymore."

"Do tell."

"Not much to tell, aye, 'bout six months back one of the merchant companies hired-on us a man good with a bow. As soon as them scum showed sail he put an arrow into their 'elmsman from three miles out. Said he didn't need to see them, only need to be able to see them. We didn't ask y'know. Anyway, now they mostly leave us alone, preferring to prey on wealthy yacht owners instead."

"I've heard about them."

"What's that?"

"Entrepreneurs, people without abilities; who pursue money."

"Ahh, well that'd be the rest of us then wouldn't it?"

# Thirty Three.

*Then did his youngest daughter, who was innocent and uncertain of the nature of the gifts of the Spirit-Father, who is the Divine, asked that she might visit the moon, for the hour was late and the telling of the story long. And the gift was denied, for she had asked for a boon.*

*Myth of the Revelation*

**28 Shabin, Y.O.D. 746**

## Council Monastery, East of Vesport, Tameria

The morning air had that slight autumn chill that so enchants late risers to linger beneath the warmth of a fine quilted spread. It was the first breath of a cold beast that would soon shake its winter fur all over the land.

Vellenia lay in her room enjoying a luxury she could seldom afford: indolence. She sighed. It was past time to rise and past time to leave and if she were to be honest with herself, she wanted to do neither. There were no servants, so no matter how long she lay in comfort, no bath would be drawn, and no breakfast would be delivered. Martsen had insisted that the trainees would not be servants to the powered, nor would they be called acolytes; the taint of religious fervor left a foul taste in his mouth.

Nor was she needed here. There were two trainee groups practicing on the wheels of wishing, though only one group had the full eight. Things were far from perfect, but Martsen had shown extraordinary diplomacy and efficiency in rebuilding the sanctuary. He was well known and liked among the people living in and beyond these mountains, and had known both Briana and Dharla. His easy style and infectious laughter had instantly calmed their fears. Within two weeks, the mountain had come alive again as news had spread and people returned.

Cal Estass had returned. He had tried his hand at extortion down in Vesport and quickly learned harsh lessons on the limits of his power. Somewhere along the way though he had learned that his acid would etch glass, and so turned his ability toward an artistic channel. His etched mirrors were in high demand and provided him with a considerable income. He preferred the isolation and safety of the mountain, and a percentage of his income went to the corporation. Martsen had incorporated the mountain retreat, arguing that a business organization provided better stability and accountability than a religious hierarchy.

Dharla and Briana were doing well. At first, they didn't know what to do with themselves. Martsen had suggested they visit their families, and that they could then travel from village to village showing off their powers and recruiting new volunteers. Accompanied by two young men, they spent four weeks away before returning and had sent over two dozen new faces to join the ranks. When they returned, they talked excitedly about making a longer journey, deeper into the great forest. Martsen had convinced them that such a trip would take a great deal of planning, and they could not make the trip until the wishing circles were back in operation.

Seth had settled back into his apartment with Tabitha. They seemed happy, but had little to do to keep them occupied. A healer had been hired from Vesport, he had announced that Tabitha was pregnant and everyone was excited over that good news. Seth had tried to get word to Derek Cantor and had been unable to reach him by FarSpeaker. Vellenia had assured him that he was probably off on some assignment and would get word back as soon as he returned.

Le Le was being a total ass, acting as if she were the monarch of the mountain. Some of the girls had complained to Martsen about being approached by Le Le. The healer had come to Martsen and confided he had trouble healing the frostbite that Le Le had been inflicting on people. Amazingly, Martsen had talked to her and not only come out still alive and with all his fingers, but actually put an end to the "incidents," as he called them. Overall, it was time to get out of bed, and time to leave, and as much as she dreaded it, she must take Le Le with her.

Vellenia crawled out of bed, put on slippers, lifted her nightdress and squatted over her chamber pot. When she was finished, she reached down and touched her waste. Using her ability, she pulled the water out of her urine and feces up into a ball in her hand, turning her waste into dry dust. She put the ball of water to her mouth, willed it to be still, so that it would be cold, and drank. Her claim to Le Le had not been a lie; the water was pure. She evaporated the rest of the water into the air.

At least emptying my own chamber pot has never been a chore, she thought. She chucked, it never failed to amuse her, that of all the people in the world, she was the only one who could honestly claim that her shit didn't stink.

She walked to the closet and selected a light robe to wear down to the kitchen for breakfast. Hunger was the main priority; she would eat, dress and find Martsen and arrange to leave. With luck, they could leave within the week, depending on tides and winds, but Martsen would arrange all that.

She looked down; her foot was wet. There was a puddle of water coming into the room under the door.

Le Le, She thought. She grabbed a robe, threw it on and opened the door. Outside stood a frozen statue; it was a young lady covered with thick ice, slowly melting and dripping. Vellenia adjusted her robe, barely believing what she was seeing. She touched the woman's face and willed the ice to move. It obeyed her, though it took more effort and left her drained. She could never understand where Cordain got the strength to flow rock.

It took Vellenia a few moments to place the face. She had not seen Tabitha much since they had arrived. Seth and his new wife had made their home in Briana's old room, where she had been held captive. Now Tabitha and her unborn child stood before her as a challenge from Le Le. She wondered if Seth was alive and realized it didn't matter. Any new owner of the power would have no experience in using it, and would be as easy to defeat as Seth had been.

Vellenia pushed past the girl, tipping her over. The young woman's body hit the stone floor and cracked in several places; Le Le had frozen her deep.

Briana, Martsen, Dharla and Le Le were all lounging in the main hall talking quietly when Vellenia stormed in. None of them looked surprised.

"Oh, look who finally got my message," Le Le said.

Vellenia launched a thin stream of water across the room. It met Le Le's frosty breath and froze, but when it touched her cheek it still bit in.

Le Le slapped at the ice and broke it, severing the connection, but it took skin with it. "You'll pay for that, bitch."

Vellenia did not reply. She had rushed into the fight unprepared. Her bladder was empty and she had taken very little water from the girl. She could pull water from her own body, but only as a last resort.

Le Le moved closer, Vellenia could feel the cold airflow around her ankles and see the fog roll over the cold stones. She waited.

"Where's your precious water now?" Le Le taunted, "Forget to bring some? Why don't you run?"

Vellenia could see Le Le had been anticipating this fight, but now she was acting on pure emotion. Perhaps she could use that to her advantage. She raised a thin film of water over the stones in the floor between them. It iced.

Le Le fell hard, twisting as she landed on her side, her arm came down to catch her fall and only found more ice. It shot out and her head thumped against the floor. Vellenia moved forward and knelt, reaching for Le Le's face.

"Stop." Dharla said.

Vellenia stopped.

"Calm her," Dharla said to Briana, and then again to Vellenia, "Back up and kneel on the floor."

Vellenia obeyed.

"Is she dead?" Dharla asked.

"No, just unconscious," Vellenia said, her voice soft and distant.

"How do you know?"

"I can feel the water move within her body, her heart still beats."

§

Le Le stirred. She moved slowly. She felt pain, a great throbbing pain in her head and ribs. She felt cold and wet. She tried to open her eyes. Her right eye remained closed; her left eye was blurry.

"Are you ok?" someone asked.

She pushed herself up, wincing in pain and felt her head. There was goose-egg sized lump near her temple. She touched it gingerly a couple times and then felt her ribs. Remembering, she snapped her head around looking for Vellenia. Her vision swam; she moaned and put her head down. "Where's Vellenia?"

"Right in front of you," Dharla said.

"Is she dead?"

"No."

"Briana is calming her," Martsen said.

Le Le considered the blurry shape of Vellenia, kneeling calmly a few feet in front of her. She called upon her power, and cried out as it brought bright bolts of pain. "I'm still going to kill you, slowly."

"You're not ready yet," Vellenia said.

"I'll be ready soon enough." She stretched and moved slowly, feeling the ache in her hip, shoulder and neck, but she could still move. There would be time for a healer later.

"What do you mean?" Dharla asked.

"The wishing room is not ready, you will lose my power."

"I will take your power, I know the words," Martsen said.

"You don't know; our families keep it a secret."

"You're lying," Le Le said.

"Tell me if you're lying," Dharla said, her will ensuring truthfulness.

"I am not lying."

"I used my power, I think she's telling us the truth."

"I don't care," Le Le said. "I'm ready to kill her now."

"Make her tell me," Martsen said, turning to Dharla, "You promised me her power."

"Tell him."

"We lie," Vellenia said in a slow dreamy voice, "we announce the power has been heired. Before the transfer. Before death. It is a lie."

"Why?"

"People, all the time, everywhere, all wishing for my power. Everyone knows the words. Kill me now. When do I die? You might wish too soon. Too late, gone, somewhere, you don't get it. We cheat, we say, 'Too late, the power is taken.'" Vellenia paused.

"Then what?"

"They give up. Stop wishing, give up. Then you kill. Quick, not slow, slow never works. Only way, or use wishing room, not ready, power will be lost."

"I don't care, I'm killing her now," Le Le said. She started to crawl towards Vellenia.

"Stop." Dharla commanded.

Le Le stopped.

"Sleep."

Briana tapped Dharla on the shoulder, pointed her finger at Vellenia and made a little "down" motion with her hand.

"Sleep."

"Divine!" Briana said. "That was tiring, holding them like that."

"Can't you talk while you use your power?" Martsen asked.

Briana looked away. "I don't think so. Maybe, it's hard."

"Le Le could, I think," Dharla said. The others shrugged.

"Look," Briana said, not wanting to be the center of attention, "What are we going to do with her?"

"I know," Dharla said, "we'll keep her locked up, and you can calm her when we need to feed her or talk to her."

"Where? The only rooms with locks are the wishing wells."

"Then that's where we'll keep her."

"How will we know when we're ready?" Martsen asked.

"She'll tell us," Dharla said.

"This did not exactly go as planned," Martsen said.

"No," Dharla finally conceded," but it could have gone worse."

§

They gave her no water, no food, and barely ever came to speak to her. She conserved as best she could, but it wasn't enough. The moisture that condensed on the cold granite walls came from her own breath, and like the water from her waste, it kept her alive, but never satisfied her thirst. She had a plan, a slim chance, but it required someone from the council to come looking for her and she didn't think anyone would. No doubt, Martsen continued to send reports on her behalf, telling them how well the project was coming along, and how things were so much better, now that he was in charge.

Le Le came from time to time, to gloat, to torment her. She would kill that woman, somehow, but the trick with the floor would not work twice. Le Le froze the stones each time she came, and would stand there and laugh, or talk about the food she had just eaten, and all the while chilling the air and the walls and all she could do was sit on the bench at the far end, knees drawn up against her chest, and shiver, and wait.

§

When they were ready, they came for her. Dharla stood to one side, Briana on the other, Le Le to the rear, while Martsen opened the door. Briana flooded calmness into the small room.

"Is it time?" Vellenia's voice was thin and raspy.

"Come where I can see you," Dharla said. Vellenia lay curled up on the small bench that circled the room. She unwound her thin arms and legs and climbed slowly to her feet, looking much as Ahten had when they first arrived.

"You will obey us. You are not allowed the use of your ability. Do you understand?"

"Yes."

"Follow us," Briana said. They walked only a short way down the hall to another wishing room. Martsen unlatched the door and held it open.

"Look inside." Vellenia looked into the room. Eight young students sat calmly as the wheel spun, making its rhythmic ticks and chimes.

"Are they ready?" Dharla asked.

Vellenia watched them chant. "Yes."

"Well give me a couple days," Le Le said, "I have to go into Vesport to meet an old friend." She counted off on her fingers. "I'll be back day after next. Don't look so annoyed. Okay?" Their silence asked the obvious.

"Look, two, okay, three more days won't make a difference."

"Oh so now you're the patient one," Dharla said, "now that we're finally ready. Tell me what's so damned important now?"

"I'm going to go pick up some guests," Le Le said, "trust me, it will be worth it."

"Guests?" Briana asked.

"Yes, an old friend, of sorts, has turned up in Vesport. I know he'll want to be here, and I let him know we would wait." Briana threw up her hands and stomped away.

"Briana! You can't walk off!" Dharla shouted.

"What?" Briana said, then, remembering Vellenia, "Oh, fine, sorry."

"Let's put her away then," Martsen said, "Come on Elly." They led Vellenia back to her cell. Le Le watched them go, mouthing, "What's so damned important?" to their backs.

# Thirty Four.

*Then did his son, who was clever, and ambitious and attentive ask that he might receive leave to visit the moon. And the gift was granted. For such is the nature of the gifts, that man must learn from them to be wise, and humble, and understanding.*

*Myth of the Revelation*

**3 Veena, Y.O.D. 746**

## City of Vesport, Tameria

Derek looked at Vesport with new eyes. The last time he had been here, it had been a waypoint, not somewhere to be noticed. He had thought about Kim's words and considered the possibility that he had been right, that travel was something worth writing about.

In some ways, it was just another dirty bustling city, but it did have character. There were the usual drab people with weathered faces going about their unknowable purposes, but there were differences. Their skin was generally darker, fewer Caucasians, more browns and blacks. Fashions were different. Men wore bright colored jackets down to their knees and short pants with long stockings. Women, those few of high class he could see, wore tight wraps of cloth wound down to their ankles, while the ubiquitous prostitutes wore short skirts and halter-tops with flashy bangles and bright colored bracelets.

Warehouses, fisheries, trade shops, and bars stood end to end along the muddy street. Stalls and even half-stalls crowded in where there was insufficient room for a building, with their proprietors often sitting on their own merchandise. Derek took it all in. It was he considered, a mystery waiting to be explored.

§

To Kim it was just another port of call, another city with the usual ethnic ghettos. One of which would supply him with information, money, labor and other resources that he might need.

He scanned the buildings thrown up around the docks. Eventually he saw the mark he was looking for, carved as if it were a decorative border around a hanging sign advertising smoked fish.

He turned to Kherlos.

"Wait with him," he said, pointing towards Derek, "I will be right back." Kherlos shrugged and walked over to watch Derek.

Kim entered the door underneath the sign. The smell of fish was powerful and reminded him of the markets back home. He examined a display of sea bass laid out on kelp and ice. A short balding man hurried over and asked in Tassis if he could help honorable master. Kim answered in his own language.

"This fish does not look fresh, show me the fresh fish, I am not here to feed my hogs."

The man smiled and replied in the same tongue.

"Honorable sirah, this fish was home, dreaming of its mother only this morning."

"I too have just set foot on land. Where would I sleep tonight that I might be at home." The man smiled a broad grin.

"The streets are poor and broken here, may I offer a boy to guide you?" he asked.

"That would be most excellent. And send me three of these, such as you would serve your honored mother." Kim held out his hand to the man, so that it was obvious that his fingers concealed coins. The man took the payment and pocketed it swiftly without a glance. He turned his head slightly away from Kim, and barked a name. A boy of maybe nine years came running.

"You will guide this honored sirah, and hold your tongue; he wishes to hear none of your chatter." Kim nodded and smiled, approving of the use of "Sirah" an honorific reserved for the powered nobility of the islands. Of course, the man was simply being obsequious, and expected to be corrected. Kim left the shop with the boy in tow and returned to the docks.

"You're being followed," Derek said.

"He will show us a place to sleep tonight. We will rest and dine well here. It may be a long time before we will again have such comfort as this city may provide. Now, we must find us a coach."

§

Their destination turned out to be a three-story brick building with a high balcony across the front. Brown skinned women in bright silk dresses leaned over and exposed their breasts to passers-by. Shirtless men in satiny pants and colored head scarves strutted about like peacocks and blew kisses to anyone who so much as glanced at them.

"This is a brothel," announced Derek.

Kim and Kherlos jumped down from the wagon.

"Yes," Kim said, "I did say we should enjoy ourselves."

"But isn't that a man?" Derek pointed at one individual with long wavy hair, painted eyes and lips, and wearing a long blue dress.

"Yes, would you like him?"

"No."

Kherlos spoke briefly with Kim, and the two laughed.

"He asks if you would prefer the boy instead," Kim said.

"Oh how the mighty have fallen," Derek said in disgust.

"You have just one wife, do you not?" Kim asked.

"Yes."

"And she does not allow you to have others? Even while you are apart?"

"No."

Kim shook his head in disbelief, and then relayed this news to Kherlos who just shrugged and looked sympathetic.

"Get your things," Kim said.

A small man with many smiles showed Derek to his room. The room itself was almost enough to stun Derek into unconsciousness. The paper on the walls was bright red with a fuzzy raised green floral pattern running in vertical stripes. The drapes covering the window were a matching green with gold embroidery and were topped with a gold valence and golden pull ropes. The bed cover matched the wallpaper. He felt dizzy and off balance whenever he moved his head. Derek quickly concluded that the best way to deal with the room was with his eyes closed. The bed proved to be cool and welcoming and he found himself suddenly more tired than he had thought.

§

Derek woke to the sound of knocking.

"Yes?"

"Ah yes, please, Dinnah Sirah" came a man's voice.

"I'll be right there."

"Ah, yes please, Dinnah Sirah." Derek looked around. There was no chamber pot and his bladder needed urgent attention. He opened the door.

"Yes, please," the man said. Derek looked at him a moment, narrowed his eyes and then made a pissing motion with his right hand. The man nodded, scuttled down the corridor to an unmarked door. He opened the door and motioned Derek inside. He was still waiting when Derek emerged.

"Dinnah?" the man asked.

"Dinnah, ah yessah please," Derek answered, mimicking the man's accent.

"Very good sir."

"You're a jerk," Derek said.

"We like to have our fun. Dinner is being served in Master Kim's room." He led Derek up two flights of stairs, and along a hallway that ended with a single door. He knocked, and a slender woman in a sensuous, silky wrap showed them in. The man spoke to this woman rapidly in Tassis, punctuating the conversation frequently with laughter, and soon they were both laughing at him.

"Please," the woman said between giggles, "come this way."

Kim's room was a palace of lacquered tables and overstuffed chairs, but otherwise empty of people. Derek turned and caught the man mocking Derek's pissing motion. Of course, he thought, what else would they be discussing? The woman led Derek further back into the apartment.

"Ah excellent," Kim said pleasantly as Derek entered. Next to Kim sat a dark eyed woman with a slender, triangular face with high cheekbones. Her black hair was gathered behind her head, held there with a carved bone comb. She wore a silky bone-colored blouse with black embroidery around the sleeves.

"Derek Cantor, this is Le Le," Kim announced.

"I am pleased to make your acquaintance." He held out his hand. Le Le rose and accepted his hand. Her breath came out frosty white in the moist warm air.

"Should I kill him?"

Kim had taken a bite of the broiled fish on his plate. He chewed thoughtfully for a second.

302

"He is still of some use to me," Kim said. Le Le let him go and sat down.

"Le Le has some very good news for me; less good for you I am afraid." Derek glared at Kim and waited. "But forgive my manners, please sit and join our dinner. Kherlos is out foraging through the city and will not be joining us." Kim clapped his hands. Immediately another young girl entered carrying a plate with a broiled fish and potatoes. Derek sat as the plate was placed before him. He was not sure how to eat whole fish. He looked at Kim's plate and saw he had broken into the flesh under the fin. He cut the fish and found the skin peeled away easily. His stomach growled in anticipation.

"Yes, it is good. Eat," Kim said. "Le Le has been to the sanctuary." Derek's fork stopped. He considered Kim's words for a second. Then he looked at Le Le who was smiling like a viper.

"Kim doesn't need his little homing pigeon anymore."

"He is a newsman," Kim replied, "He still has his uses." Derek suspected they had had this argument before and that Le Le just wanted to make sure he knew his place. If Kim had not wanted Derek along then they would not have called him for dinner. He could afford to ignore Le Le, but not antagonize her. He was hungry; the fish was good. He took another bite while they bickered.

"All men tell stories," Le Le hissed.

"Vellenia and Seth are there," Kim announced.

Kim is a braggart. Derek thought. He wondered if this was a dangerous trait for a hired assassin. "How is Seth?"

"As well as can be expected."

Derek took this as a sore subject. "What about the girl? I don't recall her name, I didn't get to meet her. Is she still captive?"

"No. She has been freed." Le Le spoke as if she had been the one who freed her.

"What did the council do to Ahten over that?" Derek asked.

"There has been a change of management since your last visit."

"Oh, Good, I never liked him. Who's in charge now?"

"Martsen, you may have known him."

Derek's mouth opened. "An odd choice, I find I harbor faint resentment towards that man as well."

"And we no longer need you to find the mountain. I'm afraid you are now unemployed." Le Le made a sympathetic face and little tut-tut noises.

"So I gathered. Am I being sent home or am I being abandoned?"

"Neither, you are coming with us, but I will no longer be paying your wife's exorbitant stipend."

"I have little money."

"For a fee, we will allow you to withdraw funds from your wife's account."

"How kind, am I to be charged for this meal."

"Don't be petulant."

"What about Kherlos?"

"I have not decided about him yet."

"Does he know that?"

"No, and it's best for your health that it stays that way," Kim said.

Derek ate for a while in silence, but the fish had lost its flavor, and he was no longer hungry.

"Tell me Derek, what are your allegiances?" Kim asked.

"What do you mean?"

"When Le Le said that there had been a change in management, she meant the council is no longer in control."

"You are," Derek accused Le Le. She nodded.

Derek shrugged. "I'm just a newsman, I write it and they sell it." The answer seemed to please them.

"We're not quite ready to let the world know yet, is what I mean," Le Le said. "So I would be personally disappointed if word got out prematurely."

"I was thinking," Derek said, thinking quickly, "that we would want simultaneous coverage, both here and in Andoline. You don't allow news like this to just happen, you plan it." They looked at him quizzically. "It's not only a front page spread, but profiles and editorials. It's about the people, their histories, the difficulties they face that make them real to our citizens." He gestured at Le Le. "We chronicle your struggle; show your humility and how you use your ability for the betterment of others." Le Le snorted at this comment, but did not look displeased.

"Editorials?" Kim asked.

"Sure, a pamphlet has no credibility if it doesn't have at least two conflicting opinions on any major story. We'll write all this up ahead of time, and then we sell it to other publishers, who pay us to reprint our stories. It's called residuals."

Le Le's eyes had a certain glassy look.

"I will handle this," Kim said, "We will talk more later. Now about these residuals, Yes?"

"Yes," answered Derek, wondering why he could not keep his own mouth shut. Kim spoke a few low words to Le Le, motioned one of the girls over and spoke to her briefly. The girl left and then returned with a large bowl of rice pudding. Kim scooped a generous portion into a serving bowl and offered it to Derek

"No, thank, you, I'm not really feeling well."

Kim offered the bowl to Le Le, who took it and then flash froze the bottom.

"It's much better chilled," she said, and offered it back to Derek.

"Really, you're too kind; I think I need more rest."

"Whatever."

Derek stood up and excused himself.

"Are you sure they will keep Vellenia alive?" Kim asked once Derek was gone.

"Well nothing's certain, is it?" she said, "but they did make me a promise."

"And Martsen will take his chances in the well?"

"Maybe." She put a spoonful of pudding in her mouth and looked pleased.

"I don't think they know what they are planning," she said, after swallowing.

Kim thought this over. It was not what he had expected, and it could be good news or bad news. A lot would depend on how well they liked Le Le. If things went wrong, his career as Kim would be famous for its brevity.

"Ironic isn't it?" Le Le asked.

"What?"

"That their pets have turned their wishing wells against their masters."

"That is not the definition of irony," Kim said. Le Le glared at him.

"Yes, it's ironic," he said.

Le Le smiled. "They want revenge, that's usually a good motive." She dipped her spoon into the large bowl of pudding and blew cold breath onto it before putting it into her mouth.

"It keeps me in business," Kim agreed.

Le Le nodded thoughtfully, and threw her spoon onto her plate. "If we're going to get back, we need to get started early."

"Yes."

"Well then, tell that girl over there that she's going to bed with me." Kim spoke briefly, the woman hardly even blinked at the suggestion; she bowed to Le Le, and then waited with her eyes on the floor until Le Le led her out.

# Thirty Five.

*And in her twelfth year, Apachawea's daughter, who had taken the
name of MoonChild, asked for the gift to see that which was far as if
it was near, so that she might gaze up on her brother, and the other
children, who had wished the moon. And the gift was granted. And
MoonChild wept.*

*Myth of the Revelation*

### 4 Veena, Y.O.D. 746

## Council Monastery, East of Vesport, Tameria

D erek!" Martsen called out from his seat at the end of the table.
They had just sat down to dinner when Le Le and her new
entourage had appeared. "What an unexpected pleasure."

Derek managed a smile; if it faltered slightly, Martsen took no notice.
He bounded out of his chair, almost tripping over one of the students just
sitting down to eat, and picked Derek up in an effusive bear hug. "I am
most honored to see you again. Le Le told us she was bringing a friend,
but I never imagined it would be you. Le Le why didn't you tell me you
knew Derek?"

Le Le ignored him, brushed past and headed over to speak with
Dharla.

"She's so moody," Martsen said. "But never mind, come, sit, we are
about to dine. Tell me who are your friends?" he dragged Derek towards
the table, and shooed the occupants out of the seats next to him.

"Sit, eat, you made Ahten very angry with your writings." He waggled
his finger at Derek, "but I don't care, I'm in charge now, everyone is
happy, no more stupid rules." Martsen waved his hand at the other people
in the room, who all nodded except Le Le who continued to look
petulant.

"Have you met Dharla and Briana?" continued Martsen. The girls
were sitting across from him. They stood and offered to shake hands.

"No, pleased to meet you. Where is everyone?"

"All the priests are gone," Martsen said.

"We don't need them," Briana said.

"Seth, Cal, Lana?" Derek asked.

"I'm here," Cal answered. He and Lana were seated at the other end of the table. Lana gave a small, unenthusiastic wave hello.

"Ah," Martsen explained, "she is sad for Seth. Yes, we all are. He is in his room, it is very sad."

"What?"

"He has recently lost his wife you see, and she was with his child."

"Very sad," Le Le said. Derek glanced her way. She wasn't even trying to look sad. He started to rise.

"No, sit, please, you must eat. I know you will want to visit him later. Soon I assure you. I know he will be very pleased to see you. He knew you were coming, and asked that you come see him after you have had your dinner."

The unexpected lie did not escape Derek's notice. He decided to let it pass. "Well, yes, okay. And what-"

"So Le Le has told you our good news then? No? Shame on you Le Le." Martsen held his hands up defensively when he saw her glare. "Okay, okay, I should tell him then."

"She said she was," Derek started, then paused. "Um, you have something special you wanted to announce, but she didn't divulge the details." He wasn't going to start them arguing over who was actually in charge.

"Yes," Marsten said. "Yes, a most auspicious night, and you Derek, here again at the start of ah… yes, well you must be tired. Tell me, who are these gentlemen you bring with you?"

"I am Kim, and this is my man Kherlos, I am sorry, but he does not speak Colovencia.

"Mr. Kim?" Martsen asked.

"Just Kim."

"I must admit, that I did not expect Le Le to bring back newsmen, but I guess it does make sense."

"I do not work for the pamphlets," Kim said.

"What then?"

"I kill people." All conversation stopped. "For money."

"Really?"

"Would you like a demonstration?"

"So I take it then you're good at it?"

"Yes."

Le Le snorted at this. Kim looked at her coolly.

"Le Le does not agree," Martsen said.

"Professional jealousy, that is all."

"Is that why you are here then? To kill one of us? Me?"

"No, I am here as Le Le's guest."

"Ah yes, well that is good." Martsen seemed to be at loss for words.

Le Le took up the slack. "I assume everything is still ready for our celebration tonight?"

"Yes," Dharla said, "everything is exactly as you left it."

"Good. Derek, why don't you run along and fetch Seth then? It's not good for him to sulk. I'm sure he'll be pleased to see you."

"Yes, certainly, I think I still know where his room is."

"I am very much interested in meeting this Seth," Kim said, "I should go with you."

Martsen's scowled at Kim. "Do you have an ability, Kim?"

"Yes."

"And your man?"

"No, nor shall he."

"Seth will be fine," Le Le said. "Derek, take your friends and go visit. Dharla, Briana, do you think you could find Vellenia?"

Derek stopped. "Vellenia is here?"

The look on their faces, the quick panic, the glances between the girls and Martsen and Le Le, and even Kim's posture all told him he had just asked the wrong question.

"Yes, she is," Le Le said. "Is that a problem?"

"No, It's very nice. I have this book you see, it's kind of a hobby of mine to get Ra-ken to write their name in it."

"Take it along," Le Le hissed. "Maybe you can get Seth to sign it."

"Take a lamp," Martsen said.

§

Derek led Kim and Kherlos into the familiar hall where he had been received once before. The floors were filthy, the air smelled of decay and rot. When he had last traveled to this place, the walls had been bright with light and the floor clean. Then the passage had been filled with fresh lamps. Now the path was dark and Derek carried the only light.

"You knew," Derek said.

"Yes," Kim said, "I usually do, but what specifically are you accusing me of knowing?"

"That we were coming here, and what we would find."

"Yes."

"When?"

"Many months ago. Shortly before Kherlos and I reached your home."

"What?"

"Keep your voice low. Yes, my family employs many people in various ways from time to time, and this includes Le Le, though she does not know this. We learned the location of the sanctuary from her. She was instructed to meet me in Vesport and to insure the death of Vellenia and Seth were delayed until we returned."

"Wait," Derek stopped, "I don't understand."

Kim grabbed his arm and moved him forward. "Your job here is not to understand, but to keep your mouth shut and observe. We have no time tonight for explanations, but one day we may."

Kim spoke to Kherlos. *"We must be careful. If Seth believes we are a threat, he might kill us all. If we are to be successful, we must surprise him, so you understand you must do exactly as I say at all times."*

Kherlos considered these words. *"Derek knows this man?"*

*"Yes, they were friends."*

*"And he will let you kill him?"*

*"He too is being paid."* Kim turned back to Derek. "Kherlos will follow my instructions. You too must do as I say."

"There's something you aren't telling me."

"Yes, many things, and if I thought you knew some of them, I would be required to kill you. So you should keep such thoughts to yourself."

"Shut up and observe?"

"It is always best when I need not repeat instructions, yes." Kim looked at the passage. "This area is not so much neglected as hated. Are you sure this is the right way?"

"Yes, I see a doorway up ahead, about where I would have expected it." There was a doorway, but no door. Derek peered into the room as Kim and Kherlos crowded behind him. "The last time I was here, Seth was bathing with two young women."

"It would seem he has fallen on somewhat harder times then. Is he here?"

"No," Derek replied. He pushed past Kim back into the hall. Kherlos put a hand up and stopped him. Wordlessly Kherlos flicked his eyes down the dark corridor and then stared back at Derek.

"Yes," Derek answered the unspoken question, "He might be down there."

"Go."

Derek moved to the doorway and held up the light. Whatever contents the room once held had been destroyed and the debris scattered about the floor. In the center lay a young man in dirty clothes.

"Seth? Divine above, is that you? It's me, Derek." He moved forward and knelt beside the disheveled man.

Kim turned to Kherlos and held one finger up to his lips. He pointed at Kherlos. "You." He pointed at the floor. "Stay."

"Hello my friend." Seth spoke in a weak voice. He pushed himself up and stared at Derek with empty sockets.

"What happened to your eyes?" Derek held the lamp up to Seth's face.

"He is blind?" Kim asked from the doorway.

"Yes, I am. Who are you? You brought friends Derek?"

"What happened?" Kim asked.

"Vellenia did this to me. She didn't trust me, they killed Tabitha."

"I didn't know," Derek said. "I'm so sorry."

Seth reached out, found Derek's arm and jerked him forward, down to his level. "Now you're sorry are you? But it was you who told. You told Vellenia where I was. You turned me in. You did this to me."

"No." Kim said, "It was his neighbor."

"What?" the two men asked together. Kim shook his head at Derek; this was no time for explanations.

"Seth, does this mean you can't use your ability?"

"Yes. They made sure of that." He let his head drop, and released Derek. "Vellenia guessed I would need eyes to use my power. She was right."

*"Ah maka oclo,"* Kherlos growled.

Derek stood and blocked Kherlos. He had not understood the words, but the intent was clear. "No, this wasn't the deal—"

Kim kicked him in the back of the knee, sending him down hard onto the floor. The hot glass of the lamp landed on his chest, fell off and burned his side. Derek rolled away, then grabbed the handle and lifted it before it could set both him and the floor on fire.

Kherlos stepped past Derek, grabbed Seth around the neck and pulled him to his feet.

*"Mine."* He pressed this thumbs into Seth's neck and squeezed. His strong arms met no resistance. He held on until the protruding tongue turned dark.

*"Not yet,"* Kim said, *"his spirit yet lingers."* Kim counted softly. *"Two, three, now."*

*"I wish I had the ability to—"*

Kim stabbed Kherlos in the thigh.

*"Damnation!"*

*"Please, continue,"* Kim said. He stepped back so that Kherlos could complete his wish.

*"I wish I had the ability to shoot beams of death with my eyes!"* Kherlos stared hard at Kim who stood there serenely, the knife held between them.

Kherlos tried again. *"I wish I had the ability to shoot beams of death with my eyes."*

"It is gone," Kim said.

Kherlos sank, defeated. *"Why?"*

*"I do what I must."*

Kherlos collapsed then onto the floor and curled up, sobbing, his power lost, betrayed and defeated.

Kim walked over, stood above the broken man, and spoke softly. *"This is not the end of you. There are many with abilities that dwell on this mountain Kherlos, a clever man might find an opportunity in that."*

He walked back to Derek. "Get up Derek. I need you to be able to walk."

"Why did you kick me?" It sounded like whining.

"You were in my way, now come, we are needed elsewhere." He walked out of the room.

Derek climbed to his feet, tested his bruised knee and found it would hold, though painfully. He limped after to Kim, stopped at the door and looked back at Kherlos, still weeping on the floor. "I'm sorry." It needed saying, even if no one heard, even if no one understood.

Kim waited for Derek in the darkened hall, took his arm and guided him along.

"I'm guessing he didn't get his ability back," Derek said. Kim said nothing.

"Okay, can I ask about Vellenia?"

"Yes. They will take her ability tonight, but it is not my doing. It is their plans. My part here is done. They will not be pleased that eyes that kill is lost to them, but I of course, could not know Kherlos would act so foolishly. You understand?"

"Shut up and watch?"

"Yes."

"I love her."

"Who?"

"Vellenia."

Kim shrugged. "My brother loved Le Le."

"Will you help me save her?"

"Le Le?"

"Vellenia!"

"No."

"Will you stop me?"

"If your actions put my life in danger, then yes, I will."

"I'll keep that in mind."

§

Kim and Derek returned to the main reception hall. The food had been cleared, the tables moved back. At the far end of the hall sat a raised platform, behind which hung a banner depicting a golden sun with emanating red and yellow rays. Inside the sun was a single eye. Sitting on the platform were Dharla and Briana. On either side were two more chairs, one empty, Le Le sat in the other, bent forward, a bright look of anticipation on her face. A few of the students stood in a small group to one side, while in the center of the room, kneeling on the stone floor in filthy rags; was Vellenia. Derek saw her there, cried out her name, and hobbled towards her.

"Leave her," Dharla said.

Derek ignored her.

"Stop," Dharla said, this time with her ability.

Derek stopped, held by the woman's power, and understood.

"You would be wise to listen to this young woman," Kim advised.

"Where's Seth?" Dharla asked Kim.

"He has had an accident, I am afraid."

"What kind of accident?" Le Le and Briana looked up from their conversation.

"I am afraid that Kherlos killed him, I tried to stop him, you understand." He showed them the bloody knife. "But I was too late."

"And his ability?" Le Le spat.

"I don't know. All of us are powered here, it could be anywhere by now."

Dharla eyed him coldly. Vellenia started to rise.

"Briana," Dharla said. Briana applied her power to Vellenia once more, and she settled back down onto her knees.

"We'll talk more about this later," Dharla said to Kim, "We have other work to do right now. Le Le?"

Dharla and Le Le rose and walked over to stand in front of the kneeling Vellenia.

"Ra-ken Vellenia Echliesties, Master of Water," Dharla said in her most formal voice, "Are we ready?"

"Yes."

"To take your ability?"

"Yes."

"The wishing wheels are in perfect operation?"

"Yes."

"Le Le, I believe this honor is yours."

Le Le smiled and stepped forward, slowly, majestically. She preened; her long black hair against her pale skin made her look exotic, beautiful and dangerous.

"Your ribs still hurt," Vellenia said.

"I promised you a slow death."

"Quicker is better."

"Not for you."

"No."

"Do you want to know why Martsen betrayed you?" Le Le held her hands up over Vellenia's head and started cooling them down.

"No. All men betray me."

"Pity, I was really looking forward to telling you. I mean, imagine that, your handpicked man turning on you and lusting after your power behind your back and all the while, you didn't even know. We all laughed at you, you thought you were so much better than we were. I'm going to enjoy this. I'm going to make you beg to die, freezing your limbs and breaking them off in front of you. I can do that you know. You think my power is simple and useless except for making ice cream; I hate ice cream. You know I murdered my master to get this power. He used to think I loved ice cream and I had to eat it and pretend, but I hated it and I hated him, and now I have his power and I never even once made ice cream, not even for the prettiest of my little girls."

Le Le continued to babble while everyone else looked puzzled.

"Le Le," Dharla shouted, "What are you doing, just kill her already."

"What? What do you want, why are you yelling at me bitch, you and your little whore friend can't tell me what to do. I'll freeze both of you little techas just you watch." Le Le slapped her hand against Vellenia's head.

"What are you doing?" Kim hissed at Derek.

"Look."

Kim saw Le Le staring at her own hand, babbling the whole time.

"It won't work, my power won't work, why can't I shut up, what's doing this? Why won't my power work? I can't kill her maybe I can kick her to death, that's no good, I can, but I want her to suffer cold, deep loving cold, where is my cold?"

"Interesting."

"Babble. All of you!" shouted Derek. He spread his power to the whole room.

"I don't need my power to kill you," Kim said. "Nobody else can do anything. Sure I can. Look at everyone else just saying the first thing that comes to mind. If they remember any of this then there are going to be many sore feelings later. I thought you had one of the stupid useless powers but this is fascinating, I can still slice you open with my blade anytime, so what is this going to accomplish? Are you going to make them talk each other to death? I need calm, I need my ability. I can kill you and use my ability. Talking doesn't stop my ability, and it doesn't stop a blade, but what about them? Le Le couldn't freeze, and Dharla can't control you, but I can still use my ability, I'll show you." Kim vanished, but Derek could hear him still talking right in front of him, moving away.

He ignored Kim; he ignored them all. Vellenia was no longer held under Briana's sway, but she couldn't focus on her power either. He couldn't hear what she was saying over Le Le's shrill hysterics. He hobbled over to Le Le and made a fist. She glared at him, fear, hatred, loathing, all of it echoed in her eyes. He punched her hard, high on the cheek, and she fell.

The room went silent. They collectively caught their breath, realized the situation, and called upon their abilities.

"Stop," Dharla shouted at the whole room. "Everyone stop, stop using your powers, whoever is doing this just stop, Kim is this your ability? Where is Kim? What is that man doing? Stop him, he's doing this, someone go get Martsen, Briana calm everyone, can't you use your power? Someone go get Martsen, stop him, Briana do something."

They were all babbling again, louder, more frantic. His power trumped their power, and he felt like a god. He looked down at Le Le and she scrambled away from him as best she could. She kicked at him, hissing and screaming at him the whole time, describing her hatred for men. Derek backed away from the flailing legs.

She rose like a fury. Bent forward, with fists thrust to her sides she cursed him, but when he stepped forward, fist raised, she cowed, turned and tried to flee. He caught her then by her long black hair, it was thick and coarse, not all what he'd expected.

He pulled, hard.

Le Le screamed, she cried, she slumped down to her knees, sobbing, pleading, begging, promising to behave, promising sex, ice cream, anything she could think of, anything that came to mind. It all came out of her mouth, promises, compliments, curses and threats all hurled one after the other rapid fire while her lungs struggled to draw breath.

He looked around. Dharla and Briana were grabbing at each other on the platform. Kim was gone. Vellenia was trying to crawl toward the outside doors.

Not a bad idea, he thought. He let go of Le Le's hair and she curled up on the floor like those little caterpillars do when frightened. He kicked her, and they both yelped in pain, but it got her attention.

"Get out!" he yelled at her. She was still talking; he couldn't understand her words but he could guess their meaning.

"Get out! There!" He pointed at the door leading back to their apartments. He didn't want them going outside.

Le Le pushed herself up and started crawling towards the door. Derek limped over to Dharla and Briana. They half-sat, clutching each other, eyes wild, faces covered in each other's spittle and blood. Derek picked up a chair and shook it at them. They too got the message.

Le Le, now on her feet, moved slowly down the hallway, one hand on the wall. Briana and Dharla rushed past, knocking her down without even noticing. The two forced their way into their room at the end of the hall and slammed the door.

Le Le lay on floor crying in great heaving sobs. He released his ability and closed the hall door, exhausted.

The room was silent. Derek looked around. Vellenia had collapsed but was still struggling. Kim appeared at his side.

"Impressive, most unexpected."

"So kill me already." He headed towards Vellenia.

"I don't understand this death wish you have." Kim walked around and stood in front of Derek, and bowed low; a stiff formal bow.

"What?"

"You have the heart of a warrior," Kim announced, "So many people think that it is the ability that makes them—" Derek brushed past Kim and reached Vellenia. He wasn't in the mood for compliments. He helped her to her feet. The feel of bones underneath her thin clothes told him much.

"We have to kill them," she said.

Where she might get the strength for this task he could not imagine. "You're welcome."

"You're stupid."

"You must now go," Kim said, "they will recover, and I will not allow you to kill them."

Vellenia pulled herself up and stepped in front of Kim, confronting him face to face. Derek noticed there was something wrong with Kim's body. The man had no right arm. He held his breath, he had no strength left, she had no strength left, and they could not win this fight. Vellenia and Kim stared at each other, and then she looked away.

Kim turned so that his right side was away from the two of them. His shirt billowed out slightly and then his right arm came into view, his hand empty. He hurried over to the wall and pulled down an oil lamp. "Martsen will soon be wondering what went wrong. He will check on the other wishing chamber and then come here. You cannot be here when he arrives." Kim handed Derek the lamp. "In the morning, they are likely come looking for you both. I may be able to stop them. They may listen to reason; they may not. It is best if you are gone."

"I'm sorry," Derek said, again to no one in particular. He put his arm around Vellenia again, and the two headed for the exit.

The outside air was cool and moist; the steps down the side of the mountain were damp.

"Wait." Vellenia knelt down carefully, holding on to Derek for support. She touched the ground, and a path of dryness rolled down the steps like an invisible carpet. A small globe of water swelled in her hand. She raised the water to her mouth and drank it greedily.

"Okay," she said, and they descended. After a few more steps she asked, "Is Seth dead?"

"Yes."

"Did Kherlos get his power back?"

"No."

"I guess that's a good thing."

Derek didn't know what to say to that, so he didn't.

Inside Kim considered his next move; he needed to restore their dignity. He opened the door to the apartments. Le Le remained on the floor, small and vulnerable; she would never forgive anyone who saw her like this. He called upon his ability, walked past her quietly and grabbed a blanket from her room. He came back and laid it gently around her, and then exited the main hall.

Across the great courtyard was the entrance to the trainee's dormitories. Kim walked in unannounced to the girls' room. A dozen pair of eyes stared at him; but no one spoke. He walked among them, looking at each. He selected a slim girl with a small chest, knowing Le Le's preference for girls who did not yet rival her as a woman.

"Come with me," he said to the girl, "leave your things, they will be brought to you in the morning. There has been an accident, No one is hurt, but no abilities were captured either. You may tell the others, but you should all sleep in your own beds tonight." Kim led the young woman back to the main hall and over to Le Le's prone form.

"Take her to bed." Kim pointed at Le Le's room. "Stay the night with her. Tell her she must come to bed with you, but nothing else."

"But I'm not—" Kim cut her off with a look.

"Yes, Ra."

Satisfied Le Le would recover, Kim set off in search of Martsen. He found two girls huddling outside the wishing chamber door, clinging like frightened mice, afraid to interrupt the people inside.

"Return to your beds." He unlatched the door and pulled it open. Martsen was the first out of the room.

"What?" Martsen demanded.

Kim looked into the chamber. "Let the others out, and all of you, return to your rooms, there will be no wishes granted tonight." Kim motioned for Martsen to follow him. He talked as they walked back to the main hall.

"Vellenia has escaped, the others are unharmed. Seth is dead."

"How did that happen?" Martsen put his hand on Kim's shoulder and turned him around. He stood there, towering above Kim, holding him firmly by the arm. Kim stared at Martsen's hand. Martsen released his grip and mumbled an apology.

"The man Derek, he was sent by the Council to rescue Vellenia. He was able to prevent us from using our powers, I do not know how this could be so, but he took the woman and they have fled."

"We must go after them," Martsen said.

"Has the Divine touched you and blessed you with an ability I am unaware of?"

"What about the eyes that kill?"

"No," Kim said. "That ability has fled."

Oh, gather round people and listen ye well,
Take heed of my words and the story I tell.
Beware of acting too soon.
Tis' the Lesson of Ra-ken who gathered the Fel,
And they found they were wishing...the moon,

Of Kherlos and Cordain and Derek you'll learn
They scrape and they bow and they all take their turn,
To dance to the Brotherhood's Tune.
We all play our parts now; it's not our concern,
'Til we find we are wishing...the moon.

From time immemorial, it's always decreed,
You can't reach the heavens until you concede:
For should you be seeking a boon,
The Divine he will grant you, whatever you need,
Just as long as it's wishing...the moon.


– Popular Ballad –

# Thirty Six.

*Kellen Ra, Oren Mah, Ana moke ku Ah, Ana fetta ku Ah, Ana tonne ku Ah.*

*Blessed Divine, hear me, I act as your servant, I carry your faith. I speak your word.*

*Book of the Divine*

**17 Rasee, Y.O.D. 746**

## Southern Island of Koolan, Vesmouth Sea

Kim's family waited for him at the docks. The shallow harbor could not accommodate the deep draft of the large sailing ships that plied the trade between the continents, and so Kim, like everything else was loaded into a shallow flat-pan boat and tendered into shore sitting among bales of cotton and tobacco. They stood in a line, his mother and father at the front. This let him know that his Grandmother had passed, or was too ill to attend his return. Behind his parents stood his brothers and sisters, each in order of birth standing with their families. Koko was there near the back, with her new son, beaming proudly as she held the infant against her breast. Behind them on the street, obstructing traffic was a long line of ornate red lacquered palanquin.

When the boat was secure, he climbed onto the dock and stood before his parents. His mother stood in a splendid flowing blue and green robe, decorated with white cranes and lilies and edged with gold thread. Her jet hair was pulled back tight with an ebony and gold comb, small diamonds glittered at the tip of each long lacquered fingernail. His father stood behind her in a simple black suit.

He bowed deep to his mother and father. He waited for her to speak. She stood impassively, enjoying the moment, enjoying the impatience of the others. This was her way of telling Kim that his grandmother was dead. That she was now head of the family. It was her way of softening the blow. Had grandmother been ill, Kim's mother would have hurried them off. Any delay would be disrespectful, an insult. Kim understood the message, and bowed again, lower, and held his bow.

"Welcome home honored son." She lifted Kim up with her thin bony fingers. "You may kiss me."

Kim stepped into his mother's arms and gave her a light kiss on the cheek. With his mother properly greeted, Kim turned and greeted his father. They two bowed as equals, with Kim bowing slightly lower, as was his place. His mother held out her arm. Kim took it and led her down the wharf to the first couple.

"Your brother AhSet and his wife Oohli," his mother announced, in case Kim had been gone so long as to have forgotten his family, a mild jab, but also a way of avoiding the embarrassment should this actually be so.

"AhSet has been appointed secretary to the Commissioner of Finance, and your nephew PiSet has been accepted at University."

"You do me great honor brother," Kim said. They exchanged bows. One by one, his mother led him down the line, re-introducing him to his brothers and sisters and their families and extolling the accomplishments and virtues of each. A variation of this scene would be repeated back at his mother's home, where his aunts and uncles and other honored guests waited. Kim led his mother to her litter.

"Ride with us," she said.

Kim bowed. "I am honored."

Inside, with the procession under way, Kim's mother dropped the formalities. "Give me the short version."

Kim told his story and waited while his mother thought. His father had said nothing the entire trip, but had listened intently.

"I believe this will bring balance and opportunity," she said. "What do they call themselves?"

"Heralds of the Divine."

"Interesting, it has just the right touch of hubris, what are your thoughts dear?"

"It is as you say, balance and opportunity."

"Did we acquire the eyes that kill?" Kim asked.

"Yes, that ability will trouble us no more."

"May I inquire as to its place in the family? Will it be used for contracts?"

"No, that has not changed, nor shall it, the Council's plan was good, but flawed. It lacked the unity of family. This ability will be safe with us, and in time, people will believe it is back with the Angels. They are so quick to believe pretty lies."

Kim held his tongue. He had asked his questions.

"And what about contracts?" she asked.

"Le Le, is the key. She will shape them into the image of the council, which is what she desires and hates the most. It is she that will teach them the advantages of letting someone else do the killing."

"And the Council?"

"There are always offers from the junior members, the elders will guide me there, but it is a large empire with many ambitious people. That has not changed."

His mother sat back, looking pleased with the answer. "A second Council Ra-ken, or whatever they call themselves will be a boon. The opportunities for spies, agents and assassins are limitless. You have done well my son. I think I shall buy a second house."

# Thirty Seven.

*Modern deification theory bases the premise of the paranormal gifts on the manifestation of the will of a divine munificent being, of omnipotent stature. The functional augmentations arise from grants of beneficence, monopolistic in nature. Intelligence and beneficence are demonstrated through the manifestation, nature and exclusivity of the augmentations.*

*Philosophica Divine - Massatti*

**25 Rasee, Y.O.D. 746**

## Chambers Council Ra-ken, City of Andoline

There are a few things I should go over with you before you go in," said the guard outside of the privy chamber of the Council Ra-ken. There were two guards, the new one was doing the talking, and the one keeping his mouth shut had been around longer. The man waiting to see the council gave the guard a quizzical look.

"Offending a member of the Council is punishable by us throwing your lifeless body into the river. And there's lots of ways to offend them."

"Tell me about it," Derek said. The older guard chuckled and the new guard gave him a dirty look.

"I am, so shut it. Now, if you have an ability, you don't ever use it, unless they directly tell you to, which they won't so that's that. Next, they speak in order. The woman wearing black's in charge, and she always speaks first. If someone else asks you a question, you look to her. If she ok's it, then you answer to her, not to the one that asked it. Got that?"

"I already–"

"Got it? Yes or no?" Derek looked to the other guard for support, who just shrugged in a "What are you going to do?" sort of way.

"I'm only doing this for your own good; it's not my skin if you take my meaning." Derek crossed his arms and waited.

"Now, it don't matter that you might know their names, you aren't in their league and you don't get all chummy. And another thing–" Derek never found out what the final warning was. The man stopped in mid-sentence and the two guards snapped to attention. The door to the council chamber pushed open a crack and familiar female voice called out.

"Derek, get in here."

"Yes, Vellenia." He sauntered into the room and closed the door behind him.

Vellenia took her seat. Tawnya Brawly, current head of the Council Ra-ken, Able to Direct the Strikes of Lightning, rose. "Sirrah Derek Duane Cantor, Able to Make Others Speak Without Reflection; the Council Ra-ken would like to thank you for the service you have rendered us in your part in saving the life of Ra-ken Vellenia Echliesties." She paused letting the message sink in. "We have agreed to a payment of a sum of twenty thousand suns, as our way of thanking you for this service."

Derek blinked. "Thank you, that is—"

"Yes, shut up," Tawnya said. "We don't like you. You've caused us embarrassment in the past, and only your familiarity with Vellenia kept that from being fatal. So we agreed that she would pay you out of her own purse, and she's not very happy about that either.

"Obviously, we don't want the details of what happened public knowledge, which is why you won't be allowed to work as a newsman from now on. It's bad enough with all the lies they print about us, but it's even worse when they print the truth, so that's just not going to happen." She paused and stared at Derek, he nodded agreement.

"Good, now that's that, about the man Kim. I understand that you managed to befriend him, is that so?"

"Sort of, it's hard to tell."

"Well he didn't kill you, and that's something. I understand that he made it quite clear to you, that your ability to make people talk would in no way hinder his ability to kill you should he so desire. Is that not so?"

"Yes."

"Well I think it's safe to say your ability is quite formidable against children and those prone to weeping. So while you might be quite the champion to send against the Heralds of the Divine, you would find yourself at somewhat less of an advantage among those of us who've earned our titles."

Derek didn't know what to say to this, which he thought, was probably best.

"Good, I'm glad I'm understood. Now get out and don't ever come to our attention again."

Derek looked at the faces in the room. Most would not meet his gaze; the others looked like they were laughing at him. Tawnya was making little shooing motions at him. He turned to leave, and a hand touched his arm.

"I'll be in touch," mouthed Fremen Bramer. Derek didn't know much about the man, and had heard little other than he didn't like the rest of the Council. Fremen winked at him, and then turned his attention back to the table. Derek left. It had worked out pretty much the way Kim had said it would, except for the bonus. Knowing Kim, he would try to find some way to deduct that sum from his payments, but knowing Clea, he would fail.

§

"Now," Tawnya sighed, "on to my least favorite topic. Shenna?"

Shenna DeCort rose from her seat. "The Heralds of the Divine…"

"Don't validate their claim by using that stupid title," Tawnya said, unaware of having just done so.

"Well what shall I call them? Your little project?"

This brought a glare from Tawnya.

"The Usurpers?" offered Cordain, anxious to keep the meeting from degenerating into bickering.

Tawnya waved agreement.

"The Usurpers then," continued Shenna, "are claiming by the treaty of Colovencia, the rights to the incomes from the lands of Epe Tianore, by rights of Briana Inno, able to control the emotions of others, as well as the income from East Moridin, by rights of Dharla Fullen. In addition, Le Le is claiming Vesport, north to some river, and eastward to some point that includes the sanctuary as her rightful lands and chattel."

"By rights," Cordain interjected, "They have to return to their lands, and lay claim. Do they intend to do that?"

Shenna shook her head. "I got the impression they were planning on staying where they were, but they did say they would make the journey if they were pressed."

Cordain slammed the table. "Which would put us right back where we started, with my friend dead, and untrained children making demands of us."

"Cordain, that's enough," Tawnya said. "There will be a forty percent administration fee, plus the cost of time and labor for building the sanctuary."

"What about the attempt on my life?" Vellenia asked, "They should pay for that."

Tawnya gave her no sympathy. "Right, good luck with that."

"They anticipated your offer," Shenna said, "and said for anything less than eighty five percent that they're willing to make the trip."

"Who do you work for?" Tawnya barked, "Them or us?"

"Don't even," she said, "I hate that man Martsen; I just want to shake him until he's a meat puppet."

"Next time, try it, you might get more favorable terms. Tell them thirty percent, or they're welcome to visit, and I'll be working up the figure on the cost of that mountain, and it won't be cheap either."

# Thirty Eight.

*Owing to the nature of augmentations to manifest Ra Accedo, as a direct indication of obtainment, abilities that would create global ruination, are shown to be unobtainable by direct evidence of continued existence. The limits thereupon the scope of abilities stand as indication of the munificent nature of the being that grants these abilities.*

*Philosophica Divine - Massatti*

**5 Veena, Y.O.D. 746**

## Council Monastery East of Vesport, Tameria

Kherlos opened his eyes. The morning light was just sneaking into the filthy cave where he lay among broken dreams, the body of a dead man, and the ghost of an old friend.

"Get Up!" Takoda snapped. The voice seemed to echo inside his head while only the sound of wind reached his ears. "Get up, if they find you here, they will kill you."

The pain in his thigh, like the emptiness, and the nagging voice of his dead friend refused to go away. He was done, his story, ended; his life, over; his ability, lost. There was no hope, no future, yet Takoda refused to let him be.

"Alright," Kherlos shouted into the vacant room, "alright." He uncurled and rolled onto his back gently. He felt the wound in the back of his right thigh.

"Use that pain," Takoda said. Takoda—his old friend, his conscience, his motivation, his burden; he had always been pushing, observing, criticizing, and his death only made it harder to silence him. "There are healers below."

"That would shut you up," Kherlos said. He had sought the comfort of healers to quiet the voice in his head and the hollowness in his soul, until Kim had decided that he was feigning illness for attention's sake.

He looked around the small room, barely more than a mountain cave strewn with debris and filth, though few caves he knew of sported barred windows. Seth's body lay next to him, its tongue protruding between blue lips, empty eye sockets staring. Kherlos grunted, at least that part of the trip had gone well. He grabbed Seth's shirt and pulled until the buttons popped. He bit a hole in the hem, and tore a wide strip of cloth to bind his leg, which was again oozing fresh blood.

"Don't leave that on too long," Takoda said.

Kherlos ignored him. He pushed his way with his good leg over to a wall, and using it for support managed to get up.

"Keep going."

Bracing himself against the wall, Kherlos tested his leg, and found he could hobble slowly along, out of the room, down the hallway, and out onto the plateau.

"You can't go down."

"You said there were healers down there."

"You'll fall down the steps."

"Isn't there some kind of contraption?"

"Do you know how to work it?

"No." Kherlos looked around. There was another door in the high cliff wall off to his right. Beyond that, the cliff curved around until it met the side of the monastery building.

"There's a path," Takoda said.

"Where?" Kherlos looked up and saw what might be a flat area running up just above where the rock face ended.

"It looks like it starts on the other side of that building."

§

Kherlos slumped down onto a soft patch of earth and rested while small flies pestered his leg. "Well Takoda, should I just stay here and let the insects eat me?" It seemed like a plan.

"Is that why you came up here?" Takoda asked, "to offer yourself to the insect gods?"

"I only believe in the Divine damn you," Kherlos said. He felt the back of his thigh where he'd been stabbed. The cloth was caked with blood. He brushed the flies away, licked his fingers and rubbed some spit on the wound. It felt closed, but he had no idea how long it would take to heal, or even if it would do that on its own.

"It will heal," Takoda said. "But you will need rest. This trail means people come up here, you will need someplace to hide for a day or two."

Kherlos looked around. The sun was up, and warm on his face, but it would not stay that way forever. He needed to get moving, and he needed to relieve himself, but this was not the place. "What about food, and water?"

"There is likely to be some fruit," Takoda said, "berries or nuts perhaps." Kherlos looked up, the peaks of the mountains high above him were covered in white.

"And there will be water."

§

"Let's say," Takoda said, "that you succeed in healing, then what?"

Kherlos grunted. Takoda had been quiet for over an hour while he limped up the trail.

"Do you speak their language?" Kherlos asked.

There was no answer.

"I thought not, well neither do I." Kherlos answered for him. "I don't need to know their words to gain their power. I know the words to that woman's power, that ice bitch."

"Yes, we do know the words for her ability," Takoda said.

The trail gave out at the far end of a shallow pool of water some twenty-five feet across and maybe five or six feet deep at the center. A thin stream of water gurgled down from a ledge overhead and a similar stream exited to his right.

"That's going to be cold," Takoda warned him.

"Bracing," Kherlos said. He pulled off his shirt, untied his belt and carefully eased his trowsers down, then stepped out of his sandals and started working his way into the water. Slowly he crouched and sat onto the wet stones, and then eased his way into the water. He spotted tiny fish darting in the water and gave a little grunt of amazement.

The water was cold. Where the fresh melt entered, the water was frigid, but it flowed slowly and picked up heat from the rocks and sun as it moved towards the shallow end, where it could safely be described as "less frigid."

"This feels good," Kherlos said aloud. Takoda declined to comment. After a little while, Kherlos felt a soft tickling on his feet. He sat up, and saw the tiny fish dart away.

"They're eating me," he said.

"That could take a while," replied Takoda. Kherlos slid further out into the water until his torso was floating. He turned over and pulled himself back to the shallows until his chest was resting on a rock. He reached back, and gently rubbed the wound. As soon as he took his hand away, he felt the soft touch of the fishes. Every few minutes he wiped away a little more dried blood and let the fish do their job.

After a while, when the cold could no longer be denied, he dragged himself out of the water into a sunny patch of grass and moss. Feeling cleaner and stronger, he laid there on the ground, absorbing its warmth while he dried.

§

"We could camp here," Kherlos remarked. He had fallen asleep and let the afternoon pass. He awoke stiff, and the wound on his leg felt tender and puffy. He dressed, and surveyed his surroundings.

"No," Takoda said. "It's too open, too popular. The trail here is frequently used."

"I don't remember seeing a lot of people."

"There is a dead man lying in a cave below us. As soon as they figure out you didn't go down, they're going to look up here."

"Where do we go?" The path ended at the edge of the pool. Looking across, he faced a steep jut of rock on the far side, the downward slope of the mountain on his right, and the path to his back.

"It looks like you could climb up there," Takoda mentally pointed out. Kherlos understood what he meant. The outcropping was steep but broken, and looked like it could be scaled. Once up, he would be on the ledge of rock where the water came down and fed the stream.

"Why not?" He slowly waded across the shallow end of the water. The rocks were black and cold, wet with spray. He climbed.

"See, perspective is everything," Takoda said.

Kherlos stood on top of the outcrop of rock and looked down. The pool below was just deep enough to jump into. He declined, but it was clear others had been here frequently. There was a trail, a thin one, possibly used only by the deer, but it was there.

He scanned the sky, there were a few hours of sun left in the day before it dipped below the peaks to the west. Below, to the south, he could see the winding valley that they had followed out from Vesport.

"Time to go," Takoda said.

The path cut back and forth up the sides. Twice he had to scrabble up outcroppings. The second time, he had to climb back down until he found it again, leading off to the side. The path exited the trees onto a teardrop-shaped field of broken rock lying against the mountainside. Hard white stones lay in a heap that rose up to meet a wide cleft. Kherlos smiled.

"This is going to hurt," Takoda said. He had been silent for some time.

"Yes it will, but I believe we are close to our goal."

"There will be loose stones."

"And sharp edges no doubt, but there is something up there."

Kherlos climbed the rocky slope. At the top, he could see why people came here. Water had carved a deep pool inside the mountain and eaten away at it until the face had broken off and become the rubble below. The water had drained and then perhaps changed course, leaving an empty half-bowl. Towards the back was a ring of blackened rocks around a patch of scorched stone, but with no trace of ash or burnt wood.

"No one's been here for a while," Takoda said.

"So I can rest here?"

"Yes."

Kherlos's stomach growled. "I don't have the tools to make a deadfall."

"There's no shortage of sharp rocks, but do you even remember how to make one?" Kherlos considered this; he had learned that skill as a young boy. "Maybe, it will come to me, but I know how to make a fire plow." The shadows stretched deep into the recess. The sun would be down soon, but the twilight would linger.

"Then you'd better hurry," Takoda observed.

§

The beast padded quietly into the cave. It knew Man. It knew Fire. Here were both. It knew sickness, and that too was here. It sat, regarded the man. It licked its paws, and lay down.

The man woke, eyes opened. Eyes met. Fear, it knew fear. The man held fear. The man held fire. Man and Fire, Fear and sickness. Fire dies.

§

In the morning, Kherlos rose and made his way to the front of his little cave. His leg was stiff, the wound was hot, and his fingers conveyed a sour odor. "We are in a bad way my friend." He scanned the tree line below and the edges of the rock faces around him. There was no sign of the tiger.

"It's there," Takoda said.

"I pray you are wrong. We need more wood." Kherlos started gingerly down the slope. The edges of the stones had given him many scrapes on his arms and shins in his hurry to gather wood the day before. After he had moved about five feet down the slope, a rock tumbled loose beneath his foot and clattered downhill, gaining momentum as it rolled until it bounded out into the trees.

The tiger emerged from the foliage. It was eight feet long, with black and white stripes, a black nose, and large yellow eyes. It looked up at him, and then casually started picking its way uphill.

"Snowcat," Takoda said, almost in awe. "What's it doing down here?"

Kherlos scrambled back uphill, heedless of Takoda's curiosity or the injury to his legs and arms. In the back of the cave, the fire was dead and cold. Only a few small stick ends remained with which he might defend himself.

"Well, my friend," Takoda said, "Start wishing."